Chocolate Cake for Breakfast

Danielle Hawkins grew up on a sheep and beef farm near Otorohanga in New Zealand, and later studied veterinary science. After graduating as a vet she met a very nice dairy farmer who became her husband. Danielle spends two days a week working as a large-animal vet and the other five as housekeeper, cook and general dogsbody. She has two small children, and when she is very lucky they nap simultaneously and she can write. Danielle's first novel, *Dinner at Rose's*, was published in 2012.

Chocolate Cake for Breakfast

DANIELLE HAWKINS

ARENA
ALLEN&UNWIN

This edition published in 2014
First published in 2013

Arena Books, an imprint of
Allen & Unwin
83 Alexander Street
Crows Nest NSW 2065
Australia
Phone: (61 2) 8425 0100
Email: info@allenandunwin.com
Web: www.allenandunwin.com

Cataloguing-in-Publication details are available
from the National Library of Australia
www.trove.nla.gov.au

ISBN 978 1 76011 134 2

Typeset in Garamond Premier Pro by Bookhouse, Sydney
Printed in Australia by McPherson's Printing Group

10 9 8 7 6 5 4 3 2 1

For Mum, who is awesome

1

WHEN THE PHONE RANG ON SATURDAY NIGHT I WAS ON my knees in the shower, scrubbing grimly at a mould stalactite I had just discovered lurking under the shelf that holds the soap. I would have liked to ignore the phone – having started on the stalactite I wanted to finish the job – but I was on call, so I stood up and reached around the shower curtain.

'Hello?'

'What are you up to?' asked my cousin Sam.

'Cleaning the shower.'

'Are you coming to Alistair Johnson's party?'

I noticed that a medium-sized waterfall was coursing from the point of my elbow onto the clean clothes on the floor, and hurriedly turned off the water. 'No, I'm on call,' I said.

'So what? It's at the fire station. Miles closer to the clinic than your place.'

'I can't be bothered,' I said feebly.

'You're pathetic,' said Sam. 'Come on. It'll be good for you.'

This annoyed me, mostly because I had a feeling he was right.

The street outside the Broadview fire station was lined with cars when I got there, and there was a cluster of youths around the front door.

Sam was watching the rugby on the big screen inside, and I went and leant on the table beside him. 'Christ,' he was saying, 'just *pass* the freaking thing . . . Shit, he's dropped it cold. Bloody idiot.'

'Hey, Sammy,' I said. Sam is my favourite cousin; he sells tractors and self-unloading trailers and other bits of serious farm equipment at Alcot's Farm Machinery. He has a cheerful round face and sticky-up brown hair and exudes fresh-faced boyish charm, and he could sell ice to Eskimos. 'Is Alison here?'

'Was half an hour ago,' said Sam. 'But then I saw Hamish Thompson collar her, so she might have topped herself by now.'

'Why didn't you save her?' But he had turned his attention back to the rugby, so I went to look for her myself.

I had only gone about three paces when I spotted Briar Coles dead ahead. Briar was in her last year of high school and wanted desperately to be a vet nurse. She had spent every Wednesday for three months with us at the clinic, until the boss couldn't take it anymore and asked the school not to send her back. She was very sweet, and very dim, and she followed you around telling you about her ponies and her dog and getting in your way until you wanted to throw something at the poor girl's head.

Her face lit up in welcome as she saw me, and taking prompt, if cowardly, action in the face of emergency I smiled, waved and ducked out through a side door.

As I hurried around the side of the building into a handy patch of deep shadow (Briar being a persistent sort of girl),

I tripped over someone's legs stretched across the path. I lurched forward, and a big hand grasped me firmly by the jersey and heaved me back upright.

'Thank you,' I said breathlessly.

'Helen?' Briar called, and I shrank back into the shadows beside the owner of the legs.

'Avoiding someone?' he asked.

'Shh!' I hissed, and he was obediently quiet. There was a short silence, happily unbroken by approaching footsteps, and I sighed with relief.

'Not very sociable, are you?'

'You can hardly talk,' I pointed out.

'True,' he said.

'Who are *you* hiding from?'

'Everyone,' he said morosely.

'Fair enough. I'll leave you to it.'

'Better give it a minute,' he advised. 'She might still be lying in wait.'

That was a good point, and I leant back against the brick wall beside him. 'You don't have to talk to me,' I said.

'Thank you.'

There was another silence, but it felt friendly rather than uncomfortable. There's nothing like lurking together in the shadows for giving you a sense of comradeship. I looked sideways at the stranger and discovered that he was about twice as big as any normal person. He was at least a foot taller than me, and built like a tank. But he had a nice voice, so with any luck he was a gentle giant rather than the sort who would tear you limb from limb as soon as look at you.

'So,' asked the giant, 'why are you hiding from this girl?'

'She's the most boring person on the surface of the planet,' I said.

'That's a big call. There's some serious competition for that spot.'

'I may be exaggerating. But she'd definitely make the top fifty. Why did *you* come to a party to skulk around a corner?'

'I was dragged,' he said. 'Kicking and screaming.' He turned his head to look at me, smiling.

'Ah,' I said wisely. 'That'd be how you got the black eye.' Even in the near-darkness it was a beauty – tight and shiny and purple. There was also a row of butterfly tapes holding together a split through his right eyebrow, and it occurred to me suddenly that chatting in dark corners to large unsociable strangers with black eyes probably wasn't all that clever.

'Nah,' he said. 'I collided with a big hairy Tongan knee.'

'That was careless.'

'It was, wasn't it?'

I pushed myself off the wall to stand straight. 'I'll leave you in peace. Nice to meet you.'

'You too,' he said, and held out a hand. 'I'm Mark.'

I took it and we shook solemnly. 'Helen.'

'What do you do when you're not hiding from the most boring girl on the planet?' he asked.

'I'm a vet,' I said. 'What about you?'

'I play rugby.'

'Oh!' That was a nice, legitimate reason for running into a Tongan knee – I had assumed it was the type of injury sustained during a pub fight. 'Professionally, you mean?'

'Yeah.'

'Where?'

'Auckland,' he said.

'For the Blues?'

'Yes.'

'That's really great,' I said warmly. 'Good for you.'

He smiled. 'Thank you.'

I went right around the building and in again through the main doors, back past the cluster of youths. Sam had turned his back on the rugby and was talking instead to my friend Alison. 'Hi, guys,' I said.

'Where did you vanish to?' Sam asked.

'Briar Coles spotted me,' I explained, 'so I went and hid for a while. Sammy, do you know someone called Mark who's about eight foot tall and plays rugby for Auckland?'

'You mean him?'

I followed his gaze across the room to where a big, dark, powerful-looking man with extensive facial bruising was standing flanked by one teenage girl while another took a photo on her cell phone. 'That's the one,' I said.

'Helen, you moron,' said Sam. 'That's Mark Tipene.'

I looked again, and went hot all over with embarrassment. It was indeed Mark Tipene, and I was indeed a moron. 'I just asked him what he did for a living.'

'What did he say?' Alison asked.

'He said he played rugby for Auckland.'

'Well,' said Sam, 'he does.' When not playing for the All Blacks, where even I knew that he had for years been regarded as the world's best lock. Whatever it was that locks did.

'What on earth is Mark Tipene doing here?' I asked. You just don't expect to find random All Blacks loitering behind the fire stations of small rural Waikato townships.

'Apparently he's Hamish Thompson's cousin,' said Alison. 'Poor bastard.' Hamish was a strapping young dairy farmer, whose advances she had been resisting ever since he moved into the district, and her patience was wearing a little thin.

Across the room Mark farewelled the teenage girls and was instantly accosted by my uncle Simon, who was Broadview's mayor and took his position very seriously. The poor bloke should have stayed lurking in the shadows.

'There you are, Helen!' said a voice from behind my left shoulder.

'Hi, Briar,' I said weakly, turning around. 'How are you?'

'Really good. Guess what?'

'What?' I asked.

'Dad's getting Millie in foal to an Arab stallion over in the Hawke's Bay!'

'Wow,' I said.

'And he says I can school the foal all by myself.'

I had heard all about Briar's father's horse-training methods and quite a lot about Briar's new western saddle when my cell phone buzzed in my jeans pocket. 'Sorry, Briar, this'll be a call . . . Hello?'

'Helen? Fenella Martin's got a cat needing a caesarean,' said the after-hours lady, who never wasted time on small talk.

This was not, it seemed, my night. Fenella Martin bred Siamese cats and was the Client from Hell. 'Okay,' I said. 'I'll see her at the clinic in five minutes.' I shut the phone. 'Sorry, Briar, I've got to go.'

Scanning the crowd for Sam or Alison to let them know I was leaving, I saw Mark Tipene still deep in conversation with Uncle Simon. It didn't seem to be his night either.

Fenella, a particularly unpleasant woman in her fifties with long red straggly hair and long black straggly skirts, was dancing up and down on the doorstep when I reached the clinic. Breeders are often a bit eccentric, but Fenella was as mad as a hatter.

'It's Farrah,' she said (all Fenella's queens had names starting with F, just like their mummy). 'It's her first litter. She had two in my bed about four this morning, but nothing since then.'

In her bed. Lovely.

'Right,' I said. 'I'll open up while you get her out of the car.'

'*You'll* have to carry the cage,' said Fenella. 'My back's playing up.'

Poor Farrah was only a kitten herself, undergrown and underfed. She lay on her side on the consult room table, panting. 'Shh, baby,' Fenella crooned. 'Mummy's here. Mummy won't let anything bad happen to you.'

Seeing as Mummy had left the poor cat in second-stage labour for fourteen hours before bothering to bring her in I was underwhelmed by this statement. I inserted a gloved and lubed fingertip gingerly into the little cat's vulva and met a nose, jammed tight against the pelvis. 'I can feel the kitten's head,' I said, 'but it's huge and her pelvis is pretty narrow. I don't think it's going to come out that way.'

'I *know* that,' said Fenella. She fished a balled-up tissue out of her cleavage and blew her nose wetly. 'Get on with it.'

Caesareans are usually quite fun, but this one wasn't. Fenella insisted on being present right through the surgery and she questioned my every move.

'Why are you putting her on fluids? Nick never puts my cats on fluids.'

'Just to make sure her blood pressure doesn't drop. And if I need to give her anything IV we've already got the vein.'

'Well, I'm not paying extra just because you're not up to speed. *Nick* doesn't have to put my cats on fluids.' The reason Nick didn't put her cats on fluids was that she paid her account off at about five dollars a month, and he disliked spending money he knew he wasn't going to get back.

Fenella adjusted her knickers and asked, '*Do* you know what you're doing?'

It would have been nice to reply with, 'Well, I've never done an operation before, but I've seen heaps on *Grey's Anatomy* and I'm really keen to give one a crack,' but the only time I manage witty repartee is in the privacy of my own bedroom, when I'm imagining how the conversation might have gone if only I was brave. 'Yes,' I said gravely, drawing anaesthetic into a syringe. 'I've done lots of caesareans. My last job was at a small-animal practice in England.'

'I just adore my animals,' said Fenella. 'The cost doesn't matter.' The cost never matters to bad debtors, because they've got no intention of paying anyway.

There was only one kitten left in the uterus, wedged so tightly into the pelvic inlet it was quite hard to retrieve. I handed it to Fenella, who wrapped it tenderly in a towel and rubbed it. This didn't help the kitten, which was well and truly dead, but it helped me quite a lot. I managed to suture the uterus and the muscle layer before she looked up again, and thus only had to endure comments like 'You should be using thicker thread than that' and 'Those stitches are too close together' while I stitched up the skin.

2

'OOH LOOK,' SAID JOHN SOMERVILLE HAPPILY. 'A WOOD pigeon. There he goes.' He turned his head to watch it, slackening his hold on the leg rope, and the steer attached to the other end of the rope kicked me in the face.

It was a good, solid kick, and it sent me sprawling backwards into the mud. There was a sharp stabbing pain in my front teeth and something warm trickled across my cheek – I suspected it was blood, and reached up to touch it. It was.

John looked at me in mild surprise. 'Are you alright, my dear?' he asked.

'I don't know,' I said a trifle shortly, exploring my teeth with the tip of my tongue. They were all still in the right place, and I pushed myself up to sit. 'I think we'll sedate him, John.'

He sighed and adjusted his towelling hat. 'If you must,' he said.

The steer in the race tried to kick me again as I sidled up to inject him – an impressive, double-barrelled kick. You don't often meet such hostility in cattle. (Horses, now, are different, and shouldn't in my opinion be trusted for a second. I was soured early in life by the small and evil Shetland pony my parents borrowed for me from the neighbours, which specialised in pulling children off its back with its teeth.) I gave him a fairly hefty dose of sedative, and eventually he grew sleepy enough to let me tie his leg back up and unwind the wire that was cutting into his fetlock.

'Could you give him a long-acting antibiotic?' John asked, tearing his attention very briefly from a cluster of white puffy clouds drifting across the afternoon sky. 'I might not manage to get him in again.'

'Yes,' I said. 'Of course. And an anti-inflammatory, and then we'll just have to keep a bit of an eye on it and hope the blood supply to his foot hasn't been too badly damaged. I'll give you a ring in a few days to see how it's going.'

'How kind,' he murmured. 'How very kind.' He picked up my drug box without fastening the lid, and syringes, needles and bottles of penicillin showered down around his feet.

'What happened this time?' Thomas asked. When you first met Thomas you just got the impression of bad skin and more Adam's apple than any one person could possibly need, but he manned the front desk of the Broadview Veterinary Centre (Your Partners in Animal Health Since 1967) with military efficiency.

'Kicked by a steer,' I said, jumping up to perch on the desk beside him. 'Pretty cool, eh?' A blood vessel in my right eye had burst, and the white of the eye was now bright red.

'You look kind of evil.'

'Imagine if it was both eyes. People might think I was a vampire.'

'I read one of those books,' said Thomas. 'It's the coloured bit of the eye that's red. And aren't vampires supposed to be incredibly beautiful?'

'Are you saying I'm not?'

'It might help if you washed the cow shit off your ear, for a start.' He pulled the accident book out from under the counter and shoved it towards me.

Mid-July is a fairly quiet time of year in large-animal practice, and at twenty to five that afternoon four of the five vets were in the big office at the back of the building. Nick was busily writing reports – he seemed to spend almost all his waking hours doing paperwork, while making distressingly little headway. Anita had small children and finished work at three, but Keri, Richard and I were eating pick 'n' mix lollies from the shop across the road and discussing Joe Watkins, the meanest farmer alive.

Little Zoe the vet nurse pushed the door open and scurried in, face bright red with emotion. 'Helen!' she said. '*Mark Tipene* is asking for you at the front desk! The All Black!'

I got to my feet, and Richard and Keri both followed suit. 'You can't *come*!' I said, appalled.

'Why not?' Keri asked. 'I need to talk to Thomas.'

'I just want to see Mark Tipene,' said Richard, who was at least honest. 'Maybe he'll autograph my gumboot.'

'Hang on,' Keri said, and the woman actually spat on her hanky and rubbed my cheek.

I batted her hand away. 'Stop that!'

'You can't go out there with cow shit on your face,' she said. 'Okay. Head up, shoulders back. Off you go.'

Crimson with embarrassment and followed by a giggling entourage I went out into the shop. Mark Tipene was standing at the front counter, looking at a notice advertising kittens free to a good home and giving the impression that he had just strayed in from the set of a James Bond movie. His black eye had faded to a sickly green, streaked with red, but instead of spoiling his looks it made him look tough and a little bit dangerous. We had a picture of Mark Tipene without a shirt pinned up in the lunch room to lift our spirits on bad days (the boys had a corresponding picture of Rihanna wearing only a couple of bits of string), and it was frankly unbelievable to have the man himself wander in off the street.

'Hi,' I said, digging my hands into the pockets of my overalls in an attempt to appear relaxed. Somehow I doubt I pulled it off.

'Hi.' He smiled at me across the counter. 'Nice red eye.'

'Thank you.'

'What happened?'

'I got kicked in the face by a steer.'

'Ouch,' he said. 'What are you doing after work?'

'Um, nothing much, I don't think,' I said stupidly.

'You're on call,' said Thomas at my elbow, where he was pretending to work on an internet order to Masterpet but actually listening avidly.

'There you go,' I said. 'I'm on call.'

'Oh,' said Mark Tipene. 'I was wondering if you could come and have a drink.'

'Yeah, go on,' said Richard, coming up to the counter beside me. 'I'll swap nights with you, so you don't get interrupted.' And the rotten lousy sod leered at me, right in front of one of our nation's sporting heroes. I kicked him in the shin.

'Ow!' he said. 'Sure you don't want to reconsider, mate?'

Mark smiled and shook his head. 'What d'you reckon?' he asked me.

'Um,' I said. 'Okay. Um. Thanks.' Gracious and articulate acceptance it was not.

Richard clapped me encouragingly on the shoulder. 'There you go,' he said. 'That wasn't so bad, was it?'

'Leave her alone,' said Keri. 'Go on, Helen, it's ten to five. I'll shut down your computer for you.'

'I – I'll just go and take off my overalls,' I muttered, and fled back into the vet room.

'What on earth is the matter?' my boss asked, glancing up from his docket book.

'I'm going out for a drink with *Mark Tipene*,' I said, feverishly shedding the overalls.

Nick looked profoundly unimpressed by this momentous news. 'I wouldn't let it go to my head, if I were you,' he said. 'Did you book in Rex's lepto vaccinations?'

'Not yet. He wasn't home when I rang.'

'Follow it up tomorrow, will you? And you might like to turn your collar out the right way.'

I did, took a couple of deep breaths for good measure and went back out.

'Bye, kids,' said Thomas. 'Have fun.'

'That's right,' Richard said. And as we reached the door, which he must have judged to be a safe distance, he called, 'Be gentle with him, Helen.'

We went silently out the automatic doors and turned up the street. 'I'm sorry about those idiots,' I said at last. My friend Alison never feels these irresistible urges to fill uncomfortable pauses. She just smiles, and thus appears poised and slightly mysterious. I admire this approach greatly but am utterly unable to replicate it.

'It's fine. They seem nice.'

'They are,' I said, and there was another uncomfortable pause while I searched desperately for a nonchalant, witty remark. Sadly, the one I came up with was, 'We've got a picture of you in the lunch room, with no shirt on.'

'Right,' said Mark blankly.

I closed my eyes in anguish. 'I'm so sorry.'

He laughed. 'Helen. Get a grip.'

I opened my eyes again before I walked into a wall, which really would cement this Complete Birdbrain impression I was crafting with such loving care. 'Yes,' I said. 'Right. Will do.'

Your choices, if you want to go out for a drink in downtown Broadview, are fairly limited. There's the Returned Servicemen's Association, where the average age of the patrons is somewhere over eighty and you can get roast hogget (which really means very old cull ewe) and boiled mixed veg from five pm on Tuesdays for $12.95, or the Broadview Hotel, where the serious drinkers lurk and where, twenty-odd years ago, a man shot his straying wife at point-blank range with a shotgun. Sam claims that you can still see the bloodstain on the carpet in front of the bar, but my cousin never lets the truth get in the way of a good story. If you wandered in and asked for a glass of chardonnay they probably wouldn't say 'Piss off, you queer' out loud, but you'd be in no doubt that they were thinking it.

That leaves the Stockman's Arms, just down the road from the vet clinic. Mark opened the door and followed me in out of the crisp July dusk, ducking to avoid the set of rusty harrows draped artistically around the doorframe. It was barely five and the place was almost empty.

'What would you like to drink?' he asked.

'Um,' I said. He was going to think I was incapable of starting a sentence with anything else. 'Ginger beer, please.' I was being quite enough of an idiot already without alcohol.

'Grab a seat while I get the drinks,' he said.

I sank into a chair at a corner table and took deep slow breaths, as advised by the small rodent-like man who taught Beginner's Yoga courses at the Broadview Community Centre. *It is better to remain silent and be thought a fool than to open your mouth and remove all doubt. It is better to remain silent . . .* In yoga classes we were urged to use 'I am a clear vessel filled with pure white light' as our mantra, but I was adapting as the situation required.

Mark pulled out the chair opposite mine and sat down, passing me a bottle of ginger beer. 'How's that eye feeling?' he asked.

I put up a hand and touched my sore cheekbone. 'Not too bad. It looks worse than it is. How about yours?'

'Oh, it's fine.'

'That's good.' I took a careful sip of ginger beer and put the bottle down, which filled up four seconds.

He arranged three cardboard coasters in a nice straight line, using up another six.

I examined the fingernails of my right hand, which had a greenish tinge and would have been improved by a few minutes' work with a nailbrush. 'It's your turn to say something now,' I said. Remaining silent was all very well in theory, but I couldn't take the strain.

'I'm trying to think of something worth saying.'

'How's that going?'

'Badly. So, how did you manage to get kicked in the face?'

'I was trying to unwind a bit of wire from around a steer's leg,' I said.

'You didn't tie it up first?'

'I did, but the man holding the leg rope got distracted by a passing wood pigeon and let go.'

'Top bloke,' he remarked.

'John's one of my very favourite farmers. Usually when you turn up you find he's rescuing worms out of a puddle and the cow's still out the back somewhere. And he has a pet chicken called Esmeralda.'

'I had a pet chicken when I was about five,' said Mark.

'What was it called?'

'Chicky.'

'Good name,' I said.

'I know. Really original.' He smiled at me across the table.

'Were you a country kid, then?'

'Yeah,' he said. 'My parents had a sheep farm out of Stratford.'

'Had?'

'Dad's still there. Mum lives in Cairns now. Where did you grow up?'

'About two blocks that way,' I said, gesturing with my ginger beer bottle. 'My dad's a dentist in town.'

Exhausted by this burst of conversation, we relapsed into silence and gulped thankfully at our drinks in preparation for the next round. Some people, I am told, actually enjoy this first-date mutual appraisal disguised as casual conversation, but I think I'd rather go to a preschool ukulele concert. Or a Brazilian waxing appointment. Or –

My mental list of the world's least enjoyable pastimes was brought up short by the bang of swinging doors and the clatter of harrows. Fenella Martin, trailing an acre or so of black crushed-velvet skirt, swept into the pub. There was a man with her but he was largely obscured by the billowing draperies. Fenella came right up to the edge of our table in a cloud of stale incense and said, 'They told me you were here.'

Those treacherous swine. 'How's Farrah?' I asked.

'She's got diarrhoea,' said Fenella. She was wearing a remarkably nasty crocheted magenta vest, which matched the magenta plastic rose nestling coyly behind her right ear.

'Oh dear,' I said. 'Is she still eating?'

She didn't answer, but bent and picked up a crocheted bag (also magenta – it's nice to see a woman accessorising with such attention to detail). She burrowed through the bag and emerged with a peanut butter jar, an inch of sinister brown material in the bottom. 'Look at this.' She shook the jar and its contents slopped up the side. 'That was this morning's – and here's one from yesterday . . .' She rummaged through the bag again. 'A bit runny, but not nearly so bad.' She put both samples down in the middle of the table for me to examine at my leisure.

'It could be the antibiotics,' I said. 'Is she still eating?'

'Yes,' Fenella admitted grudgingly.

'Then it's probably nothing to worry about. Or would you like to bring her in tomorrow for a check-up?'

'I'd have to leave her,' said Fenella. 'I'm going to Auckland for the day.'

'That's fine. She can spend the day with us.' I pushed the two jars towards the edge of the table.

'You keep them,' Fenella said with touching generosity.

3

'DID HE THINK IT WAS FUNNY?' ALISON ASKED WHEN I described this debacle during our lunchtime walk the next day.

'I think so, but they sat down at the next table, so we couldn't laugh out loud,' I said. 'And then they figured out who Mark was and turned around to talk to him. And *then* all of Undershott's Accounting came in and he had to pose for about seventeen photos. Are we going up Birch Crescent today?'

'Absolutely – now you're going to be a Wag you'll have to pay extra attention to your figure.' She turned purposefully up Broadview's steepest street, ponytail swinging from the back of her Nike cap.

'A what?' I asked, labouring behind her as she bounded gazelle-like up the hill.

'A Wag. You know – wives and girlfriends. They spend all their time shopping and making exercise DVDs. Did he ask for your number?'

'Nope,' I said. And in an attempt to act like a girl who couldn't care less whether or not the handsome and charming

All Black called I added brightly, 'I suppose I could always get *his* number off Hamish. And then we could all go out together on a double date.'

Alison shuddered. 'If that dickhead calls me Head Nurse again I'll . . . actually, I don't know what I'll do. But it won't be good.'

'What's wrong with calling you Head Nurse? You are.' Although there were only two nurses at the Broadview Medical Centre and the other one should really have been pensioned off ten years ago, so this title wasn't quite as impressive as it sounded.

'What do you call a nurse with dirty knees?'

'Huh?' I asked, puzzled by this seemingly random question.

'Head nurse,' said Alison patiently.

'Oh-h. That's actually kind of funny.'

'The first five times, perhaps.'

The cell phone in the pocket of my track pants began to ring, and I fished it out. 'It'll be Thomas with a calving,' I said, not even bothering to look at the screen. 'Hey, what's up?'

'Helen? Hi, it's Mark here.'

'Oh! Hi!'

Alison looked at me questioningly.

'I'm sorry to call you in your lunch break – the vet clinic gave me your mobile number.'

'That's fine,' I said.

'It's probably against the Privacy Act or something.'

'Thomas gives my number to all sorts of dodgy people.' I thought about that little statement as it left my mouth. 'I – I mean – not meaning that *you* are . . .'

Alison rolled her eyes, and I turned my back on her.

He laughed, which was kind of him. 'You wouldn't be free to go out for dinner tonight, would you?'

'I can't,' I said. 'I'm on call.'

'What about tomorrow?'

'I'm on call for the weekend too.'

Alison, having walked around to stand in front of me again, slumped despairingly onto the pavement and struck her forehead with the heel of her hand. An elderly gentleman hoeing his veggie garden across the street leant his hoe against the fence and started anxiously towards her.

'Oh well,' said Mark. 'Another time, maybe.'

'My dear, are you alright?' the elderly gentleman called.

'Fine,' said Alison hastily, standing back up. 'Just fine.'

'Um,' I said, 'look, d'you want to come to my place for tea? I might have to go and calve a cow or something in the middle of it, that's all.'

'That'd be great,' he said. 'I'll grab fish and chips.'

'Dog waiting for you in the kennels,' said Thomas when I got back to the clinic.

'What's wrong with it?'

'You're the vet.'

'You're so sweet and helpful,' I said.

Thomas waggled his eyebrows at me. He had evidently been squeezing a spot on his nose, which did nothing to enhance his looks. 'And Max Tarrant rang wanting his blood results.'

'I don't think they're back yet, but I'll have a look.'

'Hey, Helen, check this out,' he ordered, and I veered obediently around behind the counter to look at his computer screen. With the aid of Google he had summoned up a long list of websites. Mark Tipene Wikipedia. Mark Tipene All Blacks. Mark Tipene images. Mark Tipene articles. Mark Tipene's official Facebook site. Mark Tipene YouTube clips . . .

'Here you go,' he said, moving the mouse to enlarge a shirt-less photo of a mud-streaked, olive-skinned god, chest muscles rippling, rugby ball in one big hand and a look of grim determination on his face. Very nice, if tall, dark and muscle-bound is your thing. It never *had* been my thing – I liked 'em lean and blond and surfy. But still, very nice. 'Did he get hold of you?'

'Mm.'

'And?'

'And what?'

'What did he *say*?'

'None of your business.'

'You know,' Thomas said, 'I could always book in Hohepa's herd leptos at milking. *Morning* milking. Cups on at four.'

'That's blackmail!' I said. Michael Hohepa milked fourteen hundred cows and was legendarily grumpy.

Thomas shrugged. 'So?'

'Do your worst,' I said. 'If I start giving in to blackmail now it'll just be the start of a slippery slope.' And with that I put my nose in the air, pulled my shoulders back, and swept off towards the vet room. Unfortunately I tripped over the cord of Thomas's fan heater as I went, which rather spoilt the effect.

Thomas sniggered as he turned back to his computer. 'Would you look at this?' he said reverently, and I did before I could help myself. 'Here's a few of his girlfriends. Underwear model Nicole Rakovich – that one's only dated the thirteenth of April this year. And before that Tamara Healy . . . She plays netball, doesn't she?'

'She's the captain of the Silver Ferns,' I said.

'That's the one. Shit, you wouldn't kick *her* out of bed, would you? Legs up to her armpits. And that blonde girl who used to do the weather report, and . . .'

I turned and fled, wondering why on earth the man *did* want to see me again.

I got home at six forty-five, having been detained by a sneezing rat just on closing time and then a heifer with a prolapsed uterus at half past five. It was dark and the house was freezing. Murray the ginger cat met me at the kitchen door and wound himself insistently around my ankles.

Murray and I lived in a poky farm cottage ten kilometres west of Broadview. It was just the two of us; after six months of sharing a two-bedroom flat in central London with three other people, I'd got home quite desperate for solitude.

The place was carpeted throughout in orange nylon, which clashed horribly with everything else. An enormous and nasty conifer blocked most of the afternoon sun, the windows rattled when the tanker went past and my landlord only graded his tanker track (which was also my driveway) when the dairy company threatened to stop picking up his milk. But these were very minor flaws. When I bought food it stayed in the fridge until I wanted to eat it, and nobody ever came home drunk in the early hours of the morning to play house music at about a million decibels on the other side of the bedroom wall.

I turned on the kitchen light and discovered that Murray had killed a sparrow while I was at work and plucked it all over the room. It was hard to believe so many feathers had fitted on one small bird. I picked up the little limp corpse, hurled it out across the dark lawn and turned to fetch the vacuum cleaner. The vacuum cleaner cupboard was in the opposite direction to the fridge, and Murray yowled in protest.

'Tough,' I said. 'You can wait. You should've eaten the sparrow.'

The vacuum cleaner bag was full, and burst as I removed it from the machine. This was not entirely a surprise, since every time the vacuum cleaner had stopped sucking in the last five months I'd emptied the bag into the rubbish bin with the help of a fork, reflecting that I really *must* put vacuum cleaner bags on my shopping list.

Ten minutes' hard labour with a brush and shovel improved neither my temper nor Murray's. I finally fed him, considered lighting the fire and decided showering was far more important.

Leaving the outside door open I wrote, *Come in. In shower. Beer in fridge* on the back of last month's power bill, left it on the edge of the kitchen table and ran down the hall.

Having showered and dressed and dragged a brush through my hair, I wiped the bathroom mirror with the corner of a towel and looked critically at my reflection.

The red eye was undeniably a drawback. It was a shame, because normally my eyes are my best feature, coffee-coloured with long dark lashes.

My hair was better: long and dark and, thanks to thirty-six dollars worth of miracle serum from the hairdressers, even bordering on lustrous. I pulled a hank of it over the red eye, decided it just looked silly and tucked it back behind my ear.

Round, pink cheeks – cute on a six-year-old but less so when you're twenty-six. Freckles across nose, ditto. Skin otherwise good – family tradition states that Helen Has Lovely Skin. I've always suspected that family tradition states this mostly because I was quite overweight in my teens and my aunts wished to be encouraging. I made a face at myself in the mirror and went up the hall to find, surprisingly, not one but two men in my kitchen.

'Hey, cuz,' said Sam. 'Bloody hell, what'd you do to your face?'

'Hit it against a steer's foot,' I said. 'Hi, Mark.'

Mark was leaning against the table wearing a pair of faded jeans and a blue Adidas sweatshirt and looking far too tall, dark and handsome to trust as far as you could throw him. 'Hi,' he said.

'Have you guys met?' I asked.

'Yeah, we met on Saturday night while you were off playing with a cat,' said Sam. 'Hel, it's freezing in here.'

'I know. I'll light the fire – I got home late.'

He picked up a wodge of newspapers from the box beside the old-fashioned pot-belly stove. 'I'll do it,' he said. 'You clean your elbows.'

I peered at the backs of my forearms. 'Bugger.'

'That's our Helen,' said Sam. 'Washes once a month whether she needs to or not.'

'Are you here for any particular reason?' I enquired, running the dishcloth under the tap and scrubbing at the green stripes on the backs of my arms. Mark Tipene could never have laboured under the illusion that I was a model of wit and poise, but it did seem a shame to be making such a good job of coming across as a complete fool. Most people can at least manage to get clean while showering.

'Just passing by,' said Sam sunnily. 'Is that an Audi R8 outside?'

'It is,' said Mark.

'It's beautiful,' said Sam, sighing a long and lustful sigh.

Mark smiled. 'I know. I love it very much.'

'Where are the matches?' Sam asked as he balled up sheets of newspaper.

'In the wood box,' I said, crossing the kitchen to toss the dishcloth through the laundry door. There was a newspaper-wrapped and most delectable-smelling parcel on the table beside a bottle of red wine. 'Thank you, Mark; that smells great.'

'It might pay to heat it up a bit,' he said. 'Have you been out wrestling with another steer?'

I shook my head. 'Just putting a heifer's uterus back on the inside of the heifer. It was a nice easy one.'

'What was its uterus doing on the outside?'

'Sometimes when they push out the calf they keep pushing and the uterus comes out too, so you have to turn it back round the right way and tuck it back in.'

'That sounds complicated,' he said.

'Not really.' I perched on the edge of the table and pulled off one sock to demonstrate. 'Imagine the sock's a uterus, with a calf inside. So it's attached at the vulva, and the rest of it's just sort of flopping around inside the cow.' I stuffed one hand into my sock and wiggled my fingers. 'That's the calf. Then the calf's born –' I withdrew my hand '– and if you're unlucky he scratches the lining of the uterus on the way out and the cow keeps on straining. So the uterus comes out too, and it turns inside out as it comes because it's attached at the vulva.' I turned my sock inside out, holding the top still. 'So you give the cow an epidural so she stops pushing, and stuff it all back in.'

'What stops the cow pushing it all back out again?' he asked.

'Drugs,' I said. 'Oxytocin makes the uterus contract up –' I balled up my sock in one hand to enhance my demonstration '– so it can't flop out again. And some people sew the vulva shut, but I never bother.'

'Thank you, Dr McNeil, for that fascinating obstetrical lecture,' said Sam.

'I liked it,' Mark said mildly. 'It was very informative.'

'Thank you. So there, Sammy,' I said.

Sam attempted a sneer. It didn't really come off; he hasn't got the right kind of face for sneering. 'He's just being polite. It's part of the job description when you're a sporting legend and a role model.' He closed the door of the wood burner and stood up, dusting his hands on his thighs. 'Right. Reckon you've got it all under control?'

'I doubt it,' I said. 'Thanks for lighting the fire.'

'You're welcome.' He looked at Mark. 'Going to South Africa next week?'

'Yeah. That's the plan, at this stage.'

'Thank Christ for that. The lineout looks a bit sad without you. Okay, chaps, have a nice evening,' said Sam. He opened the kitchen door and let himself out, and we heard him whistling as he went down the porch steps.

'Nice bloke,' Mark said.

'He is. He's my favourite cousin.' I opened the warming drawer of the oven and took out my roasting dish.

'You've got quite a few relatives around here, haven't you?'

'They're everywhere,' I said. 'The district is overrun. There are twelve McNeil families in the local phone book, I think – thirty-eight of us at Christmas lunch.'

'Bloody hell.'

'I know. Sometimes I think I was insane to come back home.'

'Home from where?'

'London,' I said.

'Why did you?' he asked.

'Well, I'd been away for two years by last December, and it was cold and dark by four in the afternoon, and I didn't like my locum job much. I always wanted to be a large-animal vet, and I was sick of constipated gerbils. So when Nick – my boss at the clinic here – rang up and offered me a cow job, I quit and got the next plane home.'

'I never did a proper OE,' he said. 'I've always been a bit sad about it.'

'But you must have done some pretty cool things instead,' I said, spreading the fish and chips over the bottom of the roasting dish and stealing a chip just to make sure it was up to standard.

He reached over to take a handful. 'Spending half your life in the gym, travelling all over the world but never having time to see any of it, never-ending press conferences and schmoozing with sponsors . . .'

'Don't you enjoy it?' I asked, startled. Half the little boys in the country dream of growing up to be an All Black.

'Yeah, of course. I still can't quite believe they pay me to play rugby. But I get a bit sick of the politics and the publicity stuff sometimes.'

'I bet you do,' I said fervently. 'Is it always like last night when you go out?'

He ate a chip in a thoughtful sort of way. 'Well, I've never had someone deliver cat shit to the table before.'

'Yes,' I said, 'that was special.'

'I was a bit disappointed that you didn't rush it to the lab for further testing,' he said. I had dropped both samples smartly into the rubbish bin around the corner from the pub, having checked to make sure Fenella couldn't see me from inside.

'What I *really* should have done is taken the lids off those jars and hidden them in Richard's ute. I wish I'd thought of it at the time.'

'Who's Richard?'

27

'The tall skinny vet with the dodgy-looking goatee.' I opened the fridge door and looked inside. 'What would you like to drink? I've got beer, if you don't mind Waikato, or that very classy-looking wine you brought with you. Or milk.'

'Beer, please. I don't think milk would give the right impression.'

'I wouldn't worry,' I said, passing him a bottle. 'You could ask for a fairy drink and still make a better impression than me and my cat shit.'

'What on earth is a fairy drink?' he asked.

'Hot water and milk and sugar. Like a cup of tea without the tea.'

'It sounds revolting.'

'It is,' I said. 'But my little sister likes them.'

'How old is she?'

'Five. Fairy drinks are acceptable when you're five.'

'That's quite an age gap,' he said.

'Yeah. My dad married again, and he and my stepmother have two girls. They're great.'

'Any other brothers and sisters?'

'No,' I said. 'You?'

'One big brother.'

'I always wanted a big brother.'

'I'm not sure you'd want mine.'

'Why not?' I asked.

He made a face. 'Rob hates pretty much everyone.'

'Including you?'

'Especially me.'

'Oh,' I said. 'Well, I suppose it's a bit depressing having a world-famous little brother.'

'I'm not that famous,' he said.

'You are, too. Thomas googled you this afternoon – he's the one at the front desk with all that surplus Adam's apple.'

Mark looked pained. 'Don't you people have anything better to do?'

'Well, it's a quiet time of year,' I said. 'Calving's only just getting going, and we've finished most of the herd lepto vaccinations.' Just then my cell phone, balanced on the kitchen windowsill, started to ring. I picked it up and looked at the screen – it was Pauline the after-hours lady, which seemed a bit unfair after two calls already this evening. But perhaps it was just a quick phone query. 'Hi,' I said.

'You sound very chirpy,' Pauline remarked. 'I'll fix that. Joe Watkins has a calving. Live calf. He asked for someone who knew what they were doing.' I had never actually met Pauline face to face; she was merely a gruff cynical voice on the end of the phone. In my head she was pushing sixty, with curlers and fluffy slippers, a cigarette permanently attached to her lower lip.

'Did you tell him he was getting me?' I asked.

'Yes. He hung up.'

'I can hardly wait,' I said, but I was talking to the dial tone. Putting the phone down on the edge of the table with a peevish little thump, I pulled my sweatshirt over my head. 'I'm really sorry, I've got to go and calve a cow.'

Mark crossed my kitchen and turned off the oven. 'Can I come?' he asked.

'It'll be awful,' I said glumly, picking up the overalls hanging over the back of a chair and starting to put them on. 'The guy's our nastiest farmer, and the cows always look like toast racks, and his shed's disgusting.'

'Would you rather I just went away and let you get on with it?'

I pulled myself out of my trough of Watkins-induced gloom. 'I'd love you to come,' I said honestly. 'I expect I'll need the moral support. It's just such a lousy way for you to spend your evening.'

He smiled and shrugged. 'I've spent some pretty lousy evenings. Bet you it doesn't even crack the top ten.'

4

THE PASSENGER SIDE OF THE BENCH SEAT IN MY WORK ute was obscured beneath a pile of liver sampling forms and pregnancy testing pads. I swept the paperwork into a pile, shoved it down beside the driver's door and threw the banana underneath (mislaid the week before) over my shoulder into Rex's paddock.

'Thank you,' said Mark. 'Hang on, we've forgotten the sauce!' He put the parcel of barely warm fish and chips down on the seat, turned and ran back to the house.

We ate on the way, which improved my mental state quite a lot. Mark balled up the fish-and-chip paper as I turned into Joe's tanker entrance and drove down a narrow bumpy track which wended its way between skeletons of dead farm machinery. It was a shame it was too dark to properly appreciate Joe's fences – instead of bothering about all those pesky expensive posts and wires and insulators, he just strung lengths of baling twine from gorse bush to gorse bush.

We parked in front of the shed and climbed out. Three skinny dogs lunged, barking, against their chains, and Joe appeared from behind the vat and grunted.

'Hi, Joe,' I said. 'What've you got?'

'How the hell would I know? That's why you're here. Come on.' A greeting which, although hardly warm and welcoming, pleased me. It's so disappointing to describe someone in graphic detail as being a total prat and then have them make a liar of you by being perfectly charming.

We made our way through Joe's cramped and grubby milk room and onto the yard, where a small thin heifer was standing miserably in the race. Two feet that looked about as big as hers were sticking out from her back end. I pulled on a long plastic rectal glove and poured a dollop of lube onto my palm. 'Joe, this is Mark. Mark, Joe.'

'Hi,' said Mark, but our host had evidently exhausted his fund of chitchat and didn't even bother to grunt again.

The calf was *not* alive, and hadn't been for some time. Its head was bent so far around I couldn't reach it at all, and it had arrived at that delightful stage where the gas of decomposition had accumulated under the skin and made the whole thing expand to entirely fill the cow's pelvis. The amniotic fluid was long gone and the uterus was starting to clamp down around the calf. There are many, many types of tricky calving – uterine torsions, great big Hereford calves in small dairy heifers, cranky beef cows inadequately restrained in someone's sheep yards half a mile from the nearest water, whole textbooks worth of weird foetal malpresentations – but for that sinking, well-*that's*-this-evening-vanishing-down-the-toilet feeling, I personally think the fizzer calf is hard to beat.

I withdrew my arm and said to Joe, 'The calf's dead. I'll

need to cut off the head, for a start. And I don't know if the shoulders will fit through even without the head.'

'Better get on with it, then, hadn't you?' said Joe.

If I was a charitable person I might have wondered if he'd suffered a crushing blow in his youth to turn him against the whole human race. I'm not, so I merely thought, *I'm going to charge out this call like a wounded bull, you arsehole.*

'Could you grab a couple of buckets of warm water?' I asked.

'I've got calves to feed,' he said. 'Your boyfriend can do it.' And off he went.

There was a brief silence in the yard, broken by Mark scratching his nose and saying, 'Wow.'

The only bucket in the milk room was half full of rotten milk, and I left the world's best lock swilling it out while I went back to the ute to get my embryotome and wire, two five-litre containers of lube and a box of long gloves. Pressing a man who doesn't even have a pair of gumboots into service as a rotten-calf midwife, I thought, has to be some kind of record dating low.

'Right,' I said when we reconvened at the cow's side. 'Epidural first, and then we'll pump in about ten litres of lube – it's as dry as a bone in there – and then I'll get a wire round its neck and cut the head off. And if we're really, really lucky we'll be able to pull it out.'

'What if we're not really lucky?'

'I keep chipping bits off the calf until it's small enough to come out. Or until I tear a hole in the cow's uterus.'

'That's the way,' he said. 'Look on the bright side.'

I crouched down to get the local anaesthetic out of a Barbie lunchbox (donated by my sister Caitlin, who'd received two for her last birthday). 'Well, she's not very big, and her uterus isn't in great shape. She's been trying to calve for about three days, poor girl. And she'll probably sit down, and that'll give us even less room than we've got now.'

She did sit down, but she very considerately waited until I'd placed the wire around the calf's neck. I threaded the ends of the wire down the barrels of my embryotome (which is just a fancy name for two tubes of steel, bolted side by side, that protect the inside of the cow while you're sawing off your chosen bit of calf with piano wire) and screwed the handles on to the free ends of wire. 'I'm really sorry,' I said, 'but I need you to do the sawing while I hold everything in place. You'll probably get dirty.'

'I expect I'll cope,' said Mark, crouching down and taking a handle in each hand. 'Say when.'

I felt again to make sure my wire was in the right place, and took a firm grip on the embryotome. 'When.'

Mark pulled one handle smoothly towards him, and then the other.

'Just slow strokes for a start, then a bit quicker once the wire's bitten in . . . Far out! Stop!'

He stopped sawing. 'What's wrong?'

'You've done it,' I said, pulling the embryotome out of the cow. 'You're through. That's amazing.' If only I'd had him the week before, when my assistant was a frail elderly man with a colostomy bag.

'Stop it,' said Mark. 'You'll make me blush. What now?'

'Now I need that evil-looking hook in the bucket to grab the neck stump with, and we'll pull out the head. Actually, to be honest, I say "we" but I really just mean you.'

He stood up and rummaged through my calving bucket. 'Well, no point in keeping a dog and barking yourself. This one?'

'No, no,' I said pityingly. 'The *really* evil-looking hook. *That's* just a finger knife.'

'This gear looks like you found it in a medieval torture chamber,' he said. 'This one, then.'

'That's the one. Cheers.' After some effort I clamped it around a vertebra, and passed the end of the attached rope to my assistant. 'Pull, please.'

Having calved the head, we had only nine-tenths of the calf to go. 'Right,' I said. 'More lube. You can never have too much lube.'

Mark sniggered.

'Oh, shut up.'

'I didn't say a word!' he protested.

I put down the lube container and picked up the calving jack. 'It was a very suggestive laugh. Now we'll hook this up and I'll get you to do the pulling while I stand here at the front and pretend to be doing something important.' *Please, please, let it come out without me having to cut off a leg.*

Even with an All Black on the end of the calving jack, however, the calf didn't come. I had to cut off a front leg, and then lie on the concrete behind the heifer to work my fingers between the calf's ribs and pull out handfuls of decomposing internal organs. The smell was appalling.

'Are you doing that for any reason other than to see if you can make me throw up?' Mark asked.

I dropped something which may once have been a liver onto the ground beside me with an unpleasant wet splat. 'I'm trying to deflate the thing a bit. I *did* tell you it'd be the world's lousiest evening.'

'Nope,' he said, 'it still doesn't crack the top ten.'

'What would?'

'Losing the last World Cup was up there. And the World Cup before that.'

'Oh,' I said. 'Of course. Right, let's hook up the calving jack again.'

We did, and pulled, and the calf broke in half behind the ribs. I very nearly rested my cheek on the heifer's rump and wept. 'Can I have the evil hook again? And we'd better put in some more lube.'

'You're doing well,' he said gently.

'I'm not,' I said, and if my voice wasn't a wail I'm sure it was heading that way. 'The thing's got a bum the size of a bus, and I have to try and get a wire round and split the pelvis, and even if I can do it we've still got to get the back legs out.'

'And if we can't?'

'I'll have to put the heifer down. I'm not leaving her for Joe to shoot; I did that with a cow that had a broken leg a few months ago, and Keri saw her lurching round in a paddock a week later.'

'Is it worth carrying on?' he asked.

I pushed a wisp of hair back off my face with a dirty glove, which was an ill-considered move. 'Yeah. I'll put the hook around a vertebra and get you to pull it all a bit closer. Poor little heifer.'

After another ten minutes I pulled my left arm out of my patient and said unhappily, 'I can't do it. I can't reach, and my arms aren't working anymore. Could you try? If you can't reach either I'll put her down.'

'Yes, of course,' he said.

I got stiffly to my feet. 'I'm so sorry. You'll get filthy.'

'So I'll wash,' he said serenely, pulling a long glove out of the box. 'Tell me what to do.'

On impulse I reached up and kissed his cheek, which in hindsight would have been a nicer gesture if my face had been clean. 'Drop the introducer over behind the tail, and then pick it up from underneath. You'll need to worm your arm forward as far as you can and push the thing over, then pull your arm out and reach in again underneath. I'll give you my calving gown.'

He shook his head. 'It won't fit me,' he said, unzipping his sweatshirt and hanging it over a rail. He held out his hand for the introducer.

'You'll want some lube,' I said, pouring it liberally over his gloved arm.

'Because you can never have too much lube.' He knelt behind the heifer and felt his way into the birth canal. The heifer stared dully ahead with a look of exhausted bovine long-suffering.

'If you follow the rope in you'll find that evil hook clamped around a vertebra. And you should be able to feel the hair on the calf's back, and if you keep going back you'll feel a tail.'

He closed his eyes, frowning. 'It's enormous.'

'It's all blown up with gas. What can you feel?'

'The end of your rope and the hook . . . some bone . . .'

'Cool. So go forward from there, over the calf.'

There was a pause, and I bit my lip hard to stop myself from asking what he could feel now. Watching someone else calve a cow is a bit like watching them fumble with a knot; it leaves you twitching to elbow them aside and have a go yourself.

'I think I can feel the tail,' he said at last.

'Awesome. So push the introducer down between the calf's legs, if you can. And then the trick is not to pull it back out with you when you bring your arm back.'

'Mm,' he said. Then, 'Hah! Got it!'

'You *legend*!'

'Thank you,' he said, smiling at me. He had a particularly nice smile, swift and warm and infectious. You wouldn't think it would be possible to spend a wonderful evening dismembering a rotten calf for Horrible Joe Watkins, and yet here we were. It was the best night I'd had for months.

Half an hour later the last haunch of rotten calf slithered onto the concrete, and Mark bent to unhook it from the calving jack. I swept my arm around the heifer's cervix, pulled it out again and began to strip off my gloves. 'Well, what d'you know? We didn't rip a big hole in her uterus.'

'So she'll be okay?'

'I think so,' I said. 'I'll fill her up with penicillin and anti-inflammatories, and we'll see if she'll stand up. I wonder where Joe is?'

Mark shrugged. 'Who cares? What should I do with the bits? It looks like the scene of a chainsaw massacre.'

'Leave them,' I said firmly. 'It can be his first job in the morning.'

'Very good,' said Mark, and picking up my calving jack he vanished towards the milk room.

I chose a cocktail of nice expensive drugs for my patient, seeing as Joe wasn't there to refuse pain relief on her behalf. Then I opened the gate in front of her and she struggled gallantly to her feet. Cows really are amazing. I let her out into the paddock beside the shed and went back into the milk room to see Mark scrubbing my embryotome with hot water and an ancient brush that had lost half its bristles. It is often said that the way to a man's heart is through his stomach, and it is equally true (although less well known) that the way to a vet's heart is through cleaning her gear.

'How's the patient?' he asked.

'Up and eating,' I said, peeling off my calving gown. 'Thank you so much.'

'You're welcome. It was fun.'

'Really?'

'Yep.' He laid down the embryotome and held out a hand for the gown.

'It's okay, I can do it.'

'I'm sure you can,' he said, twitching it out of my hand in a very managing fashion.

I reached up to touch my hair. It felt crunchy, which is always a bad sign. Cupping my hands under the running water I started to wash my face.

'Want some warm water?' he asked.

'No, cold's better.'

'Why on earth?'

I scrubbed at an ear with my fingernails; there was a towel hanging up in one corner of the room, but it looked like it had been festering there unwashed for at least a decade. 'The theory is that the warm water makes your pores open, and then the smell really gets in.'

'I see. Do you have anything against soap, then?'

'Not at all,' I said. 'Is there some?'

He looked around the room. 'Ah. No.'

'Never mind; we can scrub properly at home.'

I carried an armful of gear out to the ute and retrieved my docket book, bringing it back into the milk room and opening it on top of a plastic drum in one corner. Rotten calving, head back. Full foetotomy. Time on farm: two hours. And Joe could pay for both of them, the miserable old sod. Drugs used – but at this point Mark pulled his filthy T-shirt off over his head and I temporarily lost my train of thought. He was *beautiful*: sleek and muscled and perfectly proportioned.

He looked up and caught me staring, and I felt my face get hot. This was a shame; those of us whose faces are round and rosy to start with are not improved by blushing. It makes us look far too much like peeled tomatoes.

There was a tense, electric silence. One of those really meaningful silences when you realise suddenly that if you said just the right thing – or didn't say anything – or smiled, or kissed the other person, or *something*, it could be absolutely perfect. But if you're me, you'll probably just cock it up instead.

'Sorry,' I muttered, bending again to my docket book, and the moment vanished like mist in the sun.

'What do you charge for something like this?' Mark asked, running his T-shirt under the tap and beginning to scrub his arms with it. There was a tattoo on the inside of his right forearm, a pattern of thin interlocking whorls that snaked from wrist to elbow.

'Hmm? Oh, four or five hundred dollars.'

On the way back up the driveway we got a clear view through Joe's living room window. He was lying back at his ease in an armchair in front of the TV, coffee mug in hand. I leant on the horn in the hope he'd jump and spill his coffee, but he never even glanced in the direction of the ute.

During the ten-minute drive home the conversation touched on the weather, the Super Rugby schedule and the relative merits of Neutrogena foaming facial scrub and Jif in removing the smell of dead calf from your hands. I parked the ute between Mark's beautiful car and my scruffy one and we climbed out into the frosty darkness.

'Would you like to come in for a coffee?' I asked, the blood rushing once more to my cheeks as it occurred to me that asking someone in for a coffee really just means, 'Do please come in if you feel like sex.' Hastily I added, 'Or a shower.' *Awesome. That's cleared it up nicely.*

'No, it's getting late,' said Mark. 'I'll let you get to bed.'

'Um,' I said for about the thirtieth time in our short acquaintance. Presumably refusing the coffee actually meant, 'I don't find you all that attractive.' I wished I was better at this stuff; gaucheness might be charming in the heroine of an old-fashioned romantic novel, but in the real world it's just a major turn-off. 'Okay. Thank you for coming with me – I'd never have calved that cow by myself.'

'You're welcome.' He reached out to straighten the ute's aerial, bent after an unfortunate sliding-sideways-into-a-hedge incident the month before, and said abruptly, 'Can I see you tomorrow?'

I blinked at him in surprise. 'After covering you in rotten calf?'

'Yeah. If that's okay by you.'

'I – yes, of course it is. Who knows, you might even get to do another horrible calving.'

'I can hardly wait,' he said solemnly.

'How come you're allowed to wander around the countryside calving cows instead of concentrating on rugby?' I asked.

'They try to give the guys who played in the Super Rugby final a bit of a rest before the Tri Nations games.'

'That's nice of them,' I said. 'Would you like to come for tea, or will Hamish be upset that you're not spending enough quality time with him?'

'There's only so much quality time a man can spend with Hamish before being forced to hit him over the head with something heavy.'

I smiled; too much Hamish affected me in exactly the same way. 'So why go and stay with him for a week?'

'Oh, well, it's nice to get out of Auckland. And he had a couple of big farm jobs he needed a hand with. Retagging the herd, and giving them all copper bullets.' He pulled his ear sheepishly. 'And then I met this really great girl on the weekend, and I wanted to see a bit more of her.'

'I – I'm not that great,' I stammered, and then gave myself a swift mental kick. There was just no need to take gaucheness to these new and previously unscaled heights. Or depths. 'You know, it's going to be really embarrassing if you were talking about someone else.'

'I wasn't,' said Mark, and closing the distance between us in two long strides he bent his head and kissed me.

At age twelve, or thereabouts, I had spent quite a bit of time envisaging that magical first kiss from the handsome stranger. I would be looking my best, obviously, gowned in cornflower blue and slender as a reed. The setting varied from an orchard white with blossom, to a candlelit ballroom, to a lonely shore where little waves broke hissing against the shells. (It's probably unnecessary to say that my idol, at twelve, was Anne of Green Gables.)

I *hadn't* planned to be dressed in khaki overalls and have one red eye. Neither had my imagined perfect kiss involved the handsome stranger saying conversationally, when at length he let me go, 'You smell terrible.'

I laughed. 'Well, so do you.'

'True,' he said. 'I'll try to wash before tomorrow. What should I bring?'

'Nothing. I'll ring you if I get called out, but if you make it here before me there's a key to the back door on a nail at the top left-hand side of the doorframe.'

'Thank you. It seems a bit rough that you're on call two weekends in a row.'

'It's usually only one in five,' I told him. 'And two in five over spring. But I swapped weekends, because I've got to go to Taupo in a few weeks' time.'

'I see,' said Mark. 'I thought perhaps being on call was a handy excuse when some dodgy bloke asks you out and you don't want to go.'

I shook my head, and he pulled me back up against him.

5

'SO, HOW WAS YOUR EVENING WITH MARK TIPENE?' ALISON asked the next day as we marched along the road past Broadview Nissan. A salesman paused in the act of polishing a car bonnet to admire Alison's pert lycra-clad bottom, then realised she'd noticed and began to polish with renewed vigour.

'It was really nice,' I said. 'Which is surprising, since we spent it doing a disgusting rotten calving for Joe Watkins.'

'How romantic.'

'It was. Especially the bit where Mark got to put his arm into the cow up to the shoulder, when he had no overalls or gumboots.'

'Where was Joe?' she asked.

'Inside watching TV,' I said. 'Horrible old coot.'

'I'm not actually telling you this because it would be a breach of client confidentiality, but he comes into the medical centre every couple of months for an injection and he's got a tattoo of a topless girl on his bum.'

'Is it a nice tattoo?'

'No,' she said decidedly. 'Very tasteless.'

As opposed to all those really tasteful tattoos of topless girls that you see around the place. I had a hopeful thought. 'Is the injection for some fatal disease?'

'I'm afraid not,' said Alison. 'But it *is* a painful injection, if that makes you feel better.'

'It does. Thank you.'

'You're welcome. So, are you seeing your All Black again tonight?'

'No.' I aimed a kick at a pebble, and missed. After two years of junior soccer, during which my parents spent their Saturday mornings watching me pick buttercups in my corner of the field, I was allowed to go to singing lessons instead. 'He was going to come for tea, but he rang this morning and said the guy who was supposed to be playing number four tomorrow had just fallen off his motorbike and dislocated his thumb, so he's gone to Dunedin to play rugby instead.'

'Damn,' said Alison.

We strode on past Alcot's Farm Machinery, waving to Sam, who was deep in conversation with a farmer in front of an enormous self-unloading trailer.

'He kissed me goodnight,' I said to my feet.

'*Did* he?' Alison is a most satisfactory friend; when you make some momentous announcement you can be quite confident she'll treat your news with the attention you feel it deserves. She never responds with, 'Cool. Hey, guess who I saw this morning?'

'How was it?' she asked.

'Lovely,' I said. Thrilling. Perfect, in fact, smell notwithstanding. Anything less like kissing the previous model – which was pleasant and familiar and about as exhilarating as a bowl of rice pudding – would have been difficult to imagine. 'I got the impression he's had quite a lot of practice.'

'I expect he has. When are you going to see him again?'

'Goodness only knows,' I said sadly. 'He's flying out for South Africa on Tuesday, and then they're playing Australia again on the way home the next weekend, and the weekend after *that* I've got to go to Mary-Anne's hen's weekend.' It was all very depressing.

'Oh,' said Alison, sounding discouraged. Then, rallying gamely, she offered, 'I wouldn't be surprised if that was quite a good thing. If he makes an effort to keep in touch you'll know he really likes you.'

'And if he doesn't I'll know the only reason he wanted to see me was that it was better than hanging out with Hamish.'

On leaving work that night I turned left instead of right at Broadview's only set of traffic lights, and went to visit my family. I parked the ute behind my stepmother's car and let myself in through the garage. As I rounded the corner of the hall towards the kitchen there was a piercing shriek and Em roared, 'Annabel! Stop that at once!'

'Caitlin's got my pink blanket!' Annabel wailed.

'She wasn't even using it!' Caitlin cried. 'She only wants it because I need it for my hospital!'

'Hey, munchkins,' I said, arriving at the scene. Caitlin had climbed with the blanket to the top of a bookcase, while Bel protested beneath her.

'Helen, get my blanket back!' she demanded.

'But I *need* it!' said Caitlin.

I swung my smallest sister up with a grunt of effort and sat her on one hip. Annabel has the same build as a bull terrier: compact but extremely dense. 'Come on, let's go see what your mum's doing,' I said. 'Do you think I'd be allowed to stay for tea?'

'Yeah! Can you read me *Bad Jelly the Witch* when I go to bed?'

'I'm sick of Bad Jelly,' I said. 'Can't we find something else?' Reading to Bel was deeply painful; you only ever managed half a page before she waved you imperiously to silence and took over herself. And her grasp of the text was shaky at best, so you had to wait while she furrowed her brow and muttered, 'Um . . . Um . . . No! Don't *help* me! I can do it!' I tried to stick with nice, short books like *The Very Hungry Caterpillar*, which at least kept this penance to a minimum.

'*Please?*' Bel asked.

'We'll see,' I said weakly.

'Your eye is red,' she informed me.

'I know. I got kicked by a cow. Hi, Em.'

My stepmother turned from the stove to kiss me. 'Sweetie, your *face*!'

'It's fine,' I said. 'Doesn't hurt at all. But it looks nice and impressive, don't you think?'

Em brushed my bruised cheek with beautifully manicured fingers. 'Nick shouldn't expect you to put yourself in these dangerous situations,' she said.

'Please don't ring him,' I said. 'Promise me you won't.' Sometimes, just fleetingly, I fantasise about having a traditional evil stepmother who wants nothing to do with me. It would be so much less embarrassing.

'Hmm,' said Em. 'Any weekend plans?'

'I'm on call.'

'*Again?* Sweetie, it's slave labour!'

'No it's not,' I said, letting Bel slide to the floor. 'I swapped weekends so I can go to Mary-Anne's hen's weekend in August.'

'Mary-Anne,' Em repeated. 'Which one is she?'

'The short one with curly dark hair who manages to say "my fiancé" at least twice per sentence.'

Em nodded. 'Ah, her. Now, I need a favour,' she said, giving her cheese sauce a brisk stir, then putting down the wooden spoon and tilting her chin up towards the ceiling. 'I can feel a nasty bristly hair, and I can't see it in the mirror. Can you get it for me?'

I peered obediently at her neck. 'No, you're good.'

'Look harder,' she ordered. 'I'm having lunch with Christine Marshall tomorrow, and she's got eyes like a hawk.'

I looked harder. 'There?'

Em's hand flew to the spot I had touched. 'Oh, God,' she said. 'I didn't even *notice* that one. That's it; I'm going to have to start waxing my neck.'

'No, you're not. It's minute. You'd practically need an electron microscope to see it.'

'Annabel, fetch my tweezers. Or maybe I should just go straight for your father's razor.'

'Daddy doesn't like it when you use his razor,' said Bel.

'She was only teasing,' I said.

'She *does* use his razor. It makes Daddy sad.' She shook her curly blonde head mournfully. '*Poor* Daddy.'

'Annabel! Tweezers. Now,' Em ordered. 'Helen, love, Monique Ledbetter's having an Intimo party next week. Why don't you come with me?'

'What, another sex toy thing? No *way*,' I said, leaning against the bench beside her.

'Honestly, Helen, I don't know where you developed all these hang-ups.'

'I think I got most of them at that sex toy party.'

My stepmother smiled a small and wicked smile. 'Sweetie,' she said, 'grow up. Anyway, this one isn't sex toys, it's really lovely lingerie. Just gorgeous – very feminine and flattering. And she's putting on wine and nibbles.'

'What night is it?' I asked. Not that it mattered, because if it was on a night with no prior commitments I was going to invent an engagement on the spot. I love Em very much, but her idea of feminine and flattering and mine are poles apart.

'Wednesday.'

'I can't,' I said. 'I'm going to the movies with Keri.' It's so nice not to have to lie. 'Where's Dad?'

'At your grandmother's. Apparently she's got no water.'

'Poor Dad,' I said.

'He shouldn't be far away,' Em said. 'You'll stay for tea, won't you, sweetie?'

At ten that night I was reading in bed with Murray on my feet when my phone buzzed beside me. It was a new message received from Mark T (not to be confused with Mark M, a tubby and cheerful classmate currently doing a residency in equine medicine in Ohio). I gave a happy squirm as I opened the phone, and Murray opened one golden eye and glared at me.

How many calving cows tonite?

None so far. How is Dunedin?

Cold. Sleep well x

I squirmed again, and Murray bit my toe through the duvet. 'But he sent me an x,' I explained.

Murray looked completely unimpressed.

After four minutes of intense thought I sent back: *You too x*

I picked my way through the gumboots and empty swap-a-crates at the back door of Sam's flat (where they subscribed to the Sky Sport channel) just after seven the next evening, and went into the kitchen to find his flatmates playing cards at the kitchen table.

'You cheating bastard,' said Will, whose back was to the door. Will was a thoroughly nice bloke. He was thoughtful and courteous and painfully shy, and he could only just bring himself to talk to me.

Dylan, who was loud and inconsiderate and thought he was far more attractive to women than was in fact the case, lifted one buttock off his chair and farted in greeting. 'Evening, Helen.'

'Cheers for that, Dylan,' I said, looking at the floor and deciding not to remove my shoes.

'Better out than in.'

'Dear God,' I said faintly as the smell reached my side of the kitchen. It was the sort of odour that is depicted in cartoons as an evil green mist. 'What have you been *eating*?'

'Beans and eggs,' said Dylan. 'Grab me a beer while you're next to the fridge, would you?'

'Get your own beer, you low-life,' Will said, getting up. 'Come into the lounge, Helen, before you pass out.'

Sam was lying full length on a battered couch, reading a rugby magazine, a beer on the floor beside him. 'Here you go, Hel,' he said, folding it open and passing it over.

The article was headed *Locked and Loaded*, with a picture of Mark taking up the rest of the page. It was one of those artistic publicity shots taken from so close up you can see the individual hairs in the subject's designer stubble and the faint creases around his eyes as he gazes into the middle distance.

He's worn the number four jersey for over ten years, and the farm boy from Taranaki who made the All Blacks on the strength of just one season at provincial level has never looked more dangerous. Kurt Wallis talks to Mark Tipene about the impending Tri Nations series, composure under the high ball, and that mysterious blonde hottie.

I lifted Sam's legs and sat down on the couch, letting them fall back across my lap.
'Comfortable?' he asked, just a trifle sarcastically.
'Yep. Thanks.'

He's twice been awarded New Zealand Sportsman of the Year, his picture graces the International Rugby Hall of Fame, and opposition forward packs almost wet themselves at the thought of facing him on the field. His name has been linked to a selection of the country's most luscious females – among them the delectable Tamara Healy, no mean sportswoman in her own right.

A selection of the country's most luscious females. Oh, *man.* I might, with the light behind me and in the eyes of a particularly fond observer, pass as quite cute in a girl-next-door kind of way, but in my wildest dreams I could never achieve lusciousness.

This is a man whom opposition coaches label a cheat, while in the same breath urging their players to model their game on his. A man who raises money for victims of domestic violence, who has had a beer with the Prime Minister and drunk tea with the Queen of England, and yet who recently refused a lucrative book deal on the grounds that his life wouldn't make very interesting reading.

'Do you think that perhaps the guy who wrote this has a bit of a crush on him?' I asked. The way this article was going, Mark would be leaping skyscrapers and rescuing people from burning buildings by the bottom of the page.

'I got the impression he wants to marry him and have his babies,' said Sam.

'Mm.' I bent over the magazine again, in search of further references to this mysterious blonde hottie. There was more fulsome praise to wade through, and great screeds of rugby jargon. I think the writer even said something about 'good clean ball'. As opposed, presumably, to all that nasty dirty ball that is such a blight on our national game. The hottie didn't make her reappearance until the last paragraph.

And the blonde with whom he was snapped at Auckland's waterfront last week? Tipene frowns and scratches his chin. 'Sorry,' he says finally, 'which one was that?'

I handed Sam back his magazine and rested my head despondently against the back of the couch.

He laughed. 'And you used your sock to show him how to put a prolapsed uterus back in.'

'The sock was a high point,' I told him. '*Then* I took him to a calving at Joe Watkins' and covered him in rotten afterbirth.'

'Awesome,' said my supportive cousin.

'Who'd you cover with rotten afterbirth?' Dylan asked, ambling in and throwing himself into an armchair.

'Mark Tipene,' said Sam. 'You know – him.' He waved a hand towards the TV, where in the pre-game ad break an admiring crowd of All Blacks was clustered around a dinky little car I doubt any of them would have been seen dead driving. 'The reason behind Helen's sudden interest in rugby.'

'Mark Tipene?' Dylan repeated, eyeing me sceptically.

'It's true,' said Sam. 'She met him at Alistair Johnson's party last weekend and asked him what he did for a living, and he asked her out on the strength of it. I suppose he thought it made a pleasant change from girls drooling on him.'

On screen the players ran onto the field. It was a clear, still night in Dunedin and the men's breath steamed in the cold. A pair of chilly-looking *New Zealand Idol* finalists sang the Australian and New Zealand national anthems, with added quavery bits to prove that they were serious musicians. Mark's face in the line of black-uniformed men was grim and handsome, like a storybook hero's, and my stomach gave an uncomfortable little lurch.

'Beer, Hel?' Sam asked, prodding me in the ribs with a sock-clad foot.

'Yes, please.'

'What's the difference between a ruck and a maul?' I whispered ten minutes later.

'In a maul they're passing the ball back from one to the other, and in a ruck the ball's on the ground and they're tickling it towards their side with their feet,' said Sam.

'Cool. Thank you.'

'You're welcome. Be quiet.'

Mark, in the middle of the All Black lineout, reached up as his teammates lifted him and swiped the ball casually from the hands of the Australian jumper. Then he promptly disappeared from sight under a boiling mass of black and gold jerseys. I stiffened in alarm. How on earth was *that* legal? He'd be trampled to death if the ref didn't blow the whistle . . .

The whistle blew. Well, I thought, better late than never. Presumably now one of those stomping brutes would be sent to the sin bin. In the top left-hand corner of the TV screen a little picture of a whistle appeared, with *Not rolling away* beside it. Mark was getting to his feet, and a gold-shirted player had the ball.

'*What?*'

'You've got to roll away when you've been tackled,' Sam explained. 'You're not allowed to kill the ball like that.'

'How was he supposed to roll away with ten enormous thugs lying on top of him?'

Sam shrugged. 'Those are the rules. And he probably *could* have rolled away – they all try to make it look like they couldn't help it. You get away with as much as the ref will let you.'

'I still don't see how getting squashed flat can be his fault.'

'Helen, shut up,' said Sam.

Great try. You legend.

Not the most inspiring of text messages, but its composition occupied the entire drive home and the removal of a rabbit's large intestine from the kitchen floor. Murray, the soul of generosity, always left the bits he didn't want for me.

The phone buzzed. *Thanks. Any calving boys?*

I was still frowning at the screen when it was followed by, *Or even calving cows.* Ah yes, of course. The pitfalls of predictive text.

None of either, I wrote. *How many bones broken after that game?*

None. All good.

Thats a relief. Goodnight x

And I only agonised for two minutes about the x, which was definitely progress.

Nite miss you x

I didn't actually jump up and down and squeal, but it was close.

6

SPRING IS BY FAR THE MOST INTERESTING TIME OF YEAR in large-animal practice – the work is mostly emergency rather than routine, and almost all the really cool medical conditions of cows occur around calving. The only downside is that lots of them don't occur during business hours.

It rained steadily all the first week in August and we were flat out at work. I enjoyed it; I was getting lots of good experience and it distracted me nicely from obsessing about Mark. Sitting around waiting for the boy you like to call does your mental state no good at all. Besides, it's embarrassing.

The insides of my elbows were bruised purple from calving cows, which made me feel pleasantly stoic and hardworking. I did six breech calvings in a row, operated on a calf with a twisted stomach and spent Saturday night on Sam's couch so as to watch the All Blacks play South Africa live at two thirty on Sunday morning. Sam's couch was uncomfortable and his flatmates were highly amused, and I was thankful that the following week's match against Australia was screening with a two-hour delay on poor people's TV, so I could watch it at home.

Just before three the next Friday afternoon I was sitting on the edge of Thomas's desk, drinking coffee and waiting for the next calving. We often had an early afternoon lull and then a run of calls around three thirty, once the dairy farmers had checked their calving mobs.

Anita came up the hall and vanished into the dispensary behind the front counter. 'Who's on call this weekend?' she called.

'Me,' said Richard, who was leafing through the *Auto Trader* in a corner.

'I'm on back-up,' I added.

'I've just induced six little heifers at Justin Smith's, so you might spend a bit of time there this weekend pulling out calves.'

'Thanks for that,' said Richard sourly. 'What are they in calf to?'

'Angus,' she said, reappearing with a box of thirty-mil syringes under one arm. 'Justin's already had two heifers down with pinched nerves, so we thought we'd better get the rest of the calves out before they grow any bigger.'

'Yippee fucking skip,' Richard said, closing his paper and stalking off to sulk in the lunch room.

Anita, who had three small children and a husband with two share-milking jobs, snorted. After work each day she picked up the kids, bathed them, fed them, supervised their homework, took them down to the cowshed while she examined that day's accumulated sick cows, packed each of the kids a nourishing lunch for the next day and put them to bed so she could spend a relaxing evening with the farm accounts. She had almost no sympathy for anyone else who felt they were overworked and underappreciated.

The automatic doors at the front of the shop opened and Hamish Thompson came in out of the rain. 'Afternoon, all,' he said, kicking off his gumboots.

I slid to my feet and went up to the counter. 'Hi, Hamish, how are things?'

'Bloody wet.'

'True. What can we do for you?'

'Box of Clavulox and some milk let-down stuff for heifers,' he said.

I turned towards the dispensary and found Anita already gathering the drugs. 'Are you alright for syringes and needles, Hamish?' she asked.

'Yeah.' He settled himself comfortably against the counter, crossing one ankle over the other and running a hand through his hair. He looked like Hollywood's take on the rugged, virile man of the land, and I'd have bet a reasonable sum of money that he was hoping you'd think so. 'Enjoyed your hot date the other night, did you, Helen?'

'It was great,' I said. 'There's something so romantic about cutting up a rotten calf.' When talking to Hamish it was fatal to show the slightest sign of embarrassment. He was like a hyena, prowling around the edges of the conversation in search of an opening, and if you provided one he would attack without mercy.

'So I heard,' said Hamish. 'Has he called you?'

'None of your business,' I said, although I smiled to take the edge off.

'Just taking an interest,' he said. 'Do you want me to sign something?'

I pushed his docket and a pen across the counter.

'*Has* he called?' Thomas asked from his desk.

'Of course he has,' said Anita. 'Look at her, she's blushing like a schoolgirl.'

I hadn't been, but my cheeks immediately began to grow warm. Blushes are such suggestible things.

'So you reckon he really likes her, Hamish?' Thomas asked.

'Seemed pretty keen. No accounting for taste, I suppose.' He signed his docket and handed it back to me, grinning.

'But surely he could get any woman he wanted,' said Thomas. 'No offence, Helen.'

I had a fairly quiet Saturday: two calvings, a vomiting dog and three kittens with ringworm belonging to Fenella Martin. Ringworm is hardly an after-hours emergency, but what really annoyed me was spending half an hour of my life listening to Fenella explain that mating brothers to sisters and fathers to daughters is line-breeding and not inbreeding.

I got home from this happy outing just after eight and texted Mark: *Have fun out there and don't get broken.*

The reply, twenty minutes later, was, *Will do.*

Hmm. Succinct. Well, no doubt he was busy. Although of course he might be both busy and irritated at being sent inane messages by some girl he'd kissed on impulse a fortnight ago.

Text messaging really is a lousy way to communicate with someone you don't know very well. You miss out on all the important cues, like facial expression and tone of voice, and if you don't hear back you've got no idea whether the other person hasn't got their phone on them or just doesn't have anything to say to you. It's enough to make you develop a stomach ulcer.

I managed somehow to stay awake until the replay at eleven thirty. It wasn't a very interesting game, at least for a rugby ignoramus; it was raining heavily in Brisbane and both teams spent most of their time kicking the ball from one end of the field to the other. The Wallabies won, and at one thirty, having heard nothing from Mark and unable to think of any comment he might possibly want to hear, I turned off the TV and went sadly to bed, to be woken at six with a calving.

7

MY FIRST ACT ON MONDAY MORNING WAS TO SMASH A full glass bottle of the most expensive antibiotic we stocked. Nick put his head around the door of the dispensary, closed his eyes for a second and said tiredly, 'Jesus, Helen.'

I knelt down to pick up the pieces, cutting my finger in the process. 'You can charge it to my account.'

'Oh, don't be such a bloody martyr,' he snapped.

Then I went to a calving north of town – a live Jersey calf with one front leg bent right back. I tried for half an hour to get the other leg, and then called for help.

Anita arrived in her briskest and most efficient mood, attached my calving jack to the leg that was coming the right way and winched the calf out without bothering about the other leg at all. 'Alright?' she said curtly, pulling the slimy little thing around for its mother to lick. 'Think you'll be able to manage that by yourself next time?'

'Yes. Thanks, Anita.'

'Don't just stand there. Get yourself cleaned up. You're late for those calf dehornings at Mulligan's.' And off she went, her ute screeching around the tanker loop and spraying water six feet in the air.

I had two cat speys and an abscess to lance back at the clinic, and when I went in after a seven-minute lunch break to get started the surgery was a tip. I looked at it tight-lipped for a moment and went to find Zoe, who should have been cleaning it but was instead on the phone in the vet room, winding strands of hair around her finger as she talked. Seeing me in the doorway she swivelled in her chair so her back was to me.

The blood of my Scottish ancestors, a warlike and disreputable lot whose favourite employment, I believe, was rustling English cattle from over the border, grew hot in my veins. 'Zoe,' I said. 'Excuse me, please, we've got surgery.'

There was no response.

'*Zoe!*' I repeated crossly.

Zoe muttered something into the phone and slammed it down.

'The surgery's disgusting,' I said. 'What happened?'

'I *have* had things to do,' she said. 'You could help, you know.'

'Seeing as I've been doing nothing all morning while you slaved? Clean it up, please, while I pre-med the cats.'

'Bitch,' she said and, bursting into tears, ran out of the room.

I went wearily out to the front of the shop and leant on the counter beside Thomas. '*What* is her problem?'

'Boyfriend trouble,' said Thomas. 'I'll have a word with her.'

'And in the meantime I'll go and scrub the fucking surgery.'

Thomas raised his eyebrows. 'Not like you to swear. Are you having boyfriend trouble too?'

'No,' I said shortly.

'You can tell Uncle Thomas all about it, you know.' He bent towards me, and a gust of Lynx Out of Africa made my eyes water. 'Haven't you heard from your All Black?'

'I've just got really bad period pain,' I said. This was untrue, but proved a highly effective way of horrifying Thomas and distracting him from his line of questioning.

At five twenty pm I turned down Rex's tanker track, lined up the first pothole wrong and crashed with a brain-jarring thud into the second one. It seemed a fitting conclusion to a thoroughly crappy day, unbroken by any form of communication from Mark. He'd been back in the country for more than twenty-four hours, and surely if he'd had any interest in me at all he would have been in touch by now. I had read *He's Just Not That Into You* one rainy weekend at my ex-boyfriend's parents' bach, and it was pretty obvious that he wasn't. I wondered whether Thomas would mock or commiserate, and which would be harder to bear.

Monday was yoga night, but I was in no mood for being a vessel filled with clear white light. I would have a long, hot bath with a glass of wine and a Georgette Heyer novel instead, followed by poached eggs on toast and bed by eight o'clock.

That small self-righteous inner voice whose sole job it is to make you feel guilty piped up, *You should really go to yoga.*

Oh, sod off, I told it.

Turning in through my gate I nearly hit a sleek, dangerous-looking sports car parked in front of the garage. Now *that* was unexpected. Mark was sitting on the back doorstep with Murray on his lap, and suddenly, although three seconds ago the only good thing about today had been that it was nearly finished, life was a wonderful thing.

I turned off the ute, got out and shut the door. *Don't say um. Don't you* dare *say um* . . . 'Hi.'

'Hi,' said Mark, tipping Murray lightly off his knee as he stood up. 'Sorry to just turn up.'

'You're the first nice thing that's happened all day,' I said, going across the lawn towards him.

He put his arms around me and kissed me for quite a long time, and I realised that, contrary to all expectation, today was the best day of my life to date. 'You still smell,' he said when we broke apart.

'A gentleman wouldn't keep pointing it out.'

He grinned. 'Well, I'd have thought a lady would smell better.'

'It's burnt hair,' I said. 'I've been dehorning calves. Come in and grab a drink while I have a shower. Have you been waiting long?'

'Only about ten minutes.'

I climbed the steps and reached up for the key, hanging on its nail at the top of the doorframe. 'You should have let yourself in.'

'It's just a bit creepy to get home and find some random bloke making himself comfortable in your house, don't you think?'

'Only if you were going through my knickers drawer or something.'

'That's usually the very first thing I do in someone else's house,' said Mark.

I left him making a cup of tea and went to have a shower, where I paid particular attention to my elbows. Satisfied that both they and my earlobes were clean, I pulled my wet hair back into a ponytail, and put on my favourite, bottom-flattering jeans and a green T-shirt that Alison said went nicely with brown eyes.

As I came back into the kitchen, Mark's pocket started to ring. He took out his phone, looked at it briefly and turned it off. 'Dad,' he said, putting the phone down on the bench.

'Shouldn't you get it? It might be important.'

'Nope,' he said flatly. 'He'll be ringing to tell me I should have passed the ball wide and not tried to run it, and that I was sloppy in the lineout.'

'You were not!'

He looked at me, amused. 'How would you know?'

'I watched. And they said on Radio Sport this morning that you were pretty much the only player on the field in that game who looked like he knew what he was doing.'

'You listen to Radio Sport?'

'Yes,' I said. I had been an avid follower of the sporting news for nearly three weeks now.

He smiled and reached out a long arm to pull me closer, and a pair of headlights raked the side of the cottage as a car pulled in behind my ute.

'Oh, dear Lord, *no*,' I said, stepping hurriedly back.

'What? It's your boyfriend?'

'Worse. Stepmother. And sisters,' I added, as both rear doors opened too. 'I'm so sorry.'

'Sorry for what?' Mark asked.

'Whatever they're going to say.' I opened the kitchen door as Caitlin reached the bottom step. 'Hey, munchkin, how are things?'

'Good,' she said, marching in past me. 'We've been dancing. I was a fairy, but I had to take my wings off to get in the car.'

'Very cool,' I said. 'Were you a fairy too, Bel?'

'No,' said Annabel, ascending the stairs with a stately, measured tread. 'I was a rabbit.'

'What sort of dance does a rabbit do?'

She ignored this frivolous question and fixed her eyes firmly on my visitor. 'Were you cuddling Helen?'

'Yes,' Mark admitted.

'Why?'

'Annabel,' said Em, following her in and closing the door behind her, 'that is none of your business. Hello, sweetie.'

I kissed her cheek. 'Em, this is my friend Mark. Mark, this is Emily, and the small ones are Caitlin and Annabel.'

'I'm Helen's evil stepmother,' Em said. 'How nice to meet you.'

'You too,' said Mark.

'Are you a giant?' Caitlin asked, looking him up and down thoughtfully.

'No, I'm just tall.'

'He certainly is,' said Em. 'Now, sweetie, I can see you've got things to do –' she paused and winked at me in a way that was probably meant to be subtle but really, *really* wasn't '– but I just wanted to drop in a wee something I bought for you last week. What have I done with it? Caitlin, please run back to the car and bring me the bag on the front seat.' She opened the door for Caitlin, and turned back to Mark. 'Where are you from, Mark?'

'Taranaki, originally, but I live in Auckland.'

'And what do you do for a living?'

'I play rugby,' he said.

'You're on TV,' said Bel suddenly. 'And you're on our Weetbix packet. Helen, can I have something to eat?'

'Is she allowed a piece of cake?' I asked Em. 'Or is it too close to teatime?'

'Hmm?' said Em. She sounded somewhat absentminded, no doubt because ninety-nine percent of her brain was attempting feverishly to recall the family Weetbix box. 'Yes, alright then. Just a small piece.'

I opened the pantry and removed a large chocolate cake. I had found the recipe in Thursday's *Broadview Broadcast*, labelled 'Absolutely Superb Chocolate Cake', and made it to see if they were telling the truth. They were. According to an article I once read in *Cosmopolitan*, every girl should be able to bake a good chocolate cake, use an electric drill and perform a striptease. I was currently sitting on one out of the three.

'Wicked,' said Bel. 'I want a big bit, Helen.'

'So do I,' said Mark.

I took a knife from the block on the bench and handed it to him. 'Em, would you like a cup of tea?'

'No, we'd better not stay,' she said, to my profound relief. 'I haven't done a thing about dinner, and your father will be home by now.'

Caitlin stormed back up the steps, plastic bag in hand. 'Cake! *Mean!*'

'Is that a big enough piece?' Mark asked Bel, indicating a very generous wedge with the carving knife.

'No,' said Bel.

'About half that,' said her mother firmly, taking the bag from Caitlin. 'Helen, I ordered these for you at the Intimo evening.' She pulled a couple of wisps of scarlet lace out of the bag and handed them over. 'That's such a gorgeous colour on you. Just let me know if I got the sizing wrong, and I can swap them.'

'Oh,' I said faintly. 'Thank you.'

'Perhaps your friend Mark can give you a second opinion,' she suggested.

'*Em!*'

'Have fun, sweetie,' she said, laughing and patting my cheek. 'Come along, girls. You can eat your cake in the car.'

'Beautiful cake,' Mark said, taking a large bite.

Em was backing her car around at high speed, no doubt in haste to get home and scrutinise the Weetbix packet.

'Thank you,' I said.

'She's nice.'

'Yeah, she's lovely.' I spread the scarlet wisps on the bench for closer inspection, and began to laugh helplessly. 'These are *awful*.'

'Oh, I don't know,' he said. 'They look alright to me.'

'Then they're all yours. They should be a good colour on you, too.'

'Tempting, but I don't think they'd fit.'

'I should be used to it by now,' I said. 'When I was in sixth form she rang the mothers of all the boys in my class to get me a date to the high school ball.'

'Ouch.'

'It was pretty bad,' I agreed. Although it was nothing compared to being told, at the tender age of seventeen, that my father was a tiger in the bedroom. *That* probably caused permanent psychological damage.

'This is really good,' said Mark, taking another bite of cake. 'Does your mum still live around here?'

I shook my head. 'She died when I was ten.'

'Oh. I'm sorry. What happened?'

'Car crash,' I said.

'God, that's terrible.'

'She got into the loose gravel at the side of the road and crashed into a power pole. She was probably putting on lipstick – she always did her makeup in the car.' That morning she had made my sandwiches and Dad's, done my hair in a French plait

68

and reminded Dad not to forget the milk on his way home. I was late for the school bus and ran out without kissing her goodbye. (I *always* kissed her goodbye, and for years I used to wake in the middle of the night wondering if she'd still be alive if I hadn't forgotten.) And then that afternoon a shaking, grey-faced Aunty Deb came to get me from school, and Dad's and my world fell apart.

Mark was wearing the alarmed expression of a man who finds himself dropped without warning into the middle of a deep and meaningful conversation, and taking pity on him I changed the subject. 'Would you like to stay for tea? I have venison steak.'

'How did you manage that?' he asked.

'Sam's flatmate shot a deer last week.'

'I haven't had venison steak for about ten years. Yes, please.'

We cooked dinner companionably and ate at the kitchen table, Murray supervising from the bench. 'You're a great cook,' said Mark, finishing his second pile of roast potatoes.

'It's the garlic salt,' I said. 'One of the great inventions of our age. Cake?'

He shook his head. 'It wouldn't fit.'

'You can take some home with you, if you like.'

'That'd be great,' he said. 'Thank you.'

'I thought you professional athletes were only supposed to eat health-giving and nutritious foods like steamed vegetables and brown rice?'

He grinned. 'Yeah, but they'll never know.'

We retired to the couch, a great big squashy plum-coloured thing I bought from my second cousin Kevin for twenty-four bottles of Steinlager. If my aim had been to find the piece of furniture that was going to look as hideous as possible against an orange nylon carpet I couldn't have done better, but it was very comfortable.

'Are you very sore from Saturday?' I asked. To my uneducated eye it had seemed that Mark had spent the whole eighty minutes being stamped on by big men with spiky boots. Many of whom, to add insult to injury, were on his team.

'Yeah, a bit. A few knocks; nothing major,' he said, pulling up the hem of his shirt to show me.

'Nothing *major*? How many ribs did you *break*?' He looked like he'd been run over by a truck, and any pride I might have had in a few measly elbow-bruises evaporated completely.

'Not even one,' he said.

I reached out and put a hand gently over the livid stripes on his chest. 'It's frightening.'

He didn't answer, but covered my hand with his. His skin was very warm and I could feel his heart beating through his chest wall. It seemed fast, for an athlete's.

Please don't stuff this up, I told myself desperately. *Just for once, depart from tradition and don't stuff it up . . .* 'You wouldn't consider a change of career, would you? How about playing something safer, like lawn bowls?'

'I could, I suppose, but the money would be lousy.'

There was a short silence, which neither of us dared to break. Then it occurred to me that it was my move. Gathering up all of my courage, I got up and sat down again across his lap, straddling him.

'Hi,' he said softly.

'Hi.' And then we stopped talking and just kissed each other instead, which was far better.

8

AT HALF PAST NINE MARK, WHO HAD BEEN LYING FULL-length on my couch with his head on my lap, sat up and stretched his arms above his head. 'You've got something on this weekend, haven't you?' he asked.

'Yes, I'm going to Taupo to play drinking games and make wedding dresses out of toilet paper.'

'That sounds like fun.' He stood up in one fluid movement and reached a hand down to me.

'You reckon?' I asked, taking it and letting him pull me up.

'Actually, it sounds hideous.'

'That's what I thought.' I preceded him into the kitchen and rummaged in the drawer under the microwave for plastic wrap with which to cover half a chocolate cake.

'I don't need all that,' he said.

'I was going to take it in to work, but Keri's on a diet and she'll be mad at me. Please take it.'

'Oh, well, in that case, okay.' He accepted the cake and bent his head to kiss me. 'I'd better go home and let you get to bed.'

'You could stay,' I said impulsively. 'If – if you want to . . .'

He looked at me, startled, and my cheeks burnt in shame. Hurriedly I added, 'But you've probably got an early start or something.'

'No,' he said. 'I mean yes, I want to.'

'Okay, um, cool,' I said, going abruptly from hot with embarrassment to cold with terror as I realised that, in fact, this was all moving way too fast for me. I didn't really want him to stay; I wanted him to kiss me goodnight and go away. Then I would be free to lie awake half the night, reliving every second of the evening, overanalysing his every word and agonising about how much he really liked me. The lying-awake-and-obsessing stage is an important one in any new relationship – you're not supposed to just skip it.

But I must have done a reasonable impression of one of those uninhibited, self-confident girls who view sex as merely a pleasant form of exercise, because Mark put down his cake, pulled me closer and kissed me, sliding his hands warmly up my sides under my T-shirt. I lifted my arms obediently and he tugged the shirt off over my head.

'You are so lovely,' he said against my mouth.

'Thank you,' I whispered, and because there didn't seem to be anything else to do in the circumstances (as well as because I had never been so attracted to anyone in my life), I twisted away from him and took his hand, pulling him up the hall to my bedroom.

He sat down on the edge of my bed and looked at me, and with shaking hands I reached behind my back to undo the catch of my bra. I couldn't; I was so nervous I had lost all feeling in my fingertips.

'Here,' he said softly, pulling me up between his knees and reaching around me to undo it himself. And then he sat me across his lap and kissed me with a single-minded concentration that completely changed my mind about this being a bad idea.

Ten minutes or so later he sat up and said, 'Crap, wallet's in the car.'

This remark seemed to have no relevance at all. 'W-what?' I asked unsteadily.

'Condom.'

'Oh,' I said. 'I've got some.' Getting up I crossed the room and felt around in the bottom of my wardrobe until I found a plastic grocery bag, from which I extracted one of about twenty small cellophane-wrapped boxes.

Mark was watching me in the dim light from the hall with a bemused expression on his face. 'Did you get some kind of discount for buying in bulk?' he asked.

'What? No. *No!* Alison gave them to me – my friend – she's a nurse – they're for this weekend. I mean, not to *use*; they're for the hen's party. For some stupid party game. The medical centre had about a pallet of them, and they're almost expired. Oh God, now you think I'm a crazed nymphomaniac.'

Mark started to laugh. He lay down flat on his back and laughed harder than I had ever seen anyone laugh before, and after a while I climbed into bed beside him and pulled the covers up under my chin, so as not to freeze while waiting for him to finish.

At last he pulled himself together and rolled over to put his arms around me. 'I don't think you're a crazed nymphomaniac,' he said. 'I think you're the most wonderful girl I've ever met.'

I was woken in the morning by the persistent shriek of a blackbird in the copper beech outside my bedroom window, and lay for a few minutes with my eyes shut. Bed, which is one of my favourite places in any case, always becomes exponentially warmer and more comfortable as the time to leave it approaches. I rolled drowsily onto my back, encountered a large warm shoulder and went from barely conscious to fully alert in about half a nanosecond.

I turned my head cautiously and looked at Mark, lying asleep on his stomach with one muscular brown arm curled around his head. *Wow*, I thought, then, *Dear Lord, what have I done?*

With extreme stealth I inched my way out from under the duvet, collected an armful of clothes and tiptoed down the hall to the shower.

I was making my lunch when he appeared in the kitchen doorway, dressed and with his hair sticking up in damp spikes.

'Hi,' he said, shoving his hands into the pockets of his jeans.

When I was fourteen, or thereabouts, Dad sat me down and talked to me about sex. He started by saying it was a lot of fun, and I almost combusted in horrified embarrassment. He then went on to say that, in his opinion, it was a shame to get too hung up about the whole thing, and as long as people took the right precautions he couldn't see any particular virtue in abstaining. This was unexpected, since television had led me to believe that fathers all over the world were united in their quest for daughterly celibacy.

'Although,' he'd added, 'it's not really a great idea to sleep with someone you don't know. Sex is –' he paused, and I waited apprehensively to hear what my father thought sex was '– pretty intimate.' I breathed again; that could have been a lot worse. 'It's worth taking the time to get to know the other person first. Tends to save a lot of unhappiness and regret later on.'

It occurred to me now that I really should have taken my father's advice. When you've gone to sleep in someone's arms, waking up all the way back at awkward acquaintances is truly awful.

'Hi,' I said nervously. 'Coffee?'

'God, yes.'

'How d'you have it?' I asked, spreading Vegemite to the very edges of the bread with unprecedented care and precision.

'Just milk, please.'

I put down my knife and turned to open the fridge door. 'What would you like for breakfast?' I asked. 'Muesli? Or toast, or eggs . . .' Or of course the poor bloke might want nothing more than to escape, thus avoiding half an hour of excruciating morning-after conversation across the breakfast table. 'Or you might rather just get going.'

'Can I have chocolate cake?' he asked.

I managed to look at him then, and he smiled at me. 'Of course you can,' I said, smiling back.

Mark crossed the kitchen and began to unwrap the cake on the bench. 'You're allowed cake for breakfast on special occasions,' he said.

The sun was coming up, warming a handful of little wispy clouds on the horizon to pink, and in the conifer outside the kitchen window a few hundred sparrows shouted joyfully. I knew just how they felt.

'What are you doing tonight?' he asked.

'Nothing, I – oh. Crap. I'm on call. And at this time of year I'll probably have to go out and calve a cow. What about tomorrow?'

Mark shook his head. 'I have to speak at a charity dinner thing.'

'Impressive,' I said.

He made a face and, reaching out, hooked a finger through a belt loop on my jeans and pulled me towards him.

'Th-Thursday?' I asked shakily.

'No good. Dinner with sponsors. And then you've got that hen's party on the weekend.'

'Sunday night, then.'

'That's a hell of a long way away.'

It was. Practically aeons. I covered his hand with mine. 'Yeah.'

'I'll come back down tonight,' he said.

'Are you sure? It's such a long way to come to see someone who might be calving a cow.'

He stroked my knuckles with the side of his thumb. 'I don't mind.'

'If you're too tired and you don't feel like a two-hour drive, I won't be offended,' I said.

'I'll feel like it,' said Mark.

I laughed, and he kissed me. I was late for work, and Mark must have been *really* late for training.

9

'OH, IT'S YOU,' SAID MRS DOBSON-HUGHES WITH A MARKED lack of enthusiasm, as I ushered her into the consult room.

I was surprised by this, seeing as a few weeks before I'd been the only vet in the practice who was allowed to express her horrible dog's anal glands. 'It is,' I agreed. 'What can I do for you today?'

'There's a lump on Pierre's side,' she informed me. 'It wasn't there last week – I would have noticed.'

'Right. I'll just bring up his history . . . He was in here not long ago, wasn't he, with sore eyes?' I looked at Richard's notes, which read: *Runny eyes. Chlorsig.* For Richard that was actually pretty detailed – I had recently found an entry of his saying merely, *Flat.* The Vet Council kept sending us bulletins stressing the importance of careful record-keeping, but he had yet to take their advice on board.

'The other vet – such a *professional* young man – said I brought him in *in the nick of time,*' said Mrs Dobson-Hughes. 'Pierre's eyes were so inflamed that it could have gone either way.'

'My goodness,' I murmured. 'And Richard prescribed you some ointment?'

'He did. A very strong antibiotic. I was hoping to see him today and show him how Pierre's eyes have cleared. I did just what he told me.'

'Well, his eyes look great,' I said. 'Well done.'

'We got there in the end,' she said. 'I sat up all night with him, but I don't begrudge a moment of it.'

Today the horrible Pierre had a sebaceous cyst on his side. I squeezed out a blob of greyish waxy stuff but Mrs Dobson-Hughes wasn't even slightly impressed. Evidently my bedside manner was nothing compared to Richard's.

'Em rang,' said Thomas, as the automatic doors closed behind Pierre and Mrs Dobson-Hughes. It was quite fascinating watching them walk from behind; they had identical waddles. 'She said you were to call her back urgently.'

Em answered the phone on the second ring. 'Hello?'

'Hey,' I said. 'It's me. What's up?'

'That *was* Mark Tipene in your kitchen last night, wasn't it?'

'It was.'

'Mark *Tipene*! The All Black!'

'Yep,' I said. 'Did you find him on the Weetbix box?'

But she was not to be diverted. 'And just how, pray, do you know Mark Tipene?'

I sat down cross-legged on the bench in the lunch room. 'I fell over his feet at a party a few weeks ago. His cousin's share-milking just out of town, and he was down here visiting. And then he came in to work and asked me out.'

My stepmother was temporarily stricken dumb, but I heard the sounds of laboured breathing down the phone.

'Em,' I said gently, 'you sound like a stalker.'

'You're seeing *Mark Tipene*,' she repeated.

'Um. Yes. I think so,' I said, looking across the lunch room at his picture and smiling wonderingly to myself.

'Sweetie, he's *gorgeous*.'

'I know.' His eyes looked brown but on closer inspection they were actually hazel, with gold flecks. And his back was all ropes of muscle that tightened and shifted under the skin as he moved. And he was coming back this evening . . . I pulled myself back to the present with some difficulty.

'Look, Em, I've got to go. There are about four cats waiting out the back.'

'Sweetie,' she said, 'why don't you do something about your nails? A set of acrylics? Maureen at Body Bliss does such a lovely job. My treat.'

'I don't think acrylic nails would be a starter in calving season. Think of the poor cows I'd shred.'

'Oh,' said Em. 'Well, how about your hair?'

'What's wrong with it?'

'Nothing,' she said quickly. 'It's very pretty. But what about some foils? I was thinking that a lovely warm caramel would be beautiful on you.'

'Mm, maybe,' I said. 'Talk to you soon.' And I hung up, a little deflated by these suggestions on getting me up to standard.

***

'Mrs Dobson-Hughes sends you her love,' I told Richard that afternoon, coming into the office to find him looking at cars on Trade Me. 'She says no-one has ever understood Pierre the way you do.'

Richard looked momentarily surprised, and then began to laugh.

'Why did she have to sit up all night with a dog with runny eyes?' I asked.

'I told her that if she didn't put the drops in hourly he could lose his sight.'

'Why?'

'Just to see if she would. Dog only had a bit of allergic conjunctivitis.'

'You rotten bastard,' I said admiringly.

'It's my mate Paul's technique. He had some old witch tell him he didn't know what he was talking about when he said her cat had a flea allergy, so he got her to bathe it in iodine every morning for a week.' He double-clicked on a picture of a red Holden Commodore. 'I can't believe she actually did it. That's completely made my day.'

'You might live to regret it,' I said. 'Now she'll tell all her friends about you and you'll have a whole coven of crazy ladies wanting you to look after their snappy little lap dogs.'

The weekend's hen's party was a two-day event, involving a number of university friends. I had, before the advent of a large, sexy All Black lock, been looking forward to it, but as I headed for Taupo on Friday evening I was feeling decidedly unenthusiastic about the whole thing.

I drove down with my ex-boyfriend Lance, who worked these days in a small-animal practice in Hamilton. He was going to the stag's night.

The two of us had been in the same year at vet school. We'd lived together at university, worked at different branches of the same practice after graduation and then went overseas. We'd spent two years alternately backpacking around Europe and doing short-term locums to save up for the next trip. And by the end of all that we were sick to death of one another, and we went our separate ways with mutual relief.

It had been a civilised and remarkably painless break-up. I got custody of Murray, and Lance kept our shared laptop. I didn't have to stifle the urge to call him at two am from random nightclub toilets and beg him to take me back, and I hardly ever woke desolate in the watches of the night to contemplate my impending lonely old age, death, and consumption by Alsatians. This had troubled me rather more than Lance's absence did, because if you can leave fairly cheerfully after six years together it obviously wasn't much of a relationship, and in that case what on earth was the point of spending six years in it?

'So,' I asked, holding two paper cups of coffee between my knees while I did up my seatbelt, 'what are you boys doing this weekend?'

Lance nosed his way through the crowded petrol station forecourt, which was bristling with enormous four-wheel drives en route to the ski fields. 'Fishing,' he said sadly. 'And golf.'

'Lucky you,' I said. Lance dislikes fishing, and he hates golf with a deep unswerving hatred. I don't mind it, myself – I'm not much good at any sport requiring hand–eye coordination, but with golf at least you get a pleasant stroll between whacks at the ball.

'Are you going to cover the groom in plastic wrap and shaving foam and tie him to a streetlamp?' I asked.

'Probably,' he said gloomily. 'What are you girls doing?'

'We're having cocktails and playing hen-party games and going out dancing.' I feel about dancing the way Lance feels about golf. Perhaps we could swap: I'd join the stag do and he could be a hen.

'I could have done without this, this weekend,' he said.

I handed him a coffee. 'Yeah. Me too.'

We were silent as we drank our coffee, and it was a good ten minutes later when he asked, 'How's work?'

'Good,' I said. 'I pulled triplets out of a cow yesterday. How about you?'

'Not bad. Did my first tibial crest translocation this morning, and I've been plating lots of broken legs.' *I'll see your triplets and raise you a whole pile of orthopaedic surgeries.* He *always* trumped my work stories.

'Excellent,' I said, and there was another lull in the conversation while I gazed out the window at the passing silhouettes of pine trees against the evening sky, and thought bitter thoughts about wasting one of the few weekends in the foreseeable future that didn't contain a rugby Test match at a hen's party.

'Hey, Nell?'

'Mm?' My cell phone beeped from my handbag, and I reached down to rummage for it.

'I've, uh, met someone.'

'A girl someone?' I enquired.

'Yeah.'

'Good for you,' I said, pulling two lip glosses, a box of tampons and a pocket torch without a battery from my bag before finally locating the phone. 'What's she like?'

'She's a lawyer.'

'Most impressive,' I said as I opened a text message from Mark. *Hows yr day going?*

So so. You? I replied.

'It's early days,' said Lance. 'But I wanted you to hear about it from me.'

'Thank you. That's very considerate,' I said. 'I've just met someone too.'

'So you've bowed to the inevitable and hooked up with a dairy farmer?'

'No, actually. A rugby player.'

The phone chirped again.

Not bad. Better if u were here.

'A rugby player?' he repeated.

'Um, yes, Mark Tipene,' I said, my toes curling unhappily because it sounded far too much like showing off.

Wish I was, I wrote.

I needn't have worried about the bragging, because Lance didn't believe me. 'Right,' he said in the weary, patient voice that was just as infuriating after a gap of eight months as it had been when I encountered it every day.

'You can check with Em if you like,' I said. 'She's met him. She's very concerned I'm not glamorous enough – she wants me to get acrylic nails and make an appointment with a personal shopper.'

'Honestly?'

'Honestly. But please don't say anything. It's at a fairly embryonic stage.'

'Define "fairly embryonic",' he said.

'Oh,' I said vaguely, 'we've been out for a drink, he's come for tea, he helped me with a horrible rotten calving a few weeks ago . . .'

Lance digested this for a bit, decided I might in fact be telling the truth and said, 'Be careful, won't you, Nell? I wouldn't want to see you hurt.'

'Thank you,' I said. 'I'd rather not see me hurt either.'

'I don't think those guys are known for their faithfulness.'

'And you're basing that on all the All Blacks you know?' I asked, ever so slightly crisp.

'No need to jump down my throat. They're famous, they've got big disposable incomes, and everywhere they go there are hundreds of silly little tarts lining up to sleep with them. Just – be careful, that's all.'

'I will take your advice on board,' I said solemnly.

Lance and I used to amuse ourselves by collecting phrases that mean the opposite of what they say. 'I'll certainly take that on board' actually means 'I've already made up my mind and nothing you can say will change it.' As does: 'I hear what you're saying.' And then there's: 'We really must catch up sometime,' which can be translated as, 'I will never make the slightest effort to get in touch with you.'

'I don't know why I'm wasting my breath,' he said. 'You've never listened to anything I've said in your life.'

'I have too!' I cried, stung.

'When?'

I groped for an example and, luckily, found one. 'I've never put my feet on the dashboard since you told me the airbag would ram my knees through my brain if I was in a crash.'

'Huh,' said Lance, sounding pleased. 'Well, there you go.'

10

'CUTE PUPPY,' ALISON SAID, PUTTING HER HEAD AROUND the door of the treatment room at ten past twelve on Tuesday afternoon.

'It is now,' I said darkly. 'It was less cute when it was awake.' Also considerably louder, and quite determined to draw blood.

'What's wrong with it?'

'Broken ulna. The X-ray's on the bench.'

Alison held the X-ray up to the light and squinted at it in a professional manner. 'Is that *your* hand?'

'Zoe's gone home sick,' I said defensively. 'It's hard taking X-rays by yourself.' Making cameo appearances in your patients' radiographs is not exactly consistent with best practice. 'I'm sorry about our walk; you might as well go without me.'

Alison made a face. 'It's going to rain. I'll stay and help you if you like.'

'Thank you, you're a true friend,' I said, sticking a long strip of elastoplast down one side of the puppy's foot. 'Grab the end?'

Alison stuck the end of the tape obediently to her finger. 'How was the hen's weekend?' she asked.

'It was good. Nice to catch up with everyone.' I applied a second tape stirrup to the other side of the foot and started to wind a cotton bandage up the puppy's leg. 'Although it was a bit of a shame that Mary-Anne threw up over the till at the restaurant.' On reflection, plying with cocktails a girl who gets giggly on a glass of weak shandy may have been a mistake.

'Classy,' Alison remarked.

'What did you get up to?' I asked.

'Not a whole lot. I saw your cousin at the pub.'

'Which one?'

'Sam,' she said, transferring both ends of elastoplast to the same hand and holding the end of my bandage down with the other. 'Oh, and Lydia Naylor and Tracey Reynolds had a fight.'

'What about?' I asked.

'Apparently Tracey found a whole lot of dodgy text messages on her boyfriend's phone. So she tried to pull Lydia's hair out by the roots.'

'How exciting,' I said, starting on a layer of cast padding.

'Never a dull moment,' Alison agreed. 'I must say it makes a pleasant change to have the patient asleep when you're putting on the cast. I had a little boy try to bite me last week.'

'That's why I prefer animals. If a dog does that you can jab it with a pole syringe full of ketamine through the bars of the cage. Have you got a finger spare to hold down another layer of bandage?'

'Just as long as you don't incorporate my hand into your cast,' she said, trapping the end of the padding layer under her left little finger.

'I'll try not to.'

'Thank you.'

I opened a packet of Scotchcast and dropped it into a jug of water. It's such cool stuff – water activates the resin and it heats up and hardens in mere minutes. In fact, it usually hardens about thirty seconds before you really want it to, just to keep you on your toes.

'So,' Alison asked casually, 'any more visits from random All Blacks?'

'Not one,' I said, squeezing out the roll of Scotchcast and beginning to wind it up the puppy's leg. 'But they're all in Wellington for the week, so Broadview's a bit out of the way.'

'What are they doing in Wellington?'

'Training, visiting schools, kissing babies, making old ladies cups of tea – that kind of thing. Just bend that leg a tiny bit at the elbow? Cheers.'

'When's he getting back?'

'Friday. D'you reckon I've got enough padding around the top there?'

'Heaps,' she said. 'Stop trying to change the subject. Are you going to see him this weekend?'

I nodded. 'I'm going up to Auckland on Friday night.'

'Wow. You really *are* going to be a Wag.'

'Please don't,' I said. 'You might jinx it.'

Thomas opened the door of the treatment room. 'Are you nearly done?' he asked me. 'Nick's been held up at Hollis's, so you'll have to go and see the sick cow at Ian Weber's.'

'Ian doesn't like me,' I protested.

'He doesn't like anyone. What makes you think *you're* special?' said Thomas, withdrawing and shutting the door behind him.

I sighed. 'It's so depressing going to Weber's. He never believes a word I say.'

'If Mark Tipene liked me I wouldn't give a toss about whether or not Ian Weber did,' said Alison, which I thought was an excellent point.

I got back to work at ten to five on Friday afternoon, having just spent an hour and a half making a hole in the side of a cow, draining twenty litres of nasty brown fluid from her caecum and sewing her up again. I climbed out of the ute feeling extremely pleased with myself, went in through the back door to wash my surgery kit and ran smack into Richard.

'Where the fuck did you put the blood transfusion bags?' he demanded.

This happy welcome removed just a bit of the gloss from my afternoon. 'In the box with *Blood Transfusion Bags* written on the side, on the top shelf in the drug cupboard,' I said. 'What's up?'

'Dog with rat-bait poisoning. Nick's supposed to be on call, and he's way the hell up the valley doing a calving.'

'Have we got a dog to use as a donor?' I asked.

'That thing of Keri's.'

'Okay,' I said, crossing the treatment room to open the small-animal drug cupboard and standing up on tiptoe to swat down the box. 'Whose dog is it?'

'Harvey's. Some fancy bloody heading dog.'

'Oh no. Not Nancy?'

'I don't fucking know,' snapped Richard.

'I'm not on call either!' I snapped back.

It was six o'clock by the time we'd taken blood from Keri's labrador and run it into Don Harvey's favourite, dog-trial-champion heading bitch. And six thirty once I had written out her vitamin K dosing instructions for Nick, whose small-animal medicine is fairly rusty. And five past seven, with my good mood well and truly gone, by the time I got home, showered, and threw a random assortment of clothes into a bag. Tearing back up the hall I located my cell phone in the pocket of the dirty overalls I had just flung into the washing machine and rang Mark.

'Hi,' he said.

'Hi. I'm so sorry – I'm running really late. I got stuck at work.' I held the phone between chin and shoulder and tipped a great mound of cat biscuits into Murray's dish. 'I'm just leaving now.'

'Oh,' he said. 'That's a bugger.'

'I'm really sorry,' I said unhappily.

'I just meant it's a bugger for you to have a long day and then a two-hour drive. Would you like me to come down instead?'

'No, I'm all organised. I'll see you in a couple of hours.'

I had no trouble at all finding my way to Mark's house in Mount Eden, which was right at the end of a cul-de-sac. Actually, my navigation skills would have been a considerable surprise to my boss, who firmly believes I have no sense of direction, and that when I got lost in my first weeks back in Broadview it had nothing to do with him sending me to farms via trees that had fallen down ten years ago and streams invisible from the road.

I parked my elderly green Corona on the street, pulled up the hood of my sweatshirt against the drizzle and ran down a long and poorly lit driveway with a high brick wall on one side and an ornate wrought-iron fence on the other. Mark's place was the first in a row of semi-detached townhouses, each front door approached by two shallow tiled steps and flanked by a pair of cypresses in big terracotta pots. It all looked terribly expensive and Tuscan. I thought of my weatherboard farm cottage with its peeling paint and ill-fitting windows and briefly considered turning around and running away.

Before I could decide one way or the other, Mark opened the door. 'Hey,' he said. 'You made it. How was the traffic?'

'Fine,' I said nervously. 'Lovely place.'

'You haven't seen it yet.'

'No, but the step's nice.' *Oh, for heaven's sake, girl, if you can't say anything sensible just shut up.*

'Thank you,' he said, smiling. He stood aside to let me in, and closed the door. And then he put his arms around me and kissed me, and the cold lump of worry that had been growing in the pit of my stomach quietly dissolved.

The more I found out about Mark, you see, the further out of my league he seemed. He was a proper, serious sportsman of the seen-once-in-a-generation type, whereas when I was small I was so clumsy that people kept anxiously testing my vision. He was idolised by half the country; I was idolised by Briar Coles, who, although sweet, was undeniably a few sandwiches short of a picnic.

But it was difficult to focus on these depressing truths while kissing him, so I stopped trying and concentrated on the matter at hand. Eventually we broke apart and he picked up my backpack. We went hand in hand up a staircase with sandstone treads and into a big open-plan living area. There was a kitchen in one corner – all stainless-steel appliances and granite bench tops and with a fridge that looked like the mainframe of a spaceship – and another flight of stairs led from the middle of the room up to a mezzanine floor where I assumed his bedroom must be. Beyond the stairs was a great black leather sofa, two black leather armchairs and a huge plasma-screen TV.

'Crikey,' I said.

'I'm told that this place has all the warmth and charm of a lawyer's waiting room,' said Mark.

It did, too. The walls and flooring and kitchen cabinets were all beige, and the furnishings black. The only touch of colour was provided by two big canvases on the far wall, each one sporting a single red squiggle on a white background. I find it hard to be impressed by art that looks like it took longer to hang straight on the wall than it did to produce. However, those whose living rooms are a symphony of plum and orange are in no position to criticise anybody else's interior design. And perhaps he loved it.

'Have you had a good day?' I asked.

'It's improving rapidly,' he said. 'Are you hungry?'

I shook my head.

'Drink?'

'No, thanks.'

'Anything else?'

I turned and put my arms around his neck. 'This is good.'

He smiled, resting his forehead against mine. 'Should we go to bed, then?' he asked, apparently not feeling obliged to go red, stammer or otherwise act like an idiot. A novel approach, and vastly superior to mine.

'Yes, please,' I said.

He picked me up with no apparent effort – which was especially nice; it made me feel all delicate and waif-like – and carried me to the foot of the stairs.

'Sexy,' I remarked. 'Very *Officer and a Gentleman*.'

'Good, that's what I was going for,' he said, starting up the steps.

'Are you sure you don't want to put me down?'

'Quite sure, thank you.'

'Because it'd be a blow to fall down the stairs.'

He reached the top without mishap and set me down. 'Helen?'

'Yes?'

'When I was imagining this, you talked a lot less.'

11

VERY, VERY CAUTIOUSLY, I SLID OUT FROM UNDER THE covers. I retrieved my T-shirt and knickers from the floor, put them on and padded across the room to a set of French doors leading out onto a balcony. A great web of lights stretched away beneath my feet, and away to the right was an unbroken stretch of darkness that had to be the sea.

'Okay?' Mark asked.

I turned to see him watching me, propped up on his elbows.

'Fine,' I said. 'Sorry I woke you.'

'You didn't,' he said.

'Lovely view.'

'It'd be even better if you took your top off.'

'Good line,' I said admiringly. 'Do you use it a lot?'

'No,' he said. 'Come here.'

I went back across the room to sit beside him on the edge of the bed. He reached up and brushed my cheek with the back of his index finger, and my throat tightened painfully.

'What's up?' he asked.

'Nothing,' I said. This was untrue, but I had a suspicion that it might be a bit early for, 'You are entirely perfect and completely wonderful, and I think I love you.'

He moved over to make room for me and I slid under the covers beside him. There was a short silence, and he ran his hand up my leg from knee to hip. 'I thought you didn't like these,' he said, tracing the lacy hem of the scarlet knickers.

'Oh, well, I thought you might.'

'I do. Please pass on my thanks to your stepmother.'

'Hmm,' I said. 'I think not.'

'Spoilsport.'

'You could always tell her yourself.'

'Fair enough,' he said serenely. 'I will.'

I kicked him.

'Stop that,' he ordered, rolling over and pinning my legs with his.

'You're so hot,' I said.

'Thanks,' said Mark, smiling. 'I work out.'

'I meant your body temperature, you weenie.' I lifted my head off the pillow to kiss his nose, which was nice and handy.

'What's your dad like?' he asked.

I was a little startled by this abrupt change of subject. 'Well,' I said, 'he's about six foot seven, a fundamentalist Christian, collects guns, very protective of his daughters . . . Ow!'

'We'll try that again, shall we?'

'Biting people is *not* cool,' I said sternly.

'Toughen up, McNeil, it didn't even break the skin.'

'I can see the headlines now. *Innocent Girl Bitten by Crazed All Black. Wound Turns Septic. Major Surgery Required . . .*'

'Yeah,' he said. 'Amputation at the neck.'

'The ultimate solution.'

'So,' he repeated patiently, 'what's your dad like?'

'Lovely,' I said. 'Big and kind and a little bit slow – I mean, not stupid, but he's always running late and you can't hurry him up. What's *your* dad like?'

'Big and fierce,' said Mark.

'Is he proud of you?'

He grimaced. 'Yeah, I guess.'

'And your mother?'

He rolled back onto his side and pulled me up against him. 'She still cuts out every article that says something positive about me and sticks it in a scrapbook.'

'That's really nice,' I said. 'Your parents have split up, haven't they?'

'About ten years ago.'

'Have either of them married again?'

'Dad has. His new wife's an interesting woman.'

'Really interesting, or is that a polite way of saying she's a hideous bitch?'

'Hideous bitch,' said Mark without the slightest hesitation.

'A proper evil stepmother then,' I said.

'That's right. Not like yours.'

'Yeah,' I said, 'mine is pretty cool.'

'How old were you when she came on the scene?' he asked.

'Fourteen. Poor Em – imagine finding that your new man comes as a package deal with a fat angry teenager.'

'I struggle to picture you fat and angry.'

'That's very kind, but I was,' I said. At fourteen I was *appalled* that my father thought he could replace Mum with some blonde bimbo who put her makeup on with a trowel and dressed like Erin Brockovich. And it took me a long time to figure out that if I wanted to lose weight I was going to have to do something a bit more proactive than tying a jumper around my waist to make my bottom look smaller. (It didn't.)

'What kind of hideous bitch is your stepmother?' I asked. The hideous bitch comes in so many variations: there's the brittle, lacquered type with the artificial laugh and the vicious one-liners, or the belligerent type who takes everything as a personal insult, or –

But Mark sat up and looked down at me. 'I'm not going to lie here and talk about stepmothers,' he said firmly. 'I've got better things to do.'

I laughed. 'What, like me?'

'That's the one,' he said.

The morning was dull and grey, with sharp angry squalls of rain hurling themselves at the windows. Lovely weather, I reflected, drifting into Mark's space-age chrome bathroom for a shower. And it was a gorgeous shower – completely different from mine, which was like having someone piddle on your head.

Mark wasn't in bed when I came out, and I wandered back across the room to look out the French doors at the sprawl of roofs and trees below, with the harbour beyond stretching to the horizon.

'Coffee?' he called from downstairs.

I went and looked down from the low wall overlooking the kitchen. 'Yes, please.'

'Real coffee, or instant?'

'Instant's good,' I said, and went downstairs to see him reach down two mugs from a shelf in his beige and steel kitchen.

'Milk?' he asked, spooning instant coffee from a metal canister.

'Yes, please.'

He added milk, filled both mugs from a tap in the corner of the sink and passed one over.

I looked at it doubtfully – I hadn't expected to have to request specifically that my coffee be made with hot water – and saw a reassuring wisp of steam. 'Do you have boiling water on tap?' I asked.

'Yep. Cool, eh?'

'Extremely cool,' I said.

'*And* the fridge makes its own ice.'

'Far out, brussel sprout.'

'I know. It's pretty incredible,' he said.

'Do you have a robot to do your vacuuming, like on *The Jetsons*?'

'No,' he admitted. 'Sorry.'

'Oh well, never mind. The tap's still impressive.'

'Thanks.' He leant over and kissed me. 'Good morning.'

'Good morning.'

'What do you want to do today?'

'Whatever you like,' I said dreamily. 'I don't mind.'

'You're really not the high-maintenance type, are you?'

'I'm just lulling you into a false sense of security,' I explained. 'Then I'll start demanding fur coats and Porsches.'

'I see,' said Mark.

He made me scrambled eggs the exact consistency of rubber for breakfast and rejected my offer to do the dishes. He left them piled in the sink instead, said he was exhausted from all that strenuous scrambling and that we'd better go and lie down to recover. So we did.

12

'WHERE'S MURRAY THE CAT THIS WEEKEND?' ASKED MARK that afternoon, covering a slice of bread with thick slabs of cheese.

'Home alone,' I said. 'He's not allowed back to the cattery; he screamed for the whole weekend the last time I left him there.'

'Poor Murray.'

'Poor Murray, my foot. He's probably disembowelling a rabbit on the end of my bed as we speak.' I was sitting cross-legged on a leather-topped chrome stool on the opposite side of the kitchen bench, eating yoghurt. 'That looks revolting.'

'No-one's forcing you to eat it,' he said, ladling mayonnaise onto his cheese with a tablespoon. He slapped a second piece of bread on top of the mess and mayonnaise oozed from the edges. Undeterred, he collected the drips with a finger and wiped them on the top slice.

'Charming,' I remarked.

'Always.'

'Mark,' I said, 'what do you want to do when you stop playing rugby?'

'Finish my building apprenticeship, for a start,' he said. 'I got my carpentry certificate when I was twenty, but I've still got another four thousand hours to do under a master builder.'

'Four thousand hours sounds like a lot.'

He took a large bite of sandwich, losing about quarter of a cup of mayonnaise from the far end in the process. 'Bugger,' he said. 'Yeah, especially when you consider it's taken me eight years to do the first four thousand.'

'So if you keep playing for another eight years, you'll be qualified when you retire.'

'I won't last another eight years. Four or five, maybe, if I'm lucky and I don't have any major injuries.'

'Do you mind?' I asked.

'Mind what?'

'That – well, that it's going to end.'

'Yes and no,' he said slowly. 'You're right, some guys find it pretty tough. When I started playing you didn't get any support – once you retired you just had to piss off and get on with it. But now they really encourage you to do some sort of further education and plan for your retirement. And there are plenty of people who've been through it to talk to.' He lifted the top of his sandwich and scooped the mayonnaise puddle back in with his tablespoon. 'You have to try to remember how insanely lucky you are to spend ten years doing your favourite thing and getting paid for it.'

I got down off my stool and went around the counter, pulling his head down to kiss him.

'What was that for?' he asked, putting his arms around my waist.

'Just because you're awesome,' I said.

'Thank you.'

'Except for your eating habits. They're pretty nasty.'

Just then his iPhone buzzed on the counter beside him, and he removed an arm to pick it up. 'You don't want to go out for dinner tonight, do you?' he asked.

I shook my head, having not the slightest desire to share him with anybody.

'Good.' He tapped the screen a couple of times and put the phone back on the bench.

'Who was it?'

'Alan. Jaeger. Friend of mine.'

'Oh,' I said. Alan Jaeger was the All Black captain.

Mark raised one eyebrow. 'Want to go after all?' he asked.

'Nope,' I said. 'But it *is* kind of surreal to be invited out for tea with Alan Jaeger.'

The phone buzzed again and he looked down at it. 'This one's from his wife,' he said, tilting the phone so I could read the message. *Are you ashamed of her?*

I smiled. 'Are you?'

He didn't reply, but showed me his answer before sending it. *No. Of you.*

'That's alright then,' I said as his phone started to ring.

He turned it off.

The landline started to ring instead, and he sighed. 'Might as well answer it,' he said. 'Or she'll just come round with a loudspeaker.' He plucked the phone off its charger at the end of the bench. 'What?' He listened for a moment and passed it to me.

I took it hesitantly. 'Hello?'

'Helen?' a woman asked. 'Hi, I'm Saskia. See you guys at seven, okay? Don't bring anything. Oh, hang on a minute – do you like scallops?'

'Uh, yes,' I said.

'Good.' And she hung up.

'Seven o'clock,' I said helplessly. 'We're having scallops.'

The Jaegers lived in a mansion on the side of One Tree Hill. An actual mansion, with columns and gables and even a turret stuck on one side like a beret. It made Mark's luxurious inner-city townhouse look modest, if not spartan.

We approached the mansion via a steep driveway, overhung with trees and ending in a broad sweep of tarmac at the front steps. As soon as Mark pulled up, a tiny woman with cropped blonde hair and a face like a pixie flung open the front door. 'Hello!' she said, bouncing up to kiss Mark's cheek. 'Come in, guys.' She shepherded us down a wide panelled hall into an enormous kitchen.

Alan Jaeger, like Mark, was bigger in real life than he appeared on TV. He had a neck like a bull, two cauliflower ears and a magnificent monobrow, and he looked like a hired thug. He was standing at the stove with a tea towel slung over one shoulder, frowning down into a pot.

'Hi,' he said, turning and holding out a hand to me with the easy friendliness of a man who spends large chunks of his time chatting to strangers. 'You must be Helen.'

'Hi,' I said. 'Nice to meet you.'

'You too. You're a vet, Tip says?'

'Yes,' I said, trying to think of a suitable remark so as to uphold my end of the conversation. *Lovely weather we're having, isn't it? You know, you're the first hooker I've met? Don't human doctors lance aural haematomas so your ears don't turn into solid lumps of scar tissue?* Best, I decided, to stick with remaining silent and being thought a fool.

'Big or small animals?' he asked.

'Both,' I said. 'I'm lucky; more and more jobs are one or the other these days.'

'That must be really interesting.'

'Not compared to your job.'

'Oh, I don't know about that,' he said.

'Helen, what would you like to drink?' Saskia asked. 'Wine, beer, cider, juice, soft drink . . . ?'

'Wine, please.'

'Red or white?'

'White.'

She opened the fridge. 'Sav, chardonnay, pinot gris or riesling?'

'Pinot gris, please,' I said, slightly dazed by the number of options.

'Mission Estate or Greywacke?'

'Whichever's closest.'

'They're both equally close,' she said inexorably.

'Greywacke,' I said, and accepted my glass feeling I had earned it.

'Excellent choice,' said Saskia, pouring one for herself. 'Al, how long before dinner's ready?'

'About quarter of an hour.'

'Would you like a tour of the house, Helen?' she asked.

'I'd love one,' I said.

Mark crossed the kitchen and opened the fridge, extracting a carton of orange juice from the inside of the door without having to look for it. 'Be nice,' he told Saskia over his shoulder.

'I'm always nice,' she said haughtily. 'Tip, don't even think about drinking that straight out of the box.'

Glass in hand, she led me through an archway into a small crimson antechamber. 'We're in the process of renovating,' she said. 'We bought the house a year ago – nobody had done anything to it since about 1950. I've just finished the walls in here. Alan's not sold on the colour.'

'I think it looks great,' I said.

'Did you hear that, dear?' Saskia called. 'Helen thinks it looks great.'

'That's wonderful, my petal,' Alan called back.

'Sarcastic prat,' she said, smiling.

We turned right into a big bare room papered in sickly olive-green. 'The formal lounge,' said Saskia. 'Isn't it awful? Alan doesn't know it yet, but we're going to start stripping the walls tomorrow.'

A door in the far wall led back into the hallway; crossing it, Saskia opened a heavy door, switching on a light to reveal a bathroom that could have belonged to a fairy princess. It had a full-length window curtained in shimmering gauzy stuff like a golden cobweb, and a vast claw-footed bath. The walls were cream and the floor was covered in tiny iridescent tiles, gold and green and turquoise.

'It's *gorgeous*,' I said, awed.

'Thanks. But if I'd known what little bastards those tiles were going to be to lay I'd never have started.'

'You did all this yourself?' I asked.

'Yep. It gives me something to do in the evenings when Alan's away.'

'I guess that's quite a lot of the time.'

'It sure is,' she said, running her fingers through her cropped hair. 'The Tri Nations games start a fortnight after the Super Rugby season ends, and this year the All Blacks have fourteen Test matches scheduled. And they're *all* weekend games rather than mid-week. There's just never a break. And of course next year's the World Cup, so everything will be condensed even more to fit that in. And if that wasn't enough, Argentina's joining the Tri Nations, which will mean even more games, and they want to play tests in Japan for extra revenue, and –' She broke off, shaking her head. 'If you've got any sense you'll drop Tip like a hot potato and find yourself someone you might actually get to see from time to time.' She smiled and ushered me back out into the passage. 'You won't, of course, but you can't say you weren't warned. Right, come and tell me if you think the curtains in our bedroom were a terrible mistake.'

Dinner began with the scallops, wrapped in bacon and dipped in aioli. They tasted wonderful, and so did the lamb curry that followed them.

'More?' Alan asked me, spoon poised over the dish.

I shook my head. 'I wish I could. I think that was the best thing I've ever eaten. May I have the recipe?'

He grimaced and scratched his chin. 'Now you're asking. I don't really do recipes; I just throw things in until it tastes about right.'

'Or doesn't, as the case may be,' said Saskia. 'He made some very strange pumpkin soup last night. Tip, have you heard that Jimmy Dalton's snapped his Achilles again?'

'Bloody hell,' said Mark, holding out his plate for more curry. 'When did he do that?'

'Yesterday, at training. Jimmy used to play for the Blues, Helen. He's been in England for the last couple of years.'

'He must have only just come back from his last injury,' Mark said.

'Mm,' said Saskia. 'This weekend was supposed to be his first game.'

'How long will he be out?' I asked.

'Permanently,' said Alan, and there was a brief, depressed hush around the table.

'How are you going?' Mark asked as he nosed his car out onto the street. It was raining again, and the tyres hissed on the wet tarmac.

'Good,' I said, sinking back against the soft leather seat with some relief. The Jaegers were delightful people, welcoming, unpretentious, funny . . . Still, being inspected by your new boyfriend's oldest friends is undeniably stressful. 'They're lovely. How long have you guys known each other?'

'Ten years, give or take,' Mark said. 'Alan and I made the Blues development squad together.'

'And Saskia?'

'About the same.' He looked at me sideways and added, 'I brought her home from the pub one night, and for some obscure reason she decided my flatmate was a better bet than I was.'

I gave a surprised choke of laughter. 'Really?'

'Hard to believe, I know.'

'Almost impossible,' I said honestly.

'Well, I called her Sasha. And then I threw up on her shoes.'

'Sasha's pretty close to Saskia!' I said, quite indignant on his behalf.

'Yeah, but I think they were her favourite shoes.'

'Did you mind very much?'

'I expect it was good for me,' he said. 'I was a cocky little shit.'

So he *had* minded. 'I bet you weren't,' I said, putting my hand on his knee for a second.

'Of course I was,' said Mark. 'I was eighteen years old, I'd just left home and I was making more money than I knew what to do with. I thought I was God's gift.'

I felt a sudden twinge of pity for that eighteen-year-old boy, with too much money and fame and no life experience to put it all into perspective. Getting from cocky little shit to national role model must have involved some pretty painful lessons.

Mark parked his car among a selection of other expensive European vehicles in the communal basement car park, and we went up a flight of concrete steps and out through a locked door with a six-digit combination. This place, it seemed, had been designed for the type of people who carry only a laptop and a bottle of pinot noir in from their cars, and have their groceries delivered.

'Did you have a good time tonight?' he asked, reaching for my hand as we rounded the corner of the building.

'It was really nice,' I said. 'Nearly as good as staying at home. Was it Saskia who said your house looks like a lawyer's waiting room?'

He unlocked his front door. 'Who else? Cup of tea?'

'Yes, please.' We went upstairs, and I reached down two mugs while he crossed the kitchen to press a button on his answer phone, where a red light was blinking.

'*Dad here*,' said a gruff voice. '*Give me a ring when you've got a minute, eh?*'

The machine beeped, and immediately a girl's voice continued, '*Hey, Tip, I don't know what I've done with the earphones for my MP3 player. Are they at your place, by any chance? Just flick me a text if you find them. Thanks, love.*' There was a kissing noise, and then another beep.

'*Mark, it's Becky. Call me, okay?*' This voice was soft and husky, as though its owner had either been crying or smoked forty cigarettes a day. The machine beeped again, announced '*End of messages*' in a jovial masculine tone and fell silent.

There was a brief, charged pause. 'Those ones there?' I asked, nodding towards the fruit bowl on the bench where, nestled between an apple and a wizened kiwifruit, lay a set of earphones.

'Guess so,' Mark said slowly. 'They've been there for months.'

There was another, even tenser pause.

'Who's Becky?'

'Oh, for God's sake,' he said. 'Helen –'

'*Who's Becky?*' I snapped.

'She's nobody. Just a girl I hooked up with once. Before I met you.'

'Does *she* know she's nobody?'

'She's not nobody,' he said unhappily. 'She's just not my type.'

'So did you sit her down and tell her that, or did you say "I'll call you" and then never did?'

'Of course I told her,' said Mark. 'I said she was a lovely girl but I wasn't after a relationship at the moment. Or words to that effect.'

'Might have been nice to tell her that before you slept with her,' I observed, cold as an Arctic winter.

He tilted his head back wearily. 'Yeah,' he said. 'I know. But we'd just won the final, and I was drunk – and then the next week I went to see Hamish, and he dragged me off to that thing at the fire station, and I met you.'

I wanted badly to believe him. Scarily badly – it was up there with the way I used to wish that today would be the day I'd open the back door and find Mum in the kitchen, having been forced to fake her own death in order to carry out a top-secret mission for MI5.

'The other message is from my ex-girlfriend. We're still mates, but that's it.' He picked up the earphones and put them down again. 'They really *have* been lying around for months.'

I nodded, a swift jerky nod like a puppet, and got two teabags out of the box on the bench.

'Please believe me.'

'Okay,' I said.

He looked at me for a few seconds, then came and put his arms around me.

I rested my head against his chest. He was big and warm and solid, and he smelt nice. That's a particularly dumb reason to trust someone. 'If you *were* the kind of scumbag who has three or four girls on the go at once,' I said at last, 'you probably wouldn't check your answer phone in front of one of them. Not unless you were really stupid. And you're not.'

'Thank you,' he said, and I felt him relax.

'But,' I added into his shirt, 'if you break my heart I'm going to be really pissed off.'

13

EXPERIMENTALLY, I FLEXED THE KNUCKLE A CAT HAD bitten that morning. It was stiff and sore, and I made a mental note to swing by the clinic on the way home and start myself on antibiotics.

'Nice to see them all singing along,' said Alison. 'Very patriotic.' The camera panned slowly along the row of All Blacks, each one with his arms around his neighbours' shoulders. There was Alan, and Mark a good head taller than little Sione Brown on his right.

'Mark's only pretending,' I said. 'He's not allowed to sing out loud.' Never have I come across anyone with less ability to carry a tune.

'Same again, girls?' Sam asked, getting to his feet. It was the evening of the third Friday in October and we were at the Stockman's Arms, watching the last Tri Nations game between New Zealand and South Africa on the big screen above the bar.

'No,' said Alison, bending down and groping purposefully under her stool for her handbag. 'It's my round.'

'No it's not. What do you want, Hel?'

I brandished my cell phone. 'On call. But thank you.'

'Chardonnay, wasn't it, Alison?'

'No, please, let me,' she said.

'Sit down, woman,' Sam said sternly and, skirting a table of unwary diners who were just realising that Catch of the Day actually meant defrosted, deep-fried shark in batter, made his way to the bar.

'Evening, ladies,' said Hamish, sauntering up to lean on the high table between us. 'Hi there, Head Nurse.'

Alison smiled wanly but didn't answer, thus demonstrating the upper limit of her range of nastiness. It was no wonder he persevered.

'Hi, Hamish,' I said. 'How's that heifer?'

'It's alright. It'd want to be, after what you charged me for coming to see it.'

The heifer had been at the back of the farm with a dislocated hip. I hadn't charged him any of the time taken to reach the patient from the cowshed, the hip had slid neatly back into its socket and the heifer had walked away. Just what, I wondered, *would* Hamish consider to be value for money?

'I see it's another lovely evening in Wellington,' he continued, looking idly at the screen as the rain and the haka began simultaneously. 'Looks as windy as hell. It's going to be a crap game.' Conversation with Hamish was so seldom an uplifting experience.

'That's right,' I said. 'Look on the bright side.' But he had turned away to direct the full force of his charm on my hapless friend, so I went back to the rugby.

By now I had a reasonable grasp of the rules – and I had met a few of the players during weekends at Mark's place, which made it exponentially more interesting – but I still found eighty minutes of watching my boyfriend try to smash big, hard men who were trying in return to smash him a traumatic way to spend an evening. I was well aware that this was a poor and probably unpatriotic attitude, but I couldn't help it.

South Africa got a penalty, then we did, and then they attempted a drop goal, which was whisked to the right of the posts by the wind. Alan's eyebrow, as he addressed his forward pack, rose and fell like a raft on a storm-tossed sea.

Mark won the ball in the lineout and was immediately charged by a South African prop. As he fell he flicked the ball out sideways to Miles Lalu. Miles kicked it up high, which wasn't very bright considering they were playing in a howling gale, and it dropped back neatly into the arms of South African winger Jacques du Foure (according to Mark one of the funniest men alive), who sprinted nearly the whole length of the field before he was tackled.

There was a major drawback to watching rugby games on TV rather than in the flesh. Instead of focusing on player number four as they should, the cameras had this highly irritating habit of slavishly following the ball. Was Mark up? Was he alright? It was a good twenty seconds before he appeared back in the defensive line and I could breathe again.

At half-time the score was 11–9 to South Africa. The players jogged off the field, and I looked away from the big screen.

'What are you up to this weekend, Head Nurse?' Hamish was asking.

'Oh,' said Alison weakly, 'this and that.'

'There's drag racing up at Meremere on Sunday,' he said. 'Why don't you come along?'

Alison looked like a baby rabbit caught in the headlights of an oncoming car. She was appallingly bad at declining invitations – in seventh form she went out with Jason Faber, with whom she had not one single thing in common, for the whole of term two because she couldn't bear to hurt his feelings. 'That's very –' she started.

I opened my mouth to intervene. A true friend couldn't let the poor girl spend a day watching cars with Hamish Thompson without at least *trying* to save her. But Sam was way ahead of me. Straightening from where he had been leaning against the table (Hamish having commandeered his seat), he jerked his chin at Alison and said, 'Get up, babe.'

She stared at him in blank amazement.

'Let me sit down for a bit,' he said. 'You can sit on my knee.'

She slid to her feet, and Sam sat down. 'Thanks, hon,' he said, patting his knee. Moving with all the speed and agility of a woman wading through knee-deep porridge, Alison clambered onto his lap.

Sam slung a proprietary arm around her waist, picked up his beer mug and turned to Hamish, who was opening and closing his mouth like a goldfish. 'So, have you shut up much grass for silage?' he asked.

Good man, my cousin.

14

WHEN MARK ARRIVED ON TUESDAY EVENING I WAS LYING on the lawn under the copper beech with Murray draped across my stomach. I sat up and waved as the car pulled in, earning a reproachful feline stare.

'Hi,' said Mark, coming across the grass and sitting down beside me.

I leant over and kissed him. 'Hi.'

'How's things?' he asked.

'Very good. Nice shirt.'

'There's nothing wrong with my shirt,' he said defensively.

'Not a thing,' I agreed. 'Years of life left in it.' This evening he was wearing an ancient pair of paint-smeared shorts and a Stratford High School leavers rugby jumper with holes under the arms and the collar ripped off. Whenever he could get away with it Mark went barefoot, in clothes most people would be ashamed to put in a clothing bin.

'I'm afraid we've got the munchkins for the evening,' I said. 'Dad and Em are going to a Rotary Club dinner.'

'Cool,' he said, tickling Murray between the ears. 'Did you get tomorrow off?'

'I did indeed.' And Keri, noble woman, was going to castrate the three bull calves belonging to a mad lifestyle-blocker with no facilities which had been booked into my column.

'Good girl.'

'Thank you.' I lay back down again, and he lay beside me.

'Any particular reason we're lying under a tree?' he asked.

'Because it's beautiful,' I said, reaching for his hand. The late afternoon light filtered softly down through young red-gold leaves and gave each one its own personal halo. Lying under a copper beech in springtime and looking up gives me the awestruck feeling otherwise achieved by visiting the cathedrals of Europe, but for considerably less exertion and expense.

'It's also wet.'

I smiled. 'Are you worried you'll spoil your clothes?'

A car turned in off the road, and we both sat up. 'Helenhelenhelen!' shouted Bel, flinging open a rear door and leaping out. Murray, who had lived with Dad and Em for the two years I was overseas, now disliked children in general and Annabel in particular, shot across the lawn and vanished under the house. 'Look at my tattoo!' She jumped at me from a metre away, landed firmly on my solar plexus and brandished one chubby forearm, around which she had stuck a bracelet of Hello Kitty stickers.

'Lovely,' I wheezed.

'Look!' she ordered Mark.

'Beautiful,' he said solemnly.

'But I haven't got enough left to share,' she said, evidently fearing we might be overcome with cravings for Hello Kitty body art of our own.

'That's okay,' I said, getting to my feet. 'I expect we'll learn to live with it. Hi, guys.'

Em, in a very tight skirt and very high heels, leant over to retrieve the girls' bags from the back seat and then had to lever herself back off the doorframe because she couldn't bend at the hips. 'Mark, how lovely to see you again,' she said. 'We watched you play on Friday night – you were brilliant. Wasn't he, Tim?'

'Hmm?' said Dad, climbing out from behind the steering wheel. 'Yes, certainly.' He nodded to Mark across the car bonnet. 'Nice to meet you.'

'You too,' said Mark, and they reached out and shook hands.

'*We* already know him,' said Caitlin. 'We met him *ages* ago.'

'Aren't you lucky?' Dad said. 'That's a very smart car you have there.'

'Thank you,' said Mark.

'Don't let Helen drive it, will you?' my doting parent added.

'I backed his car into a post,' I told Mark. 'It was about ten years ago, but he's still not over it.'

'It was the way she approached it,' said Dad pensively. 'Acres of room, and she lined the thing up from about thirty feet and put her foot to the floor. Frightening.'

We had spaghetti and meatballs for tea, followed by lemon syrup cake. Then we played gin rummy – which would have been more fun had Bel not picked up and shed cards entirely at random, with complete disregard for the rules.

'I win,' she said smugly.

'You do not!' said Caitlin. 'You've still got three cards left!'

'*You've* only got one. So I win.'

'You're supposed to get *rid* of your cards,' said Caitlin with withering scorn.

'There,' said Bel, immediately tossing her three cards onto the pile. '*Now* I win.'

'He-*len*!' cried Caitlin.

'I know,' I said. 'She's a menace. Come on, it's bedtime.'

'I want Mark to brush my teeth,' Bel announced.

'Can't you brush your own?' he asked.

'But I'm only a little girl,' she said, looking up at him with big mournful eyes.

'Actually,' I said, 'you're a manipulative horror.'

'Come on, then, horror,' said Mark. He picked her up and slung her over his shoulder to carry her shrieking with laughter up the hall.

Caitlin looked after them wistfully – it's tough being a good girl with a smaller, cuter and naughtier sister – but Mark, having deposited Bel in the bathroom, came back and scooped her up in turn.

That section of the female brain that assesses men for good father potential (it just comes standard with two X chromosomes; you can't help it) noted this and nodded approvingly to itself.

'I've tried and tried to sleep,' declared Bel, appearing in the doorway of the lounge half an hour later. 'But I just can't.'

'Snuggle up under the covers, then close your eyes and think about nice things,' I said.

'What nice things?'

'Princesses. Fairies. That sort of thing.'

'What about fairy princesses?' Bel asked.

'Perfect,' I said. 'Goodnight.'

She pattered off down the hall, and Mark yawned and said, 'I'd have gone for fast cars and hot women myself.'

'Whatever floats your boat, I guess.'

'Mm,' he said, stretching himself out on the couch and laying his head on my knee. 'Toulon and Racing Metro have both upped their offers.'

'To?' I asked. It would be a lot, I knew; European – particularly French – rugby clubs seemed to have insane amounts of money to spend on player salaries.

'Racing's is four million dollars for three years,' said Mark. 'Give or take.' He might have been remarking on the weather – surely that offhand delivery had taken some practice in front of the bathroom mirror. His management team, who worked on commission, must have been beside themselves with delight.

'I don't want to think about fairy princesses,' said Bel, suddenly materialising at my elbow.

'Then think about something else,' said Mark.

'Are – are you going to accept?' I croaked.

'What should I think about?' asked Bel.

'Racing cars and girls in short skirts,' Mark told her. 'Go back to bed.'

'But I'm scared,' said Bel, sidling closer and laying a small pink hand on his.

'Scared of what, sprat?'

Bel cast around hurriedly for something to be scared of. 'Dragons,' she said.

'We don't have dragons in New Zealand,' said Mark firmly. 'Not one.'

'They could fly here,' she suggested.

'Nope,' he said. 'Too far. They'd never make it all the way over the Pacific. Go back to bed.'

Bel abandoned the dragons. 'Helen, could you sing me a song?'

'Annabel Jane, stop making excuses and *go to bed*.'

'Just one teensy-weensy song, and I will,' she said, producing her most winning smile.

Annabel's most winning smile, along with pink fluffy pyjamas, two stubby pigtails and a missing front tooth, was too much for me. '"Inchworm"?' I asked. I am very fond of the inchworm song, especially when sung by Danny Kaye with a Muppet backing group.

'No. "Close your eyes and give me your hand".'

So I sang 'Eternal Flame', and leant forward to kiss her on her freckled nose. 'Bed.'

'Goodnight, Helen. Goodnight, Mark,' she said, and trotted off back down the hall.

'You've got a lovely voice, McNeil,' said Mark.

'Thank you. Look, *are* you going to go and play in France?'

He made a face. 'I doubt it.'

'Why not?'

'I've always felt like getting paid to play rugby's just a bonus, because I'd do it anyway,' he said. 'But if I went and played for a club over there I'd only be doing it for the money. And I can't get my head around the idea of watching the guys playing on TV instead of being out there myself.' He picked up my hand and drew circles on the palm with one fingertip. 'And then I didn't think I'd be able to talk you into moving to Paris. Not enough dairy cows.'

'I would,' I said. 'Move to Paris, I mean. If you wanted me to.' I would have moved to the bottom of a hole if Mark had happened to decide that the bottom of a hole was the place to be.

'Would you?'

I nodded, and he sat up and kissed me at some length.

'Helen?' said a voice from about thirty centimetres away. Mark and I jumped simultaneously, smacking our noses together just like characters in a cheesy sitcom.

'Jesus,' he said. 'What *now*?'

'Bel won't let me go to sleep,' Caitlin informed us. 'She won't stay on her side.' My sisters, when they stayed, shared the double bed in my tiny spare room.

'Then go and sleep in my bed,' I said, carefully feeling my nose. It hurt quite a lot.

'But Bel will be scared all by herself.'

'Caitlin,' said Mark, 'I don't get to see your big sister very often, and the day after tomorrow I'm going to Europe for six weeks. Please be somewhere else.'

'Do you want to kiss Helen?'

'Yes.'

'And don't you want me watching?'

'No.'

'Oh,' said Caitlin.

'Tell your partner in crime that if she doesn't stay on her side I'll come and beat her,' I said. 'Okay?'

Caitlin giggled. 'Okay.'

'Goodnight, McMunchkin.'

'Goodnight.' We heard her scurry down the hall, and then the slam of the spare-room door.

Somewhat to our surprise, there were no further forays from the spare bedroom. Murray ventured back in and curled himself into a tight marmalade-coloured ball of fur on the battered cane armchair, and Mark and I went to sleep on the couch. We seemed to spend a significant portion of our time together asleep on either his couch or mine, which I suppose is only to be expected if most of your time together follows a day's work and a two-hour drive.

I was woken by the crunch of car tyres on gravel, and slid out from underneath Mark's arm to stagger zombie-like out to the kitchen and open the door.

'Were you asleep, sweetie?' Em asked.

I rubbed my eyes. 'Mm. How was your dinner?'

'Very pleasant. Did the girls behave themselves?'

'Of course,' I said. 'We had fun. Their bags are just here.'

As Dad and Em came back down the hall with a comatose child apiece, Mark appeared in the kitchen doorway with his hair standing all on end, looking at least three-quarters asleep.

'You survived the invasion?' Dad asked.

'Yeah,' said Mark, 'they were great.'

Caitlin lifted her head off Dad's shoulder and said, 'We played cards and rugby tackles and circuses. And Bel was kicking and kicking me in bed, but Mark said I had to go away so he could kiss Helen.'

'Lucky Helen,' Em murmured, looking Mark up and down appreciatively. 'Come on, Tim, love, let's leave these two alone.'

'Your stepmother is scary,' said Mark. He yawned and stretched, and the seams of his shirt split another inch or so under the arms. It was lucky Em had gone: the glimpse of bare chest through the holes might well have been too much for her.

I waved at my departing relatives through the kitchen window. 'Many years ago, when Lance and I had only been going out for a couple of months, I brought him home for the weekend,' I said. 'Caitlin was about eighteen months old, and she tipped everything out of his bag and spread it all over the floor. And Em picked up his tube of K-Y jelly and said, "Sonny, if you're doing it right you don't need this stuff."'

'The poor bugger,' said Mark, laughing. 'Come on, let's go to bed.'

15

'DOING ANYTHING TONIGHT?' I ASKED AS ALISON AND I descended Birch Crescent at a jog-trot one warm afternoon in early November. The breeze was fragrant with the scent of rhododendrons, and the soft baby shoots of Mrs Taylor's wisteria tickled our knees as we passed her fence.

'Dinner with Mum and Dad. How about you?'

'Not a thing. Maybe I'll go and annoy Sam.'

'When does Mark get back?' she asked.

'Twenty-two days, seven hours, and –' I looked at my watch '– about nineteen minutes. Not that I'm counting or anything.'

'That's just the price you have to pay for being a Wag.'

'Scrummy,' I corrected. 'Soccer players' girlfriends are Wags; rugby players' are scrummies.'

Alison laughed. 'What about the ugly ones?' she asked.

Sam's reply, when I texted him regarding his plans for Friday evening, was brief and to the point. *Busy.*

Keri had gone hiking and it's a bit sad to spend two consecutive Friday nights at home alone watching *Dirty Dancing* on DVD, so after work I went to see Dad and Em. I found my father at the table with the paper spread before him and his glasses balanced on the very end of his nose.

'Hullo, senior daughter,' he said, leaning back in his chair and pushing his glasses back up. 'What's new?'

I sat down on the edge of the table. 'Almost nothing. Where are the girls?'

'Emily has gone to the gym, and the small ones are in the bath.'

'Any exciting new advances in the field of dentistry?'

Dad scratched an ear in a thoughtful fashion. 'I did remove most of last Sunday's dinner from behind a woman's plate this afternoon,' he said. 'Although I'm not sure you'd call that exciting.'

'Did she not realise she was supposed to take it out and clean it?'

'She's losing the plot, poor old soul. I've spoken to her daughter and she's going to keep an eye on things. How about you? Pushed back the frontiers of veterinary science in the last week?'

'Well, I had a long talk with a woman who wants us to castrate her dog and implant a pair of silicone testicles,' I said.

'Can you *get* silicone testicles?' Dad asked.

'Yep. Wouldn't have thought there'd be a huge market for them, myself, but apparently there is. And I'm treating John Somerville's pet chicken for bumblefoot.'

'Groundbreaking stuff,' he said. 'I see Mark's in today's paper.'

'Is he?'

Dad passed me the sports section. On the back page was a picture of the All Blacks at a training session; Mark, in tracksuit pants and padded jacket, was talking to one of the assistant coaches at the side of the field. 'It says he's hurt his shoulder and he's out for tomorrow's game.'

'I talked to him this morning, and he said it was just a twinge,' I said. He had sounded tired and annoyed, and it had been an unsatisfactory sort of conversation. From down the hall came a loud splash, followed by a shriek. 'Want me to go and investigate?'

November crawled by. Buttercups grew thick along the roadsides, and the snowball bush beside my porch steps was a vision of loveliness. At work the non-cycling cow calls slowed to a trickle and the lame bull calls increased sharply. Keri started the Ketosis Diet, losing both five kilograms and her sense of humour. Mark and Alan lunched with Prince William in Cardiff. I lunched with Lance's mother at the Stockman's Arms. Their lunch attracted considerably more media attention, but I think mine was more awkward.

One Monday night, eight days before Mark was due home, I made myself a truly superb prawn stir-fry. I had two fork-fuls before going off the whole idea of food. Which was odd, because I'm the sort of person who starts planning dinner as I finish lunch.

The next morning I poured myself a glass of orange juice, sat down to peruse yesterday's *Broadview Broadcast*, and then had to make a wild dash outside to throw up over the edge of the porch. I decided, tipping the rest of the glass sadly down the sink, that I must have caught one of those unpleasant twenty-four-hour bugs.

On Thursday I vomited into the rubbish bin in the surgery halfway through a bitch spey, which impressed Zoe not one bit. And on Friday afternoon, wending my seedy way along Mohapi

Road to see a sick bull, I decided enough was enough and pulled
the ute off the road into a gateway. I opened my phone and texted
Alison. *Can u nick preg test from work? If buy one Aunty Deb will
see.* Aunty Deb – Sam's mum – worked at the pharmacy, and
not so much as a cough lolly could be obtained in Broadview
without her guidance and support.

I pressed send, dropped the phone back in the breast pocket of
my overalls and sat with my forehead resting against the steering
wheel, nauseous and panicking. I couldn't be pregnant. It was
unthinkable. It was just some random bug. The kind that makes
your breasts tender and turns you right off the smell of coffee.

The phone buzzed in my pocket, and I sat up to retrieve it.
Of course. Come round after work.

Thanks, I wrote, pulling out one-handed across the road.
A van going the other way swept around the corner and swerved
wildly to avoid the nose of the ute. I caught just a glimpse of the
man driving it, white-faced and shouting abuse I fully deserved.
Dropping the phone, I crept back onto the grass verge and shook
like a leaf.

Alison lived on the outskirts of Broadview in a picturesque
but draughty villa, with an inoffensive vegan couple who wore
Roman sandals all year round. I was on her front porch at five
past five that evening, biting my fingernails and jittering.

A small white car pulled into the villa's driveway and Alison
got out, looking slim and cool in her black three-quarter pants
and blue medical centre scrub top. 'Hey,' she said.

I came to rest and removed my left thumbnail from between
my teeth. 'Hey.'

'Come on in.'

I followed her through the house to the bathroom, where she dug in her purse and found a foil sachet. 'I'll get you a cup to pee in,' she said, and disappeared down the hall.

She was back in a moment with a china teacup. 'Okay,' she said, holding it out. 'Nice mid-stream sample, please.'

I took it silently and vanished into the loo.

When I emerged she put out a hand for the cup. 'I'll do it,' she said. 'I do about ten of these a day.'

My fingers tightened on the handle. 'I won't be,' I said desperately. If I didn't do the test it couldn't come true. I had changed my mind – give me the agony of doubt over the crushing blow of confirmation any day. 'I'm just being an idiot – imagining things . . .'

Alison nodded and prised the cup gently from my hand.

We stood together at the bathroom sink while she placed a few drops of urine in the well of the little plastic pregnancy test with a disposable pipette. 'It's five eleven now,' she said, looking at her watch. 'We'll give it five minutes, and look for two pink lines.' But, even as she spoke, two fuzzy pink stripes coalesced and darkened in the test well.

'Like those ones?' I whispered.

'Oh, hon,' said Alison helplessly. 'I'll make you a cup of tea.'

I sat, while she made it, on a wooden kitchen chair, looking unseeingly at the floor. 'I never forget the pill,' I said. 'Never.'

'Did you have diarrhoea at any stage?' she asked, dunking a teabag. 'Or a vomiting bug?'

'No. Well, only this last week. And that seems to be an effect of pregnancy, not a cause.'

'Have you been on antibiotics?'

'No – oh, shit. Yes. A cat bit me, and I put myself on Vetamox.' I had entirely forgotten the antibiotic clause.

'When was that?' she asked, setting the tea down on the table at my elbow.

'I don't know . . . Just before Mark went to England. Seventeenth of October.'

She counted on her fingers. 'So you'll be – what? Seven weeks pregnant, give or take.'

'No, he's only been away five weeks.'

'They measure pregnancy from your period,' said Alison. 'Even though you conceive at your next ovulation. That makes it forty weeks from your last period to giving birth.'

'Ali, I can't have a baby,' I wailed. Mark and I had only been going out for a few months, and we saw each other once a week if we were lucky. I hadn't met his family, I didn't know his middle name – I didn't even know if he *had* a middle name. His friends called him Tip, but I didn't. He had only once said he loved me, and I don't think you're allowed to count it if it's while you're having sex. I'd been apprehensive about our future even before this catastrophe, because chances were he would decide before too long that his ideal woman would have cheekbones, good hand–eye coordination and the figure of a swimwear model. I started to cry hopelessly.

Alison rubbed my shoulder in wordless sympathy. After a while I mopped my face on my shirt, tilted my head back and pressed the heels of my hands to hot, aching eyes.

'When's Mark back?' she asked.

'Tuesday.' Oh, good God, I was going to have to tell him.

Someone came whistling up the porch steps, and I got hastily to my feet. It's probably a bit disconcerting to find a woman sobbing in your kitchen when you want to crack on with your lentil mousse, or whatever it was that Alison's flatmates subsisted on. But, unexpectedly, my cousin Sam put his head around the kitchen door. He looked taken aback, and then concerned.

'Hey!' he said, putting down a bulging grocery bag on the bench. 'Hel, what's up?'

Alison shook her head at him.

So my two best friends were a couple, and they hadn't told me. No wonder they were both busy all the time. That hurt, which surprised me, in a dull sort of way; I wouldn't have thought I'd have the least scrap of emotion to spare from my own personal disaster.

'You can tell him,' I said. ''Night, guys.'

'Helen, don't go,' said Alison.

'No, I – I need to think. Thank you.' I made for the door, and she barred my way.

'Stop that. Sit back down. You're not driving yourself home.'

'I'm pregnant,' I said tiredly. 'Not drunk.'

'Holy shit,' said Sam.

They were very kind. They tried hard to get me to stay, and Alison accompanied me anxiously to the ute. 'Please stay,' she said again. 'I don't think you should be by yourself.'

'I'll be fine.' I was going to cry again; I could feel the tears building, relentless as a tidal wave, and was suddenly frantic to get away. Alison would be nothing but supportive. She would organise an appointment with a midwife or an abortion clinic or a king-sized block of Caramello chocolate or anything else I might want, and she wouldn't judge me by so much as the flicker of an eyelid. But I thought hysterically that right now her tactful sympathy was more than I could bear.

'Can I come over a bit later and stay the night?' she asked.

'No!' I said. 'No. I'm fine.'

'You're not.'

'But I don't think ruining your Friday night's going to help.'

'You are *not* ruining my Friday night. Don't be an idiot.'

'Thank you,' I said, hugging her. 'Honestly, I'd like to be by myself.'

'I'll ring you in the morning,' she said. 'It – it'll be okay.'

I nodded. It wouldn't, but she couldn't help that.

16

THAT WAS A TERRIBLE, TERRIBLE WEEKEND. I SPENT IT
seesawing between blind panic and flat despair. I wrote lists of
the options, screwed them up and wrote more lists. I chewed my
nails down to the quick and cried myself sick – or, to be precise,
sicker. Murray had no patience with this pathetic self-pitying
behaviour, and left home to camp at a rabbit hole in Rex's bull
paddock until such time as I pulled myself together.

Sam arrived on Saturday morning with three Crunchie bars
and a cyclamen in a pot. I was almost certain Alison had sent
him, and quite sure the flowers were her idea. She came just after
lunch and sat beside me on my ugly plum couch, not talking
much but exuding sympathy from every pore. They were both
shining examples of all that friends should be, but when they
drove up together on Sunday afternoon I hid in the spare-room
wardrobe so they would think I'd gone for a walk.

I didn't want to have a baby. I wanted to be a good dairy
vet, the one farmers wanted to see rather than the one they
settled for if Nick or Anita was unavailable. I was signed up

for an extension course in cattle nutrition in the new year and I wanted to get another calving season under my belt.

Reproducing had *not* featured in my short- to medium-term career plans, and I was quite certain it hadn't featured in Mark's. Next year was the World Cup, and chances were it would be his last. Winning it was his whole focus and ambition. The last thing on earth he needed was some stupid girl – one who'd studied both pharmacology and reproductive physiology at university, for goodness' sake, and so really should have been able to keep her eggs unfertilised – announcing that she was having his child.

I thought hard about having an abortion. One quick visit to the nearest clinic, one minor surgical procedure, and voilà, crisis averted. You couldn't really ask for a tidier solution to a problem than that. Except . . . except I was going on twenty-seven, and that's old enough to act like a grown-up and deal with the consequences of your actions.

I can't do it, I thought miserably. *I just can't. I don't want a baby – it'll ruin everything – but that's not a good enough reason. And I suppose I'll like it when it's born.* I was feeling quite noble about this, in a dismal sort of way, when it dawned on me that I had no right to make the decision by myself. Mark deserved a say in the fate of his offspring, and I had not the least intention of giving him one. Which made me less of a brave, selfless, Joan-of-Arc type and more of an egotistical high-handed bitch. *Crap.*

I tried and tried to concoct scenarios where Mark might forgive me and stay around. Surely it wasn't impossible that we would make it work; we were adults, after all, not poor terrified sixteen-year-olds. And anyway, sometimes even terrified sixteen-year-olds stay together and live happily ever after. My mother's cousin did – she 'got herself in trouble' (such an unfair way to put it, when she obviously had help) and was sent off to stay with distant relatives 'until she was decent again'. And the boy who'd helped her into the trouble tracked her down and arrived at the nursing home with a bunch of flowers, and they were married and went on to have another four children. As a matter of fact, they were still living happily in Temuka, growing heirloom fruit trees and playing golf.

We were good together, Mark and I. We laughed at the same things; I enjoyed baking, he enjoyed eating things I baked – there was a shared interest right there, and they say shared interests are vital. But I knew perfectly well that in all likelihood this would be the end of us. A baby is too big and too serious a thing for a fragile new relationship.

He called on Sunday night, New Zealand time, which was Sunday morning for him in London. I had finished my latest crying jag half an hour previously, for which I was drearily grateful.

'Hi,' he said. 'How's it going?'

'Good.' It had never been worse, but good's a relatively easy word to get out without your voice giving you away. 'How about you?'

'Oh, alright. Shoulder's a bit sore.'

'Did you hurt it again?' I asked.

'Fell on it. It'll be right; it's got plenty of time to heal.'

'I only heard the game on the radio,' I said. I didn't have Sky TV and wasn't currently fit company for anyone who did. 'They didn't say you were hurt. Have you had an X-ray?'

'No, not yet. They'll check it out properly when we get home. You'll be up on Tuesday night?'

Tuesday was marked on the calendar with red felt pen and I had booked annual leave for the Wednesday almost two months ago, but I said feebly, 'I was wondering if it'd be better to come on Wednesday, and let you have a sleep first.' Jet lag, I thought, could only make our impending conversation worse.

'I can sleep on the plane,' said Mark. 'Please come. Or do you want me to come down?'

'No! No, I'll come up after work.'

'You alright, McNeil?' he asked.

I bit my lip hard, and managed, 'Yeah. Miss you.'

'You too. Only two more days.'

❦

Never had I greeted Monday morning with such relief. If I'd spent any longer alone with my thoughts I would have gone mad. At work I had to hold myself together and act like a professional, which meant I was forced to take a break from my new and all-absorbing pastimes of crying and throwing up. (Sometimes, just for variation, I'd been doing the two together, but I really wouldn't recommend it. It makes breathing almost impossible, and you tend to end up with spew coming out your nose, which is not only disgusting but very painful.)

Thomas informed me that my eyes looked like piss-holes in the snow, but he didn't feel any urge to find out why, and nobody else noticed anything wrong as far as I could tell.

❦

At half past four on Tuesday afternoon, Nick turned from his computer screen, raised his eyebrows at me and said, 'What are you doing here? Isn't your boyfriend back in the country?'

'I'm going up after work,' I said.

'Go on, then, bugger off. You can tell him that tackle just before half-time in that Welsh Test was poetry in motion, by the way.'

'I will,' I said, standing up. 'Thanks, Nick.'

'Blatant favouritism,' Richard complained. 'Just because she's shagging an All Black.'

'When you're shagging an All Black you can leave early too,' said Nick, turning back to his computer screen. 'And in the meantime you can stop pissing around on Trade Me and go wash your ute.'

It was just on seven when I parked in the street outside Mark's place, and late sunlight slanted golden through the wrought-iron fence bordering his driveway. I got out of the car and went slowly down the drive, counting the tall spiked dividers between sections of fence. *Seventeen, eighteen, nineteen – oh shit, oh shit – twenty, twenty-one . . .*

His door opened and he came out, wearing one of his elderly faded T-shirts and a pair of board shorts with holes in the knees. 'Hi,' he said, and smiled with such obvious pleasure that I ran the last twenty metres and threw myself at him headlong.

He picked me up and hugged me, and I clung to him with my face buried in the curve of his shoulder. His skin was very warm. *Don't cry*, I told myself savagely. *Don't you dare.*

'God, I missed you, McNeil,' he said, carrying me back up the steps and inside. He removed one arm to shut the door, and put it back around me.

'You too,' I said into his neck.

'Oi,' he said, loosening his arms so I slid to my feet. 'Look up.'

I did, and he took my face in his hands and kissed me.

'I love you,' I said when I could talk again, departing from my rehearsed script right at the start.

'I love you too.' He kissed me again. 'I got you something.' He dug in the pocket of his scruffy shorts and pulled out a tiny gauze bag, tied with a ribbon.

'Mark . . .' I said shakily.

'Open it.'

And because I was a snivelling coward, and I couldn't bear to ruin everything just yet, I undid the ribbon and tipped a gold chain and delicate enamelled pendant into the palm of my hand.

'I found it in this tiny little shop in Cardiff,' he said. 'I'm not very good at jewellery, but I thought maybe it was your kind of thing.'

'It is. It's beautiful. It's perfect.' I shut my eyes, trying to scrape together a few pitiful crumbs of courage. 'Mark, I have to tell you something.'

He rested his chin on the top of my head. 'You're leaving me for Hamish?'

'I'm pregnant,' I said.

Mark didn't move, and he didn't speak. He went very still, and I backed away from him. Something was hurting my hand – after a few seconds I realised it was the edge of the pendant, which I was clutching as if for dear life. I put it down on the table beside the front door, amid the junk mail and strapping tape and spare mouthguards, and said hurriedly, 'It's my fault. A cat bit me and I put myself on antibiotics, and I forgot that stuffs up the pill. I'm so sorry.'

'How long have you known?' he asked. His voice was flat and remote, as though it was coming from a long way away.

'Friday. I did a test. I – Mark, I couldn't tell you on the phone.'

'Do you want to have it?'

'No,' I whispered.

'You mean you want an abortion?'

I shook my head. 'I don't think I could live with myself. It's not its fault, it's mine.'

'Right,' he said, and he sounded suddenly very, very tired.

'This isn't your problem. I mean, I won't ask you for anything. It's all my fault – we can get your lawyers to draw something up to say it's my fault and you don't owe me anything. I'll –'

'For fuck's sake!' he snapped, interrupting this torrent of selfless eloquence. 'Just what kind of arsehole do you think I am?'

I had never seen him angry before, and I stared at him with my mouth open. 'I – I *don't*. But you didn't sign up for this.'

'Yeah, well,' he said grimly, 'neither did you. Come on, I made tea.'

A rich, meaty smell filled the kitchen. He had set the breakfast bar with two knives and forks, two wineglasses and a tea light in a glass dish. That tea light made the tears well up again, and I choked them back. He opened the oven door to remove a lasagne that looked to be all you could ever ask for in a lasagne, baked golden on top and bubbling at the edges. My stomach gave an ominous lurch, and I turned and bolted for the downstairs bathroom.

When, five minutes later, I crept back up the stairs, Mark had removed the lasagne from sight and was leaning against the bench with a beer in his hand.

'Sorry,' I whispered. 'Morning sickness. It smells b-beautiful . . .' And I burst into tears.

'Do you want some toast or something?' he asked.

I shook my head.

'Drink?'

'No, I – can I have a shower?'

'Of course.'

I stood under the hot water for a long time, but I couldn't get warm. At last I gave it up and got out, and a parboiled, wretched specimen with dark hair plastered down over its scalp and huge dark-circled eyes faced me in the bathroom mirror. *Bloody marvellous*, I told myself bitterly. *You could be Gollum's twin sister. This'll really encourage him to keep you on.*

A hair dryer might have helped, and some serious, industrial-strength makeup. I had neither, so I bundled my wet hair up in an untidy knot, took a sweatshirt from the suitcase lying open across Mark's bed and went slowly back downstairs.

He had removed all traces of food and cleaned the kitchen, and as I approached he tossed the dishcloth into the empty sink and said, 'Think you'd keep down a cup of tea?'

I nodded, and he turned to make it. 'Any idea when this baby's due?' he asked, filling a mug from the amazing boiling-water tap.

'Middle of July, I think. I'll have to have a scan and find out exactly.'

'I'll come with you.'

'You don't have to,' I started, and then saw his face and stopped. 'Thank you.'

'Biscuit?'

'No, thanks. I don't think it'd stay down.'

'How long've you been throwing up?'

'About a week,' I said. 'Throwing up and crying. Hormones, I guess.'

'Sounds like a riot,' he said, passing me my tea.

'Yeah, it's great.' I took a cautious sip. 'I don't know why they call this *morning* sickness; it's constant.'

Mark stretched himself out on the couch, and I curled up in one of his enormous leather armchairs with my tea. We didn't talk as the light faded from golden to pink to silver, and at last I unfolded myself and crept upstairs to bed.

He came up twenty minutes later, shed his clothes without speaking and got into bed beside me.

'What's your middle name?' I asked, watching the shadows move across the ceiling as a car passed beneath the French doors with a throaty expensive purr. Mark's neighbours' cars all sounded like that.

'Russell.'

'What's your favourite colour?'

'I don't know – blue. Why?'

'We don't know each other very well, do we?'

He was silent for a minute, and then he said, 'Your middle name is Olivia.'

'How do you know?'

'It's written on your degree. Helen Olivia McNeil, Bachelor of Veterinary Science with Distinction.'

'Full marks to you,' I said. All of our degrees hung on the wall behind the front counter at work, in order to try to convince the public that we knew what we were talking about.

'Thank you.'

'Olivia was my grandmother's name.' Mum's mum, my nice grandmother.

'Apparently I was conceived in Russell,' said Mark. 'Yuck.'

I gave a small, watery gulp of laughter.

'That's better,' he said, rolling over and putting his arms around me.

I hugged him back tightly. 'I'm so, so sorry.'

Mark wiped my eyes with a corner of sheet and said, 'Apologise again, McNeil, and you're sleeping on the floor.'

17

'WHAT NOW?' I ASKED. 'DOCTOR'S APPOINTMENT?'

'No,' said Alison, 'you need a midwife. Eloise Morgan's lovely, and she's been doing it for twenty-five years – I'll get you her number.'

'Thank you.' We had abandoned our lunchtime walk and were sitting cross-legged on the grass in front of the Broadview War Memorial, Alison with a Tupperware container of salad and me with a Vegemite sandwich. Bread was good, I had discovered; it tended to stay down.

'You told him?' she asked, carefully spearing a cherry tomato.

'Yep.'

She glanced at me for a moment, and then turned her attention back to her tomato so as not to pry. Very tactful girl, Alison.

'Well,' I said, 'he hasn't broken up with me yet. And it must have been fairly tempting, when the first thing I did was burst into tears and throw up.'

She smiled. 'Did you really?'

'Yep.'

'I'm sure he's not going to break up with you.'

'It'd be a miracle if he didn't,' I said morosely.

'I think you're being just a tad pessimistic,' said Alison.

'You try starting the day by spewing out the bedroom window, and we'll see how optimistic *you* feel.' The alarm on my phone had gone off at five that morning, and then to make absolutely sure Mark was awake I had stumbled to his bedroom window (that being closer than the bathroom) and thrown up copiously into the garden below. There may be a better way to dispel the mystery and romance of a relationship, but I can't think of it offhand.

'I haven't done that since I was seventeen and Leah Koroheke and I drank about twenty of those revolting Purple Goanna things,' she said.

I shook my head. 'Fine behaviour from the head girl, I must say. So, when were you planning to tell me about you and Sam?' It would be impossible to compete with Alison for tact and reticence, so I don't try.

'Soon. When the moment was right.' She foraged through her salad and added, blushing a delicate shade of pink, 'He – I really like him.'

'I'm so glad,' I said. 'And you could have done a lot worse. I was starting to worry that Hamish would grind you down.'

'Never.'

'You'd have gone drag racing with him if Sam hadn't rescued you,' I pointed out.

'I would *not*,' said Alison. 'I would have developed a terrible stomach bug the night before and been forced to stay home.'

'What star sign are you?' Keri asked that afternoon, picking up the newspaper on Thomas's desk. Jill Murphy was due any minute with a constipated Maltese terrier, and we were hanging around out the front waiting for her to arrive.

'Aries,' I said.

'With Venus and Mercury about to leave your work sector, now is the time to say what you mean and mean what you say,' she read.

'Thanks,' I said. 'That's so helpful.' My personal theory is that next week's horoscopes are a collaborative effort between everyone in the newsroom, written late on Friday afternoons after the first half dozen beers.

'Read mine,' Thomas ordered. 'Aquarius.'

'Aquarius,' said Keri. 'Hmm. Oh, here we are. You're under the influence of the waning moon, and you need to be careful not to take your loved ones for granted.'

'So it's okay to take them for granted when the moon's waxing?' I asked.

'S'pose so.'

'What a heap of shit,' Thomas said.

The automatic doors slid open and Jill Murphy came in, small fluffy dog under her arm. 'With any luck,' said Keri brightly, 'that'll be just what we say when Buffy's had his enema.'

Buffy, as it happened, was quite impressively constipated. According to his owner he had spent most of the previous weekend working his way through a rotten possum – which was no mean feat, seeing as he was only the size of a medium-sized possum himself. Sadly, though, the possum's fur had failed to navigate the length of his digestive tract, and his large intestine was blocked from end to end. We could feel the hard, distended loops of bowel through his abdominal wall. Why, I wondered, hadn't he left the fur behind? Surely it's not all that tasty. And imagine the feel of it in the back of your throat . . . I did imagine it for a moment, and then wished I hadn't.

We knocked Buffy right out to unblock him. It's not a very sophisticated job; you administer enema solution per rectum to grease everything up a bit, knead the abdomen to break the blockage down and winkle the bits out with a gloved finger. Keri and I took turns kneading and winkling, swapping every five minutes or so, while Zoe stood at the patient's head to monitor the anaesthetic.

It was hot in the treatment room and I was concentrating on keeping my Vegemite sandwich down when Keri shouted, '*Zoe!* Turn him *down*!'

Zoe jumped and dropped her cell phone into the pocket of her scrub top. 'What?'

Keri yanked off her gloves and made a dive for the anaesthetic machine's dial. 'He's on *four*! Is he still breathing?' She turned off the gas, pushed the button that floods the machine's circuit with pure oxygen and began to squeeze the rebreathing bag.

I snatched a stethoscope off the table and pressed it feverishly to Buffy's chest – his heartbeat was slow and faint, but it was there. 'His heart's beating.'

'What's his colour like?' Keri asked.

I peeled back the little dog's upper lip. His gums were pale grey. 'Terrible.' And offering up a fervent prayer of thanksgiving for having put the dog on IV fluids before anaesthetising him, I increased the flow from his drip. *Shock rates are ninety mil per kilo per hour – he's seven kilos – nine times seven is sixty-three – six hundred and thirty mil per hour is about ten mil a minute – a hundred drips in sixty seconds – almost two drips per second . . .* There's nothing like panic for speeding up your mental arithmetic.

For several tense minutes Keri breathed for Buffy while I listened to his heart. 'Eighty beats per minute . . . ninety . . . a hundred and ten . . . He's getting pinker. Stop breathing for him for a minute, Keri – see if he'll do it himself.'

He wouldn't, but after another five minutes we tried again, and were rewarded by a quick heave of breath. I turned down the drip and we regarded one another wide-eyed across the patient. And then, as one, our gazes swivelled towards Zoe.

'Did you look *once* at that dog?' said Keri in a soft, menacing voice.

Zoe opened her mouth, shut it again, burst into tears and fled. Bel does that too – defensive crying in an effort to divert blame from its rightful source.

'She never looked away from that bloody phone,' said Keri.

'Nope,' I agreed.

'And if he'd died it would've still been our fault.'

I nodded. Ultimately, the responsibility lies with the vet, not the nurse. 'I didn't look at him either. If you hadn't noticed he'd be dead.'

Keri let out a long, shaky breath. 'Okay,' she said. 'I'll watch the anaesthetic; you look after the back end.'

By half past four the aftershocks of Buffy's near-death experience were fading. He had gone home, de-constipated, along with a prescription for laxatives and some anti-inflammatories for his poor pummelled colon. Zoe was folding washing out the back in icy offended silence, and Nick had agreed to have a word with her about the advantages of the nurse monitoring the patient rather than the social lives of her forty closest friends. He had then hurriedly left the building, muttering something about needing to revisit a sick bull.

'He won't say anything to her,' said Keri, jumping up to sit on the counter and glaring at our leader's departing back. 'He's such a wimp.'

'Never mind,' I said. 'She's had a fright. She won't do it again.'

'Of course she will. That bloody phone should be constipated.'

'Confiscated,' I corrected, grinning.

'Oh, whatever. What's on tomorrow, Thomas?'

But Thomas's attention was elsewhere. 'Hey, Helen,' he said. 'Your boyfriend's here.'

I turned in surprise and looked through the window. Mark was crossing the car park, looking unusually respectable in dress trousers and a white business shirt with the sleeves rolled up above his elbows. He had been scheduled to spend the day with his management team (he had not one but three people looking after his contracts and sponsorship deals and investment portfolio; it was scary), so he must have come straight on from there. I'd never seen him in corporate get-up before, and I wasn't at all sure I liked it. He looked like he belonged not with me but in the kind of trendy waterfront bar where Beautiful People hang out, with a martini in one hand and a supermodel in the other.

Nick changed direction and hurried towards him, hand outstretched.

'God, he's gorgeous,' said Keri dreamily. 'Mark, I mean, not Nick. Helen, what've you got that I haven't?'

'Tits, for a start,' Thomas said.

She scowled at him. 'When I want your input, zit-face, I'll ask for it.'

'Careful,' he said. 'I've only got to say the word and you're dehorning Joe Watkins' calves.' A horrible, horrible threat: Joe liked to wait until the calves were at least six months old before they were dehorned, and you had to chase them around a tumbledown shed through bits of old machinery to catch them.

Luckily the automatic doors opened before hostilities could develop any further. 'Thomas!' called Nick. 'Grab a box of beer out of the chiller, there's a good chap.'

'What about that bull?' Keri asked, but she spoke too softly for him to hear.

Mark came and leant on the counter beside me, and I rested my head against his white cotton shoulder for just a second. 'Hey.'

He gave me a swift one-armed hug. 'Hey. Hi, guys.'

'Hi,' said Keri. 'How was the UK?'

'Great. Freezing cold. It's good to be home.'

'More importantly, how's that shoulder?' Nick asked.

Entirely preoccupied with pregnancy, I hadn't even asked, and it occurred to me that I really was a lousy girlfriend.

'Coming right,' said Mark. 'By the time it's had a month's rest it'll be good as new.'

'What'd you do to it, exactly?'

'It's the AC joint,' Mark said, digging his left thumb into the point of his right shoulder. 'Round there somewhere. They X-rayed it this morning. The doctor called it a grade-two dislocation – it shouldn't need surgery or anything like that.'

'So you'll manage it with physio?' Nick asked.

'Yeah.'

Thomas returned with a box of beer and fished in the drawer under the till for the bottle opener he kept there in readiness for just such occasions. Opening the first bottle, he passed it to me, since I happened to be closest. I passed it on to Mark.

It was five thirty when we extricated ourselves, and since Thomas never believes anyone who says they're not in a beer mood, Mark had drunk mine as well as his. I swapped bottles with him at intervals and took the odd micro-sip, and was quite proud of my powers of deception.

'How are you feeling?' Mark asked as we crossed the car park.

'Oh, alright,' I said. 'Are you going to be the new face of Tip Top ice cream?'

'Yes.'

'Congratulations. Wearing only a pair of Speedos and three girls in teensy little bikinis?'

'Just the one girl, actually,' he said, pulling his keys out of his pocket and tossing them idly on the palm of his hand. 'Tam Healy.'

A vision appeared ready-made in my head, in which he and the delectable Tamara were frolicking in the surf with an ice cream apiece. Or, even worse, an ice cream between them.

'Want me to pick something up for tea?' he asked.

The Tamara of my imagination shook her hair out of her eyes, laughing, and the evening sunlight turned her smooth wet skin to gold. 'Hmm?' I said. 'No, don't worry, I've got stuff at home.'

'Okay,' said Mark, 'see you there.'

I walked into my kitchen ten minutes later to find him trying to feed my cat. This would have been simpler had Murray's head not already been in the bowl.

'Don't you ever feed this poor animal?' he asked, trickling cat biscuits between Murray's ears.

'I didn't have time to come home before work this morning,' I said. 'I left him heaps to eat, but he's never grasped the concept of rationing. Breathe, little dude.'

'Can't breathe; must eat,' said Mark, putting the cat biscuits down on the bench.

'How *is* your shoulder?' I asked abruptly.

'Bit sore. It'll be right; it's no big deal.'

'Really?'

'Really.'

'That's good.'

'Alan and Saskia have invited us out on their yacht for a few days after Christmas,' he said. 'Are you keen?'

The mere thought of a few days on a boat made my stomach stir uneasily. 'I think it'd probably be the end of me,' I said. 'I get seasick even when I'm not pregnant.'

'Right.'

'You go,' I said. 'It sounds wonderful.'

He shook his head, and my tears welled up quietly and overflowed.

'Look, it's no big deal, we'll do something else,' he said, just a trifle impatiently.

I rubbed my eyes with the back of my hand. 'Sorry. Ignore it, it's just h-hormones, and I feel so s-sick . . .'

Mark sighed and put his arms around me. 'I know,' he said.

'Are you going to tell them why I can't go?'

'I won't if you don't want me to.'

'I guess you might as well,' I said. 'It's going to become obvious in a few months, anyway.'

'Mm,' he said. 'You know, I think your breasts are getting bigger already.' And he ran his hands up my front in an investigative sort of way.

'Bigger than Tamara's?' I asked, regretting the words even as they left my mouth.

He let me go. 'Helen, it's just an ad.'

'I know,' I said.

Later that night, in bed, where deep-and-meaningful conversations don't feel quite so much like scenes from *Days of Our Lives* as they do in daylight, I said into the darkness, 'It's just that having a baby makes everything so much more serious. All of a sudden we're not just cruising along and enjoying it anymore – it's like we have to decide whether we love each other enough to stay together for the rest of our lives, and it's too soon to have to think about it. I'm not putting it very well, but do you know what I mean?'

And Mark, in the voice of someone who is at least nine-tenths asleep and has heard your words as merely a murmur on the edge of hearing, said, 'Unghf. Nigh',' as his arm slackened around my waist and he dropped the rest of the way into unconsciousness.

18

AT THREE THIRTY ON MONDAY AFTERNOON, HAVING written *Doctor* across my column on the day sheet, I walked straight past the door of the medical centre. I paused along the street beneath a small faded sign reading *E. Morgan and J. Bennett, Broadview Independent Midwives*, looked furtively from left to right, pushed the door for a few seconds before thinking to pull it, and at last scurried inside. A buzzer sounded, and someone called, 'Helen? I'll be with you in a minute. Just take a seat.'

I sank onto a plastic chair and nodded to the woman across the waiting room. She was both overweight and hugely pregnant, and had chosen for some reason to swathe herself in purple lycra. I was just deciding she looked like Violet Beauregarde and sniggering internally when her stomach rippled, which made me think less of Violet Beauregarde and more of *Alien*.

The woman rubbed her side and remarked, 'Little sod's trying to kick his way out.'

'Does it hurt?' I asked, fascinated.

'Nah, just pisses you off when you're trying to sleep,' she said. 'You're the vet, aren't you?'

'Um, yes,' I said, having not the faintest recollection of ever having seen her before. This was surprising, because she wasn't the type you'd have thought you could forget.

'When are you due?'

'July, I think,' I said unwillingly. 'But no-one really knows yet; it's very early.'

'I won't say a word,' she assured me.

'Thank you. What about you?'

'Tenth of January.'

Crikey. Almost a month to go. I couldn't for the life of me imagine how she was going to get any bigger without exploding.

A door opened beside my new acquaintance, and a pleasant-looking woman in her fifties with smooth brown hair came out. 'Hello, Sharon,' she said. 'I'm sure Janet won't be long. Helen, come on in.'

She closed the door behind us and sat down gracefully at her desk, knees together and feet crossed at the ankles. 'Do sit down,' she said, gesturing for me to sit on the bed in the middle of the room. 'I'm Eloise Morgan. I don't suppose you're Tim and Glenys McNeil's daughter, by any chance?'

'Yes,' I said, and she smiled.

'I wondered if you might be. My dear, I delivered you. Or, to be more accurate, I *tried* to deliver you. But you decided to turn around at the last moment and come out bottom first, and your poor parents were rushed to Waikato Hospital for an emergency caesarean. You were my first really difficult birth, and you scared me nearly to death.'

'I'm sorry,' I said, smiling back.

'Apology accepted,' said Eloise. 'It only seems like last week, and yet here you are, expecting a baby of your own.' She flicked an imaginary speck of dust from the knee of her trousers and added, 'I'm sorry your mother isn't here to be a part of your pregnancy. She was a lovely, lovely person.'

'Thank you,' I said, restraining myself with some difficulty from throwing my arms around her neck and bursting into tears.

She turned and picked up a plastic wheel from her desk. I had a very similar one on my own desk, except that mine was for working out bovine gestation dates instead of human. 'Now, how far along are you, according to your dates? Did you take note of when the first day of your last period was?'

'I was on the pill,' I said. 'But I took a course of antibiotics around the fifteenth of October, and I can't possibly have got pregnant after the twenty-first because my boyfriend wasn't in the country. I – I forgot you're supposed to take extra precautions with antibiotics.'

'Did your doctor not remind you?'

'I didn't go to the doctor. I just put myself on amoxicillin for a cat bite. I'm a vet.'

'I see,' said Eloise, putting her plastic wheel back down on her desk. 'And how do you know you're pregnant?'

'I did a test,' I said. 'Actually my friend Alison did it for me, and she's a nurse at the medical centre. And I feel awful, and my breasts hurt.'

'That does sound fairly conclusive,' she said. 'So you weren't planning on having a baby just now. But you've decided to go through with the pregnancy?'

I nodded.

'Alright,' she said evenly. 'Well, my dear, the first thing to do will be to book you in for an ultrasound. This week, if possible – the smaller the baby the more accurately they can give you your due date. Are you taking folate?'

'No.'

'It's recommended that you do, both before you get pregnant and for the first twelve weeks. It's been proven to decrease the risk of spina bifida. You can get it at the chemist's.'

'Okay,' I said. I would have to visit a chemist in Hamilton; I might as well announce I was pregnant on national television as buy folate from Aunty Deb.

'Well,' she said, 'let's fill in the paperwork. You'll need some blood tests, just to confirm the pregnancy and make sure you're healthy.' She turned in her chair and pulled a pad towards her. 'What's your full name and date of birth? I should remember, I know, but I've met a lot of babies between then and now.'

'Helen Olivia McNeil,' I said. 'Twenty-ninth of March, 1985.'

'Who is your doctor?'

'Dr Hollis.'

She wrote busily for a few seconds, and then looked up at me. 'And your partner's name?'

'Mark Russell Tipene.' Lucky I asked.

'Just like the All Black,' Eloise observed brightly.

'No, he *is* the All Black,' I said.

She sat back in her chair and blinked at me.

'Honestly. I'm not some delusional rugby groupie, I promise.'

'Right,' she said. 'Okay. Right. And – and you've spoken to him about the baby?'

'How was the midwife?' Mark asked that night.

I held the phone between ear and shoulder and opened the bread bin. It contained one stale crust and the end of a baguette

I'd bought at least a week ago, which was a bit of a blow. 'I don't think she believed you were the baby's father,' I said, checking the crust for obvious mould before putting it into the toaster. 'I think she thinks I'm mentally unstable. But she's lovely.'

'She doesn't sound lovely.'

'She is, really. She delivered me – or actually she didn't, because I ended up being a caesarean, but she was Mum's midwife. She's written me a referral for a scan and for some blood tests.'

'When's your scan?'

'Five thirty pm on Wednesday.'

'Wednesday,' he said. 'Oh, shit, that's the night of the Mangere Christmas parade. Is that the only appointment they had?'

'The lady on the phone said it was the last one this week,' I said. 'And I think I'd better take it, because the longer I leave it the less accurate they can be about when the baby's due. I'm sorry.'

'Okay.'

'I'll make sure I get a photo to show you. I don't think they look like much at this stage, anyway. How's the visit going?' He was spending a few days at his father's place.

'Fine, if you like spraying blackberry.'

'Is that good for your shoulder?' I asked.

'Yeah, it's okay. And it beats hanging out with Jude,' Mark said.

All I knew about Jude was that she and his father had been married for six years and that Mark hated her with a deep implacable hatred. 'What *wouldn't* you think was better than hanging out with Jude?' I asked.

'Nothing probably. No, it's all good.' From somewhere beyond him came the sound of voices raised in some indistinguishable query. 'Look, I've got to go. Are you feeling a bit better?'

'Yes, a bit,' I said. I wasn't, but there was nothing he could do about it. My toast popped up and I looked at it without enthusiasm.

'That's good. Talk to you tomorrow, okay?'

'Okay. Bye.'

The next morning I was texting with one hand and wiping the kitchen bench with the other. I had written *Need blood test c* when I had to pause and hang over the sink for a while, breathing deeply. But the wave of nausea ebbed, and I picked the phone back up to continue.

ant walk lunchtime. Sorry.

After work? Alison replied.

Cool.

Hope you get Raewyn x

At seven minutes past five that evening, when we met at the post office corner halfway between the vet clinic and the medical centre, I held my arm out wordlessly to show off the deep purple bruise in the crease of my elbow.

'Heather?' she asked.

'Yep.'

'Bad luck.'

We had two phlebotomists in Broadview, and Heather's technique consisted of shoving the needle through her victim's skin and then making vigorous subcutaneous sweeping motions in the hope of meeting a blood vessel. It was hideous.

'I don't know why she doesn't just make a cut in your ear and hold a dish underneath to catch the blood,' I said. 'It'd be a lot less traumatic.'

Alison smiled. 'Booked in your scan yet?' she asked.

'It's tomorrow night,' I said. 'Mark can't come; he's going to be on a float in the Mangere Christmas parade.'

'Will he be wearing a tutu?'

'Just his Blues uniform, I think,' I said. 'Was it Sam's tutu that first caught your eye?' During last year's Broadview Christmas parade, which I'd got home from London just in time to see, Sam had driven the length of the main street on a tractor, towing a urea spreader and dressed as a Christmas angel.

'Of course,' she said. 'He's going to be an elf this year.'

'Sexy,' I remarked.

'We can't *all* go out with gorgeous All Black locks,' she said. 'Some of us have to make do with elves. Now, are you up to Birch Crescent today?'

'I'll try,' I said bravely.

꧁

'Job for you,' Thomas said on Wednesday afternoon, looking up as I passed the front counter on my way in from restocking the drugs in the back of my ute. 'John Somerville's got a steer with woody tongue, and he'd like you to take another look at that chook while you're there.'

I came around the counter to look at the day sheet. It was three forty-five now, which meant that even if I left right away I wouldn't get to John's until four twenty, and no call there ever took less than an hour. 'I can't,' I said. 'I've got an appointment in Hamilton at half past five.'

'Doing what?' Thomas asked.

There were so many plausible lies I could have told him. I could have said I was going to visit the optician, or to look at a car, or even to have my hair done. But in the stress of the moment I managed only to go red and mutter, 'Um, I – none of your business.'

'Fine,' said Thomas huffily. '*You* call John and change it, then. He asked for you.'

John wasn't in, and he didn't have an answer phone. 'Richard?' I said, running my colleague to ground in the lunch room, where he was tipping stale biscuit crumbs out of the tin into his cupped palm.

'Mm?' He shovelled the crumbs in, rolled them around in his mouth for a while, grimaced and swallowed them anyway. 'Yuck.'

'Could you do me a favour? John Somerville's got a steer with woody tongue to look at, and I've got to be in Hamilton at five thirty.'

Richard looked at his watch. 'Who's on call?' he asked. 'Get them to do it.'

'I am,' I said, suddenly remembering. 'Shit. Look, can you swap?'

'I was on last night.'

'Please? I'll do your next two nights.'

'I'm shattered,' said Richard, who had spent the hours between one and three pm tending his virtual garden on Facebook.

'*Please?*'

'Oh, alright. You owe me.'

'I know,' I said. 'Thank you so much. While you're there can you have just a quick look at Esmeralda's bumblefoot for me?'

'Jesus Christ,' he said heavily, as if I'd asked him to give me a kidney.

'Just get John to pick her up, and take a picture of the bad foot on your phone so I can see if it's improving. Okay? Please?'

'Anything else, Your Majesty?' he said over his shoulder as he left the room.

I made it to the imaging centre at five twenty-eight, overshot the turn into the car park and hurried breathlessly through the front door at five thirty-three. 'I'm Helen McNeil,' I told the woman behind the counter. 'I've got a five-thirty appointment.'

'Take a seat,' she said. 'They'll call you.'

I sat down gingerly on the edge of a chair so as not to put undue pressure on my bladder, and picked up a year-old copy of *Woman's Day*. I had read an article on Jennifer Aniston's baby bump (which looked less like a bump and more like a loose-ish chiffon blouse to me) and was flicking through the pictures of celebrities in haute couture gowns at the back when a very pretty Indian girl of about my age came down the hall and said, 'Helen?'

She arranged me on the bed in a small dark room, minus my shorts and with a towel draped discreetly over my thighs. 'Ready? The gel's cold,' she said cheerfully, squeezing ultrasound gel onto my bare stomach. 'Right, let's see what we've got.' And she placed the head of her ultrasound machine firmly on my bladder.

I made a small involuntary squeak.

She took the probe away again. 'Do you need to go to the toilet?'

'Yes, but the lady on the phone said I needed a full bladder.'

'Well,' she said, 'there's full and then there's dangerously close to bursting. Why don't you go to the toilet next door and let some out, and we'll try again?' She wiped my stomach with a paper towel, and I slunk out of the room, holding up my towel with one hand.

'Better?' she asked when I reappeared.

'Much,' I said, climbing back onto the bed.

'Good.' She reapplied the gel with a generous hand, and dug the probe back into my abdomen. 'Okay, the big black circle's your bladder – fluid shows up as black on ultrasound – and there's your baby.'

I had seen it already, a white comma inside a dark circle. I had expected a skeletal seahorse-shaped thing something like a calf in early gestation, on the grounds that we mammals all develop along similar lines, at least at the start, but it looked like an actual baby. It had a round head with a tiny nose, and it waved two arms with recognisable hands at the ends.

'It – it looks like a baby,' I said stupidly.

The technician was evidently a kind girl. Instead of asking just what I'd been expecting it to look like, she smiled and said, 'It's amazing, isn't it? And all the organs are already nearly formed – liver and kidneys and everything. The baby's even got a tiny tongue. In a couple of weeks it will be big enough to suck its thumb.'

The thought of that teeny little embryo sucking his or her thumb brought tears to my eyes. Of course, almost everything *did* bring tears to my eyes just at the moment – I had found a dead silvereye on the living room floor that morning, courtesy of Murray, and wept over the tiny corpse.

'How old is it?' I asked.

'I'll just do some measurements . . .' She turned to her computer screen. 'Right . . . so your due date is . . . the tenth of July. Lovely.'

I tried to smile back at her, but I don't think it came out very well.

19

'WHAT'S THE MATTER WITH *YOU*?' NICK ASKED, COMING into the vet room the next afternoon to find me resting my cheek on the cool shiny cellophane wrapping of a drug company mailout.

'Nothing,' I said, lifting my head hastily up off my desk.

'You look terrible,' he said. 'For heaven's sake, go home and put yourself to bed.'

I opened my mouth to demur, and then thought better of it and stood up. 'Thanks.'

Out the front, Thomas was on the phone and Anita was filling the pockets of her overalls with tubes of pink-eye ointment while Richard decorated tomorrow's day sheet with a green highlighter. He finished adding some careful shading to the side of a column and looked critically at his artwork.

'Oh,' he said as I approached, 'I had a look at that bird's foot for you.'

'How was it?'

'Looked good to me. I didn't take a picture, but the swelling's gone right down and she's not limping.'

'Cool,' I said. 'Thank you.'

'John was bleating on about some other thing with a limp – a duck or something. I said I'd get you to ring him.'

As I took my diary out from under my arm to write myself a note to call John tomorrow, the door to the consult room opened. Keri ushered out a vast woman wearing a white broderie anglaise tent and carrying a toddler, following in her wake with a small tabby cat in a cage. The woman surged up to the counter beside me.

'Hi,' I said.

'Hi,' said Sharon from the midwife's waiting room. 'You'll have to walk, honey, Mummy can't carry you and Pixie.' She put down the little girl, who buried her face in her mother's skirt and wailed.

'If you have any problem with those tablets,' said Keri, setting the cat cage on the counter and speaking up to be heard over the crying child, 'just give us a ring and we'll give him the long-acting injection.'

'He just takes 'em out of my hand,' Sharon said. 'I've got a real way with animals.' The toddler's wails became more insistent and higher pitched, and Sharon patted her vaguely.

'That's great,' shouted Keri. 'Now, he should be much better by Saturday morning, so if he's not bring him in to the morning clinic between nine and twelve.'

Richard, who was on call this weekend and would thus be manning the Saturday clinic, bared his teeth at her over the client's head.

Happily, Sharon was fishing through her purse and missed this shining example of customer service. 'What's the damage?' she asked, taking out her credit card.

Keri came around the counter and looked it up on the computer. 'Seventy-nine dollars sixty.'

Handing over her card, Sharon wiped her damp forehead with the back of a pudgy forearm. 'Warm, isn't it?' she said, and turning towards me added companionably, 'It'll be winter when you get to this stage, lucky girl.'

I went rigid with horror. *They might not have noticed*, I thought feverishly. *I'll say I've never seen her before – they probably didn't notice . . .*

Sharon winced and clapped a hand to her mouth. 'Oops,' she said.

They would, however, have noticed *that*. As indeed they had: four heads had turned in unison towards me, like deer at a bird's alarm call.

'If, ah, if you could just enter your pin number?' said Keri, wresting her eyes from my face to the customer's. 'Thank you. Would you like your receipt?'

'No, I won't bother.' Sharon hefted her child up to sit on her hip, waved Keri away as she tried to pick up the cat cage and took it herself. 'I can manage. See you.'

We watched her waddle across the polished floor and out through the automatic doors, and my nausea was temporarily swept away by a wave of hot hate.

'Helen?' said Thomas.

And here we go. 'Yes, Thomas?'

'Are you up the duff?'

I considered denial for about half a second before deciding it was a complete waste of time. Also, I lacked the energy. 'Yes,' I said flatly.

Thomas laughed.

'Hah,' said Anita with evident satisfaction. 'Thought so.'

Richard gave a long, low whistle, and Nick, coming down the hall from the back of the building, raised his brows in enquiry.

'Helen's pregnant,' Thomas said gleefully.

Nick opened and shut his mouth like a goldfish for quite some time. '*Are* you?' he finally asked.

I nodded.

'Good Lord,' he said. 'When are you due?'

'Tenth of July.'

'Hmm,' said Nick. 'So you're not going to be calving many cows this year.'

'We'll have to get a locum,' said Richard.

'We'll see,' said Nick in discouraging tones.

'Oh, come on, we'll be run off our feet. Every second weekend on call over calving?'

'I worked every other weekend for nine years and it didn't do me any irreparable damage, as far as I'm aware,' said Nick.

I closed my diary and picked it up, and Keri reached across the counter to touch my hand. 'You okay?' she asked softly.

'Mm,' I said, because if I'd attempted anything more I would have burst into tears. The Huggies pregnancy website had assured me that both weepiness and nausea would recede in the second trimester, and I was clinging to that hope.

'Hey, Helen, you'll be able to do one of those *Woman's Weekly* photo shoots, with you and Mark and the baby,' said Thomas. 'They'd probably give you ten grand.'

It was actually far easier to be teased than sympathised with. 'Awesome,' I said. 'Thanks.'

'Shit, I would. Ten grand is ten grand.'

'Thomas, nobody would pay ten *cents* to see a picture of your offspring,' said Keri.

The phone started to ring, and Thomas skated backwards across the polished floor in his wheeled chair to pick it up. 'Broadview Vets, Thomas speaking . . . Hi.' There was a pause, and then he said, 'Look, she's in consult at the moment, but I'll pass the message on, and she'll give you a call back in about quarter of an hour. Thanks, John.' He hung up and propelled himself rapidly back to where the action was.

'Call John Somerville,' he told me. 'Right, what'd I miss?'

In the end I was the last to leave work, after a forty-minute phone conversation with John Somerville about limping ducks. When, finally, I made it out to the ute, I rested my head on the hot steering wheel and cried. All that prevarication and micro-sipping of beer and wringing my hands about anyone finding out I was pregnant, and it was out. Just like that. And although they'd promised not to say a word, of course everyone would – they would tell just a handful of people apiece, in the very strictest of confidence, which meant three-quarters of Broadview would know by tomorrow lunchtime.

From there it would be but a short step to the national news. Mark's ingrown toenail had made the papers a couple of years ago, so presumably his unborn child would be at least equally newsworthy. I might well wake up tomorrow morning to find the lawn covered in reporters and cameramen. (Besides nausea and exhaustion, pregnancy appeared to have granted me a new and special flair for exaggeration.)

I spent a few minutes brooding on all the awful misfortunes that would, if there was any justice in the world, befall Fat Sharon. Then I sat up, wiped my eyes on the hem of my shirt and opened my phone to call Mark.

His phone didn't ring, which meant that either he'd turned it off or the battery had gone flat. *'Hi,'* said his voice. *'Leave me a message and I'll get back to you.'*

'It's me,' I said. 'Everyone at work knows. A horrible pregnant woman I met at the midwife's came in and told them. I – I just thought you might want to tell your parents before they hear it on Radio Sport or something. I'm sorry.'

I shut my phone and dropped it on the seat beside me. And then, just to set the seal on an already bad day, I went to tell Dad and Em.

I was never the type of kid who got into trouble. I was a plump and anxious teenager, and I expect Dad was more worried that I might never leave home at all than that I was going to fall in with the wrong crowd and spend my weekends experimenting with sex and alcohol. Admittedly I did once crash his car, but he watched me do it. I had no experience with serious parental confessions.

Caitlin met me at the door, wearing pink Barbie swimming togs and pink water wings. 'Can you swim with me?' she asked.

'Not today,' I said, and she slumped.

'Please?'

'I'm not feeling very well. Sorry, munchkin.'

'Do you want some Pamol?' she asked.

'No, thanks,' I said.

'It's strawberry flavour,' she coaxed, ushering me tenderly up the hall. 'Mum, Helen's sick.'

The rest of the family were in the kitchen. Bel was seated on the bench while Dad adjusted her swimming goggles, and Em turned from the open fridge with a bottle of wine in one hand.

'Sick of what?' she asked. 'Would wine help?'

I shook my head.

'Must be serious, then,' said Dad.

'Yeah,' I said. 'Hi, Bel.'

'Will you come swimming?' she asked.

'She *can't*,' said Caitlin. 'She's *sick*.'

'So am I,' said Bel hopefully. Annabel adores Pamol, both because it's sweet and because taking medicine makes her feel important.

'You are not.'

'Are too!'

'Into the pool with you both,' ordered Dad.

'But someone has to watch us,' said Caitlin. 'We can't just swim by *ourselves*. We might *drown*.'

'Yes, and you wouldn't want that,' said Bel, glaring through her goggles at each adult in turn to ensure we were suitably sobered by this hideous thought.

'We would not,' her mother agreed. 'It would be terrible. We'll watch you from the deck.' She opened a cupboard, swept up a handful of wineglasses and followed the girls out through the French doors.

'Everything alright?' Dad asked me.

'No,' I said, dissolving once more into tears.

He looked a little taken aback, but he put his arms around me and patted me on the back. 'Come on, now,' he said kindly. 'Come and sit down and tell us what's wrong.'

Caitlin and Bel had launched themselves into the pool, and Em was pouring the wine at the big outdoor table on the deck above them. 'Tim, here's yours . . . Bel! Less splashing, please! Helen, you'll have one, won't you?' She turned and saw my face. 'What's wrong, love?'

'I'm pregnant,' I said.

Em dropped the wine bottle back onto the table with a thud. 'Oh, sweetie.'

Dad said nothing at all. He took off his glasses and began absently to polish the lenses on the hem of his nasty Hawaiian shirt, his invariable custom when at a loss. In the first year after Mum died, when he was trying to work and look after me and keep us both clean and fed and clothed, he nearly polished them away to nothing.

'Nine weeks,' I added. 'I had a scan yesterday.'

My stepmother came around the table and enfolded me in a warm, coconut-oil-scented hug. 'Oh, *sweetie*,' she said, and I laid my head on her shoulder and wept.

For quite some time I cried while Em stroked my hair, and then something wet and cold pressed itself against my legs. On inspection it proved to be Bel, complete with goggles and Dora the Explorer flotation ring, and howling like a car alarm.

'Annabel,' said Dad. 'Stop that, please.'

'Is Helen going to die?' she wailed.

'Of course not!' Em said.

'Well, not imminently, as far as we know,' corrected Dad. 'But everyone dies eventually.'

The wails increased in both volume and frequency. 'I – don't – want – to – die!'

'Oh, well *done*, Tim,' said his wife.

'Bel, you womble,' I said, crouching down level with her small crimson face. 'I'm not going to die; I was just a bit sad. But I'm better now, see?' I pulled a tattered ball of tissue from the pocket of my shorts and wiped my eyes.

'Why were you sad?' asked Caitlin, approaching across the deck.

'I'm just not feeling very well. I've got a sore tummy.'

'I don't like it when you cry,' said Bel, snivelling gently. 'You're a big girl. You're not supposed to cry.'

'I know,' I said. 'I'm not crying anymore.'

'You need to have some Pamol,' Caitlin said firmly, and trotted inside to get it, leaving a trail of wet footprints behind her.

I sat down in an outdoor chair and Bel began to climb into my lap. 'Hey,' I protested, fending her off, 'you're all wet and cold.'

'I just want to give you a cuddle,' she said plaintively, putting on her starving-orphan-all-alone-in-the-world face. I was moved less to remorse than to admiration – pulling off that expression with dimples and a round rosy face like a Renaissance cherub was impressive.

'I'll cuddle you when you're dry,' I told her.

'If you don't want to swim, Annabel, you'd better have a bath and get into your pyjamas,' said Dad.

Faced with this dire threat, Bel scampered back across the deck and into the pool, where she lay crocodile-style at the shallow end by the steps, submerged up to her nose.

'Here you go, Helen,' said Caitlin, coming back out of the house armed with a medicine bottle and a tablespoon.

'No, thank you,' I said.

'It won't hurt you,' Em said. 'Paracetamol's completely safe.'

'It's good for you,' said Caitlin sternly, putting her spoon down on the table to wrestle with the child-proof cap of the bottle.

'Caitlin, I swear if you make me drink that revolting stuff I'll throw up.'

'But then how are you going to get better?' she asked, in the sort of voice used for reasoning with the very young or the very dim.

'I think I'll be better soon if I just sit here quietly,' I said.

'Go and get back in the pool, sweetie,' said Em. 'It was kind of you to think of it.'

Caitlin sighed and went, leaving behind a dense uncomfortable silence. When I couldn't bear it any longer I said, 'Your glasses are probably pretty clean by now, Dad.'

'What? Oh, yes.' He stopped polishing and settled them back on his nose. 'So they are.'

'Are you going to say anything else?' I asked, flippant with shame and unhappiness. 'Or is that it?'

Dad looked at me gravely across the table. 'Just what do you expect me to say, Helen?'

'I don't know. I sort of hoped you knew how this conversation was supposed to go.'

'No,' he said. ''Fraid not.' And the silence seeped back to surround us again.

Em took a sip from her wineglass and set it carefully back down. 'Have you told Mark?' she asked.

'Yes. I told him last week, when he got back from England.'

'How did he take it?'

'He was lovely,' I said to my hands. 'He's being so nice. Far nicer than I deserve.'

'It does take two,' said Dad drily.

'But it's my fault. I stuffed up the pill.'

Em smiled at me very kindly. 'These things happen.'

'I didn't think they'd happen to me!' Smart career women aren't supposed to get themselves knocked up – it's the sort of thing that happens to silly teenage girls who fear that telling their silly teenage boyfriends to wear a condom will brand them as losers. I mopped my eyes again with the wad of tissue and said miserably, 'People will think I did it on purpose – that I thought I'd get my fifteen minutes of fame by having Mark Tipene's baby.'

'Of course they won't!' Em said.

'I think you've got enough actual problems without inventing extra things to worry about,' said Dad.

This was no doubt true, but not even slightly comforting.

'So, when is this baby due?'

'The tenth of July,' I said.

'A winter baby,' said Em. 'That's nice.'

'Nice,' I repeated scathingly. '*Really?*' She was only trying to be kind, but I was tired and sick and teetering on the brink of hysteria, and it seemed a stunningly inane comment.

Em and Dad exchanged a long look but said nothing, and I shoved back my chair and stood up.

'Helen,' said Dad gently. 'Sit down.'

I shook my head. I was going to cry again, and when Caitlin tried to dose me with Pamol I would almost certainly shout at her, and then I'd have that to feel bad about on top of all the rest. I rushed into the house, tripped over Bel's toy stroller and banged my hip hard against the edge of the table.

'Hey,' said Dad behind me. 'Come on, love. Hang on a minute.'

I shook my head again, crying too hard to speak, and he gathered me up against him and hugged me.

'Shh,' he said. 'It'll be alright.' There was a short pause while he searched for some uplifting comment, and then he said tentatively, 'I'm sure it will be a very nice baby.'

'I d-don't *want* a baby!'

'Well,' he said levelly, 'you don't have to have one.'

I straightened with a jerk. 'I can't do that!'

'Why not?'

I pushed myself away from him, failed to locate my tissue and had to wipe my nose on the back of my hand instead. 'What – what if I had another baby one day? A wanted, planned-for one. Every time I looked at it I would think about the one I killed because it wasn't convenient.'

My dad has almost no time for self-pity, and in response to this speech I more than half expected him to suggest that, if I felt like that about it, I might like to stop throwing tantrums and start acting like an adult. But he didn't; he smiled a small crooked half-smile and reached out to ruffle my hair. 'You are so like your mother at times,' he said, and I cried harder than ever.

20

'HOW WAS YOUR DOWN COW?' KERI ASKED, LOOKING UP from the paper as I came into the lunch room early the next afternoon.

'Good,' I said. 'I gave her two bags of calcium, and she got up and chased Doug through a fence.'

'Did she get him?'

I took a glass from the cupboard above the sink and filled it with water. 'Not quite.'

'Pity,' said Keri.

'He did tear his overalls,' I said, sitting down at the table. Doug Harcourt was a self-important little man, and I had enjoyed watching him try and fail to clear a seven-wire fence. 'What have you been doing?'

'Lame cows at Hohepa's,' she said. 'Are you going to Mark's this weekend?'

I nodded.

'Cool.'

'Mm,' I said.

'He seems like a really lovely guy,' she said tentatively.

I nodded again.

'How are you doing?' she asked.

I picked at the side of a fingernail. 'I keep hoping I'll wake up.'

'Oh, Helen,' she said, reaching across the table for my hand.

'Don't,' I said. 'Sorry . . .' And getting up I turned and went blindly out of the room.

It could have been so much worse. I wasn't going to be sent to some grim workhouse for unmarried mothers, ostracised by society, forced to eke out a precarious living on the streets until killed by consumption and/or syphilis, or any of the awful fates that used to await unmarried pregnant girls. In fact still *did* await unmarried pregnant girls who weren't lucky enough to get themselves knocked up in parts of the world where sex before marriage was socially acceptable. Mark hadn't greeted the news with happy cries, but neither had he turned and run screaming for the hills. I had a loving, supportive family and a good job.

And none of those things made me feel the slightest bit better.

At quarter past five I let myself wearily into my kitchen and took two cereal bowls from the cupboard beside the fridge. I filled one with water and the other with jellymeat, and turned to see Murray watching me with accusing eyes.

'Sorry,' I said, pouring out Young Neutered Male cat biscuits (specially balanced for weight control, although the control becomes questionable when you're doling out enough for the whole weekend, plus extra out of guilt at abandoning your pet). 'I promise I'll be back on Monday morning. You won't even have time to miss me.'

Murray turned his back and stalked down the hall, stiff with outrage.

My handbag began to ring on the bench behind me. Hunting through it I found the spare keys to the garage, a tube of flea treatment I should have given Murray a fortnight ago and, unexpectedly, a green plastic turtle, before finally emerging with my cell phone. 'Hello?'

'Hey, Nell,' said Lance.

'Hi. What's up?'

'I was just wondering how things are with you.'

'Fine,' I said warily. Lance and I got on perfectly well these days, but we didn't ring one another to chat.

'Everything alright?'

'Who told you?' I asked.

'Told me what?'

'Lance!'

'Vet nurse,' he admitted. 'She's friends with yours. Is it true?'

'Yes.' If Zoe had fought a battle with her conscience before spreading my business far and wide, it must have been a short one.

'Congratulations.'

'Please don't,' I said.

'How are you doing?'

I put the water bowl on the floor and straightened to pick up the jellymeat. 'I'm sick as a dog. Morning sickness sucks.'

'So I hear,' said Lance. 'Kate's due in April.'

Lance's older sister Kate was the kind of person I wanted to be when I grew up. She was smart and funny, grew her own vegetables, rode a motorbike and bought fabulous clothes for three dollars fifty in op shops. She also had a very nice husband, and was no doubt having a baby because she wanted one. 'That's great,' I said, trying hard to sound properly enthusiastic. 'Please give her my congratulations.'

'Will do,' he said. 'Got anything planned for the weekend?'

'I'm just on my way to Mark's.'

'You're not driving while you're on the phone, are you?'

'No.'

'Well, don't.'

'You don't get to tell me what to do anymore,' I said.

'Old habits die hard.'

'I'm actually fairly capable, you know,' I said, which, considering my current predicament, was a fairly optimistic claim.

'You can't have changed *that* much,' said Lance.

'It's unkind to ring people up and sneer at them,' I said severely. 'Especially when they're feeling like death warmed up.'

'Sorry. So, are you freaking out?'

'Yep.'

'Biting your nails again?'

'Of course.'

'What does Mark think about your bloody fingerprints all over his good shirts?'

I hadn't actually made a habit of bleeding on Lance during our time together, whatever he might imply. I did, however, annihilate my fingernails in times of extreme stress, and it was true that the night before my equine medicine oral exam I'd left a fingerprint or two on his shirt. He had told me that biting your nails till they bled was a sign of mental illness, but he had also put plasters on my fingertips and spent an hour talking me through the diagnosis and treatment of colic.

'He doesn't wear good shirts, so it wouldn't matter,' I said.

'Probably still best not to bleed on him. It's a bit of a turn-off.'

'Thanks,' I said cordially. 'I'll take that on board.'

'Is he – ah – okay with all of this?'

'He's being wonderful,' I said.

'That's good,' said Lance. 'Otherwise I suppose I'd have to have a quiet word, and he's a hell of a lot bigger than me.'

'You do realise,' I said, 'that you're an egg?' But I said it fondly, because calling to check that his replacement was treating me right was really quite sweet.

'You're just wishing you hadn't let me slip through your fingers.'

'Yeah,' I said. 'It's eating me up inside. Hey, thank you for ringing.'

'That's alright. You take care, okay?'

'You too.'

'Right,' said Mark. 'Let's see this baby.'

I began to search through the handbag I had just dropped on his kitchen bench. 'It doesn't look like much. It's not quite an inch long yet.'

He took the envelope silently and looked at the grainy black and white photo inside. 'The uterus is the black circle,' I said helpfully, 'and the baby's the little white tadpole in the middle.'

'Wow,' said Mark. Then, spoiling the poignancy of the moment ever so slightly, 'Which end is which?'

'That's the head,' I said, pointing. 'There's an arm, and there's the umbilical cord.'

'Yeah, okay.'

'And the ultrasound technician said the tail will vanish in another week.'

'That's a relief.' He put an arm around me, and I leant back against him.

'Have you told your parents?' I asked.

'No, not yet.'

'I told Dad.'

'How did that go?'

I sighed. 'Oh, alright. He was just sort of quietly disappointed.'

Mark said nothing, but his arm tightened around my waist.

'At work everyone stops talking when I come into the room.'

'Don't worry about it,' he said. 'They'll find something new to talk about in a week or two.'

'Have any reporters rung you up yet?'

'No. I don't think they will. Babies aren't really big news.'

'Even yours?' I asked.

'I think you overestimate people's interest in my life,' said Mark. 'As long as I turn up on the rugby field and don't arse it up completely, they couldn't care less.'

I nodded, although a bit doubtfully, and turned in his arms to hug him. 'How was physio?'

'Good,' he said. 'Coming along nicely. How's the morning sickness?'

'I haven't thrown up all day.'

'Well done.'

'Thank you,' I said.

He smiled and kissed me. It was a slow, serious, eleven-on-a-scale-of-one-to-ten sort of kiss, and it left me quite weak with relief that he still found me reasonably attractive. And then someone knocked on the front door.

'Oh, piss off, whoever you are,' muttered Mark.

'It'll be the first reporter,' I said.

'It'd better not be.' Letting me go he went slowly downstairs and opened the door. 'What are you doing here?' I heard him say.

It must be so nice to be a boy, and therefore not to have to bother with social niceties when you're not in the mood.

'Came up to look at a car,' said the visitor, coming in past him and taking the stairs two at a time. I slid the ultrasound picture under the fruit bowl and out of sight. 'Piece of shit. Waste of fucking time.' Reaching the kitchen he looked me briefly up and down, an exercise that appeared to give him very little pleasure. 'Who are you?'

'Helen,' I said. 'Hi.'

'Hi.' He turned away and opened the fridge, taking out two bottles of beer.

'This is my brother Rob,' Mark told me, catching a bottle as it skated across the granite bench top towards him. 'Rob, Helen.' His voice was flat and slightly wary.

Robert and Mark Tipene must have looked very much alike when they were younger: they had the same dark unruly hair and hazel eyes under eyebrows that slanted up at the corners, and the same rangy, broad-shouldered frame. Mark was a couple of inches taller and Rob was quite a bit thicker through the middle, with half an inch of beard and puffy dissatisfied eyes, and I thought that seeing them together was the best illustration I had ever seen of how people's natures affect their looks. If Mark had spent the last ten years drinking too much and feeling hard done by he would have looked just like his brother.

'You want one?' Rob asked me as an afterthought, waving his beer bottle in my direction.

'No, thanks.'

'Suit yourself.' He turned back to Mark. 'How was Dad's?'

'About the same as usual,' said Mark. 'How's work?'

'It's a fucking nightmare. The boss is a tool. Hasn't got a clue.'

'Pretty much like the last place, then,' Mark said drily.

'I'm thinking of setting up on my own.'

'Doing what?'

Rob shrugged. 'Auto electrics, car stereos . . . all that shit.'

'Right,' said Mark.

'I've got my eye on a workshop,' said Rob, tipping beer expertly down his throat. 'Do you remember Dennis Cope?'

Mark shook his head.

'Weedy little bloke. Sparky. Had that place in behind the petrol station at the north end of town.'

'Oh, yeah.'

'He's selling up. The place is a bit rundown, but the location's good.' He eyed his brother sideways over his beer bottle. 'I'd put in an offer if I had the capital.'

'Have you talked to the bank?' Mark asked.

'Wankers,' Rob said. And then, in an entirely unconvincing portrayal of a man who has just been struck out of the blue by an idea, he added, 'Hey, do you want to chuck some money in?'

'No, thanks.'

'Hang on, it's a really tidy business.'

'No,' said Mark again, with no particular expression in his voice.

'Fuck,' said Rob into his beer bottle. 'It's not like it'd be any skin off *your* nose.' He turned to me. 'You're the vet, right?'

'Yes,' I said.

'You must be pretty smart.'

'Not really,' I said uncomfortably.

'He failed sixth form,' said Rob, nodding towards his brother. 'Twice.'

'So?' I said.

He widened his eyes at me mockingly. 'Settle down. Just making conversation.'

177

'He's a gem,' I said as Mark came slowly back upstairs after accompanying Rob to the door.

'Isn't he just?'

'What's he like when he *doesn't* want something?' I said. If the last half hour had been a demonstration of Cajoling Rob, Hostile Rob must be something quite special.

Mark smiled tiredly. 'I wouldn't know,' he said. 'What d'you want for tea?'

'Toast. It's my new staple diet. How about you?'

'Oh, I don't know. Spaghetti on toast will do.' He opened the pantry. Inside were two tins, one of beetroot and the other of four-bean mix. 'Bugger.'

'Macaroni cheese?' I offered, sliding off my stool to look in the fridge. 'Except you've got no cheese.' Or bacon, or eggs, or in fact anything that looked even faintly like dinner. 'Takeaways, then.'

Mark closed the pantry door. 'No bread either,' he said. 'What takeaways do you reckon you might keep down?'

He had rogan josh with rice and naan bread, and I had rice. Apart from my daily folate tablet I don't think I'd eaten a vitamin in weeks. The Huggies website was big on a healthy balanced diet during pregnancy, but the Huggies website could take a running jump. The thought of food that tasted of anything in particular was quite simply out of the question.

After my rice I showered and crawled exhaustedly into Mark's big bed. The enamel pendant he had brought me from Cardiff was on the bedside table, and I sat up again to put it on.

I had just managed to do up the clasp – no easy task without fingernails – when footsteps crossed the room below. They didn't reach the stairs but were followed by a squeak of leather as Mark lay down on the couch and then the sudden clamour of canned laughter from the TV. Every night we had ever spent together, up until the night I told him about the baby, we had gone to bed together as a matter of course.

I lay there, turning the little pendant between my fingers, wondering if he wanted out and was hoping I'd get the message without him actually having to say it in so many words. Let's face it: you do have grounds for concern when your boyfriend prefers *Everybody Hates Chris* to you. The idea of a life without Mark, or a life where I saw him only for child handovers, hurt so much that I didn't see how I was going to bear it, and tears trickled across my cheeks to pool in my ears.

I was being foolish and melodramatic, of course; people bear all sorts of unbearable things. But sometimes it's easier to tell yourself you're not going to get through a thing than it is to contemplate the pain and effort that the getting-through will take.

※

It was a very long hour later when Mark came quietly upstairs, undressed and got into bed.

Just leave him alone, I told myself miserably. *He's hoping you're asleep.* But I reached out a tentative hand for his, on the slim off-chance that I might be wrong.

His fingers closed around mine. 'Feeling a bit better?'

'Yes,' I said.

'That's good.'

I wriggled across the mattress and propped myself up on one elbow to kiss him.

'Sure you're not going to spew?' he asked, running a hand over my hair.

'Pretty sure,' I said.

'I'm not sure pretty sure is sure enough.' But I could hear that he was smiling, and he pulled me down on top of him. 'Oh, what the hell. I like living dangerously.'

21

'WHERE'S DHAKA?' I ASKED THE NEXT MORNING, TURNING over the world news section of the paper to see a photo of a small shirtless coffee-coloured boy kicking a soccer ball along a muddy street. 'India?'

'Capital of Bangladesh,' Mark said, stretching his arms above his head and wincing as his sore shoulder caught.

'That's not bad for someone who failed sixth form twice.'

'What do you feel like doing today?'

I looked out through the kitchen window at the clean bright sky above the neighbour's roof. 'Beach?'

'Okay,' he said. 'East coast or west?'

We went west, over the Waitakere Ranges to Piha. It was a winding and very scenic drive, although I would have enjoyed it more without the stop halfway down to throw up into the long grass at the roadside. Car sickness and morning sickness are not a happy combination.

We walked to the far end of the beach and sat down in the warm black sand. The sea was a deep purplish-blue in the sunlight and the breakers a lovely clear green, edged with crisp white foam. A pair of gannets were fishing, gliding effortlessly above the waves and then folding their wings to plummet head first into the sea. I've always thought gannets are most superior birds, clean and white and beautifully streamlined, as if they were designed by a Danish furniture maker.

'You're on call for Christmas, aren't you?' asked Mark, breaking into my musings on gannet design.

'Yep,' I said. 'Lunch at Uncle Simon and Aunty Laura's, as long as nobody runs over their dog. What are you doing?'

'No plans,' he said, leaning back on his elbows and yawning.

'You're welcome to come and hang out with me. But I won't be offended if you don't want to.'

'Okay.'

I drew circles in the sand with a stem of marram grass. 'Okay you'll come, or okay you won't?'

'I'll come.'

'Are you sure? My whole family will know I'm pregnant by then.'

'It's not 1950,' he pointed out. 'Your relatives probably aren't going to horsewhip me for knocking you up.'

'No, they'll just all look at us sideways and wonder when it's going to go pear-shaped.'

'Who cares?'

I looked at him curiously. 'Do you honestly not worry about what people think?'

Mark pushed his sunglasses thoughtfully up his nose. 'Well, I can't help what people think, so what's the point of stressing about it?'

'Wow,' I said in only half-pretend awe. 'You are so cool.'

On the way home we went to the supermarket, where Mark spent five minutes in earnest conversation with a small boy who played rugby for Edendale Primary and planned to be an All Black when he grew up.

Mark unloaded me and the groceries at the front door and went to park the car, and I was just carrying in the last two bags when Alan and Saskia came strolling hand in hand down the driveway.

'Hi,' I said nervously. Mark's reasoning on the futility of worrying about what people thought was excellent, but still I was damned if I could help it.

'Hi,' said Saskia. 'We need coffee. We're completely shattered.' She was wearing a pale green linen sundress and silver sandals, with her cropped blonde hair artfully tousled, and she was the least shattered-looking person I had ever seen. She looked like Tinker Bell, dainty and flawless.

'What shattered you?' I asked.

'Door handles,' said Alan bitterly. 'You just wouldn't think it could be that hard, would you? You'd think you'd wander into the nearest shop and pick something that looked about right, and that would be that.'

'But no?'

'Don't even ask.'

'It's important to get the details right,' said Saskia.

'It's not,' Alan said. 'Once the bloody things are on the doors you'll never notice them again.'

'*I* will. Be quiet. Hey, Tip.'

'Hey,' said Mark, appearing around the corner of the building. 'Aren't you supposed to be in Queenstown?'

'Next weekend,' Saskia said.

'How did *you* get out of it?' Alan demanded.

'Wasn't invited,' Mark said, sounding distinctly smug.

'Why not?'

'Because he used to sleep with the bride, you cretin,' said Saskia. 'About five years ago, Helen; don't worry.'

'So what?' asked Alan. 'Half of Auckland used to sleep with the bride. A fair few probably still do.'

'Pay no attention to him,' Saskia told me. 'He's just sulking about having to go to Queenstown when he could be at home choosing doorknobs. Tip, my new office shelving arrived on Thursday.'

'That's nice,' said Mark.

'I'd love to have it up by Christmas,' she said hopefully.

'Reckon you can hold out till Monday?'

'You're wonderful,' she said. 'I'll be at work, but Alan will help you. Right. Coffee.' And she led the way purposefully inside.

A quick hunt through the cupboards revealed a complete absence of plunger coffee. 'Instant?' I offered.

Saskia shuddered eloquently.

'Just add sugar,' Mark said. 'It's still got caffeine in it; it'll do the same job.'

'It won't,' she said. 'I'll go and get some proper stuff from the cafe round the corner. Come and keep me company, Helen.'

Obediently, I followed her downstairs. I admired Saskia immensely; in fact, I suspected that my *Cosmopolitan* article about power tools and chocolate cakes and stripteases had been penned with her in mind. And her rugby knowledge was encyclopaedic. Back in September I'd gone with her to watch the boys play, and when the whistle blew she had made impressive comments like, 'Hah! Serves him right. Tiny's bind's been crap all season.'

I usually couldn't even tell which side had been penalised until the ref's arm went up, let alone being able to critique the way the tighthead prop was holding on to his opponent in the scrum.

'It feels like ages since we saw you,' she said. 'Have you been doing anything exciting?'

So Mark hadn't told them about the baby. And he hadn't told his parents either, which suggested that perhaps he cared more about what people thought than he claimed to. I realised suddenly that she was waiting for an answer to her question, and said, 'No. Non-cycling cows, mostly.'

We let ourselves out into the bright sunlight and started up the driveway. 'What's a non-cycling cow when it's at home?' she asked.

'One that doesn't come back on heat after calving in time for mating,' I said. 'Usually it's because they're too thin.'

'What do you do with them?'

'Treat them with hormones to get them started.'

'What, cow IVF?'

I smiled, never having thought about it quite like that. 'Well, yeah, sort of. It's not the most exciting time of year; it's pretty repetitive work.' It was also pretty depressing work on those occasional farms where we treated a third of the herd every year because the people in charge felt that actually giving the cows enough to eat would be a criminal extravagance.

'Well, there you go,' said Saskia. 'Who knew? Oh, did Tip tell you we're going out on the boat over New Year's? It would be great if you guys could come.'

'He did,' I said. 'It's so kind of you, but I'm a lousy sailor.'

'Have you tried Sea Legs? Tiny white pills – you get them at the chemist's. They're magic.'

'Um –' I said, and stopped.

'We're going to Great Barrier Island. Have you been there?'
I shook my head.

'It's really beautiful,' she said. 'A sort of unspoilt paradise. The water's incredibly clear, and the fishing's amazing. Not that fishing's really my cup of Ribena, but Alan loves it. Please come.'

'It sounds wonderful,' I said unhappily to my feet. 'But I – I'm pregnant, so I can't take anything, and I've got the most appalling morning sickness . . .'

Saskia said nothing at all, and with some effort I lifted my eyes from my toes to look at her. I was expecting her to look shocked, and quite possibly taken aback, but I was unprepared for stricken.

'It's all my fault,' I said, tumbling mouth first into the void of horrified silence that had just opened in the conversation. 'I messed up the pill. I'm honestly not expecting Mark to settle down and play happy families when we've only been going out for about half an hour . . .' She was still looking at me as if I had just announced that whale was my favourite meat, and I trailed off again, wishing fervently that for once – just for *once* – I had kept my big, stupid mouth shut.

'Congratulations,' said Saskia hoarsely. 'No, I mean condolences, or something . . . oh, shit, Helen, I'm sorry. Are you okay?'

'Not – not very.'

'No, I guess not.' She opened her bag and rummaged through it for a lip gloss she didn't want, in a vain attempt to lessen the awkwardness of the moment.

'I'm sorry,' I said wretchedly. 'Mark should have told you, not me.'

'No,' she said, dropping the lip gloss back into her purse. 'No, that's – look, I'm so sorry. It's just that our third round of IVF didn't work, and I'm still –' She choked and stopped.

'Oh, Sask,' I whispered, appalled.

She lifted her head and blinked hard. 'We can't stand here bawling in the middle of Mount Eden,' she said. 'Let's go and bawl somewhere else.'

When we returned three-quarters of an hour later, minus the coffee and with suspiciously pink-rimmed eyes, Alan and Mark were drinking beer on the balcony with their feet on the railing and their chairs tipped back on two legs against the wall. Neither of them remarked on either the lack of coffee or the time we'd been gone, but I saw Alan watching his wife, and his expression made my throat close up.

Alan and Saskia only stayed another ten minutes, and as the front door closed behind them Mark moved his sore shoulder experimentally and said, 'Told her, huh?'

'Did you not think that it might have been worth letting me know they've been trying to have a baby for the last *four years*?' I meant to speak with icy calm, but the calm slipped partway through and I finished on an indignant squeak.

His left eyebrow shot up, and for a moment he looked scarily like his brother. 'To be honest, it didn't occur to me that you'd feel you had to tell one of my friends you were pregnant, when you barely even know the woman.'

One of my friends. None of our friends were mutual ones. 'I *wouldn't* have, if you'd bothered to tell her yourself! She asked me about Great Barrier, and said she knew a great cure for seasickness, and please would we come. What was I *supposed* to say?'

'Look, it's done now,' he said. 'Just forget about it.'

'Why *didn't* you tell them?' I snapped. 'Seeing as you're so unconcerned about people's opinions?'

'Because they found out on Wednesday that their latest round of IVF had failed,' said Mark acidly. 'It really didn't seem like a good time to say, "Oh, by the way, guys, my girlfriend's pregnant."'

'In a way it's not as bad as last time,' Saskia had said, expertly fixing her eyeliner in a pocket mirror with the tip of her little finger. 'We didn't even get any fertilised eggs to implant, so at least we missed that horrible fortnight of waiting and hoping before your next period.' And snapping the mirror shut she had smiled a bright, brittle smile that was rather more pitiful than tears would have been.

Now I looked down at my hands. 'You're right. It was a really bad time, and I feel completely shit about it.'

He sighed. 'I should have told you.'

'Mark,' I said heavily.

'What?'

'Do you want to just call this whole thing off?' It was almost a relief to say it; the wild swings from cautious optimism to flat despair were so exhausting.

'*What?*'

'Well, it's not great, is it? I can't do anything except cry and throw up, and you've got the World Cup and everything – you don't need this as well.' After all, it didn't actually hurt that much. No doubt it would soon, but right now I wanted only to lie down somewhere dark and quiet and not to have to think about anything. I turned towards the steps.

'Where are you going?' he asked.

'Upstairs, to get my stuff.'

'Jesus, McNeil! Would you just hang on a minute?'

I stopped and turned slowly back to face him.

'Please don't do this,' he said.

'If – if we're going to break up maybe we should just get it over with. It'll be harder when the b-baby's born . . .'

He came across the room and put his arms around me. 'Helen. Stop it.'

It felt very, very nice to be held, and resting my head against his shoulder I closed my eyes. He must care a little bit, at least, or he would have let me go.

'Can we just . . . see how things go for a while?' said Mark quietly.

Seeing how things go comes about as naturally to me as pole dancing. I prefer the rush-in-guns-blazing-and-sort-this-thing-out-once-and-for-all approach. But I said, 'Okay,' into his shirt, and even managed not to ask how long he thought 'for a bit' would be.

22

CHRISTMAS THAT YEAR WAS ON A FRIDAY, AND WORK ON the Wednesday was manic. Keri was on holiday already, somewhere up a mountain in the Southern Alps. Nick was at, of all things, a veterinary business management seminar in Hamilton, and Zoe went home at lunchtime with a headache. The rest of us spent the day running around in small circles, and at three, just as it looked like things were easing off, a woman brought in a comatose cat with a blocked bladder. It was the best day I'd had for weeks; I was far too busy to think about myself.

At twenty past five I vaccinated the last of a litter of seven puppies and poked the last worm pill down the last small throat. I shut down the computer in the consult room and went slowly out the front to find Thomas writing up tomorrow's day sheet.

'You've got to go to Peter Drummond's,' he said. 'He's got a horse that's just gone through a fence and shredded its leg.'

I forgot all about the benefits of being too busy to think and stared at him in horror. 'You're kidding.'

'Yes,' he admitted. 'You can go home.'

I went not home but to Dad and Em's.

'Hi, sweetie,' Em said, meeting me at the door with a full washing basket on her hip and a slightly flustered expression. 'How are you feeling?'

'A bit better,' I said. I still couldn't imagine ever wanting a green vegetable or a cup of coffee to pass my lips again, but I hadn't been sick all day. 'What are you guys up to?'

'We're baking. Let's go and see what's happened while I was out at the washing line.'

'Mum!' Caitlin shouted down the hall. 'Bel's eating all the icing!'

We reached the kitchen in time to see Bel cram a huge spoonful of chocolate icing into her mouth. She eyed us over the spoon, apprehensive but unrepentant.

'That's disgusting,' I said.

'Now I haven't got enough left for my muffins,' said Caitlin. She had wrested the bowl away from her sister but, alas, only a meagre scraping of icing remained. '*And* Bel's teeth will all go rotten.'

'It will serve her right,' Em said. 'She's a very naughty little girl. Helen, would you be up to making some more?'

As I put my bag down on the big butcher's block in the middle of the kitchen it beeped at me. Rummaging through it for the phone I found the plastic turtle again, and pulled it out. 'Guys, is this yours?'

'Turty!' Bel cried rapturously. 'My baby turtle! I've missed her so much!' And clutching the turtle to her chest she peppered it with chocolatey kisses.

'You don't even like that turtle,' said Caitlin. 'You put it in Helen's bag ages ago.'

'I do,' Bel said. 'I *love* her.' Upon which she opened a drawer, dropped the turtle in and shut the drawer again with a slam.

'That's a funny way to treat a turtle you love,' I remarked.

'She needs a sleep,' said Bel firmly. 'Helen, can I play with your phone?'

'Only after you wash your hands.' I found the phone in the depths of my handbag, opened it in the hope the message was from Mark, and learnt instead that Keri was wishing everybody a merry Christmas before she lost cell phone coverage for the next few days.

'Did Laura ring you?' Em asked.

'Yes, last night.' Aunty Laura had called to order bean salad as my contribution to Christmas lunch. Honestly, *bean salad*? You're not supposed to have to eat stuff like that at Christmas time.

'I thought we'd do cold ham and salads,' she had said. 'Nobody wants all that heavy stodge.' Which saddened me deeply, because I've always felt that the roast potatoes and gravy and bread sauce are major highlights of the whole Christmas experience.

'What are you taking?' I asked.

'Tabouleh,' said Em.

'What's that?' Caitlin asked.

'Couscous and parsley and tomatoes and things.'

'Gross.'

'Yep,' I said. 'Where's the icing sugar?'

'It's labelled *Rice*,' Em said. 'We broke the proper container. It's nice that Mark is coming for Christmas, isn't it?'

'I hope so,' I said, picking up the rice container in one hand and a tin of cocoa in the other.

'Hope he's coming, or hope it will be nice?'

'Both.'

'Has he said he might not make it?'

'No,' I said. 'No, I'm sure he will.'

'Sweetie,' said Em gently, 'he wouldn't be coming if he didn't care about you.'

I nodded. 'Right, how much icing do we need, Caitlin?'

'Enough for eight more muffins,' she said.

Em rinsed the dishcloth under the tap and began to scrub chocolate icing off her youngest daughter. 'Annabel, just how exactly did you manage to get icing on your eyelids?'

'You're hurting me!' protested Bel from the depths of the cloth.

'Well, it has to come off. Helen, love, try not to worry so much.'

'I am trying,' I said tightly, tipping icing sugar into a bowl.

'Mark seems like such a nice boy,' she said.

'Boy? He's only twelve years younger than you are.'

Em put down the dishcloth and looked critically at Bel's face. 'Well, there you go. Perhaps I'll make a pass at him.'

'I thought you liked older men,' I said.

'I could make an exception for that one. Does he give a decent foot rub?'

'No idea,' I said. Mark had never shown the slightest inclination to rub my feet. Should he have? Was it something all good boyfriends did? 'Why?'

'Christine Marshall's husband massages her feet when she's in the bath.'

'*Neil Marshall?*' Neil was loud and beery and, I would have thought, the complete antithesis of the Sensitive New Age Guy.

'So she says,' said Em.

'I don't believe it.'

'Your father *might* come into the bathroom while I was in the bath,' she said pensively. 'But only if I'd died in there several days ago and he'd started to notice a nasty smell.'

'Cake?' Mark offered through the open kitchen window.

It was eight pm on Christmas Eve and I was sitting on the top step of my tiny porch, idly watching the leaves of the poplars along the roadside dance and quiver in the evening light. 'No, thanks,' I said. 'But could you grab me a cracker while you're up?'

'I thought you were feeling better.'

I propped my elbows on my knees and my chin in my hands. 'Only sort of. You know, I've been fantasising for about the last fifteen years about how great it would be not to feel hungry, and now I'm not, and it *sucks*.'

He wandered outside and sat on the step beside me, passing me my cracker. 'I bet it does.'

'What sucks even more is that I can't even tell myself that at least I'm getting thinner.' After my shower that evening I had pulled on my favourite bottom-flattering jeans, only to find that they didn't quite do up. Presumably this was due to my uterus now being the size of a grapefruit, and home to a lime-sized foetus. (Week Eleven on the Huggies website had a definite citrus theme.)

'It probably doesn't make you feel any better,' Mark said, 'but this is really good cake.'

'That's good.'

'Nice of you to make it when you can't eat any yourself.'

'Consider it compensation for spending Christmas with my extended family,' I said.

'If it's going to be that grim, why *are* we spending Christmas with your family?'

'I'm not sure. Force of habit, maybe. If it's too dire we'll leave.'

Uncle Simon and Aunty Laura lived on the outskirts of town, in a large and pretentious brick house on top of a hill. We got there at half past eleven on Christmas morning and left the ute out on the roadside so as to avoid being parked in.

The driveway was lined with cars, and I had a spasm of that horror you get in dreams where you stand up to give a speech and realise you forgot to put your trousers on. I must have been mad to think of subjecting us both to the scrutiny of the extended family. 'I could just drop off the bean salad and say I've got a call,' I said.

'Get a grip, McNeil,' said Mark, taking the salad bowl as we started up the driveway.

Uncle Simon met us at the edge of the lawn. 'Welcome,' he said solemnly, shaking Mark by the hand. 'Merry Christmas. Good to see you again.'

'Merry Christmas,' said Mark.

'Simon McNeil, mayor.' Uncle Simon likes to be absolutely sure people realise who they're speaking to. 'Good of you to come today. Meeting all the relatives, eh? And how are you, Helen?'

'Good, thank you,' I said.

'People are congregating on the patio. Come and say hello,' he said, relieving Mark of the salad bowl and giving it to me. He led Mark around the side of the house, and I went meekly in the back door with my salad.

The kitchen was full of hurrying aunts. Aunty Laura, short and squat and wearing a silk tunic that looked like an expensive floral tent, was fossicking in a drawer for cutlery. 'That's your salad?' she said briskly. 'Put it on the table. Leave it covered for now and find a suitable serving spoon.'

I repressed the urge to salute and turned left into the dining room, where the table was already laden with a discouraging array of salads. Aunty Deb followed me in and hugged me. 'Merry Christmas, love,' she said.

'Merry Christmas. Nice top.'

'Thank you. A Christmas present from myself. Have you brought Mark with you?'

'Yes,' I said. 'Uncle Simon mustered him round to the patio.'

'Poor man,' she said. 'How's the morning sickness?'

'Still there.'

'Is the ginger tea helping?'

'A little bit,' I said. It wasn't – I had drunk it solidly for a week and gained only a deep aversion to ginger – but it seemed a shame to hurt her feelings.

From the kitchen came the sound of high-pitched bickering. '*I* want to carry it!'

'You're tipping it! Mum, Bel's dropping sauce on the floor!'

'Annabel,' Em said wearily, 'put it on the bench. Now.'

'But *Mu-um . . .*'

Em must have taken the dish, because loud wails rent the air, followed by an almighty crash of metal on metal. Granny's voice rose shrill above the uproar. 'What's all this? *What's* all this?'

Even at her most amiable my grandmother's voice couldn't be described as dulcet, and when displeased she sounded just like the wicked witch in a pantomime. Aunty Deb and I looked at one another and giggled.

'We could get out through the window,' I suggested.

'Wimp,' she said, and led the way back into the kitchen.

The crash proved to have been a stack of baking trays, dislodged while rummaging for a platter. Granny was sitting squarely on her walker, blocking the outside door, and Bel was still roaring open-mouthed as Em mopped the tiles around her feet.

'Helen,' Bel sobbed, casting herself against me and burying her head in my skirt. My baby sister is not the girl to let the chance of a dramatic gesture pass her by.

'You're quite a stranger, Helen,' Granny said.

This was true. Visiting my grandmother required both courage and resilience, and lately I'd had neither. 'Merry Christmas, Granny,' I said, patting Bel.

'Got yourself in trouble, I hear.'

I had the sudden and unpleasant feeling that the ears of everyone in the room were straining in my direction. 'Mm,' I said.

'Helen's not in trouble, Granny,' said Caitlin. 'She's a good girl.'

'She is indeed,' said Em, wrapping a protective arm around my shoulders.

Granny snorted.

Escaping outside, I made my way around the side of the house to the patio and found Uncle Peter talking to Mark. Uncle Peter once played a game of rugby for Waikato and would, we are told, have certainly been an All Black if not for the stupidity and lack of vision of that year's selectors.

Sam, his sister Maree, Dad and Uncle Bruce (actually a first cousin once removed rather than a bona fide uncle) were grouped around the Water Feature. This was a new addition to the patio since I had last visited, a polished stone ball atop a metre-high concrete plinth, with a trickle of water spouting from its top and dribbling down the sides into a shallow bath at the bottom.

'Apparently it cost two and a half thousand dollars,' Sam was saying.

'It makes me want to pee,' Maree said. 'Hey, Helen!'

'Hi, guys,' I said. 'Merry Christmas.'

'Ah,' said Dad. 'You would be the woman who gave her sister a tambourine for Christmas.'

'She wanted a harmonica. You should be grateful.'

'I'd be more grateful if I hadn't been woken at six by someone banging a bloody tambourine two inches from my left ear.'

'Sorry. How long has Uncle Peter been talking to Mark?'

'About ten minutes,' said Maree.

'I'd better rescue him,' I said.

'How?' she asked.

'He'll be alright,' said Sam. 'I'm sure he's coped with worse.'

'Lunchtime!' called Caitlin, coming around the corner of the house. 'Aunty Laura says you've all got to come now!'

⁂

'So,' Em hissed, spooning potato salad onto her plate, 'what did Mark get you for Christmas?'

'A book, some body lotion and four boxes of Cabin Bread,' I said. The Broadview supermarket didn't stock the large dry crackers, and they were perfect for giving an upset stomach something to do apart from trying to digest its own lining.

'Oh.' In Em's opinion, lingerie, jewellery and perfume are the only valid gifts for a man to bestow on the woman in his life. Anything else means he doesn't think she's sexy.

'It was just what I wanted!' I protested, picking up a bread roll.

'Annabel, there's nothing green on your plate,' said Aunty Laura, who was stationed at the head of the big table, serving slices of ham that appeared to have been cut with a microtome.

'I don't like salad,' said Bel.

'It's good for you.'

Bel looked mutinous. 'Daddy says salad isn't food, it's what food eats.'

'Well, you need to eat this –' she snared a leaf of fancy lettuce in her tongs, and dropped it on Bel's plate '– before you can have pudding.'

'But I don't *like* –' Bel started.

'Annabel,' said Em warningly. Then, in a low angry mutter, 'Who does that woman think she is?'

After Uncle Simon's lengthy Christmas grace I made it to Mark's side for the first time since we had arrived.

'How are you doing?' I asked.

'Fine.' He looked at the bread roll in my hand. 'Is that all you're having?'

I nodded sadly.

'Bummer,' he said, smiling at me as he speared a lump of camembert with his fork.

'Helen!' Granny called from Uncle Simon's big armchair. 'Come here!'

I went, and Mark, poor innocent, put down his plate and came too. 'So you're the rugby player, are you?' she asked, looking him up and down.

'Yes,' he said.

'Can you do anything else?'

Mark looked somewhat nonplussed. 'I can knit,' he said after a moment's thought.

Like Queen Victoria, Granny was not amused. 'I dislike tattoos,' she said, looking pointedly at his bare arm. 'Very low class.'

'Granny!' I said.

'I dare say he can take it,' she said drily. 'Looking forward to fatherhood, are you?'

There was a breathless, delighted hush as everyone within earshot fell silent, the better to hear Mark's response. I used the time to tweak my Most Hated People list, moving Granny to first place ahead of both Joe Watkins and Fat Sharon. But Mark, who after years of media training and press conferences was very difficult to rattle, just looked at her evenly and said, 'Of course.'

'Humph,' said Granny, and the phone in my shorts pocket began to ring.

23

NEVER, NOT EVEN IN THOSE FIRST FEW MONTHS POST-graduation when after-hours calls were wildly exciting rather than a major drawback of the job, have I been more grateful for a call. 'Hello?' I said, opening the phone as I hastened out through the French doors.

'Hi,' replied a voice that didn't, strangely, belong to Pauline. 'I've got a really sick dog here that needs looking at.'

'Oh. What's the prob –?' And then I realised who it was on the other end of the line and broke off, smiling.

'I think it's got a broken leg or something,' said Sam.

Truly, the boy was a pearl among cousins. 'I'll be at the clinic in five minutes,' I said warmly.

'There you go. Don't ever say I don't do anything for you.'

'You're wonderful,' I told him.

'Yeah,' he said cheerfully. 'I know.'

'Call?' Mark asked as I came back in.

Aunty Deb was standing between us, so I only nodded. 'Do you want to come, or would you rather not?'

'I'll come,' he said.

'You've not even had your lunch!' said Aunty Deb. 'At least eat something first.'

Mark broke open his bread roll, transferred a pile of ham shavings and a wedge of cheese into the split and closed it again. 'Good to go,' he said.

'Let me put the rest in the fridge for you,' she said, bustling forward to relieve him of his plate. 'You can have it when you get back. Good luck!'

'What is it?' he asked as we crossed the lawn.

'Nothing,' I admitted. 'It was Sam, rescuing us from Granny. Did you want to be rescued, or would you rather go back and finish lunch? I can easily say they've rung back and changed their minds.'

'Nah, let's go home,' he said. He looked at his roll. 'I think I've got all the best bits here anyway.'

We had barely reached the ute when the phone rang again. 'A woman's just called with a fitting dog,' said Pauline. 'Where are you?'

'In town,' I said.

'Good. I told her to go straight to the clinic.'

'Did you get her name?' I asked, remembering my last fitting-dog call, when the owners hung up before Pauline could get any details and I waited in vain at the clinic for an hour in the dead of night, getting steadily colder and sourer.

'Beryl Stewart,' she said.

I stuffed the phone back into my pocket and dug frantically for the keys.

'What is it?' Mark asked.

'Fitting dog,' I said, wrenching the driver's door open. 'The owner's a lovely old lady who just lost her husband.'

'What makes dogs start fitting?' he asked, reaching up and grasping the handle above his door as we swung left at the bottom of the hill.

'Poison,' I said. 'Or epilepsy, or a brain tumour . . . Nothing good. She *loves* that dog. I did a house call there a few months ago, and she had her husband's ashes in an urn on the mantelpiece, and she told me hers and Taffy's are going to go in there too. She's had it put specially into her will, because she doesn't trust her son to do it.'

Beryl Stewart was waiting at the clinic, a fragile, silver-haired wisp of a woman in a powder-blue twinset and pearls. She was bent over the back seat of her car, but straightened as I tumbled out of the ute. 'My dear,' she said shakily, 'I do apologise for spoiling your Christmas.'

'Of course you haven't,' I said.

Taffy the Bichon Frisé was stretched out flat on the back seat of the car, every muscle in spasm and with her lips drawn back in a horrible fixed, grand-mal-seizure snarl. I bent and scooped the small shuddering body into my arms. 'Could she have got into anything?' I asked over my shoulder, running towards the back door.

'I don't know! I was out all morning with friends. I left Taffy inside, but she can get in and out of her little door whenever she needs to. I found her on the kitchen floor when I came in.'

I grappled with my keys and an armful of seizuring dog, and Mark twitched the key ring out of my hand. 'It's the big silver one,' I told him. 'Could she have left the section?'

'No,' said Mrs Stewart. 'It's completely fenced.'

'Have you put down any slug bait in the veggie garden?'

'I – I put some down yesterday, but she's never touched it before.'

'Alarm code?' Mark asked.

'Two-four-six-five-stay.' I ran past him up the hall, dropped Taffy on the treatment room table and switched on the lights. 'I need to sedate her, Mrs Stewart, so she'll stop seizuring.'

The anaesthetic drugs were in a drawer under the table – they should have been locked in the safe at the end of every day, but neither Zoe nor I ever remembered to do it. I pulled up four mils of diazepam and reached for the clippers to shave the skin over the vein on Taffy's foreleg.

'Mark,' I said, 'could you put your thumb across the crook of her leg – here – and hold up the vein for me? Try and keep her leg still . . . no, like this.'

A small, old, seizuring dog is not the ideal subject for vet-nursing practice, but he did pretty well, and I managed to get in half the diazepam before blowing the vein. I gave the rest into a thigh muscle, and then recalled that, for some reason that I probably knew the night before my pharmacology exam, it would have been absorbed faster per rectum.

'Was she herself at breakfast time, Mrs Stewart?' I asked, keeping my thumb over the needle hole in Taffy's foreleg.

'She didn't finish her biscuits, but she often doesn't. She's always been a fussy eater. I didn't worry about it.' She laid a hand on the little dog's head. 'She was like this when I found her. She might have been like this for hours.' A tear rolled down the soft wrinkled cheek, and she wiped it away with a trembling hand.

'I know it looks awful, but she honestly isn't feeling it,' I said. 'She's unconscious.' I opened the nearest cupboard with my foot. 'Mark, could you put a bag of fluids in the microwave for a minute and a half?'

He bent to get one, and vanished silently up the hall.

'We'll get her on a drip, Mrs Stewart, and keep her anaesthetised. Every time the drugs start to wear off I'll see whether she starts shaking again, and when she doesn't I'll let her wake up.'

'She's not – she's not responding,' she whispered.

'She will, I promise. I'll give her something stronger; I've just got to wait a few more minutes to see how well that first dose is going to work.' I flew around the treatment room, opening and shutting drawers. IV-giving set, catheter, a second catheter in case I spoilt the first one, tape . . . Where was Mark? Surely by now he'd had time to warm a dozen bags. Finally he opened the door and, snatching the fluids, I started to connect up the giving set.

'If she's eaten slug bait there's an antibody, surely?' said Mrs Stewart.

I shook my head. 'I'm afraid there isn't. It's just a case of keeping her asleep until it wears off, and running in lots of fluids to flush it out of the system. Could you bear to leave her, and go home to see if the bait you put down is gone?'

'Yes, of course,' she said, taking a cobweb of linen handkerchief from her sleeve and wiping her eyes. 'I'm only getting in your way here.'

'You're not in the way at all,' I said, running fluid through the line to flush out the air. 'But it's awful to watch your dog like this. Would you like to come back, or would you rather stay at home and keep in touch on the phone?'

'I – I'm not sure,' she said helplessly.

'Perhaps you could ring me from home about the slug bait, and then come back if you'd like to,' I said. 'Mark, could you write down my mobile number for Mrs Stewart? There should be a post-it note somewhere over by the computer.'

'Thank you both so much,' she said, taking it. 'I know you'll do your best.'

I stopped myself from saying, 'She'll be fine, I promise,' when I couldn't actually promise anything of the sort, and nodded instead.

'Right,' I said as Mrs Stewart's footsteps faded down the hall. 'Catheter. We'll try the other leg. You've got to hold it really firm.'

Mark immediately clamped the leg in a vice-like hold.

'Just let me shave it,' I said. 'And you'll need to give me some space to put the catheter in.' I repositioned his hand. 'That's better – now hold it still – cool . . .' I pushed the catheter through the skin, and blood ran back to fill the hub. 'Thumb up. Thank you.' I threaded the catheter up the vein and taped it in, started the drip running and ran to the safe.

The Nembutal bottle wasn't in the safe, and I rummaged frantically through the drug cupboard for a good minute before remembering that Nick had finally thrown it away a month ago, in anticipation of a best practice audit. Auditors tend to frown on the use of drugs that are five years out of date.

'Shit,' I said.

'What?'

'Can't find the stuff I want,' I said, returning to the table and pulling a mil each of ketamine and diazepam into a syringe. I injected slowly into the port on Taffy's giving set, and the small woolly body went limp.

'Good work,' said Mark.

'No it's not,' I said tiredly. Poor work at best. I should have had all the right drugs to hand, and their doses written down for quick reference. 'Watch her for me?'

'Watch her for what?'

'Breathing!' I snapped, and hurried up the hall for my toxicology book.

The book wasn't on the shelf above my desk, or on Keri's, or Richard's. This was becoming a recurring theme. I gave up the search and pulled out my phone to call my customary fount of veterinary wisdom.

'Hey, Nell,' he said. 'Merry Christmas.'

'I'm so sorry to ring you on Christmas Day,' I said, leaning back against my desk. 'Work question.'

'No worries,' said Lance.

'I've got a seizuring dog, twelve years old, probably slug bait.'

'Yuck,' he said.

'Yeah, she's pretty bad. I've knocked her out with ketamine-diazepam – I know it was the wrong thing to use but –'

'Not at all.'

'I thought you weren't supposed to use ketamine in animals with neurological signs?'

'Old wives' tale,' said Lance briskly. 'Newer studies have found that it actually decreases ICP – intracranial pressure. Top it up with Nembutal.'

I went back down the hall to the treatment room, where Mark was standing over Taffy, watching her chest rise and fall. 'Haven't got any. Can I use pentobarb?'

'I wouldn't,' said Lance. 'The concentration of that stuff's a bit variable. You might as well stick with ketamine, if it's working. Got the dog on a drip?'

'Yes.'

'Good. What brand of bait was it?'

'Don't know. The owner's checking and ringing back.'

'Some have carbamate in them,' he said. 'Has your dog got pinpoint pupils?'

I looked. 'No.'

'Okay. No point in giving atropine then. Might be worth trying gastric lavage, if it's been less than four hours since it ate the stuff.'

I looked at my watch – it was one thirty. 'It might be. Good idea.'

'Got anyone to help you?' he asked.

'Mark,' I said, smiling at him across the patient. 'He's a pretty good vet nurse.'

'Good on him. You might have to keep the dog sedated for a few days: metaldehyde takes a long time to wear off.'

'Will do. Thanks, Lance.'

'You're welcome. Oh, Kate's yelling about something, hang on . . . She wants to know if you're feeling better.'

'Not much,' I said. 'Is she?'

'Yeah, she's great. She says you should try vitamin B6.'

'Does it help?'

'So she says.'

'I'll give it a go,' I said. 'Thank you.'

'You're welcome. Take care, okay?'

'You too. Merry Christmas.' I closed the phone and put it back in my pocket. 'Thank you for watching her for me. I'm sorry I snapped at you.'

'So K-Y man told you what you needed to know?' Mark asked.

Lance was a bit pedantic, and prone to experimenting with nasty straggly tufts of facial hair, but he was a better person than I was. He wouldn't have told his new girlfriend my embarrassing secrets, and I shouldn't have told Mark any of his. 'Please don't,' I said unhappily.

Beryl Stewart rang just then to say that the ground around her primulas was indeed devoid of slug bait, so we spent an unpleasant half hour with a bucket and a stomach tube, washing out Taffy's stomach. Then I packed a box of supplies and we headed home, dog and all. I laid Taffy on a pile of newspapers and blankets in one corner of the kitchen, with the drip bag tied to a cupboard door handle.

'Drink?' I asked.

'Yeah,' said Mark, crossing the kitchen to put the kettle on. 'What do you want?'

'Tea, please.' I opened the pantry to retrieve the cake. 'I'm sorry; this is a lousy Christmas.'

'It's fine,' he said.

'Did you have a nice talk with Uncle Peter?' I asked.

'Which one was he?'

'The one who should have been an All Black.'

'That's right. Yeah, it was great.'

'Sorry,' I said.

'I liked your aunty Deb.'

'She's lovely, isn't she?'

He put an arm around me. 'She told me all about how clever you are, and how you were dux at high school.'

She would. Sam won the Accounting Cup one year, and she carried it around in her handbag and showed it to people.

'There were only about twenty of us in seventh form,' I said, resting my head against his shoulder. 'It's not all that impressive.'

'It's a lot better than I could do.'

I reached up and kissed his cheek. 'But you can knit.'

'So I can,' said Mark, letting me go.

I was sick and tired and self-absorbed, and it didn't occur to me that he honestly thought he was stupid. So instead of pointing out that he was the smartest, most logical person I'd ever met, and that he would have passed sixth form on his ear if he'd bothered to devote a fraction of his brain to schoolwork rather than rugby, I turned away and went to check Taffy's heart rate.

It was a lovely summer afternoon, warm and sunny, with a light breeze ruffling the leaves of Rex's poplars. All over the country, happy overfed people were playing cricket on their lawns and nibbling on leftover pavlova and chocolate truffles. Mark went to help Hamish milk, and I considered making something amazing for dinner for about four seconds before nausea won and I retired to the couch instead.

In the end, Mark dined on mayonnaise-and-salami sandwiches (had Em known I'd given him a litre of condensed-milk mayonnaise and an illustrated history of the Persian empire for Christmas she would have predicted the rapid and inevitable downfall of our relationship), and I had banana on toast. As we finished eating, Taffy's anaesthetic began to wear off and she started to paddle again. I topped her up for the fifth time, rang Mrs Stewart with a progress report and moved Taffy to the floor at the end of my bed.

It was not a restful night. About the seventeenth time Taffy stirred, somewhere around three in the morning, I rolled over and buried my face in the pillow.

'Your dog's twitching again,' said Mark sleepily.

'Mm,' I said, rolling back. 'I think I'll be sick when I stand up.'

He pushed himself up to sit. 'Tell me what to do, then.'

'No, it's okay.' I swung my legs out of bed, took a few deep breaths and switched on the bedside light. I had swathed it in a pair of pyjama pants so as not to wake Mark every time I turned it on, and then proceeded to wake him anyway by blundering around the room and falling over things.

The drip bag needed changing, and Taffy's body temperature was down to thirty-six degrees. I filled a hot water bottle and covered her with an extra blanket, and crawled back into bed, nibbling furtively on a Cabin Bread.

'What are you doing?' Mark enquired.

'Eating Cabin Bread to settle my stomach,' I said. 'Sorry.'

He sighed and sat up again.

'Where are you going?' I asked.

'Couch.'

'No, please don't! I'll stop.'

He got out of bed. 'Don't bother,' he said shortly, and went up the hall.

I lay and watched the numbers change on the digital alarm clock beside the bed: 3:40, 3:52, 4:09, 4:17 . . . Finally I got up and padded after him.

He was lying on his back on the couch, slowly rubbing his sore shoulder with the heel of the opposite hand. A square of yellow light from the hall framed his feet but his face was in shadow.

'Is it very sore?' I asked, stopping in the doorway.

'It's alright.'

'Would you like a heat pack?'

He shook his head.

'Lucky it happened now, I guess, if it had to happen,' I said tentatively.

'Helen, being injured now isn't insurance against being injured later.'

I bit my lip. 'I know.'

'Go back to bed,' he said. 'I'll be there soon.'

He hadn't come by the time I went to sleep, and he wasn't there when I woke up. I pushed myself up on my elbows – the clock said 7:05, bright sunlight outlined the curtains, and on the floor at the end of the bed lay a little white dog, watching me warily with her chin on her paws.

24

Injury Woes Leave Blues Blue

The season's barely started, but mounting injury lists are keeping Blues head coach Bob Grantham awake at nights. There's Mark Tipene's shoulder, of course, partially dislocated in last year's final Irish Test and then reinjured against the Crusaders last weekend. Tipene's management are talking about a four- to six-week rehab, but with the World Cup looming the All Black coaching team is unlikely to want to take any chances rushing its star lock back into play.

Then there's prop Luke Sia'alo's torn hamstring, fullback Sean Jones's dodgy ankle and several senior players unavailable due to extended holiday leave. Blues captain and All Black skipper Jaeger set a good example by choosing not to take advantage of his contract's holiday clause but was in disappointingly poor form last weekend, a mere shadow of his relentless and rock-solid best.

Bastards, I thought, refolding the paper and slapping it back down on the coffee table between a tattered copy of the *Listener* and a *Little Tots* parenting magazine.

'What's up?' Mark asked.

'Some prat saying Alan played badly last weekend.'

'Well, he didn't have a great game.'

'He wasn't *bad*.'

'I don't think you should read the sports news,' he said. 'You take it all way too personally.' He leant forward and picked up *Little Tots* with his left hand, his right arm being currently in a sling. 'Read this instead.'

'No, thank you,' I said. Being pregnant was daunting enough without starting to think about how to raise the child when it arrived. This was a pretty stupid approach, and even I could see that I was eventually going to have to give the matter some thought, but just now I was far too busy comparing life as it was to life as it might have been.

Imagine if I *hadn't* decided to flick that bit of tartar off that cat's molar with my fingernail. I wouldn't have got myself bitten, wouldn't have started that stupid course of Vetamox, wouldn't have bloody ovulated, wouldn't have stuffed up Mark's life as well as mine, wouldn't now be keeping up my last pair of respectable work shorts with a row of hair ties looped through the buttonholes on one side and around the buttons on the other . . . It was a particularly stupid train of thought, as depressing as it was pointless.

Mark shrugged, settled back in his plastic chair and opened *Little Tots* himself.

It was the evening of the first Wednesday in February, and we had met at the Anglesea imaging centre for my week twenty ultrasound scan. Week *twenty*. It really is incredible how time flies when you're wasting it in futile regret. We were the only people in the waiting room, and after a few minutes the receptionist, a slim grey-haired woman who'd been examining Mark surreptitiously through her lashes, stood up and approached.

'You – you *are* Mark Tipene, aren't you?' she said.

Mark lowered *Little Tots*. 'Yes,' he said. 'Hi.'

'Could I just take your picture for my son? He's a huge fan.'

'Of course,' said Mark.

'Thank you so much!'

'Why don't I take one of you both?' I suggested. After seven months with New Zealand's sexiest sportsman (*News on Sunday* said that, not just me), I had a good working knowledge of pretty much every available piece of photographic equipment on the market.

'That would be wonderful,' the receptionist said, handing me her camera.

Mark stood up, and I took the photograph.

'Oh, thank you, dear,' she said. 'How's your shoulder, Mark?'

'Not too bad,' he said, as he always did.

'So you'll be fighting fit in time for the World Cup?'

'I hope so.'

'Jack – Jack's my son – was so upset when you hurt it again last week,' she told him. 'Those shoulder injuries can be so slow to heal if they need surgery.'

Lucky you mentioned it, I thought sourly. *After all, he might not have realised.*

'And you'll really be wanting to be at your best this year, won't you?'

'That's right,' said Mark patiently.

'Well, best of luck. And congratulations to you both.'

'Thank you,' he said.

'First baby?' she said to me.

I nodded, and her smile grew even wider.

'Oh, now *that's* exciting. And it looks as if Leanne's ready for you. Go on down.'

'Okay, guys, there's a foot. Spine . . . ribs . . . arm coming across the screen now . . . there's the head, see?'

'Yes,' said Mark, almost under his breath.

I reached out for his hand, and his fingers folded tightly around mine. Although of course you know that pregnancy results in a baby, and that a baby is a little person, actually seeing the little person is quite a revelation.

'That's a nice shot of the head,' said Leanne, pressing a button so that the picture on the screen froze. 'I'll just take a few measurements.'

'It's not *that* nice,' I murmured. The baby's face didn't show up very well, being soft tissue over bone, so that we saw a skull rather than tiny cute features.

'I think it takes after you,' said Mark. I stuck out my tongue at him, and he grinned.

'Are you hoping to find out the baby's sex?' Leanne asked, busily drawing lines across the head on the screen with her mouse.

I said 'Yes,' as Mark said 'No,' and we looked at each other in dismay.

Proper couples probably manage to discuss stuff like this before-hand, I thought wearily. 'Why not?'

'I just like the idea of waiting till it comes out,' he said. 'Why do you want to know?'

'I – I just do.'

'Fine. Whatever.'

'No, it's okay,' I said.

'Look, it doesn't really worry me.'

'Sometimes we can't tell anyway,' said Leanne soothingly.

Having measured the baby's arms and legs, the blood flow through the heart and the size of the internal organs, Leanne printed off a CD of ultrasound pictures for us to take away. While we were waiting for it, Mark signed her coffee mug, the calendar on the reception desk and a diary belonging to one of the sports physicians next door. It was all terribly social, but eventually we made it back out to the car park.

'Shit,' he said, kissing the top of my head. 'I'm late.'

'For what?'

'Dinner with World Cup sponsors.'

'That's right,' I said. The World Cup had added another great heap of meetings and ad campaigns to the existing load, and even now, seven months out, the national sporting media seemed incapable of covering any story without slipping in a reference to the likelihood of the world's best rugby team failing once more to win it. The World Cup was starting to feel like a great brooding presence on the horizon, blocking all view of life afterwards.

'You're still coming up on Friday?' he asked.

'Yes.'

'Cool. Love you.' And pulling his keys from his pocket he sped across the car park.

A cranky ginger cat and half of last night's lemon spaghetti awaited me at home, but postponing our reunion, I stopped at Dad and Em's.

'Daddy's at a meeting,' Bel told me, coming down the hall. 'Lachlan Johnson was very naughty at school today.'

'What did he do?' I asked.

'I don't know, but it was *very* naughty. His mum came and got him after play time.'

'How exciting,' I said as we went into the living room together. The TV was on, Caitlin was writing carefully in a notebook and Em lay on the couch with a book.

'Hi, sweetie,' said Em, looking up. 'What's exciting?'

'Lachlan Johnson. What did he do?'

'I have no idea, but they're holding an emergency Board of Trustees meeting as we speak. I can hardly wait to find out.' She sat up, letting her book slide to the floor. 'How was your scan?'

'It seems to have the right number of fingers and toes, so that's nice,' I said, sitting down in Dad's big armchair. Bel climbed onto my lap and snuggled her face into the side of my neck. I stroked her hair absently, and then stiffened. 'Annabel McNeil, did you just *lick* me?'

She giggled.

'Yuck!' I said.

'I'm a baby kitten,' she explained. 'I'm washing you.'

'Well, how about you stop?'

'Annabel, don't lick your sister,' said Em. 'Boy or girl?'

'We didn't find out. Mark didn't want to know.'

'But you did.'

'It was the first thing he'd had any say in, so it seemed fair enough.'

'What hasn't he had a say in?' asked Em.

'Having the thing in the first place, for a start!'

'For God's sake, Helen, it's not a thing, it's a baby.'

'I know,' I muttered.

'Sweetie, it's time you started to think about what you're going to do. Are you going to stay here or move in with Mark?'

217

I rested my cheek on the top of Bel's curly head. 'I don't know, I . . . Stay here, I think.'

She frowned. 'Haven't you talked about it?'

'He just wanted to see how things went for a while,' I said very quietly.

'You can come and live with us,' Caitlin offered, looking up suddenly from her notebook. 'I'll help you look after your baby when I'm not at school.'

'I want to look after the baby too,' said Bel. 'Can I, Helen?' She squirmed around in my lap to throw her arms around my neck, kneeing me firmly in the stomach as she went.

'*Bel!*' I cried, doubling over. 'Be *careful!*'

'Go to your room,' Em ordered. 'Right this instant.'

Bel fled, sobbing, and I pushed myself up to follow her.

'Leave her, she's alright,' said Em. 'Helen, love, I really think you need to talk to Mark about what you're going to do.'

'I know. It's just – he's hurt his shoulder again, and he's really stressed about it.' At least, I assumed he was – he hadn't said so, and I hadn't pursued the subject. Asking people if they're worried about their potentially career-ending injuries seems just a bit too much like prodding their open wounds to see if they hurt.

'Well, why not put your name down at the day-care centre in town in the meantime?' Em said. 'Christine Marshall tells me there's a waiting list of up to a year.'

'Yeah, okay,' I said without enthusiasm.

❦

I got home just on dusk – a beautiful clear, pink dusk with one star out – and found Murray waiting on the deck.

'Hi,' I said. 'Sorry I'm late again.'

Murray rose gracefully and wound himself around my ankles. Picking him up, I sat down on the top step and rubbed him behind the ears, and he began to purr in approval. Just then, low in my abdomen, something quivered. I sat very still, holding my breath. There it was again: a faint stirring sensation as the baby moved. Oh. Wow.

I thought, as I sat with one hand pressed to my stomach, watching the stars come out, that this really was a revoltingly sappy way to behave. Woman resents unborn child, child quickens, woman has epiphany and is suffused with tenderness for the innocent new life burgeoning within her. How corny. How unoriginal. How *wet*. But there you go.

Eventually I got up, fed Murray and fetched the lemon spaghetti from the fridge. I ate it cold, standing at the kitchen bench, and then washed the plate and went to get the phone.

'Hello?' Em said.

'Hi. It's me. I – I just wanted to say you don't have to worry anymore. I'm going to be a good mother.'

'Helen, sweetie, of course you are!' she cried.

'I know I've been acting like a dick, and I'm sorry.'

'You have *not* been acting like a dick. Has she, Tim?'

'No more so than usual, as far as I'm aware,' came Dad's voice.

'Sweetie, you're doing just fine,' said Em. 'When I was pregnant with Caitlin I spent the first two trimesters crying and eating potato-and-gravy from KFC. And she was *planned*.'

This information was surprisingly comforting. 'Thanks, Em,' I said. 'Hey, what did Lachlan Johnson do?'

'He rubbed poo in another child's hair. His own poo. He brought it to school in a little container.'

'What – "Here's one I prepared earlier"?'

'Exactly,' said Em solemnly. 'It was a premeditated act.'

25

'ARE YOU DOING ANYTHING THIS WEEKEND?' ALISON ASKED the next day, vaulting lightly over a stile into the Broadview Wildlife Park. This optimistically named spot was a smallish paddock on the southern edge of town, home to three sheep, several roosters and one tatty peacock. However, it was reached by a flat, tree-lined road, which made it a far nicer summer destination than the sun-baked heights of Birch Crescent.

'Going to the Blues–Chiefs game tomorrow night, and then on to someone's engagement party,' I replied, jumping down after her with a thud.

'How glamorous.'

'Except that none of my good clothes fit anymore. I'll probably have to wear Nick's overalls.'

'Who knows? You might start a trend.'

'Somehow I doubt it,' I said morosely. 'What are you guys doing this weekend?'

'Having dinner with your grandmother.'

I looked at her in flat disbelief. 'You're kidding.'

'I'm not.'

'Huh,' I said. 'Well, there you go. And I thought Sam liked you.'

'I think your grandmother's hilarious,' said Alison. 'I do her diabetic checks. She always calls me "young lady", and she never does anything I suggest.'

'She'll probably cook you tripe,' I said.

'We're taking fish and chips.'

'That's no guarantee. There might be a tripe entree.'

'What *is* tripe, anyway?' she asked.

'The stomach lining of a cow. You boil it for a week or so and serve it with onions.'

'Yummy,' said Alison.

At ten past seven on Friday evening I stood in Mark's gleaming chrome bathroom, looking despairingly at my reflection.

'Ready?' he called from the bedroom.

'No!' I called back.

He looked around the bathroom door. 'What's up?'

'I can't go out like this,' I said, turning to face him. 'Look at me.'

'What's wrong with you?'

I looked down at the paisley wraparound skirt I had found in the back of my wardrobe the previous night. I'd tried it on with sandals and a long cream singlet and decided it was actually quite an elegant look, reminiscent of Gisele Bündchen. Now I could only assume I had been in some kind of pregnancy-induced hallucinogenic state. 'I look like a whale wrapped in a curtain!'

'You do not,' he said.

'I do too!'

'Well, then, wear something else.'

'Nothing else fits!' I wailed.

Mark sighed. 'Could we finish this conversation in the car? We're late.'

I nodded sadly and went past him down the stairs. At the front door he turned me around with his good arm and kissed me. 'Stop stressing, McNeil,' he said. 'You look beautiful.'

I put my arms up around his neck and hugged him tightly.

※

Saskia winced. 'Not straight, Alan,' she muttered.

Blue number four caught the lineout ball and lobbed it to the halfback. 'Straight enough,' said Mark. Then he winced in turn as a mob of red, black and gold players fell on the poor halfback like maddened wasps and turned the ball over.

'Offside!' Saskia barked, just before the whistle blew. 'Good . . . Don't waste it . . . Oh, for God's sake! What a piss-poor excuse for a kick!'

'Settle down, woman,' Mark said. 'It's his first start, poor little sod.'

'It'll be his last if he can't do better than that.'

Someone in the row behind us squealed, and I turned to see a woman with bright blue eye shadow waving frantically at the big screen above our heads.

The camera was of course centred on Mark, who glanced up for a moment, smiled in a friendly sort of way and turned back to Saskia. She looked up too, and waved. Wonderful ambassadors for New Zealand Rugby, the pair of them. I, however, spent my second and a half on national television staring in horror at my own reddening face.

As the coverage flicked back to the field, Mark looked at me and began to laugh. 'It's your fault,' I told him, pressing the palms of my hands to burning cheeks. 'You know what I'm like; you should have left me in the car.'

'*I* once lost a Malteser down my front at an All Black game,' Saskia said, 'and the whole country got to watch me fish for it before I realised I was on TV.'

'Really?' I asked. 'Or are you just trying to make me feel better?'

'Really,' she said.

'She loved it,' said Mark. 'Probably did it on purpose. Some people'll do anything for fifteen minutes of fame.'

In the next twenty minutes we were treated to two opposition tries and a single penalty kick by the Blues, which missed. 'Shit,' said Mark as the half-time hooter blew.

'It could be worse,' Saskia said. 'They could be winning without you.'

'Oh, shut up,' he said.

The second half was very tense, as the Blues clawed their way back into the game. But they never clawed their way into the lead, and in the end they lost by two points.

'Crap,' said Saskia, as the Chiefs fullback kicked the ball into touch, ending the game. She got to her feet and stretched. 'Want to come with me, Helen, or wait for Tip to sign autographs?'

'I'll wait, but thank you.'

'No, you'd better go,' Mark said. 'I'll be a while.'

When we got to the bottom of the steps I stopped and looked back – Mark was posing for photos with a couple in their fifties at the end of our row of seats, and a queue was forming in the aisle.

'We were having tea at a restaurant in Cook's Beach a few weeks ago, and a woman came and sat beside him and put her hand on his thigh,' I told Saskia. A fairly brazen move, I had felt, when he was dining with another woman at a table for two.

'Classy,' she said.

'She didn't even look like she was drunk.'

Saskia grinned. 'That's just an occupational hazard of hanging out with Tip in public. I remember once when he and Alan were flatting together we got home from the pub and counted fourteen phone numbers written on Tip's arm.'

'Did he copy them all down and work his way through the list?' I asked.

'I wouldn't be at all surprised,' she said, evading a pack of blue-clad teenagers who were making their way up the steps against the tide of people leaving the stadium. 'But he was only about nineteen, and nineteen-year-old boys aren't usually known for their taste and discrimination.'

'What was he like back then? He told me he was a cocky little shit.'

'When I met him I thought he was an arrogant dickhead. And then I got to know him a bit better, and figured out that he was actually just a scared kid.'

'Scared of what?' I asked.

Saskia shrugged. 'Failure. Getting kicked off the team.'

'But he was really good, wasn't he?'

'He was amazing. He was an All Black three years before Alan was. But when you get told your whole life that you're useless, you start to believe it.'

'Saskia!' called a cheerful-looking Samoan woman from the top of the steps, forcing me to abandon this fascinating line of questioning.

'Hey, Maria!' Saskia called back. 'Helen, this is Maria Mamoe, Aleki's wife. Helen's Tip's partner, Maria.'

Aleki Mamoe was the Blues' starting openside flanker. A top bloke, Mark said, who always played in his lucky boxer shorts.

I liked the thought of one hundred and twenty kilograms of muscle-bound rugby player needing to wear his lucky undies on the field. 'Hi,' I said.

'Nice to meet you,' said Maria. 'Pretty crap game, eh? I'm going to kick that man's bum when he gets home. He gave away two penalties.'

Mark's friends' engagement party was being held at a bar in Newmarket, and it was nearly ten when Saskia and I got there. We were met at the door by the wall of noise you get when a couple of hundred people are screaming at the tops of their lungs over a live band in a space about twenty metres square.

It was very hot inside, and Saskia was immediately drawn into a circle of people. She introduced me to the man on my right and we roared pleasantries at one another.

'Sorry? What was your –? Oh, hi, Greg. Oh, *Craig*. Sorry. Nice to meet you. I'm Helen. *Helen* . . . Never mind.'

Almost any remark sounds completely inane after you've repeated it three times at the top of your voice. After a while I stopped trying and settled for nodding and smiling. And a while after that I realised my smile had become fixed and my nod was turning into a nervous tic, and slunk off to the toilets to regroup.

Putting my bag down on the edge of the bathroom sink, I rummaged through it in search of a hairbrush. A pen . . . Bel's turtle, mysteriously returned . . . a box of Tampax – now that was ironic . . . a cheque book for an account I had closed a year ago . . . It was just possible that, one of these days, it mightn't hurt to have a cleanout.

Behind me a toilet flushed, and I glanced up at the mirror to see a startlingly beautiful blonde girl emerge from a cubicle. She wore a little black dress with a halter neck – a sleek, clinging, sophisticated dress, unmarred by the merest wrinkle of knicker line – and her hair fell in glossy waves over her slim brown shoulders. I'm sure I would have been a trifle dispirited by the contrast between this radiant vision and myself in any case, but I recognised her, and I almost crumpled into the sink.

Of course I had known that Tamara Healy was a pretty girl. I had seen her playing netball on TV, lithe and blonde and coordinated and no doubt all sorts of other good things I wasn't. But done up for a party she wasn't just pretty, she was stunning.

Our eyes met in the mirror, and she smiled. She had a chipped front tooth, and the effect was oddly endearing. It seemed unfair that the woman's only visible flaw should actually enhance her good looks. 'Hot out there, isn't it?' she said.

'Um, yes,' I whispered. 'Very.'

Once she'd gone I hunted through my bag with renewed fervour and found not only my hairbrush but a tube of Lash Defying mascara. I brushed my hair until it shone, put on two coats of mascara and pulled the neck of my singlet down an inch, on the grounds that if cleavage is your distinguishing feature you might as well show it off. Then I picked up my bag and swept out of the toilets.

The band was taking a break, which decreased the noise level from deafening to merely loud. I was standing on the outskirts of the crowd, looking at a dense wall of shoulder blades and planning my route, when Alan Jaeger came in through the door to my left. He had the pink, scrubbed look of someone not long out of the shower and an angry red graze on his forehead.

'Hi, Helen,' he said, stopping beside me. 'How are you?'

'Very good. Hey, you were really great out there tonight.'

'Thanks.'

'The scrum looked awesome,' I said.

'Pity nothing else did. Drink?'

'Not for me, thanks, but they're handing out champagne over there,' I said, pointing towards the far end of the bar.

Alan made a face. 'Good on them.'

'Alan,' said the breathtaking Tamara Healy, appearing from behind a pillar. 'Tough luck tonight. I hear you were legendary, as usual.' She leant in to kiss his cheek.

'Thanks,' said Alan.

Straightening, she turned to me. 'Hi,' she said. 'I'm Tamara.'

'Helen. Hi.'

'Oh!' she said. 'Tip's Helen? Nice to meet you!'

'You too,' I said.

She turned back to Alan. 'Jules was talking about going up to Pakiri on Sunday for a surf,' she said. 'Tommo and Becs are up there all week. Would you guys be keen if the weather's good?'

'Better check with the boss,' said Alan. 'There was talk of sanding window frames or something.'

Tamara laughed. 'You two are so cute.'

Alan was hailed just then by a small round man in a Danger Mouse T-shirt and turned away, leaving the radiant vision and me alone.

'He's such a lovely guy,' she said.

'He is,' I agreed.

'And Saskia's great, isn't she? Although every time she and I go out for a quiet drink we end up dancing on the tables in some dodgy bar in the CBD at two am.'

I smiled, though a small, cold, loser-ish feeling formed in the pit of my stomach. Saskia had never asked me out to dance on tables. And the fact that table-dancing is about the last thing

I would ever want to be doing at two am – or at any other time – was no consolation at all.

'You're a vet, aren't you?' Tamara asked, and when I nodded said, 'I couldn't do your job. I'd just turn into a blubbering mess if I had to put an animal down.'

I fought down an impulse to reply with, 'Oh, I *love* killing things. It's a real high point of my job,' and said instead, 'You teach, don't you?'

'Yeah, I've got thirty-one new entrance kids this year. Five of them don't speak English.'

'Crikey.'

'I know,' she said, laughing. 'It's craziness. But so rewarding. I love it. It's not just a job, it's a vocation. Do you feel like that too?'

I had spent that morning following Anita up and down the pit of a herringbone cowshed, rectally palpating any cows she couldn't confirm pregnant with the scanner. And in the afternoon I'd cleaned the post-mortem room freezer and ferried a trailerload of frozen cows' feet from last year's lameness training workshop to the clinic's offal hole. 'Absolutely,' I said.

'Oh, there's Tip,' said Tamara, waving.

Mark was easy to spot, being the tallest person in the place by about four inches. He was on the other side of the room talking to a man with a shiny bald head, and he smiled as our eyes met.

'Isn't his shoulder just the *worst* luck?' Tamara continued. 'Just when he was getting on top of that wrist thing, too.'

'Wrist thing?' I asked, surprised.

'Oh, he broke his scaphoid when we were in Cairns last Christmas, being an idiot on a skateboard. His mum was *so* cross with him. I thought she was going to send him to his room without any pudding. It was hilarious. Is she very excited about the baby?'

'I – um – haven't met her,' I said hoarsely. Mark had never suggested that I meet either of his parents, and our most exotic holiday destination had been a weekend in the Coromandel in January, during which a strong easterly wind had turned the sea into a sort of pulverised-jellyfish soup.

'She's lovely,' said Tamara, smiling at me kindly.

'That's good.'

'And Tip's great, isn't he? He'll be a brilliant dad.'

⁂

'Tamara's really beautiful,' I said, as Mark pulled the car out onto the street just before midnight. Such a stereotypical insecure-girlfriend remark, but it slipped out before I could catch it.

There was blank silence from the driver's seat.

'Isn't she?' I pressed. If you're going to be an insecure nagging girlfriend you might as well do it properly.

'Yeah, I suppose so.'

I drummed my fingertips on the window ledge of the car, and then stopped because it hurt my poor chewed nail beds. 'Why *did* you guys break up?'

Mark rested his head back against the car seat. 'Could you just not?' he asked.

I very, very nearly burst into tears. 'Fine.'

⁂

He was already in bed when I came out of the bathroom, lying on his back with one arm behind his head. I switched off the lights and skirted the end of the bed in the dim orange glow of the security light outside. The baby began to squirm as soon as

I lay down, and taking Mark's hand I pressed it to my stomach so he could feel it too.

'*Fuck!*' he said, jerking his arm back. 'Be careful!'

'I'm sorry!'

He removed his good arm from behind his head and massaged the bad shoulder. '*Please* don't do that.'

'Sorry. I forgot. I wanted you to feel the baby kicking.'

He sighed, sat up and laid his palm against my stomach. 'Where?'

'It's stopped now.'

He gave my stomach a quick rub, the kind you give a puppy to make up for growling at it. 'Oh well, next time. 'Night, love.'

26

MARK WAS OUT FOR ANOTHER SIX WEEKS WHILE HIS shoulder healed. He spent the time getting faster and fitter, going to physio and answering all questions on the progress of his injury, from me or anyone else, with, 'Good, thanks.'

We talked on the phone every day or so and saw each other most weekends, but things felt fragile and uneasy. We didn't discuss moving in together or life post-birth, and eventually I pulled myself together and started researching my local childcare options.

I began to look pregnant, which was an improvement on merely looking thick around the middle, and at work everyone got used to the new status quo, moved on to fresher gossip and stopped breaking off their conversations when I came into the room.

On a dull and windy Tuesday afternoon in early April I parked the ute behind the clinic and climbed stiffly out from behind the steering wheel. I peeled off a dirty pair of Nick's overalls, having now grown out of my own, collected an armful of muddy ropes to put through the washing machine and let myself in through the back door.

'How'd it go?' Thomas asked, leaning back in his chair and yawning as I came into the shop.

'Disaster,' I said shortly. After forty minutes of grappling with a calving jack, assisted by an unwilling farmer who really wanted to be covering his maize stack instead, I had managed to get the cow's dislocated hip back into its socket. This led to great satisfaction all round for about fifteen seconds, until I moved the cow's leg and the hip fell straight back out again. 'We got it in, but it wouldn't stay there. The socket must have been smashed to bits.'

'Oh, well, there's a dog coming in,' said Thomas. 'And your grandmother called. She wants you to go round after work.'

'Why?' I asked, rubbing my aching side. I must have pulled something while wrestling with that cow.

'Dunno,' he said. 'Maybe she's been knitting you baby clothes.'

Granny lived just down from the supermarket, in one of a line of orange-brick units surrounded entirely by asphalt. I left the ute on the side of the road and crossed this tarseal wasteland to knock on her living room door.

'Come in!' she called.

I let myself into the cluttered gloom and pulled the door shut behind me. Granny's living room was always overheated and under-lit. She kept the blinds closed to stop the carpet fading, and every flat surface sported a group of brass elephants or paua-shell ashtrays, a case of ornamental teaspoons or a doll with frilly Victorian petticoats and staring eyes.

'Hi, Granny,' I said. 'How are you?'

Granny pulled her cardigan more tightly around her. 'My back's killing me and it's been about seven years since my bowels worked properly,' she said flatly.

Well, that would depress anyone, I thought, wending my way around a small lacquered table to her armchair and bending to kiss her cheek. 'Cup of tea?'

'Yes, alright. You'll find biscuits in the big red tin in the pantry.'

The big red tin contained half a packet of very whiskery ginger kisses. Watched from the top of the fridge by a sinister-looking rag doll and a crocheted chicken, I threw them out, made the tea and carried two mugs back into the living room. 'Your biscuits were growing mould,' I said, passing her a mug.

'Just as well, probably,' she said. 'That little dark snip of a nurse doesn't like me eating anything I might actually enjoy. And I shouldn't think *you'd* need to be putting on any more weight.'

I sat down on the edge of the sofa and took a small resentful sip of tea.

'When's this baby due again?' she asked.

'July,' I said.

'What's that – another three months?' She looked at me over the rim of her mug. 'Is that boyfriend of yours still on the scene?'

'Yes.'

'Planning on moving in with him, are you?'

I kept my eyes firmly on an African violet in a brown macramé-sheathed pot. Who, pray tell, would choose to spend their free time knotting a pot jacket out of hairy brown string? And *why*? 'No.'

'So – what? You raise the child, and he can pop in if and when it suits him?'

I bit my lip. Never have I known anyone else with Granny's aptitude for finding and prodding a person's very tenderest spots.

'Well?' she asked.

'Something like that,' I said.

'What kind of stable home is that for a child?'

'Granny, I'm doing my best!'

'I dare say,' she said, shaking her head. 'Seeing as you're here, you might as well take a look at Tibby for me. She's gone off her food.'

Tibby (or 'the old witch's familiar' if you were talking to Em, who disliked being referred to as 'Timothy's trophy wife'; I did once point out that 'Timothy's trophy wife' was a step up from 'Timothy's fancy piece', but for some reason this failed to placate her) was curled on the spare-room bed in a patch of late afternoon sunlight. She was a small cat with dusty black fur and an uncertain temper, and she opened her eyes and glared at me as I sat down beside her.

I ran a soothing hand down her back and felt every vertebra, which was not a good start. I opened her mouth – quite a bit of tartar on her back teeth but only mild gingivitis. Mucous membrane colour reasonable. Eyes okay. Lymph nodes not enlarged. No nasty lumps in the abdomen. I took a pinch of skin between finger and thumb, and it stayed tented. At least ten percent dehydrated, then. Tibby batted my hand irritably with a paw to let me know her patience was wearing thin.

'Granny,' I said, going back into the living room, 'have you noticed her drinking?'

'She drinks like a fish,' said Granny. 'She's always at her bowl. She drinks the water in the bottom of the shower, too.'

Oh. Crap.

'What is it?' she asked.

'I think her kidneys might be packing up,' I said. 'I'd like to take a blood test and make sure.'

'And how much is that going to set me back?' Granny asked.

'Actually, maybe I can tell from a urine sample. Hang on.' I let myself out and hurried across the asphalt to get a small needle and syringe from the back of the ute, then returned to the living room. 'I'll just see if I can get a sample by popping a needle into her bladder through her side. She'll hardly even feel it.'

'Go on, then,' said Granny.

Tibby had curled herself back up into a tight black ball of fur, and was unimpressed at being disturbed again. She tried to scratch my wrist with a back foot when I felt for her bladder, but the thing was the size of a ping-pong ball and I hit it easily enough. The urine I pulled back into my syringe was very, very pale yellow, and capping the needle I went slowly back into the living room.

'She's got kidney failure,' I said, sidling between a glass-fronted cabinet and an ottoman and holding out the syringe for Granny's inspection. 'She's very dehydrated, but her urine's really dilute. It should be dark orange and it's like water. Her kidneys aren't doing their job.'

'What can you do about it?'

'Well, we can give her fluids and something to stop her feeling sick, and there are tablets you can give to increase the blood flow through the kidneys and make the best of the kidney function she's got left, but it will keep getting worse. The treatment might give her a few more months.'

'And if we don't treat her?'

'Weeks,' I said. 'Maybe. But it's a pretty miserable way to go. She'll be feeling really sick because her kidneys aren't getting rid of all the toxins they're supposed to. That's why she's not eating.'

'So she's suffering,' said Granny.

'Yes.'

'Can you put her to sleep?'

'I could give her fluids, and an injection to make her feel better,' I offered. 'Then you could think about it for a couple of days and see how much she improves with treatment. You don't have to decide today.'

'I have decided,' she said. 'Put her to sleep now.'

'Are you sure?'

'Can you do it or can't you?' she snapped.

I nodded and went out to the ute.

'Should I bring her out to you, so you can say goodbye?' I asked, re-entering Granny's stuffy little living room with pentobarb, stethoscope, syringe and needles.

'No, leave her be,' she said. She pushed herself slowly and painfully to her feet and shuffled out into the hall. 'Come along, girl!'

I followed her into the spare room and found her stroking Tibby's small black head with the side of a crooked finger. She pulled her hand back and turned to face me. 'Alright. Go on.'

'Would you like me to take her away and bury her?' I asked. 'Or you could have her cremated.' It always feels so insensitive to ask, but it's worse asking over the body of someone's pet.

'What nonsense,' said Granny. 'Cremating a cat.' She sniffed and went past me out of the room.

I pulled up five mil of pentobarb, stroked Tibby softly between the ears and, rather than trying to get a vein by myself, gave the injection through her side into the liver. She flinched as I put the needle in but went limp almost at once, and by the time I put the stethoscope to her chest there was no heartbeat. I fetched a towel from the cupboard in the hall and wrapped the small body to carry it back into the living room.

'Very much obliged to you,' Granny said crisply. 'What do I owe you?'

'Nothing.'

She nodded.

'I'm so sorry, Granny,' I said.

'Here.' She held out a plastic bag, knotted firmly at the top. 'Off you go. Don't open it now.'

I looked at her doubtfully as I took the bag. 'I'll make you another cup of tea.'

'I don't want another cup of tea.'

'What are you having for dinner?'

'I'm quite capable of getting my own dinner, thank you!'

'I know you are,' I said. 'But there's no reason someone else can't peel you a potato from time to time.'

'No, thank you. Goodnight.'

Back in the ute I tried to unpick the knot in the bag, gave up and tore it open instead. Inside was a tiny knitted vest and hat made of fine, soft cream wool. The knitter had dropped a fair number of stitches, due perhaps to a combination of arthritic hands and working in a carpet-sparing gloom, and as I held up the vest, a hole in the front unravelled a little further. I refolded it carefully, laid it on the seat beside the towel-swathed Tibby and got back out of the ute.

'Forget something?' Granny asked sharply as I opened the door yet again.

'Thank you,' I said, bending to hug her. 'Thank you for the clothes. They're lovely.'

'I thought I told you not to open that,' said Granny. But her cheek was wet against mine, and she caught my hand fleetingly in hers. 'Yes, alright. Go on, now.'

It was after six when I got home, and nearly dark. A couple of hundred sparrows were settling down for the night in the big conifer, chattering at the tops of their small shrill voices. I crossed the lawn wearily and fetched a spade from the carport, so as to bury Tibby under the copper beech rather than slipping her into the post-mortem freezer at work.

I had just cut out a square of turf when a car started up at my landlord's house, a hundred metres up the road. It turned left at the bottom of their driveway and then left again up the tanker track beside my cottage. I expected it to go past on the way to the cowshed for milk, but it came in through my gate and stopped. Spade in hand, I crossed the lawn towards it.

Rex got out of the car, stiffly because he needed a new hip, and then jumped backwards as I approached. '*Christ*,' he said, steadying himself with a hand on the bonnet. 'You gave me a shock! What are you doing? Burying the body?'

'Um, yes,' I said.

He roared with laughter. 'Only joking, my dear. How are you keeping?'

'Very well, thank you.'

'Good to hear it,' he said. 'You're looking well. I'm glad I've caught you, as a matter of fact; I've been wanting a word.'

I began mentally to frame a polite rejection, on Mark's behalf, to the impending invitation to speak at this year's pre-calving do at the club. But I needn't have bothered, because Rex said instead, 'You've been an excellent tenant, Helen. No trouble with the rent, no old mattresses on the lawn . . .'

'Thank you,' I said, since some response seemed to be expected.

'You're welcome. I expect you'll be off up to Auckland as soon as you stop work?'

I felt the blood rush to my cheeks, and was grateful it was too dark for him to see it. 'No, I –'

'The thing is,' he continued, 'Daniel's coming home on the first of June. He and his wife have a little one now, and he wants to have a go at managing the farm. So I'm afraid we're going to need your house.'

'Oh,' I said blankly. 'Right. When do you want me out?'

'Well, officially we need to give you six weeks' notice in writing,' said Rex, scuffing at the grass with the toe of his gumboot. 'But we'd really like to get the builders in and tidy the place up a bit – put in some insulation, that kind of thing . . . So if you were happy to be out by – oh, I don't know, the end of the month?'

27

'*WHAT?*' EM YELPED.

I moved the phone further from my ear. 'He was very apologetic,' I said.

'He can't do that! That's only two weeks' notice!'

'Nearly three.'

'He hasn't got a leg to stand on, legally.'

'Well, I said it would be fine.'

'Now why doesn't *that* surprise me?' she said. 'Honestly, sweetie, you've got to start sticking up for yourself. You need –'

But I missed just what it was that Em thought I needed, because Zoe put her head around the lunch room door and said, 'Nick wants you in his office.'

I nodded and, seeing as Em seemed to have paused for breath at the other end of the line, said, 'I know. Look, sorry, I've got to go. Talk to you later, okay?'

'Come for tea.'

'I can't. Mark's coming down. He's going to South Africa tomorrow.'

Dropping off the portable phone en route, I went down the hall to the tiny, filing-cabinet-lined room that was officially Nick's office and that he used mostly for storing things which didn't work but that he couldn't bring himself to throw away.

'Come on in and have a seat,' he said as I appeared in the doorway.

I made my way around an elderly photocopier and a bent calving jack to sit down. A small heel pushed hard against my abdominal wall from the inside, withdrew when I pressed back, and kicked me in the liver instead.

'I've just had Andre van der Pasch in,' Nick said. 'He had a few concerns about that cow you saw yesterday.'

'What concerns?' I said, forgetting all about my ill-behaved foetus and stiffening in my chair.

Nick, who loathes confrontation, drew squiggles on the edge of a teat-spray flyer and looked unhappy. 'Just a couple of queries about the amount of time you spent there. He feels it would have been better if you'd called in someone more experienced earlier rather than struggling on yourself.'

'But I didn't *need* anyone else! I knew what was wrong with her – the head of the femur was stuck under the wing of the ilium. It took us a while to get it out, and then we got it into the socket, and then it fell out again and I realised the whole joint must be smashed. Nick, I honestly think you'd have done exactly the same thing.'

'I don't think there's any problem with your decision to put the cow down,' said Nick carefully. 'Andre just feels that he's a busy man, with a lot of things on his plate, and spending an hour and a half messing around with a cow that was never going to be a starter wasn't a good use of his time. Perhaps we just need to be a bit more aware that our clients have businesses to run, and that our input is only a small part of their overall operations.'

'But I –' I started, and then stopped abruptly because the tears were building behind my eyes and crying is a crappy, crappy way of dealing with constructive criticism.

'Helen, I don't think for a minute that you did anything wrong. Your clinical skills are excellent, you're thorough and sensible, you do a really good job of explaining to clients what you're doing and why, but –'

Ah, the dreaded 'but'. I once went to a marketing seminar at which the presenter explained that when you insert a 'but' into a sentence it magically turns everything that went before it into bullshit. It's true, too – just try it. 'Of *course* your bottom doesn't look big in that, but . . .' Or, 'I really like your mother, but . . .' See?

'– but you need to work on your confidence,' he said, starting on a row of triangles, which he shaded carefully as he spoke. 'Sometimes you come across as just a bit hesitant. I always remember the old vet I worked for as a new graduate. He was rough as guts and he never made any attempt to keep up with new treatments or techniques, but the cockies loved him. If he had no idea what was wrong with the cow he told them it had intestinal ringworm or malignant hepatitis or some other condition he'd made up on the spur of the moment, and they absolutely lapped it up. Used to drive me mad. I remember once I wanted to take bloods from a herd pre-calving, and the farmer told me that Bruce could tell if they were getting enough magnesium by just looking at their tongues.' He looked up from his colouring-in to smile at me encouragingly.

I smiled back. 'Okay,' I said. 'I'll work on it. Thank you.'

Nick bent his head and began drawing circles between his triangles. 'And the other thing I wanted to catch up with you about is your parental leave.'

'I put the form on your desk last week.'

'You did,' he agreed. 'Thank you. You're thinking you'll be back in October?'

I nodded. 'I'm skipping the whole of calving. I'm so sorry.'

'It's fine. We'll be fine. But that isn't very long. You're entitled to twelve months' maternity leave.'

'Yes, but I only get paid for fourteen weeks of it,' I said.

Nick looked up at me and his eyebrows twitched in surprise. I realised that now he would think that Mark, who earned a cool half-million a year without counting sponsorship, wasn't prepared to contribute anything towards the upkeep of his own child, and added quickly, 'Mark would support me – us. I just don't think it's fair that he should have to.'

My boss opened his mouth, thought better of whatever it was he'd been going to say, and shut it again.

It was half past eight when Mark's car turned in through my gate and parked behind the ute. I pulled my hands out of the sink and wiped them on the thighs of my maternity jeans, and went to the door to meet him.

'Is the car alright there?' he asked. 'You're not on call?'

'No, it's fine. How was the fitness test?'

'All clear.'

'Awesome,' I said, reaching up to kiss him. 'So you're starting in Cape Town?'

'No, I'm on the bench.'

'Bob easing you back in?'

'Mm,' he said. 'I hate the bench.'

I had no problem with Mark being on the bench – it meant he wasn't on the field, where he might get hurt – but I wasn't quite stupid enough to say so. 'Have you had tea?' I asked.

'I had something after training.'

'There's a chicken pie in the fridge.'

'Oh,' he said. 'Well, in that case . . .'

While he retrieved the pie I went back to my dishes. 'My landlord came to see me last night,' I said, scrubbing vigorously at the potato pot. 'I have to be out of here by the end of the month so he can do the place up for his son to move into on the first of June.'

'What, this month?' Mark asked over his shoulder.

'Yes.'

'Any idea where you'll go?'

I shook my head. 'I haven't even looked yet. If all else fails I'll hang out at Dad and Em's for a couple of weeks.'

'You could come and stay with me for a while,' he offered, putting the pie dish down on the bench and reaching for a plate.

For a while. I hadn't realised I still possessed the tiniest sliver of hope that one day Mark would go down on bended knee and beg me to move in with him so we could raise our child in the good old-fashioned, two-parent way. But the hope must have been there, because I felt it shrivel up and vanish, and the world became just a smidgeon darker and bleaker than it already was. 'It might be a bit too far to commute to work,' I said.

A silence grew, during which Mark spooned chicken pie and mashed potato onto his plate and I attacked the cheese grater with a dish brush. 'Anyway,' I said, 'the midwife is here, and the antenatal classes. And my name's on the waiting list for the day-care centre here when I go back to work.'

'When are the antenatal classes?'

'It's a whole weekend. Fourteenth and fifteenth of May, at the scout hall in town.'

'Why didn't you say?'

'Because you're playing rugby in Brisbane,' I said tiredly.

'Sorry.'

'I'm used to it.'

'It *is* my job,' he said.

'I *know*.'

Mark picked up a fork from the pile on the draining board and speared it into his pile of mashed potato.

'Aren't you going to warm it up?' I asked as he retreated to the table.

'It's not very cold,' he said, sitting down.

I blinked fiercely as I started to dry the dishes. Yesterday had been awful, and today no better, and Mark was going away for a fortnight, and he didn't love me anymore, if indeed he ever had, and –

'You're going to put the baby into day care five days a week?' he asked suddenly.

I looked up and saw him turn over the application form at the end of the table. 'I'll take ten weeks off when it's born,' I said. 'At least.'

'And then you want to go back to work full-time?'

'My job *is* full-time,' I said. 'They've got no obligation to offer me a part-time position.'

'Well, have you asked?'

'No,' I admitted.

'Right,' he said. 'So have you ever had any intention at all of giving me a say in any of this?'

I looked at him sharply. 'What's that supposed to mean?'

He didn't bother to reply in words, but lifted an eyebrow and ate a forkful of mashed potato. It was a move calculated to annoy, and boy did it succeed.

'At what point, exactly, have you *wanted* a say in anything?' I demanded.

'And what's *that* supposed to mean?' he said, putting down his fork.

'You said you wanted to just see how things were going to go. And you've been just seeing for the last four months, and I still don't know if you're in or out, and this baby's arriving soon and I don't even know where I'm going to l-live . . .' My voice cracked and I swiped a furious hand across my eyes. For four months now I'd been holding my breath while he slipped away, misunderstanding by misunderstanding. Four months of constant worry, of sidestepping my family's concerned or avid questions, depending on the questioner, and of guilt that the excited anticipation I should be feeling was entirely passing me by. You can become quite seriously bitter in four months. 'This has stuffed up my *whole life*, and then you swan in and say you don't want your kid in day care when you've got no intention of doing *anything* to help look after it yourself –'

'That's just bullshit, and you know it!'

'You haven't even got a car you can put a baby seat into!' I cried. 'You're still just wandering around enjoying your perfect little playboy lifestyle and being World Cup pin-up guy. You haven't had to give up *anything*, you're –'

'Yeah,' he broke in icily, 'well, I'm not the one who fucked everything up in the first place.'

Snatching the grater off the bench, I flung it at his head. I missed, although he was only about three metres away, and it bounced harmlessly off a curtain without even having the decency to clatter.

He gave a sarcastic snort of laughter.

'Get out!' I shouted. 'Just get *out*!'

'Oh, with pleasure, believe me,' he said, shoving back his chair.

I reached up and gave the chain around my neck a savage jerk. It broke, and I hurled his pendant across the room at him. Through sheer fluke it hit his chest, and fell in a small glittering heap at his feet.

He looked neither at it nor at me. He opened the door, went out and slammed it behind him with a force that shook the house. The baby leapt beneath my ribs like a hooked fish.

I didn't move as his car started. There was a low, angry snarl as he revved the engine, a screech as the car turned onto the road, and he was gone.

28

MY HOT CHOKING FURY VANISHED ABOUT TWENTY
seconds after Mark did, swamped by the appalled realisation
that I'd finally lost him, and since people apparently don't die
of broken hearts I might have to live without him for another
sixty years. Leaving the chicken pie on the bench for Murray to
dismantle at his leisure I crept blindly up the hall and into bed.

I suppose I must have got up the next morning and gone to
work, although I have no recollection of anything that happened
there. The day after that was a Friday, and at four fifty pm I
looked at the clock on my computer screen and thought with
exhausted relief that soon I'd be able to go home and cry.

'Come on,' said Keri, putting her head around the vet room
door. 'Drinks.'

'Be there in a minute,' Nick said, typing intently with
one finger.

'I'm just looking something up,' I told her, with every intention of slipping out the back door and bolting for home as soon
as they left the room.

'Can't you do it on Monday?' She looked as though she would be more than happy to stand there and heckle, and I was far too fragile to withstand heckling. I shut down the computer and pushed myself up to stand.

'What are we having, ladies?' Thomas asked as we came into the shop.

'Wine,' said Keri.

'You'll have to grab a glass. Helen? Ginger beer?'

'No thanks, I'm good.'

The printer in the corner whirred, and Nick sauntered out of the vet room behind us to collect a few sheets of paper from its tray. 'Right, chaps,' he said, handing them round. 'New roster.'

We perused it in silence for a few moments before Richard said, 'You're fucking joking.'

'I never joke,' said Nick.

'Every other weekend, two nights a week and no lieu days? That's slave labour!'

'It's only for a couple of months,' said Nick. 'I'm reasonably confident you'll survive.'

'Survive what?' Keri asked, coming back down the hall with a dusty-looking wineglass in her hand.

'Spring,' said Thomas. 'Blame Helen – it's all her fault for having unprotected sex.' He was doubtless hoping for a reaction, but I was too miserable to oblige.

Keri picked up a copy of the roster and looked at it. 'Bloody hell, Nick, couldn't you get a locum?'

'Why pay good money for a locum when you can just work your existing staff to death?' said Richard bitterly.

'Listen here, you whining Gen Y brats,' said Nick. 'I've been looking for a locum since Christmas, and there aren't any. So how about we all just stiffen our upper lips and get on with it?'

'If that was supposed to inspire us, it failed,' said Keri.

'I *was* thinking about paying you some sort of bonus to make up for losing your lieu days, but I may yet change my mind.'

'Oh,' she said. 'Well, that would be a nice gesture.'

Just then a small red car pulled up outside and Mrs Dobson-Hughes got out, the horrible Pierre clasped to her bosom.

'Aren't you on call?' Richard asked Nick.

'Yes.'

'Hah! She's all yours.'

Nick sighed as the automatic doors opened. 'Hello, Maggie,' he called. 'What can we do for you?'

'Pierre's been sick twice since yesterday,' she said. 'We're supposed to be going out tonight, and I couldn't leave him without having him seen.'

'Come on into the consult room and I'll look him over,' said Nick.

'I'd prefer to see Richard.'

'Of course,' Nick said graciously. 'Dr Fleming?' And as the consult room door closed behind the three of them he sank into a chair and beamed at us. 'There you go,' he murmured. 'Proof that karma *does* exist.'

It started to rain just as I reached home, which seemed appropriate. It would be twenty to eight in the morning in South Africa, and Mark would be getting up. He would not, however, be calling to ask how my day had gone, tell me about his trip and complain about sharing a room with Sione Brown, whose hair-care products overflowed the bathroom sink to lie in piles on the floor. Unhappiness rolled over me in a great cold wave.

My phone beeped and I pulled it out of my shorts pocket. The message was from Alison, and read, *6.30 ok 4 u?*

Oh, good God, no. I could no sooner go out this evening and act like a rational human being than I could have grown wings and flown to the moon.

Sorry really shattered going to stay home and have early night.

Ok hope ur better 2moro x

Thanks have a good one.

I put the phone back in my pocket, dropped my head onto the steering wheel and cried.

Sobbing in the dark while the rain beats against the windscreen certainly is marvellously atmospheric, but eventually I tired of it, climbed laboriously out of the ute and went inside. I changed into pyjamas, fed Murray and sat down at the kitchen table to write a list.

Place to live
- Check in Broadcast
- Ask Em
- Aunty Deb?
- Real estate agent?

Although if I *did* find a new place I would have to pack, cut off and reconnect the electricity and phone, clean the oven . . . Seeing as getting up and dressed in the mornings was almost more than I could manage, my chances of achieving all that seemed, frankly, slim. I put down my pen and got up to put the kettle on.

A car turned in through the gate, its headlights raking the shadowy kitchen. At least, I thought crossly, homelessness would prevent people from popping in unannounced to spoil my Friday night plans of eating a kilo or so of pasta with cheese and crying myself to sleep. I stamped across the kitchen to open the door.

'Hi,' said Sam, coming in past me and unloading a plastic bag full of styrofoam containers onto the table. 'We brought food.'

'Um, thanks,' I said stupidly.

Alison ran up the porch steps behind him. 'Nice PJs,' she said.

I looked down – this evening's pyjamas were very old and very threadbare, and gaped in a most unladylike fashion where the fly buttons had come off. Mark, on seeing them, had suggested it might be time to throw them down a deep hole and buy a new pair. I was just pointing out the breathtaking hypocrisy of this statement when he sat me on the edge of the table and started taking them off, and I sort of lost the thread of my argument.

'I'll go and change,' I muttered now, hurrying up the hall.

When I came back into the kitchen, dressed more respectably in sweatshirt and jeans, they had set out the food and found an assortment of plates. Murray was watching with interest from the end of the kitchen bench.

'It's the Stockman's Arms' new sharing platter,' Alison explained. 'It sounded quite nice. Sorry to just turn up.'

'No, it's lovely to see you. And the food looks great – what would you like to drink?' I opened the fridge. 'Beer?'

'I thought you weren't supposed to be drinking, in your condition,' said Sam.

'It's Mark's,' I said, and my voice hardly wobbled at all. 'It's been there for months. Help yourself.'

'Where's he playing this weekend again?' Alison asked.

'Cape Town. And then Pretoria the weekend after.'

'Tomorrow night will be a tough game,' said Sam, plucking his beer of choice from the fridge. 'The Stormers haven't lost all season. How does Mark feel about Reuben Scott starting?'

Reuben was the third lock in the Blues squad, a pleasant young man with a slight shortage of chin, but more than ample nose to make up for it.

'Not all that thrilled. He hates the bench. Ali, would you like a beer?'

'No, thanks,' she said. 'Come and eat before it gets cold.'

'Have you guys heard of any places to rent?' I asked, tickling Murray between the ears on my way to the table.

'Not that I can think of,' said Alison. 'Why, are you thinking of moving?'

'I have to. Rex wants the cottage for his son and I've got to be out by the end of the month.'

'Good,' said Sam. 'This place is grim.'

'Not as grim as moving back in with Dad and Em.'

'Why on earth don't you get your act together and move in with Mark?' Then he jumped, as people do when kicked under the table.

I tried to tell him why not, found that my throat had clamped shut and shook my head instead.

'Oh, Helen,' said Alison, leaping up to come around the table and hug me. 'Oh *no*.'

'Well, it's not really a s-surprise – sorry . . .'

'Arsehole,' said Sam.

'No he's not,' I gasped, lifting my head from Alison's shoulder.

'Yeah, he is,' he said coolly. 'Only arseholes leave their pregnant girlfriends.'

'He tried. You c-can't make yourself care about someone just because they're having a baby.'

'Well, if that's how he feels I suppose you're better off without him,' said Sam, frowning.

And I came to the conclusion, lying in bed later in that state of desolate calm that you reach when you've temporarily cried yourself out, that he was right. There's no point in just wishing indefinitely for someone to love you when they don't – eventually you've got to give up and start building yourself a new life.

'Well,' said Em a few days later, putting her bottle of nail polish down on the coffee table and looking critically at her handiwork, 'personally, I never thought he was much of a rugby player.'

Seeing as Em's knowledge of rugby was probably somewhere on a par with Kim Kardashian's, this was not a particularly damning condemnation.

'He's big and strong,' she continued, 'but all he does is run into people and try to rip the ball off them.'

'Em, that's pretty much the job description,' I said. Rugby's really fairly straightforward – the forwards try to pulverise each other, and then the backs skip lightly through the holes in the opposition's defence to score the tries. Forwards *can* score tries, but it's not their key role and they like to pretend it's no big deal. A manly nod of acknowledgement once the ball is planted over the line is acceptable, but victory dances, like fancy hairstyles, are left to the backs.

She sniffed. 'And then if *he* has the ball he doesn't throw it to anyone else, or kick it, or anything clever – he just charges straight into the biggest, hairiest thug he can find. I'm sorry, but I fail to see what's so impressive about that.'

'If I were you, I'd bring up those concerns with the All Black coaching panel,' said Dad from the big armchair across the room.

'Tim, don't be patronising. Sweetie, is he at least going to pay you some sort of child support?'

'I don't want his money!' I said.

'Oh, for goodness' sake, Helen! It's not for you, it's for the baby.'

'People raise babies on a lot less than I earn.'

'That is not the point,' she said. 'Look, I'll ring him if you like. You don't have to talk to him yourself.'

I didn't answer this straight away, being temporarily distracted by the tragedy of having lost the right to talk to Mark about anything except child support. Once we'd had long in-depth arguments about which series of *Blackadder* was the funniest, and whether icing a double chocolate muffin would improve it or push it over the edge.

'What's his number?' she asked.

'No,' I said hastily. 'No, I'll call him when he gets back from South Africa and sort it all out.'

Dad accompanied me out and walked around my car, peering at the tyres in the light of the security bulb at the corner of the garage. 'Huh,' he said. 'Not bad.'

'I had them checked last week.'

'How very mature and responsible of you.'

'Thank you,' I said graciously. I'd had my tyres checked solely because my cousin Kevin had left a rude note on the windscreen while I was in the supermarket, saying three out of four of them were bald and if I didn't do something about it he would come around and give me a good kicking, but I kept this detail to myself.

'Did you go and have a look at that house of Kaye Upton's?'

'Yes,' I said. 'It's okay.' Kaye's rental property was a small wooden box with aluminium joinery, built up on poles on the south side of a hill. It had looked dank and charmless when viewed through the drizzle, but I was in no position to be picky. Besides, it suited my frame of mind.

'Should I go and inspect it?' Dad asked.

I shook my head. 'No, it's fine. It will do for now.'

Dad put an arm around me and gave me a quick squeeze. 'Chin up, sausage,' he said. 'It'll get better. Things do.'

The back door opened, and Em came down the steps holding my handbag. 'You forgot this,' she said. 'Now, I just had a thought. How about we have a girls' day out on Saturday? We'll go to Hamilton and hit the shops, and then have a nice lunch.'

'I'm not really in a shopping mood,' I said.

'Never mind; it will do you good.'

'I need to do some packing.'

'How much packing can you do when you're not moving for another week? Anyway, Monday's a holiday; you can pack then. Tim, you'll look after the girls, won't you?'

'Yes, dear,' said Dad.

'Good. I'll pick you up at nine, Helen.'

29

I CANNOT POSSIBLY HAVE BEEN A PLEASURE TO BE AROUND just then. It was really quite heroic of Em to spend a day with me of her own free will – I should have appreciated it, but I was far too busy being miserable to appreciate anything.

'Yes,' she said as I emerged from a changing room in a dark blue tunic thing with a scoop neck. 'Just gorgeous. You can wear it over jeans, and it will be fabulous with tights and boots.'

I cast an apathetic glance at the mirror. 'It'll be too small in another month.'

'Of course it won't. If you wear your clothes so big that nobody can see your bump you'll find you look fat instead of pregnant. I think you should buy it.'

'Okay,' I said. I was going to have to buy *something* if I didn't want to spend the last three months of pregnancy in a large green sweatshirt with *Broadview Dental Fun Run 2006* across the back.

'Don't get dressed again just yet,' she said. 'I'll bring you a few other things to try.'

Having Em pass things into the cubicle and whisk them away again was quite a restful way to shop, and I tried on everything she brought me with unprecedented docility.

'I like that colour on you, sweetie,' she said, tweaking the hem of a long pink cardigan.

I screwed up my nose. 'Em, I look like a prawn.'

'Helen Olivia McNeil!' she snapped, straightening up with a jerk. 'If you put yourself down *once* more I will brain you with my handbag, so help me God!'

I stood and gaped at her in shock.

'Just *look* at yourself!' She pulled me around by one shoulder to face the mirror. 'You are *beautiful*. I would *kill* for your hair and skin. And honestly, sweetie, brushing off every compliment starts to make you look very ungracious after a while. People get tired of constantly having to reassure you – if they didn't mean it they wouldn't have said it in the first place. It's not pleasant to say something nice to someone and have it thrown right back in your face.'

'Sorry,' I whispered.

'That's alright,' she said, tucking a strand of hair back behind my ear. 'Now, you'll take the cardigan? And the navy tunic, and the wide belt?'

I nodded. I would have nodded if she'd suggested I take the purple velour jumpsuit with the orange stripes.

'Now, why don't you leave that on?'

'Okay.'

'Wonderful. Let's go and get some lunch.'

She swept through the Saturday morning crowd with her handbag dangling Hollywood-style from one wrist and me following meekly in her wake. Reaching a cafe with outside tables she smiled winsomely at a couple sitting over their coffee until they realised they had in fact finished, and sat down.

'Well, that was a successful morning,' she said. 'What do you feel like to eat?' She pushed the unfortunate couple's cups to one side and passed a laminated menu card across the table.

I looked at it without interest. 'Whatever.' And then meeting her eye I added hastily, 'Eggs Benedict. How about you?'

'I might try the Thai beef salad. I'll go up and order, shall I?'

'No, I'll go.'

'You will not,' she said. 'What would you like to drink?'

'Water, please.'

'Right,' she said, getting to her feet. 'I won't be long.'

In an attempt to really plumb the depths of woe, I passed the time she was gone in scrolling through the inbox of my phone to look for messages from Mark.

Ok

Will do

Yep

Oh, how depressingly succinct.

Late be there by 9 x

That one was two weeks old. So a fortnight ago I had been worthy of at least an x in passing.

Nite love x

Three weeks ago.

'Oh, sweetie, I hate seeing you so unhappy,' said Em, slipping back into the chair opposite mine and reaching across the table for my hand.

My throat tightened ominously. Having no wish to dissolve amid our fellow diners I pulled away and said, 'Well, let's face it, it was always going to end like this.'

'Why?' she demanded. She folded her arms and leant on the tabletop, thus increasing her cleavage exposure from excessive to borderline obscene.

'Because getting pregnant when you've been together for about three minutes tends to put a bit of a dampener on a relationship!'

'I'm sorry to break it to you, sweetie, but you're hardly the first couple in the world to have to deal with an unplanned pregnancy.'

'I know that.'

'It's been one of the leading reasons for marriage for hundreds of years. *Thousands* of years, probably.'

'Except that these days you don't get forced to the altar at shotgun-point.'

'No,' she said patiently. 'But I don't see why having a baby means your relationship is automatically doomed, either.'

I looked down at my hands. 'I guess it just put too much pressure on everything. Mark wasn't ready to do the whole settling-down-and-having-a-family thing. Not with me, anyway.'

'Wasn't he?'

'Well, obviously not!'

'Were *you*?'

'Em, please don't do this amateur psychology stuff on me,' I said tiredly.

'Did you want to settle down with him?' she persisted.

'Yes! Of course I did.'

'Because, sweetie, sometimes it didn't really look like it from where I was standing.'

I looked up sharply.

'How do you think it might have made Mark feel that you've never expected him to be there for you?'

'I –' I said, and stopped.

'You've been so determined to cope with this all by yourself. But it's his baby too. Don't you think he might have got the impression that you didn't really want his input at all?'

'I just – I didn't want to pressure him! I didn't want him staying just because he thought he should.'

'I've always remembered the celebrant at my friend Eileen's wedding saying that one of the most important things in marriage is for the woman to *abandon* herself to her husband,' Em said. 'Not to submit to him, or obey his every wish, but just to trust him completely with her heart. And don't say you weren't married, because the principle's the same.'

'Yeah, well, it's a bit hard to abandon yourself to someone who hasn't even bothered to introduce you to his parents.'

'*Hasn't* he?'

I shook my head. 'His family's not close like we are, but – but he took Tamara Healy to his mum's in Australia for Christmas.'

'Well, he spent this last Christmas with you.'

'And it was a disaster. Em, he never wanted to be with me for good. He – he said that he wasn't the one who fucked everything up.'

'People say all sorts of things they don't mean when they're upset.'

'He meant it. And it wasn't just the fight – that was just the last straw. Things have been bad for months.'

She sighed. 'Maybe it's just as well. You're very different people.'

Considering I'd just spent ten minutes trying to convince her that Mark and I had never had a snowflake's chance in hell of staying together, it was unreasonable to feel as offended by this remark as I did.

'You're such a clever girl,' she continued, smiling up at a young and spotty waiter as he placed a bowl of salad in front of her. 'And he's not at all academic, is he?'

'He's really smart!' I cried. 'I don't know why you seem to think rugby players are all just a bunch of thugs! He's well-read, and funny, and he can *always* see the best way to approach a problem. He's the most logical person I've ever met. And those guys do business training, and personal development, and learn how to deal with the media and – and *heaps* of stuff! They don't just practise chucking a ball around.'

Em's response to this little tirade was most unsatisfactory; she merely unwrapped the serviette from around my knife and fork, passed them across the table and said soothingly, 'Eat your eggs, sweetie, before they get cold.'

30

ON ANZAC DAY, FOR THE FIRST TIME DURING MY SIXTEEN months' occupancy of Rex's cottage, I inched the stove out from the wall and looked behind it. It wasn't good. Still, there are worse ways to spend a morning than exhuming a petrified mouse from behind the stove; Dad and Em, for example, were listening to Caitlin and twenty other children playing either 'The Entertainer' or 'Flight of the Bumblebee' at a piano recital in the scout hall.

I fetched a pair of latex gloves from the back of the ute and clambered over the bench into the gap behind the stove. I had removed the mouse and was scrubbing drearily at the floor with a pot scourer when I heard a car pull in, and levered myself up to see who it was.

'Hey, Nell,' said Lance, putting his head around the door. 'What's new?'

'Not a lot,' I said. 'How are you?'

'Good. Just on my way back to Hamilton from Mum and Dad's. You've got cobwebs in your hair.'

I ran a hand over my head to dislodge them. 'Coffee?'

He nodded, came across the kitchen and filled the kettle, looking distastefully at the mouse. 'Are you keeping that for a special occasion, or can I chuck it?'

'Please chuck it. How are your parents?'

'Good,' he said. 'They miss you.'

'That's nice of them. But what about your lawyer?'

'Lawyer?' he asked, opening the kitchen window and flinging the mouse out across the lawn.

'Weren't you seeing a lawyer?'

'Only briefly. Tea?'

'Coffee, please,' I said.

'Are you supposed to be drinking coffee?'

'The midwife said it was fine.'

'It's just that Kate's been steering clear of caffeine.'

'Good on her,' I said shortly. 'I'm sure her baby will turn out much better than mine.' I dropped my filthy scourer into an equally filthy basin of water and pushed it across the bench.

Lance picked up the basin and poured the water down the sink, maintaining a tactful silence.

'Sorry,' I said.

'No, fair enough,' he said. 'It's none of my business.'

That irritated me, either due to extreme prickliness on my part or because 'It's none of my business' is another of those magic statements that doesn't mean what it says. I climbed back over the kitchen bench as Murray sauntered in and wound himself around Lance's ankles.

'G'day, Murray,' he said. 'You're getting fat, mate.'

'He's probably going out in sympathy,' I said.

'Those neutered-male cat biscuits from Royal Canin are good for weight loss.'

'He's on them.'

'He should be on less of them, then. Try decreasing the amount you're feeding him by a third.'

'Yes, Lance,' I snapped.

'You're in a lovely mood today, aren't you?' he remarked.

'Sorry. It's been a crappy couple of weeks.'

'How come?'

'Because Mark's finally got sick of it all and left.'

'That's no good,' said Lance.

The complete absence of surprise in his voice stung. Which seemed unfair, because you'd think that abject misery would at least ensure that nothing else anyone might say or do could hurt you. 'Mm,' I said.

He reached out and rubbed my shoulder. 'Is he going to have anything to do with the baby?'

'I don't know. We've only got as far as screaming at each other.'

'I imagine that having Mark Tipene screaming at you would be fairly scary,' he said thoughtfully. 'Shit, he's big.'

'I think I was the one doing most of the screaming,' I said.

He grinned. 'Now, why doesn't that surprise me?'

Had Lance always been this annoying, I wondered, or was I just becoming crankier and less tolerant as I aged?

'I was watching the highlights of his game yesterday,' he said. 'He smashed some poor innocent bloke's knee to bits.'

I, too, had watched the highlights of that game. 'Not on purpose!' I cried.

'What do you mean "not on purpose"? He lined him up from about twenty metres away!'

'He *tackled* him! It's a contact sport!'

'Keep your hair on,' said Lance. 'Well, I hope he's at least going to pay you some child support.'

'I'm sure he will,' I said wearily. Then, because if the subject wasn't changed I was going to do a whole lot more screaming, I added, 'Would you be able to give me a hand to take my bed apart?'

'Why are you taking your bed apart?'

'So I can get it through the door. I'm moving – my landlord wants this place for his son.'

Lance sighed. That bed had slats on a wooden box framework, and it was a pig of a thing to dismantle and put up again. 'Got a spanner?' he asked.

'You can have your coffee first,' I said. 'I'll even give you a biscuit.'

'No,' he said sadly. 'Let's just get it over with.'

We went up the hall and manhandled the mattress off the base of the bed to lean it against the wall. 'I'll undo the bolts if you'll stop it falling on me,' I said.

'Nell, there's no way you'll fit under there.' He plucked the spanner from my hand and slid under the bed to attack the first bolt. 'You know, it's poor form to ask a man to lie on someone else's underpants.' And a pair of grey cotton boxer shorts came flying out across the room.

'Sorry,' I said, bending to pick them up and straightening again with a little grunt. What are you supposed to do with your ex-boyfriend's undies? Wash them and post them back? Burn them on their own little funeral pyre, as part of the quest for healing and closure? Keep them under your pillow to cuddle up to as you fall asleep? In the meantime I settled for putting them down on the windowsill.

'Don't mention it. Do you think they'd be worth anything on Trade Me?'

'I doubt it,' I said. 'It'd be hard to prove whose they were.'

'DNA testing?' Lance suggested, and I smiled despite myself.

There was a short silence while he wrestled with a bolt, and then he said, 'How many times have I done this now?'

'Um. Four, I think.'

'Is that all?'

'End of third year, end of fourth year, end of fifth year and before we went overseas.'

'It just feels like more,' he said. 'Can you steady the end?'

I crouched down and held the corner of the bed's frame. 'Is that okay?'

'Yeah, fine. You know, I reckon you've had a narrow escape. I was reading an article about early-onset arthritis in rugby players, and apparently the whole lot of them are cripples by the time they get to sixty. And they're the ones who are sixty *now*; they played a hell of a lot less games forty years ago.'

'But they patch them up a lot better these days,' I pointed out.

'There's still not much you can do about having no cartilage left in any of your joints.'

'They can replace knees and hips.'

'Not shoulders. Or fingers. How many of them has he dislocated?'

'I don't know. A few.'

'There you go. Those'll all be buggered in another ten years. You would have ended up wiping his bum for him.'

'I wouldn't have minded,' I muttered.

He passed me out a handful of bolts and shuffled along to the next corner. 'You're pathetic. And there's another reason you should have been heading for the hills.'

'What?' I asked.

'Do you know what the All Blacks' motto is?'

'"Feed your backs"?'

'Nope. It is – and I kid you not – "Subdue and penetrate".'

'I don't believe you.'

'Google it then.'

'Maybe it didn't sound so dodgy a hundred years ago when they came up with it,' I said weakly.

'Of course it did. It's not like human biology's changed since then. Very shady people, rugby players. Can you move along a bit?'

Turning to drop the handful of bolts on the floor behind me I glimpsed two large bare feet crossed one over the other in the bedroom doorway. Mark was leaning against the doorframe with his arms folded, and as my startled gaze lifted to his face he looked at me with a mixture of uncertainty and amusement and love that nearly stopped my heart.

As I got shakily to my feet, Lance said, 'Hold the thing steady, would you?'

Mark pushed himself away from the door and held his arms out, and I hurled myself across the room at him and clung like a limpet. He wrapped his arms hard around me, dropping his face into my hair.

'Nell!' said Lance, but I barely even heard his voice.

The baby, compressed in a feverish embrace, began to drum its heels against my abdominal wall in protest. Mark took half a step back and moved his hands to my stomach.

'He doesn't like being squished,' I whispered.

'Sorry.'

'*I* like it.'

'Good,' he said, and kissed me.

From somewhere far, far away came a muffled shout. Mark pulled his mouth away from mine and went across the room to lift the collapsed bed frame off poor Lance, who didn't, it seemed, like being squished any more than the baby did. He crawled out of the wreckage and scrambled to his feet, looking both angry and embarrassed.

'Are you okay?' Mark asked him.

'Fine.'

The tumult of joy receded a little – only a little, but enough to let in a touch of remorse. Being rescued from underneath a bed by a man six inches taller and forty kilograms heavier than you are can't be good for a chap's self-respect.

'I'm so sorry,' I said. 'Are you sure you're okay?'

'Just dandy,' said Lance.

'Mark, Lance,' I said. 'Lance, Mark.'

'Hi,' said Mark with an almost complete lack of enthusiasm.

'Hi.'

'I'm really sorry,' I said humbly.

'It's fine,' said Lance, massaging his elbow. 'It looks like you're all sorted here – I'll be off.'

I caught up with him at the kitchen door. 'Thank you.'

'You're welcome. You can just call the kid after me or something.'

'I'll take that on board,' I said. 'And, hey, cool sideburns.'

'You reckon?' asked Mark, coming to the door behind me as Lance turned his car.

I waved and shut the door. 'Reckon what?'

'That his sideburns are cool. I thought they made him look like a total dick.'

'Total dick' was a bit harsh – Lance's sideburns were really no worse than mildly silly. With an old-fashioned cravat around his neck he would have made a lovely Regency dandy. 'I was just trying to say something nice,' I said. 'It seemed the least I could do, after dropping a bed on him.'

'Ah,' said Mark. 'Right.'

There were tired creases at the corners of his eyes, and the knuckles of his right hand were grazed and swollen. He looked tough and sexy and grown-up. 'Is your shoulder okay?' I asked.

'Yeah.'

'What happened to your hand?'

'Stomped on in a ruck.'

'Is it very sore?'

'It's alright. It'll just mean the arthritis sets in a bit quicker, I suppose. A few less years of being able to wipe my own bum.'

I smiled. 'How long were you there before I saw you?'

'K-Y man was just going to put my boxers on Trade Me.'

'Poor Lance. He'll probably never get over it.'

'Good,' said Mark grimly.

'He was only trying to make me feel better.'

'He wasn't. He was trying to weasel his way back into your knickers.'

'Of course he wasn't,' I said.

'I know weaselling when I see it.'

'Well, I suppose you've done plenty of it yourself over the years.'

'Almost none,' he said haughtily.

'Liar,' I said, and hugged him.

He hugged me back, dropping his chin onto the top of my head. 'I love you.'

And only five minutes before, the years were stretching grey and bleak before me, to be spent watching Mark's expressions on his child's face and furtively tracking his love life via the internet. 'Same,' I whispered.

His arms tightened. 'Well, that's a good start,' he said, and taking half a step backwards he picked me up.

'Mark, don't! You'll hurt your shoulder.'

'It's fine.' He carried me across the kitchen and up the hall. I kissed his ear. 'My bed's all in pieces.'

He stopped in my bedroom doorway and let me slide to my feet. 'I'm pretty confident we'll figure something out,' he said.

31

MY ROOM WAS HOT AND STILL, AND THROUGH THE OPEN window came the soft tearing sound of Rex's big white-faced steer pulling up grass on the other side of the fence. Mark was asleep in a broad stripe of sunlight, lying on his side with his arm heavy across my chest. The skin under his eyes looked grey and papery with exhaustion. Normally his ability to sleep anywhere, at any time, was legendary, but perhaps he too had spent the nights of the last fortnight staring at the ceiling.

It was very warm, especially underneath a large hot arm. I began to edge out from underneath it, and Mark stirred, frowning, and pulled me closer. I smiled to myself, threaded my fingers down between his and closed my eyes.

When, blearily, I opened them again, the light had changed. It slanted across the far wall, the dull warm gold of evening, and gleamed on the battered varnish of the chest of drawers in the corner. The wrong corner, now that I came to think of it, and the window was in the wrong place too. It was too high and too far away, and I was drowsily wondering why when the hand cupping my left breast moved down to rest on my stomach instead.

I had, until then, failed entirely to notice that hand. It was big and very brown against my skin, crisscrossed with the faint silvery lines of old scars. I looked at it wonderingly for a few seconds, and then covered it with mine.

'Hey,' said Mark.

Tears rose, stinging, behind my eyelids. 'Hey.'

'Nice bump.'

I moved his hand sideways. 'Feel there. You have to press quite hard.'

He did. 'Foot?'

'No, I think it's a bottom. There's a foot over here somewhere.' I felt for it in its normal spot, beneath my ribs. 'There. He's started getting the hiccups – it feels really weird.'

He prodded the little foot gently, and it withdrew. 'I bet it does,' he said. Then, almost under his breath, 'In a couple of months we're going to be parents.'

'It's terrifying, isn't it?'

'Yep,' he said.

I squirmed around in his arms to face him. 'Em says I've been acting like the baby's none of your business. Have I?'

There was a short silence, which effectively answered the question before he spoke. 'Yeah. A bit.'

'Mark, I'm so sorry,' I said.

He smiled at me. 'That's okay.'

'I just – I didn't want to pressure you, when you've got the World Cup and your shoulder and everything else to worry about already. I didn't want you staying just because I'd guilted you into it.'

'I'm not that noble, McNeil. And I don't think staying with someone you're not happy with does your children any favours.'

'Is that what your parents did?' I asked.

He was silent for so long I thought he wasn't going to reply at all. 'Mum used to say that if it wasn't for Rob and me she'd leave,' he said finally. 'But why the hell she thought having divorced parents would be worse for us than growing up with that shit is completely beyond me.'

I lay very, very still, holding my breath lest he stop talking.

'We spent our whole time creeping around trying not to make a noise,' he said. 'When they weren't fighting you could feel the pressure building up until you almost wished they were. They'd get pissed and start shouting at each other – sometimes I think Mum did it on purpose. It was like if she could wind him up enough to make him lose it and thump her, she'd won.' His voice was level and matter-of-fact, and he turned his head to rub his cheek against my hair. 'Once Rob got in between them. I was about five, so he must have been seven or eight. Mum was screaming – he'd split her lip, I think; her face was covered in blood, anyway – and Rob ran in, and Dad picked him up and threw him against the wall.'

I buried my head in the hollow of his shoulder and hugged him tighter. His skin was hot and smooth, and he smelt faintly of Deep Heat. When I was five I was my mother's best helper, and my father's right-hand girl, and I had never seen either of them drink more than a glass or two of wine with a meal.

'Broke his collarbone, poor little sod,' he added.

'What about you?' I asked.

'Me? I was fine. I probably ran away and hid. I wasn't the bravest kid.'

'You were *five*! Did it happen very often?'

'Not really. I think the threat of violence was worse than the violence itself, if that makes sense.'

I nodded.

There was a short silence, and then he said quietly, 'I wouldn't ever hit you or the baby.'

I stiffened, horrified that he should think I needed reassurance. '*Mark!* I know that!'

'Well, you know what they say about the cycle of domestic violence. And then rugby players are pretty dodgy. All that subduing and penetrating.'

I giggled, and then sobered abruptly. 'That's not funny.'

'No,' he agreed. 'Would you sing something for me?'

'Sure,' I said. 'What?'

'That thing you sang for Bel about closing your eyes.'

I sang it, and he lay and watched me in the fading light as though I was something rare and precious that he couldn't quite believe was his.

I will never forget this, I told myself. *I will never forget how this feels, right this moment.*

He reached for my hand. 'Thank you,' he said. And then, in order to save us from being overwhelmed completely by the beauty and significance of the moment, he added, 'You don't know any Megadeth songs, do you, McNeil?'

'How was your flight back from South Africa?' I asked, reaching a tin of crushed pineapple down from the top shelf of the pantry.

Mark, who was buttering bread shirtless and with his hair standing up on end, yawned and scratched his stomach. 'Long,' he said. 'We left Jo'burg at around six on Saturday evening and got in last night about ten.'

'That's hideous.'

'Well, you lose half a day with the time difference.' He put down his knife and turned to open the fridge. 'What do you want on your toasted sandwich?'

'Pineapple and cheese, please. Do you want bacon?'

'Hmm,' he said. 'Why not? The Hawaiian toastie.'

'I only saw the highlights of your last game,' I said, putting my tin of pineapple down on the bench beside him. 'But that try off the end of the lineout was brilliant.'

'Yeah, it worked out well. It always makes Bob happy when his set-piece moves come off. Do you want me to put the stove back?'

'Yes, please.'

As he pushed the stove back into its corner, the phone began to ring, and I crossed the kitchen to retrieve it from the end of the table. 'Hello?'

'Hi, sweetie.'

'Hi,' I said. 'How was the concert?'

'It was fine,' said Em. 'Caitlin did very well. Now, how are you?'

'Really good.'

'*Are* you?'

'Yes,' I said, smiling. I went back across the kitchen to lean against Mark, because any moment not spent touching him was a moment wasted. He slid his arms around me and pulled me back against him. 'Mark's here.'

'Oh, *sweetie*,' Em cried. 'That's just *wonderful*.'

'I know.'

'So you've managed to sort yourselves out?'

'Yeah, I think so,' I said. I tilted my head back to look at him, and he kissed my nose.

'Thank heavens for that. Well, I won't hold you up – I'm sure you have *far* better things to do than talk to me.' Her voice fairly oozed innuendo, and Mark grinned.

'I'll call you tomorrow,' I said.

'Yes, you do that. Have a lovely evening. Has he asked you to move in with him yet?'

I began profoundly to regret holding this conversation eight inches from the man's left ear. 'Um –' I started.

'Bring it up in bed,' she said firmly. 'Now's the time, while you're still on a high from making up. All those endorphins, or pheromones, or whatever they're called, will be zinging around the place – give him a blow job and he'll probably *propose*.'

I made a small strangled gulping noise, which she interpreted as embarrassment.

'Good grief, sweetie,' she said. 'If you weren't pregnant I would seriously question whether you understood the facts of life at all.' And, with a parting snigger, she hung up.

'I'd say anyone who'd spent more than half an hour with that woman would have a fairly good grasp of the facts of life,' Mark said thoughtfully, resting his chin on the top of my head.

I put the phone down on the bench. 'They sure would.'

'Do you want to move in?'

'Yes,' I said recklessly.

'Awesome. When?'

I twisted out of his arms and stared at him. 'Really?'

He laughed. 'Yes!'

'Are you *sure*?'

'Of course I'm sure. I think it's time we stopped mucking around and did this properly, don't you?'

'Um, yes,' I said, slightly dazed.

'Why don't you come this weekend?' he said. 'Then you won't have to move twice.'

I began to laugh helplessly. 'I'm on call this weekend, for a start. And I can't leave work with less than a week's notice.'

'A couple of weeks, then.'

'The baby's not due for nearly three months! I can't just swan around on holiday at your place for three months.'

'Why not?' Mark said. 'You can get things ready for the baby – make me nice things to eat . . . It'll be great.'

It sounded wonderful. 'I'll talk to Nick,' I said.

'Thank you.'

I smiled. 'How are we going to fit a baby into your place, by the way?'

Mark shrugged. 'Babies are pretty small.'

'Yeah, but they come with such a lot of equipment.'

'We'll empty out a drawer or something. It'll be fine. And we'll move after the World Cup.'

'You've really thought this through, haven't you?' I said.

He took my face in his hands. 'Yeah,' he said softly. 'I really have.'

32

MARK LEFT FOR TRAINING AT SEVEN THE NEXT MORNING with extreme reluctance. One day off seemed a little harsh after a fortnight overseas, but apparently a special lineout-overhauling session was needed before Saturday's game. I spent from seven to seven-fifty drifting around the house in a pink-tinged sentimental daze, and then floated out to the ute and off to work.

'Good morning, Thomas!' I said as I passed his desk.

He was frowning at his computer screen, and didn't look up. 'Have you got any BVD vaccine in your ute?' he asked.

'No.'

'*Fuck*,' he said. 'The computer says we've got two hundred doses in stock, and there's fucking none in the fridge.'

'Didn't Keri use some last Friday on those calves at Townsend's? That won't have been charged yet.'

Thomas dropped his head into his hands. 'Why can't you lot let me know when you take the last bottle off the shelf? It's not *that* fucking hard, is it?'

I thought it safest not to reply, and edged past him to look at the day sheet. At the top of my column were the words *Pryor take parcel 8.30.*

'What am I taking out to Pryor's?' I asked.

'Bag behind the counter.'

'What's the call for?'

'Why don't you go and find out?' he snapped. 'Where the hell is Keri?'

Thus I arrived at Kelvin Pryor's cowshed with no idea of what I was there to do. Kelvin was a gnome-like fellow in his fifties who farmed ten minutes north of town. He walked like a pigeon, with his chest well forward and his bottom well back, and he had a touching faith in his own irresistibility to women.

As I pulled in he appeared in the milk room doorway and beamed at me across the gravel. 'And how are we today, my dear?' he asked.

'Very well, thanks,' I said. 'How are you?'

'Oh, can't complain. No point: nobody listens.'

I smiled. 'What can I do for you today, Kelvin?'

'One old girl with a cold, and a couple of empties to check. Think you can handle that?'

In the race was an elderly Jersey cow with a nasty-smelling nasal discharge, and after catching her in the head bail I pulled three long spiky sticks from her left nostril with a pair of curved forceps. I love pulling sticks out of cows' noses; not only do you get a pleasant self-congratulatory glow from having done the cow a major service, but removing thirty centimetres of thistle stalk from a nostril looks so nice and impressive. It's almost as good as lancing a really serious abscess.

I had just removed stick number three and was feeling around cautiously with my forceps for more when the cow sneezed, hitting me squarely in the chest with about a cupful of bloody snot. Squarely in the chest isn't too much of a worry – it's squarely in the face that puts you off your stride – and I continued probing undeterred until Kelvin pulled a handkerchief from his trouser pocket, bustled forward and began to wipe me down.

That *did* deter me, and taking a hasty step backwards I turned to rummage in my drug box. 'Um, right,' I said. 'Antibiotics – and we'd better give her an anti-inflammatory, or she'll push another stick up there to try and stop it itching.'

'Whatever you feel is best, my dear,' he said warmly. 'You're the professional.'

I had cleaned up and was writing a docket on the milk room bench when he approached again, holding out a spray bottle. 'What do you think of this stuff?' he asked.

I looked at the bottle and discovered that it contained a miracle udder liniment, guaranteed to reduce pain and swelling. 'I've seen the ad in the *Dairy Exporter*, but that's about it,' I said. 'Does it work?' Personally I doubted that it would, since it's a bit of a stretch to ask something you rub on the skin to kill the bacteria lurking in the tissues ten centimetres down, but I had learnt through bitter experience that belittling someone's pet alternative treatment is almost as offensive as telling them their kid looks funny. (My all-time low was attending a cat after-hours wearing a T-shirt which read *Homeopathy, making damn-all difference since 1796*, and then learning that the cat's owner was a certified homeopath.)

'It's marvellous,' said Kelvin. 'Absolutely marvellous. I even used it on my daughter when she had a touch of mastitis after her little one was born. You just massage it in . . .'

'What happened to *you*?' asked Richard half an hour later, pausing en route to the back door of the clinic to look me up and down.

'Fell into a bucket of zinc oxide,' I said, scrubbing at the backs of my legs with a wet towel.

'I suppose you get that when you can't see your feet.'

'No, you get that when Kelvin Pryor tried to do a special, hands-on demonstration of how to rub your breasts with udder cream, and you trip over a hose as you're trying to escape.' And even worse than being felt up by Kelvin the Gnome was the recollection that rather than getting up and slapping him, I'd apologised for my clumsiness as I climbed out of my overalls and tipped white slurry from my gumboots. Being brought up to always be nice to people can be a terrible handicap. And *then*, just to really add insult to injury, I'd had to go back because I'd forgotten to give him his parcel.

'It's your own fault,' said Richard, stepping into his gumboots. 'You're too nice to him – he probably thinks you've got a crush on him.'

'Oh, shut up.'

The seat of my shorts was caked in zinc slurry, so I took them off and put them in the washing machine, and donned a clean pair of Nick's overalls. This, however, only partly solved my clothing problems, because when I bent down the overalls gaped at the sides, showing my knickers. In a burst of inspiration I went along the hall into the vet room, took a stapler from Anita's top drawer and stapled up the side vents.

Nick was at his desk, immersed as usual in paperwork. 'What on earth are you doing?' he asked, turning in his chair.

'I sat down in a bucket of drenching zinc and had to wash my shorts, and I thought walking around with my undies showing through the slits in my overalls – well, actually your overalls – wasn't the most professional look,' I said.

'Right. I see.' He looked me up and down. 'Whereas your current look is *highly* professional.'

I grinned. 'Sorry, boss. It's the best I can do until my shorts dry. Have you got a minute?'

'What's up?' he asked.

'Would you mind if I went on maternity leave a bit earlier than I was going to?'

'When were you thinking?'

'Another few weeks?' I asked tentatively.

Nick sat back in his chair and looked at me. 'I thought you were planning to stop on the side of the road somewhere between calvings to produce this child, and then tie it on your back and keep going,' he said.

'There's been a slight change of plan. I'm going to go and live with Mark instead.'

'Are you now? Well, that would have to be a step in the right direction.'

'Mm,' I said, feeling my cheeks get hot. It would have been nice to think I'd succeeded in hiding the shambles of my love life from my colleagues behind a facade of dignified calm, but evidently I hadn't.

'So presumably you won't be coming back to work,' he said.

I shook my head. 'I'm so sorry to be leaving you in the lurch.'

'That's alright,' said Nick. 'We'll manage. Although I must say it would have been a lot more considerate of you to get yourself knocked up by someone local.'

'Then you'd never have got rid of me,' I pointed out.

'Well, there is that,' he said, returning to his paperwork.

I left him to it and went along the hall to the shop to see if Thomas had recovered from the vaccine debacle. He had the portable phone in his hand, but on seeing me he put it down and said crisply, 'Cat for you to see.'

So that would be a no. I let myself into the consult room, where I found Fenella Martin.

Awesome, I thought, and meant it. It wasn't even morning tea time, and I'd already been sexually harassed, and now my veterinary skills were about to be examined and found wanting. If I had needed some kind of sign from above to reassure me that leaving was the right move, here it was.

'Hi, Fenella,' I said, closing the door behind me. 'How are you?'

'*I'm* fine. It's Fiona who has the problem.' She opened the door of the wicker cat cage on the table and bent to peer in. 'Come on, precious. Come on out for Mummy. Yes, I know it's scary.'

While she extracted Fiona I admired her new haircut. She had mowed a patch on top of her head, fifteen centimetres square and a precise half-inch long, leaving the sides and back untouched. It looked like a landing pad for tiny helicopters.

'What's Fiona's problem?' I asked.

'She's got a nasty urine infection,' said Fenella, unhooking the last claw from the farthest corner of the box and dragging the patient out into the open.

'Have you seen blood in her urine?'

'I've been finding little red spots on the carpet for weeks, but I didn't know which cat it was,' she said. 'I put garlic in all of their food, and it did help, but this morning I caught her weeing on my bed, and she cried when I picked her up. Didn't you, baby?' She picked up the cat and rubbed its cheek against hers.

'Is she a nervous cat?' I asked.

Fenella stiffened. 'None of my animals are nervous. They're all loved and secure. Every one of them is special. People who aren't prepared to care for their animals shouldn't be allowed to have them.'

'The reason I ask is that cats are quite prone to getting a funny irritable bladder syndrome,' I said. 'You tend to see it in more highly strung animals.'

'She *is* very sensitive,' said Fenella. 'She was mistreated as a kitten before I got her, you know.'

This came as no surprise – Fenella claimed that every animal she owned had been mistreated before she got it.

Fiona's bladder, when palpated through the abdominal wall, was the size and shape of a walnut, and she cried when I pressed it.

'You're hurting her!' Fenella snapped.

'I'm sorry.' I stroked the little cat between the ears. 'I won't touch it again. You're quite right: she's got cystitis.'

'I don't want those little pink tablets. They don't work. Give me the paste.'

'Actually, I don't think she's got an infection,' I said. 'Feline cystitis seems to be an inflammatory reaction – you know how some people get eczema when they're stressed? Cats get inflamed bladders.'

'She's not under any stress.'

'All sorts of things can set it off,' I continued doggedly. 'A new pet in the house is the most common one – have you got a new kitten or anything like that?'

'I've got two new queens,' said Fenella. 'One's a sister to Florence, my little seal-point. Marvellous bloodline. Lovely long, tapering faces – their mother was best in show at Central Districts last year, you know.'

'Wow,' I murmured.

'And she *should* have won in Napier, but the judging there was appalling. I laid a formal complaint.'

Of course she did. 'Well, I expect that'll be why Fiona's cystitis has flared up,' I said. 'There *are* other reasons for blood in the urine, but that's the most common one. So either we can do blood and urine tests now, or we can start her on pain relief and a special cystitis diet, and if it all settles down we'll know we're on the right track.'

'And if it doesn't settle down?'

'That's when we'd do the tests, to rule out things like diabetes. But ninety percent of the time we don't need to.'

'Alright,' said Fenella. 'We'll try that.'

'The only thing that's going to be a hassle for you is making sure that she only eats the special food,' I said.

'That's fine. I can feed her separately.'

'And she's not allowed to eat anything else, so you can't leave normal cat biscuits out between meals.'

'But my cats are snackers,' she said. 'They come and go as they please, and help themselves. Animals shouldn't be forced to work in with human routines.'

'Perhaps you could leave biscuits out for the others during the day, and shut this little girl in your room with a litter tray. That way she would get a bit of time out from the others, too.'

'I couldn't,' said Fenella. 'She would be beside herself with loneliness.'

'Cats do tend to be solitary animals,' I said.

'Not *my* cats.'

'Well, the others can eat the special cystitis biscuits, if you like. It's just quite an expensive diet for animals that don't need it.'

'I'm not made of money, you know.'

I took a deep breath and turned to get a box of cat pain-relief drops from the cupboard behind me. 'How about giving it a try for a week? I expect she'd be quite happy to have a little bit of time on her own. Now, you've had these drops before, haven't you?'

'I don't remember,' said Fenella sulkily. 'And I want the paste, not the tablets.'

'She doesn't need antibiotics,' I said.

'But you just said she's got a bladder infection.'

Yep, I thought, *definitely a sign*.

33

ON MY WAY ALONG DAD AND EM'S HALL THAT EVENING I
met Caitlin coming the other way, naked and with a towel
wrapped around her head. 'Hi, Helen,' she said. 'Can you help
me make fudge?'

'Sure. If your mum says it's okay.'

'Mum!' she roared, and I felt the baby jerk in alarm. 'Can I
make fudge with Helen?'

'Is Helen here?' Em shouted back from upstairs.

'Yes!' I called.

'Come here!'

'Me or Helen?' Caitlin yelled.

'Helen!'

I headed stairwards, and Caitlin turned and came too. 'Where
were you going?' I asked, curious.

'To get my sneakers out of the car,' she said. 'But I can do
it later.'

'I hear your piano piece yesterday went really well.'

'Yes,' she said complacently. 'Mum's in the bathroom.'

Em was seated on the edge of the bath in knickers, singlet and latex gloves, rubbing fake tan into her legs. 'Well?' she asked, looking up and smiling at me.

I smiled back. 'It's all good.'

'*Details*, sweetie! Come on!'

'He came back, and he loves me, and we're going to move in together and do this properly.'

Em squealed, raised both arms in celebration and fell backwards into the empty bath. 'I'm okay!' she called.

Caitlin and I rushed forward to help her up. 'Don't touch my hands!' she ordered. 'You'll be covered in fake tan.' We took a forearm each and pulled her up to sit. 'Sweetie, that's *fabulous* news.'

'I know,' I said, laughing.

'Helen, is Mark going to come and live at your new house?' Caitlin asked.

'No, I'm going to go and live at his house.'

'Are you going to get married?'

'No.'

'Let's not run before we walk, my darling,' Em said briskly, stripping off her gloves and getting to her feet. 'All in due course.'

'You're *supposed* to get married before you have a baby,' said Caitlin. 'Now can we make fudge?'

'Caitlin, it's nearly tea time,' said her mother. 'We're not making fudge right now.'

'*Mum!* If we don't make it before Bel gets home she'll want to help, and she'll make a really big mess.'

'No.'

'But *Mu-um* . . .'

'*No*, Caitlin!' said Em as a door slammed downstairs.

'Mum!' Bel shouted. 'Caitlin! I got a sticker at dancing!'

'That's wonderful, sweetie!' Em called. 'Caitlin, how about you go and put some clothes on?'

'I have to go and see Bel's sticker first,' Caitlin said, stalking from the bathroom with a hand clapped to the towel on her head.

'Horrible child,' said Em. 'Why don't you go and tell your father the good news while I make myself decent?'

I followed Caitlin downstairs into the kitchen, where Dad was filling the kettle. Bel, in stripy leggings and a purple T-shirt with a good inch of tummy showing between the two, solemnly extended the back of her hand.

'Cool,' said Caitlin.

'I *know*,' said Bel. She threw her arms around her sister and the two of them performed a celebratory caper, during which the towel on Caitlin's head slithered to the floor. 'Look, Helen!'

'It's beautiful,' I said, duly admiring the sticker. It read *Dancing Queen!* and was both pink *and* sparkly. 'What did you do to get it?'

'I was a tree, with wind in my branches.'

'Wow. Can you show me?'

Bel looked at me pityingly. 'Of course not,' she said. 'I need the music. Daddy, I'm starving to death.'

'Would you like a piece of cheese?' he asked. Dentists don't really approve of eating between meals, but if you must snack at least let it be dairy. Or bread. But never raisins – the very thought almost prostrates them with horror.

'Yes!'

'I'm starving too,' Caitlin said.

'Aren't you cold?' Dad asked, getting a block of cheese out of the fridge.

She shook her head. 'Just hungry.'

'Poor little waif,' said Dad, and she giggled. He cut two slices of cheese and handed them out. 'Now vamoose. Go and get dressed.'

'Take your towel!' I called after them, but Caitlin, who can detect the rustle of a crisp packet at a hundred metres, continued serenely up the stairs.

'So,' said Dad, 'I hear it's all back on.'

'Yes.'

'Very good.' He cut a third slice of cheese, speared it on the end of his knife and held it out to me.

'Thank you,' I said. 'How was work?'

'Oh, about the usual. Nothing too startling. You?'

'Well, I did get felt up by Kelvin Pryor. That was pretty startling.'

An expression of mild surprise crossed Dad's face. 'Wouldn't have thought he had it in him,' he said.

'A proper father would roar round there and beat him to a pulp,' I remarked.

'Did he frighten you?'

'No,' I said, nibbling my cheese. 'It was just all a bit unpleasant.'

'I'm sure it was. You know, he's coming in next week for a root canal. It's funny how sometimes the local doesn't work as well as you'd expect.'

'I love you, Dad,' I said. 'Hey, would it be okay with you and Em if I came and stayed for a couple of weeks from this weekend?'

'I expect so. Why?'

'I'm going to finish work on the thirteenth of May and go and live with Mark, so it seems a bit pointless to move into a new place for two weeks.'

'Go and live with him permanently?' he asked.

'Yep.'

'Are you sure you've thought this out? That's a fairly drastic step, considering that last week it was all over.'

'I know,' I said.

'You've got nobody in Auckland except him,' said Dad. 'And he's not there half the time.'

'I can always come and annoy you if I get lonely.'

'And babies change everything. They're incredibly demanding little things.'

'I know,' I said again. I didn't – I had all but left home by the time Caitlin was born – but I had been imagining the worst for some months now. 'Dad, I'm scared out of my tiny mind. But – but if it all turns to custard, at least I'll know we gave it a really good try.'

My father took off his glasses and began to polish them on the hem of his shirt, which was disheartening.

'I love him a lot,' I offered.

'Yes,' he said heavily. 'I know.'

Em came downstairs, swathed from throat to ankle in a very glamorous pink satin dressing gown that cried out for a pair of pink feathered mules. 'Have you told him?' she asked, pulling the sash tight around her waist.

'Yes,' I said. 'He's polishing. Not a good sign.'

She looked at Dad with her head on one side. 'Tim?'

'Hmm?' He ceased to polish and swung his glasses by one stem instead.

'What's wrong, love?' asked Em.

'Nothing's wrong,' he said testily. 'I'm just not convinced that Helen rushing off to live in Auckland at a moment's notice is the best move.'

'Oh, for pity's sake,' she said. 'It's the first sign of intelligence she's shown for months!'

Harsh, I thought. *True, quite possibly, but harsh nonetheless.*

'And anyway, it's got to be better than having her mope around here with big, lost eyes like a baby seal's.'

'Hey!' I said indignantly.

'You *have* been. For *months*! We've been *beside* ourselves with worry!'

'I'm so sorry.'

'That's alright. We love you. But it's high time you did something a bit more proactive.'

'I *am*!' I cried.

'Good,' she said. 'Tim, they'll be fine.'

I was quite touched for a moment, until she added, 'And if it doesn't work out, sweetie, remember you've always got us.'

⁂

Torn between amusement and affront, I went home to my small cold house and found Murray waiting at the door with his tail wrapped around his feet. He sat companionably beside me on the bench while I transformed a packet of two-minute noodles, one limp carrot, half an onion and the dregs of a frozen bag of mixed veggies into possibly the world's least interesting stir-fry, then draped himself across my lap when I sat down on the sofa to try to eat it. I took a mouthful, grimaced and pulled my phone from my pocket to text Mark.

Good day?

He answered straight away. *Yes esp waking up and u there.*

Same. Love you.

Yr door locked?

Yes.

Actually, no. But good point. I put down my stir-fry, and Murray, who ate almost everything but lettuce, didn't even glance at it. Instead he yawned and began to wash his bottom. 'It's not *that* bad,' I told him, struggling to my feet.

The kitchen door opened with a click and a groan, and I jumped about a foot.

'Liar,' Mark called.

34

'DID YOU GET THE LINEOUT SORTED?' I ASKED WHEN WE'D finished acting like the reunion scene from *The Notebook* and settled on the couch.

'Yep,' said Mark, pulling me more closely up against him. 'Running like a well-oiled machine. Hey, I've been thinking about you moving this weekend –'

'All organised. I rang the second-hand shop this afternoon, and they're happy to take all my furniture.' At a fraction of the price they had originally charged me for it, but you get that.

'Yeah, but –'

'And Sam and Alison are coming on Saturday afternoon to help me load it all up. Everything else'll fit in the car, and I'll just have to do a bit of cleaning between after-hours calls. Easy.' I slid my fingers down between his.

'You are not loading furniture in your state.'

'I'm pregnant,' I pointed out. 'Not crippled.'

'Look, why not wait till Sunday, when I can give you a hand?'

'*You'll* be crippled on Sunday.' Post-match blood tests of professional rugby players, according to an article that had done nothing for my enjoyment of Mark's games, show levels of muscle damage comparable to those of car-crash victims. 'Anyway, Sam and Alison are going to the beach. Honestly, love, it'll be fine. I promise not to lift anything heavy.'

'Hmm,' said Mark. He detached his hand from mine, took his iPhone out of his pocket and googled *commercial cleaners Broadview*.

'Are you casting aspersions on my housekeeping skills?' I asked.

'No, I'm trying to help.'

'It's very sweet of you, but the cleaning really won't be a big deal.'

He lowered the phone and looked at me. 'Would you please stop being so bloody self-sufficient and let me do something for you?'

Oh. 'Sorry,' I said meekly. 'Yes. Thank you.'

⁂

I spent Saturday morning from nine till twelve at the clinic, where I microchipped one puppy and admired the speed at which Zoe's thumbs moved across the keypad of her cell phone (a speed she never exhibited when doing anything else).

Sam, Alison and her mother's horse float arrived promptly at one. We loaded up the furniture, and Sam, although he obviously thought I was burning my bridges to a crisp, drove the lot to the second-hand shop while Alison and I packed everything else into my car.

Everything else consisted of three boxes of kitchen equipment, four of books, a wicker laundry basket full of shoes, a shoebox of CDs, three green shot-silk cushions, a black plastic rubbish bag full of bedding and another of towels, my mother's spade, a vacuum cleaner and two suitcases of clothes, most of which didn't fit me. Also one pissed-off cat, yelling from his cage on the porch. It seemed a fairly meagre haul – I had intended to start accumulating grown-up stuff like lounge suites and nice crockery when I got home from overseas, but I was distracted by an All Black.

I crammed the last cushion into the last available bit of space, and Alison sat on the boot to close it. 'Done,' she said.

'Thank you. You're wonderful.'

'You're welcome.'

My cell phone beeped, and I extracted it from my jeans pocket.

Hows it going?

All packed. You? I wrote back. 'Sorry, Ali.'

'It's fine,' she said. 'Is that Mark?'

'Yeah.'

The phone beeped again. *All good x*

xx, I typed. Then I thought for a moment, deleted an x in case he should think I was starting one of those tiresome 'no, I love *you* more' exchanges, pressed send and put the phone back in my pocket.

'Has your dad got used to the idea of you leaving yet?' Alison asked.

'No,' I said. 'He's still shaking his head and muttering. Poor Dad – I can totally see his point. Last week it was all over, and this week we're moving in together. It's enough to worry any parent.'

She smiled.

'Do *you* think I'm making a terrible mistake?' I asked.

'Of course not,' she said. 'But it doesn't matter what I think, as long as you're sure.'

'I am.'

'Good.'

She left for Dad and Em's in my car, and I went slowly back across the lawn and up the porch steps. Empty, the cottage looked smaller, shabbier and depressingly unloved. I made a little farewell tour, retrieving a stray sock and a bottle of body wash as I went, and in a burst of sentimentality kissed the kitchen doorframe on the way back out.

I left the key in the door for the cleaners and turned to look out over the lawn. The grass was the lovely luminous green of autumn and a flock of goldfinches swirled past to settle in rows on the wires of the fence. Just the setting for a bit of pensive contemplation on the closing of a chapter in one's life – except that it's impossible to be properly pensive with a caged cat wailing at your feet. I gave up the attempt, carried Murray out to the ute and went to Dad and Em's, where I spent the rest of the day making plaster-of-Paris fridge magnets, having my toenails painted Smurf blue and stitching up a wounded pig dog.

I had a midwife's appointment on Wednesday afternoon. Originally billed as the Birth Plan appointment, it had, due to my imminent departure from the district, been scaled down to a referral and farewell chat. Mark came, which was particularly nice. I wanted to show him to Eloise and prove I honestly wasn't a delusional rugby groupie, and he and Dad were well overdue for a catch-up. I'd been so morbidly aware of pressuring Mark that I had carefully shielded him from all family contact since Christmas, which probably isn't the best way to reassure your father that your boyfriend's a top bloke.

Mark arrived at the clinic at four twenty, and my cunning time-saving plan to meet him in the car park was foiled by a phone call from a woman whose dog may or may not have eaten the plastic wrapping from around a bacon hock. Once inside the clinic, Mark was instantly surrounded and it was quite difficult to extract him again, but it was only four thirty-three when we left for our four-thirty appointment.

We sped across town to the maternity unit, a white-painted prefab tucked in behind the rest home. We parked and made our way along a concrete path between beds of ornamental cabbages to the door, where a handwritten sign on yellowed A4 paper informed us that visiting was strictly by appointment only.

There was nobody in reception, but a buzzer sounded as the door opened and we could hear the murmur of voices from somewhere down the hall. I hadn't been here since visiting Em and a tiny crumpled Annabel six years before – my midwife's appointments to date had been at Eloise's office on the main street – but the decor had changed very little. Even the *Breast Is Best* poster on the wall across the room was the same.

'Lovely,' Mark said, eyeing it doubtfully as we sat down.

'Isn't it just?' The poster was of a large woman sitting on a park bench with her knees spread, a toddler on tiptoe beside her straining to reach the large white boob she was liberating from her shirt. Startling stuff. 'Oh, how was your photo shoot?'

'Pretty heavy going,' he said. 'I had to spray on about four cans of deodorant before they got the shot they wanted. If anyone had struck a match I would've gone up like a torch. Probably still would.'

Publicity shots of Mark were invariably of his head and bare torso, and deodorant is the ideal prop if you want to focus on someone's upper body. I leant over to sniff his neck. 'You're good. You smell nice – sort of citrus-y.'

He smiled. 'I washed with lemon-scented Jif. Good tip.'

'Wonderful stuff, isn't it? You can use it to clean your stove, your toilet, yourself . . .'

Just then a woman screamed somewhere down the hall. It wasn't a loud scream, but rather a breathless high-pitched gasp that suggested she was trying really, really hard to be brave but that it really, *really* hurt. Mark and I stiffened in our plastic chairs.

The sound stopped abruptly, and there was silence. Then a deep agonised groan, fading to a whimper. Then silence. Then another, louder scream, and a burst of panicked sobbing.

Of course I had known that labour hurts. As Kirstie Alley once put it so beautifully, you're pushing something the size of a watermelon out of an opening the size of a lemon, so it's hardly going to be an enjoyable experience. Then again, I'd delivered quite a few calves and lambs and puppies and I'd never heard any animal make a noise like that. And I'd thought, in so far as I'd thought about it at all, that it couldn't be *that* bad. Most women have more than one child, after all. But as we listened to that poor tortured girl down the hall, it occurred to me that perhaps this was going to be a lot nastier than I'd imagined.

Mark put an arm around my shoulders.

'Why don't they *give* her something?' I whispered. 'I thought they had gas and stuff.'

'I don't know.'

I began to time her on the clock above the reception desk. Quiet for forty seconds, leg-being-severed-with-a-hacksaw for twenty-five. Quiet, hacksaw. Quiet, hacksaw.

'Jesus Christ,' Mark muttered. 'Let's go.'

We got to our feet, although it seemed a horribly craven thing to do. Perhaps we shouldn't just slink away – we should burst into the room and demand that the poor woman be given some decent pain relief. Surely as a society we were well past the notion that childbirth was a woman's cross to bear and lessening the agony was somehow immoral.

'Helen, my dear, I'm so sorry, we're going to have to reschedule,' said Eloise, appearing in the doorway from the passage in a blue disposable gown. Her face lit up as she saw Mark beside me. 'Hel-*lo*! Mark? How lovely to meet you!'

There was another scream from the depths of the building.

'You'll have gathered we're a wee bit tied up just now,' she said, smiling. 'All ready for the World Cup?'

There are times when social chitchat is wildly inappropriate, and this was clearly one of them. 'Huh? Yes – look, we'll get out of your way,' said Mark.

'Oh, it'll be a little while before we deliver.'

'Can't you give her something?' I asked.

Eloise looked puzzled.

'For the pain.'

'Yes, of course,' she said. 'She's got the gas.'

'It doesn't seem to be working very well!'

Eloise smiled at me and patted my arm. 'She's doing just fine. Don't you worry. Now, I've organised for your notes to be sent to a midwife at National Women's Hospital – I'll give you a ring a bit later this evening. Okay?'

I nodded.

'Mark, it's *such* a pleasure to meet you,' she said. 'I'm a huge fan.' And with obvious reluctance she went back down the hall.

35

WHEN WE CAME INTO THE KITCHEN TEN MINUTES LATER Em was on the phone. '... Caitlin from music at five, at the Anglican church hall – you go round the back past ... Oh, hang on, Helen's just come in.' She lowered the phone. 'Sweetie, is there any chance you can go and pick up Caitlin? Bel's hurt her arm and your father's been held up at work.'

'Of course,' I said.

'Deb, don't worry, Helen can do it. No, no, we're fine. You're wonderful. Thank you so much – okay, talk soon, take care.' She dropped the phone on the bench and hurried into the lounge, calling back over her shoulder, 'Mark, how lovely to see you. I'm afraid we're having a bit of a crisis.'

Bel lay on the long sofa, wrapped in a pink velour blanket and looking alarmingly pale. 'I fell off the jungle gym,' she whispered, not without pride.

'Did you hurt your arm, McMunchkin?' I asked.

'Mummy thinks it's broken.'

'There's a funny lump above her wrist,' said Em. 'Come on, darling girl, let's get you to the doctor.'

'Want me to carry you to the car, sprat?' Mark asked.

'Yes, but don't bump my arm!' said Bel.

'Yeah, broken arms are pretty sore,' he said, picking her up. 'I was about your size the first time I broke mine.'

'Did you have a cast?' she asked.

'Yep.'

'Did people write on it?'

'Sure did. My brother wrote *Mark sucks*. So he got sent to his room, and my mum drew a shark over the top to hide it.'

'I don't want a shark,' said Bel as they went up the hall. 'I want a unicorn and a princess with a tiara.'

'What about a Humvee with a surface-to-air missile launcher?'

There was a thoughtful pause before Bel said, 'No thank you.'

'How gorgeous,' Em hissed. 'Bless him.'

'What else can we do?' I asked. 'Anything for dinner?'

'No, it's all done, the casserole's in the oven . . . Oh, you wouldn't be able to drop Granny hers, would you? It's all ready for her on the bench, and I was going to take her some carrot cake. It's in the blue Tupperware container in the fridge. She likes to eat by five thirty.'

'No problem,' I said.

'Thanks. You're an angel.' And she hastened down the hallway.

Mark and I should have realised that Caitlin wouldn't fit into his car before the three of us were standing on the pavement outside the Anglican church hall. We didn't, for which our only excuse was that neither of us had quite recovered from our recent brush with childbirth.

'Where am I going to sit?' Caitlin asked.

'Good question,' said Mark. 'Hang on, your ute's just round the corner, McNeil.'

So it was, parked behind the clinic where we had forgotten to collect it after the midwife's appointment. 'I'll go and get it while you two take Granny her tea,' I said.

'I'll come with you,' said Caitlin hastily.

'I'm not taking her her tea!' said Mark. 'She's *your* grandmother.'

'Wimp,' I said, and he smiled.

'Tell you what, you take my car to your grandmother's and I'll go and get your ute.' He handed me his car keys. 'Man, I must love you.'

'I'm honoured,' I said. 'But I've just remembered the ute keys are in my handbag on Dad and Em's kitchen bench.'

The whole operation was only slightly less complicated than the D-Day landings, but in the end a reluctant Caitlin and I set off on foot with Granny's dinner while Mark shuffled vehicles.

Granny's mood that evening was more than usually acidic, and Caitlin and I were quite crushed by the time we emerged from her living room. We found Mark leaning against the ute's bonnet at the kerb.

'All good?' he said.

'She told Caitlin she has a sway back – you don't, Caitlin – and she told me about how the doctor broke her tailbone when he delivered Uncle Simon with forceps.'

'Just what you needed to hear,' Mark said.

'We forgot the plate!' Caitlin cried. 'Mummy always puts the food on one of Granny's plates, because Granny never gives ours back!'

'Run back in and get it,' I suggested.

'No way! *You* go.'

'We'll get it another time,' I said feebly.

❧

The rest of the family were home when we returned. Bel's self-importance knew no bounds; her cast was fluorescent pink and her arm had been X-rayed. She sat in state in Dad's armchair, which had been moved across the big open-plan living area so that it was beside the table, with her blanket draped over her legs and her broken arm in a sling.

'Janelle's allowed to write on my cast, but not Courtney,' she announced.

'Why not?' Mark asked.

'She didn't let me have a turn on the computer at school, even when I said please.'

'Fair enough,' he said.

'I was *very* brave when my arm got X-rayed. Dr Hollis said I was a star. Didn't he, Mummy?'

'Yes, darling,' Em said absently, tipping broccoli from a pot into a china serving dish.

'And then after my arm got X-rayed I – Daddy!'

'Hmm?' said Dad, who was poking around in the depths of the fridge.

'I had to sit on a bed while Alison was winding the bandage up around my arm, and there was a picture of lots of different sore eyes, and one person's eye looked like a hard-boiled egg. And Dr Hollis had a runny nose.'

'How thrilling,' Dad said. He found a bottle of beer and offered it to Mark. 'Drink?'

'No, thanks,' Mark said.

'Right, everyone, come and sit up,' said Em.

'*I* can't,' said Bel importantly.

'No, you can have your dinner in Daddy's chair. Daddy will put some paper across your lap in case of spills.'

Dad put the beer back in the fridge, shut the door and turned to get a newspaper from the basket in the corner. He spread it across Bel's lap and she cried, 'There's a picture of Mark!'

'So there is,' said Dad, picking the paper back up.

'What does the article say?' asked Em.

'It's about sports stars' income from sponsorship deals,' said Dad, skimming through it. 'It's not about Mark in particular.'

'Can I cut out the picture?' asked Bel. 'I want to take it to school for News.'

'Tell them about your arm,' Mark said. 'That's way more interesting.'

'And you *always* take pictures of Mark for News,' said Caitlin.

Mark looked somewhat taken aback.

'Right, sit down, everybody,' Em said. 'I'm afraid dinner tonight's not all I'd hoped.'

'It looks lovely,' I said.

'I *was* planning to make that potato dish with smoked paprika and something nice for dessert, but somebody went and broke her arm.'

Bel giggled.

'Now, Mark, you're off to Christchurch this weekend, aren't you?' Em said, helping him lavishly to casserole.

'Yes,' he said. 'Then Brisbane the weekend after, and then home for a bit.'

'All that travel must get tiring,' Em said.

'I like going on planes,' said Caitlin. 'I've been on two, but Bel hasn't been on any.'

'So what happens when this baby's due?' Dad said abruptly to Mark. 'Are you planning to stay home, or just hoping it's not born while you're on the other side of the world?'

I looked at him in surprise, never having seen my father act even slightly like a heavy parent before.

'Stay home,' said Mark. 'The baby's due the day of the Super Rugby final, so if we're in it, and it's an away game, I won't go. Management's known about it for months; it won't be a problem.'

In response to this eminently reasonable answer Dad only grunted, and I said hurriedly, 'Actually, I'm reconsidering this whole giving-birth thing. I might just stay pregnant instead.'

'I expect you'll change your mind about that over the next couple of months,' said Em. 'Being nine months pregnant isn't all that much fun.'

'It's got to be more fun than labour. There was someone having a baby at the birthing unit this afternoon, and it sounded like they were trying to eviscerate the poor woman.'

'What does eviscerate mean?' Caitlin asked.

'It means you cut a hole in someone's tummy and pull all their insides out,' I said.

She grinned widely. 'Gross.'

'Helen,' said Em reprovingly. 'We're eating.'

'Sorry.'

'Labour's not that bad, sweetie.'

Mark's eyes and mine met across the table in silent mutual scepticism.

'I came out of *your* tummy, didn't I, Mummy?' said Bel, twitching a wrinkle from her blanket.

'Yes, you did.'

'But I came out first,' said Caitlin. 'The first one is always the most special.'

'You're both equally special,' said Em. 'And you will both go to your rooms if you're going to argue about it.'

'I can't,' said Bel. 'My arm is broken. I could *die* in my room by myself.'

'I doubt it.'

'I might!'

'Well, anything is possible, I suppose,' said Em.

'How long were your labours?' I asked her.

'Let me see,' she said thoughtfully. 'With Caitlin I started having contractions around seven at night; my waters broke at four . . . And she was born at nine seventeen in the morning. Bel was quicker, of course, being the second one.'

'You were in second-stage labour for more than *five hours*?'

'That's not bad, for a first baby. I was lucky.'

'Proper full-on contractions?' I asked. 'For all that time?'

Em nodded.

'And it wasn't that bad?'

She shook her head, smiling.

'Dad?' I asked suspiciously. 'Is this true?'

'Not having been the one doing it, I couldn't tell you. But I must say it didn't look like a whole lot of fun from where I was standing,' said Dad.

'I *knew* it!'

'It's just the price humans pay for walking on our hind legs and having large brains,' said Dad. 'Very poor design, really – mothers with narrow pelvises and babies with big heads. I read somewhere that childbirth used to kill about one woman in ten. The rate of stillborn babies would have been much higher again, of course.'

'One in ten?' Mark repeated faintly.

'About that. Not really a problem if you're thinking survival of the species, but pretty rough on the individual. Don't worry, Helen, medicine's come a long way in the last couple of hundred years.'

'Dad, I'm not scared I'm going to die. I'm just scared it's going to hurt a lot.'

'And she'll probably get torn from arsehole to breakfast,' Caitlin put in, carefully pushing her green beans to the side of her plate.

Mark choked.

'Pardon *me*?' Em said.

'Granny said it.'

'Granny,' said Em grimly, 'is an old witch.'

Getting Bel to bed that evening was quite a performance. Her favourite pyjama top wouldn't go on over the cast and nobody could find *The Children's Treasury of Verse*, without which it seemed her life was barely worth living. The book was eventually retrieved from under the couch, Caitlin provided Mabel the china doll on a short-term loan, and Bel, with the air of a princess granting a rare favour, chose Mark to read her a bedtime story.

'This one?' he asked, picking up the *Treasury of Verse*.

'No,' said Bel. '*Sleeping Beauty*.'

'So why did you need the other one?'

'I just did.'

So Mark read *Sleeping Beauty*, and I sang 'Doe, a Deer', 'Bridge Over Troubled Water' and 'I Kissed a Girl and I Liked It'. Then we were dismissed, and made our way downstairs to send up Dad and Em.

'I suppose I'd better think about heading back,' said Mark.

I sighed. 'I wish I was coming with you.'

He stopped at the bottom of the stairs, out of sight of the living room, and put his arms around me. 'Ten more days,' he said softly.

I was reading in my fold-out bed in Em's sewing room when someone tapped on the door. Murray, who had been stretched out beside me, slithered rapidly over the side of the bed and vanished.

'Come in,' I said.

Em pushed the door open and looked around it. 'Everything okay, sweetie?'

'Fine. Is Bel asleep?'

'Out like a light,' she said.

The baby began its nightly tattoo against my abdominal wall, and I smiled. 'Hey, settle down, you little punk.'

Em sat down beside me and laid a hand over my stomach. 'It really is magical, isn't it?' she said. 'That's a little person in there. It can hear your voice, it has its own heartbeat . . .'

'He pushes back when I push on his feet.'

'He?' she asked.

'He – she – who knows?'

'I'd really appreciate it if you had a girl. Then I could empty three cubic metres of pink baby clothes out of the garage, give it all to you and put away the camping gear.'

'I'll see what I can do,' I said solemnly.

'Thank you. Sweetie, try not to worry about labour. You know Granny – upsetting us all is her favourite pastime. It's nice for her to have a hobby, really. It gives her an interest in life.'

'True. Em, thank you.'

'For?' she asked.

'Everything. You've always been so nice to me, even when I was a complete toe-rag.'

'You were not!'

'Yeah, I was.' Imagine trying to iron out the kinks in a new relationship under the suspicious glare of an angry teenager. It was no thanks whatsoever to me that my father wasn't currently shuffling around the house eating baked beans cold from the tin and going on sad, furtive little dates with unsuitable women from the Lonely Hearts column of the paper.

Em giggled. 'You did cause a certain amount of sexual frustration, I will admit.'

I think it says a lot for how much I love my stepmother that I managed to repress a shudder. 'Em,' I said, 'if the baby decides to come early and Mark *is* away, would you be there with me?'

Her eyes filled. 'Oh, *sweetie*,' she said tremulously. 'Of course I will.'

36

ON MY LAST MORNING AT WORK I CLEANED AND EMPTIED my ute, finding a selection of hair ties, socks and, sadly, a Thermos flask of soup that had slipped beneath the driver's seat about seven months ago. Even before finding the flask I was feeling a bit flat – last days are melancholy things. You realise that Monday will roll around with a whole raft of fresh crises that you won't know anything about, and that everyone will cope just fine without you. The clients who only wanted to see you will attach themselves perfectly cheerfully to somebody else, and you'll inevitably drift out of touch with your workmates.

These gloomy reflections were interrupted by Thomas, who appeared at the back door and said, 'Can you go and vaccinate Hamish's herd with the TB read?'

'Sure. When?'

'The cows are waiting on the yard.'

I looked at my watch. 'I'm seeing Mrs Stewart at ten.'

'I've rung her and changed it to eleven,' said Thomas.

'But she's got her book group at ten thirty – we organised it specially.'

'Well, she said eleven would be fine.'

I went, muttering darkly, and was asked when I got there what the hell had taken me so long. It would, I thought, be nice not to be Hamish's vet anymore. It would also have been nice to say goodbye permanently at the end of the call, but you can't have everything.

Mrs Stewart brought me a pair of tiny crystal vases as a goodbye present, Briar Coles dropped in to present me with my very own framed picture of her horse, and a delightful woman whose dog had chronically infected ears brought in a basket of scones with cream and jam and a knitted baby's jacket. It was all very touching, and after work, when my colleagues presented me with a Merino-wool baby's blanket, a copy of Jamie Oliver's latest and shiniest cookbook and a card that sang 'Brown-Eyed Girl', I wept gently into my sparkling grape juice.

'Cheer up,' said Richard bracingly, folding over a slice of pizza and stuffing it into his mouth. 'You can always come back. Nick'll have to give you a job, seeing as you're related to half the clients.'

'Helen can come back any time she likes,' said Nick. 'Relations or no relations.'

'Thank you,' I said.

'I'm so jealous,' said Keri. 'No more work, living with Mark Tipene . . . Shopping with Mark Tipene's credit card . . .'

'That's right,' I said, wiping my eyes. 'I'll just float from lunch date to hair appointment to Pilates class.'

'You might want to wash the cow shit off your neck first,' Nick said. 'Pass the pizza, would you, Richard?'

'I've been in the clinic all afternoon,' I said. 'Could you not have mentioned the cow shit earlier?'

'It's only a little smear. And it brings out your eyes.'

'Thank you. That's so sweet.'

'So you're heading up to Auckland tomorrow?' asked Anita, who had come back in to say goodbye. She captured a passing toddler and held a tissue to his face. 'Blow. Through your *nose*, Liam, not your mouth.'

'Sunday,' I said. 'Mark's playing in Brisbane tomorrow night, and I'm going to an antenatal weekend thing.'

'That one Janet Bennett runs?'

I nodded.

'I wonder if she's still showing the same DVD of a woman giving birth. It was enough to give you nightmares – this awful-looking woman with pubic hair down to her knees, squatting over a video camera.'

'Please, we're trying to eat here,' said Thomas.

'And she'll read you a little book about poo,' Anita continued.

'Why?' I asked.

'Because you'll have to change shitty nappies,' said Keri.

'No, because chances are you'll squeeze one out during the birth.'

Thomas looked like he was going to faint, and I said, 'There's just *nothing* good about childbirth, is there?'

'It's worth it,' said Anita.

There were six couples at the antenatal class when Alison and I got to the scout hall the next morning, none of whom I knew. We sat on cushions in a circle on the floor with the draughts whipping around our ankles and introduced ourselves, and then listened as Janet spoke at some length about our rights. We had lots, apparently, and it was our job to be our babies' advocates. We could refuse blood tests if we wanted to – although why you'd want to was beyond me – and we should insist on being treated with respect and empathy at all times. Then she touched lightly on the desirability of a medication-free birth and we paused for tea and biscuits.

'This is *dire*,' I whispered to Alison.

'Sh!' Alison hissed back. 'She's just behind you.'

Breastfeeding was the first topic after morning tea, and we brainstormed a long list of all the reasons to breastfeed if we could, while Janet wrote them on a whiteboard. 'Bonding – between – mother – and – baby,' she said, scribbling hard. 'Strengthens – baby's – immune – system. Cost – yes, that's right. Formula isn't cheap. Excellent stuff, guys. And that's not all. Breastfed babies have lower obesity rates. They have a *fifty* percent decrease in cancer rates. They're brighter than bottle-fed babies. But you mustn't feel guilty if it doesn't work for you.'

By the end of the day we'd discussed postnatal depression, examined a silicone model of the human uterus and placenta, split into teams for put-the-nappy-on-the-teddy-bear competitions and read the book about poo.

'Ali, I'm sorry,' I said as we went down the steps.

'It was fun,' she said.

'Man, you need to get out more.'

She laughed and stretched her arms above her head. 'I've been sitting down for too long,' she said. 'Walk?'

'Sounds good.' Waving to our fellow students as they climbed into their cars, we crossed the road and headed up Moa Street in the late afternoon sunlight. 'I've got some serious catching up to do,' I said, plucking a dead grass stem and snapping off inch-long sections as we walked. 'All those girls have spent the last six months shopping for baby stuff on the internet, and I've spent the last six months worrying about being pregnant in the first place.' There had been a spirited discussion on the respective merits of the Phil and Ted's Explorer versus the Sport at lunchtime, until which point I had been entirely ignorant of the fact that Phil and Ted's was a brand of stroller. Not just any stroller, either, but the classy ergonomic type that would carry your baby in slumbering comfort over any terrain you might care to attempt. If I'd been asked yesterday I would have guessed that Phil and Ted were a dopey pair who once went on an excellent adventure.

'Are you feeling okay about it all now?' Alison asked.

'Better,' I said. 'Still scared, but definitely better.'

'I think scared is normal. *I'm* scared after all that talk about sleep deprivation and postnatal depression.'

'It all sounds so serious. We haven't even *considered* what kind of car seat to put the baby into and which brand of mattress protector is rated best by *Consumer* magazine. And then there's Janet telling us to try to have a shower and get dressed every day, and that it'll probably take eight hours a day to feed one small baby.'

'I don't believe that for a second,' said Alison firmly. 'Leah's got a six-month-old and she's got plenty of free time.'

My phone beeped, and I pulled it out of my pocket to read the message. *How is anti natel thing? SB doing hair conditioning treatment been in bthrm 1 hr so far.*

I smiled and showed it to Alison. 'SB?' she asked.

'Sione Brown. The little fullback with the long ringlets.'

'Oh, I know,' she said. 'He does have lovely hair. Can you ask what brand of conditioner he uses?'

Pls find out brand of conditioner 4 Alison. Have learnt to put nappy on teddy bear. Good luck tonight 1 more sleep x

Dove c u 2moro love u x

'Dove,' I said, smiling mistily and walking into a tree.

That evening Em made a special goodbye dinner, and Caitlin made, unassisted, a special goodbye chocolate self-saucing pudding so tough you could barely cut it with a spoon.

'Lovely flavour,' said Dad tactfully, chiselling a second mouthful off his portion.

'It's horrible!' said Caitlin, and burst into tears.

'Sweetie, it's *not*,' Em said.

'I wanted it to be perfect,' she sobbed. 'I stirred it and stirred it –'

'I think it's lovely,' I said.

'You're just trying to make me feel better!' And flinging down her spoon she fled the table.

However, this crisis passed fairly quickly, and the girls and I played Beauty Salons until bedtime. We read two chapters of *The Lion, the Witch and the Wardrobe* and they both felt the baby kicking.

I went back downstairs feeling like a model sister, and made Dad and Em a cup of tea each to continue the theme.

'Aren't you going round to Sam's to watch your boyfriend on TV?' Dad asked.

'No, I thought I'd hang out with you guys,' I said. I hated missing Mark's games – I had a furtive and irrational feeling that he was more likely to get hurt if I wasn't watching – but sacrifices must be made to soothe a concerned parent.

'We're honoured,' said the concerned parent drily, accepting his tea.

I handed the other mug to Em and sat down beside her on the couch. 'Em?'

'Mm?'

'How long d'you reckon it'll take him to come round?'

'Your father? Not long, I wouldn't think. Have a scorched almond, sweetie.'

I took one, and passed the box to my father. 'Dad, Mark's really nice. He's kind to animals, he helps little old ladies across the road . . .'

'Good on him,' Dad said.

'He gives money to lots of charities. And he gives me the peach Fruit Bursts even though they're his favourite.'

'Helen, you talk a lot of drivel,' said Dad, but he was trying not to smile.

The climax of the antenatal weekend was the real-life birth DVD. It was just as Anita had described, and we watched in appalled silence as a dark purple baby emerged from between its mother's hairy thighs. As the head crowned, one of the men bolted for the door of the scout hall and threw up.

Janet wrapped up with a few uplifting words on the joys of parenthood, we stacked our beanbags tidily in a corner and made our way thankfully out into the fresh air to say our goodbyes.

'Thank you for coming to this thing with me,' I said as we got into the car.

'You're welcome,' Alison said. 'It was a pleasure.'

'That might be going a bit far.'

'It was,' she insisted. 'Well, except for Hairy Mary at the end. When are you heading off?'

'I've just got to pick up Murray and my bag, and say goodbye. Do you know if Sam's home?'

'He should be. You can drop me off there if you like.'

The kitchen bench and stovetop at Sam's flat were entirely covered with dirty dishes, and the overflow was creeping across the table. A roasting dish was wedged across the sink, half full of scummy greyish water and with beads of congealed fat floating on top. Standards, it seemed, had fallen to a new low.

We found Sam in the lounge, perusing a tractor manual as thick as a phone book. 'Hey,' he said, looking up as we appeared in the doorway. 'Learnt all there is to know about having babies?'

'Pretty much,' I said. 'Are you going to clean the kitchen, or just burn it down and start again?'

'That's up to Dylan. It's his turn to sort it out.' He stood up, stretched and yawned. 'So you're off to Auckland?'

'Yep,' I said. 'Hey, guys, thanks for putting up with me the last few months.'

'Yeah, it was really tough,' said Sam. 'Don't be a dick, Hel.'

I went and kissed his cheek, and he hugged me. 'He's lucky to have you, okay?' he said.

'Thanks.'

'I mean it. You're great. I heard a guy in the supermarket the other day tell his mate that the hot pregnant vet fixed his dog.'

'That may be the nicest compliment I've ever had,' I said.

'Believe it,' said Alison sternly.

'I will,' I said, hugging her in turn. 'Thank you.'

'You're welcome. Drive safe. See you soon.'

'Do you want to watch *Mamma Mia*?' Bel asked, flinging open the front door as I came up the path.

'No thanks, munchkin,' I said. 'I need to get going.' It was three o'clock already, which meant that even if I left this instant, and even if nobody else in the country happened to be using the

Southern Motorway this afternoon, it would be after five by the time I got to Mark's. Precious time that could have been spent with him had already been frittered away watching Hairy Mary give birth, and the thought of any further delay was, frankly, unbearable.

'Get going to where?' Bel asked.

'Mark's house.'

'Can't you go after we watch it?'

I bent and kissed the top of her head. 'No.'

'*Please?*'

I shook my head, and she burst into tears. 'Helen won't watch my movie with me,' she wailed, preceding me into the kitchen.

'Well, she doesn't have to if she doesn't want to,' said Dad, lifting his head from the newspaper crossword.

'Drink, sweetie?' Em asked.

'No, thanks.'

Caitlin, who was doing a jigsaw puzzle on the floor, looked up and said brightly, 'Can we make fudge now?'

'No.'

'You said you'd make fudge with me! Weeks ago, and you never have!'

'Caitlin,' I said, 'I have made biscuits and cupcakes and kites and read that *dire* Pony Club book –'

'You *said* you'd make fudge.'

'Well then, I lied,' I said, and went upstairs for my bag.

Murray was asleep in the middle of the fold-out bed, visible only as a small bulge beneath the duvet. I scooped him up and dropped him into his carry cage, and he glared at me through the bars with fixed unblinking hatred. Both my sisters followed me into the room to stand one on either side of the door, drooping with sorrow and disappointment.

Ignoring the lot of them I stripped the bed and folded it away. Then I gathered up the bed linen, slung my bag across one shoulder and picked up Murray's cage in the other hand. 'Right, are you coming down to say goodbye?'

'My arm is broken,' Bel said, a tear trickling down each cheek. 'Why aren't you nice to me?'

Caitlin lifted great wet eyes to my face. 'We don't want you to go,' she whispered.

Man, they were good. 'Oh, munchkins,' I said, putting everything back down and holding my arms out. Both girls ran at me and clung. 'I'll come back and see you really soon. And you're going to come to Auckland to stay, remember?'

'For the night?' Bel asked, her voice muffled against my neck.

'Yep. And we'll go out for tea, and stay up late, and play on the flying fox in the park down the road.'

'And make fudge?' said Caitlin hopefully.

'Yes.'

In a touching demonstration of family solidarity, all four of them accompanied me to the car. 'Well,' said Dad, lifting Murray's cage into the passenger seat and closing the door, 'be good. Have fun. Is that horrible animal going to make that noise all the way there?'

'It doesn't matter; I'll just turn up the radio.'

'Just as long as you don't drive off the road.'

'I won't,' I promised.

'Good. Oh well, come back if it all turns pear-shaped.'

I hugged him. At least he'd said 'if', not 'when'.

'Tim! Of course it won't!' Em said, kissing me tenderly. 'Everything's going to be *fine*.' She stepped back and looked at me, and reached out to pull down the neckline of my top by an inch. 'Better. Okay, sweetie, go knock him dead.'

37

MOVING IN WITH MARK WAS THE BEST THING I'D EVER done. He had the first two days free, thanks to the following weekend's bye, and the weather was nasty enough to hibernate indoors with a clear conscience. We went to bed early and got up late and lived on cereal and pancakes, leaving the dishes in the sink. We did nothing even slightly productive. It was lovely.

'We should have done this months ago,' he said on Tuesday night, coming out of the bathroom and stretching himself out full length on the bed beside me.

I squirmed closer and rubbed my cheek against his shoulder. 'Yep.'

We were silent for a little while, and then I said, 'You know how in romantic movies they do those montage scenes of couples wandering around hand in hand and staring into each other's eyes and watching the sun set over the sea from the end of a wharf?'

'Doesn't sound like my kind of movie.'

'But you know the kind I mean. They have pillow fights, and a pillow bursts and fills the room with feathers, and in the morning he wears his pyjama bottoms while she wears the top.

And then they go to a market somewhere and he tries to juggle with tomatoes, and drops them on the ground.'

'*Definitely* not my kind of movie.'

'That's what this feels like,' I persisted. 'Like the too-good-to-be-true Hollywood version instead of real life.'

'It'll wear off,' said Mark comfortingly. 'Give it a couple of weeks and I'll be lying on the couch ignoring you while you nag me to take the rubbish out.' And he rolled over and kissed me, sliding his hands up under my shirt.

When he went back to work I pottered around being domestic, which made a delightful change from working full-time and skimming resentfully over the housework on the weekends. I rearranged the kitchen and made us fiddly, time-consuming things to eat, just because I could. In the mornings I walked up Mount Eden, and in the afternoons I assured Em over the phone that my nails were growing back, that I would nevertheless think about a set of acrylics and that I couldn't be happier. And then Mark would get home from training or meetings or PR appointments, and life would be entirely perfect.

Murray approved wholeheartedly of his new munchkin-free home, although I fear the Siamese next door was less than thrilled.

'Should we go and look at baby stuff tomorrow?' I asked on Friday night, dropping my book off the edge of the couch and rubbing my side as the baby began his evening exercise routine.

'Yeah, why not,' said Mark. He rearranged me more comfortably against him. 'What's that child doing? Star jumps?'

'Backflips, I think. Pushing off from my liver.'

He smiled and tickled a small foot through my abdominal

wall. 'Stop it, you. I guess we'll have to think about names at some point.'

'Have you got anything in mind?' I asked.

'Not really. You?'

'I quite like Julie, for a girl.'

'There was a Julie in my biology class,' he said. 'Sat just in front of me. She used to wind up her hair and stick a pencil through it. She was pretty hot.'

'Right. So not Julie.'

'You could do that,' he said, gathering my hair up and twisting it into a clumsy knot.

It was very nice, but I was distracted by Tamara Healy. She was skipping across the TV screen on the far wall, dressed in a skimpy white bikini and looking exceptionally sun-kissed and gorgeous. 'Hey, is that your ad?' I asked, sitting up straight.

Mark dropped my hair and reached for the remote. 'No,' he said.

I wrested it from his grasp as he jogged up the beach behind Tamara, a Greek god in board shorts. Obviously not his own board shorts: they were neither ripped nor faded. 'Very nice,' I said. 'But why wasn't it on TV in summer? Wouldn't that be a better time of year to advertise ice cream?'

He shrugged. 'Maybe they couldn't get the slot they wanted. You see that?'

'Mm,' I said, watching him rise from the surf and shake his head vigorously so that water droplets flew shining from his dark hair.

'They made me do that take about seventy times. I think it damaged my brain.'

Tamara took a long, suggestive lick of her ice cream, smiled dazzlingly up at him and snatched it back, laughing, as he made a grab for it. What marvellous on-screen chemistry. The producers must have been thrilled.

'Mark, why *did* you guys break up?' I asked.

He looked at me in a slightly pained sort of way, and then sighed and said, 'Same reason most people break up, I guess. Not enough in common. Come on, surely you're not still worried about Tam.'

'I'm not, it's just . . . you *do* have lots in common. You both play professional sport, you've got heaps of mutual friends . . .'

'She liked the idea of going out with an All Black,' he said slowly. 'She likes going to parties and being seen by the right people, and that stuff does my head in. Okay?'

'Okay,' I said. 'Thank you.'

When I came downstairs the next morning the sky outside was flat and grey, and he was standing at the kitchen bench digging chocolate slice out of my sponge-roll tin with the bread knife. 'Want some?' he asked.

I kissed his shoulder in passing and opened the fridge door to get out the yoghurt. 'No, thanks. What would Donna say if she saw you?' Donna was the Blues' dietician, a charming woman with burgundy hair and a passion for big-game fishing.

'Very little,' said Mark, offering a bit of icing to Murray, who was sitting on a bar stool with an expectant look on his face.

'So she's quite happy about you starting your day with chocolate slice?'

'I don't on game days,' he said.

'Oh well, that's alright then.' I put the yoghurt down on the bench and reached over to stroke Murray, who ignored me and kept his eyes fixed adoringly on the provider of chocolate icing.

'I used to worry about all that shit,' Mark said. 'Counting calories and protein–carb ratios. Back in the days when I used to read tactical manuals in bed.'

'Why'd you stop?' I asked.

'It takes over your life. After a year or two I figured out that it works best for me if I go hard at training and then come home and think about other things, and don't worry too much about what I eat. Within reason, anyway.'

'Work–life balance,' I said, nodding wisely.

'That's the one.'

'I guess that's why you're still doing it after eleven years.'

'Partly,' he said. 'And partly I've been lucky, and I haven't irrevocably munted myself.'

'Irrevocably munted,' I repeated. 'Nice phrase.'

⁂

Seeing as Mark's car was short on boot space we took mine baby shopping. We went to an enormous Baby Factory on the North Shore, where we were inundated by attentive shop assistants. They showed us cots and car seats, strollers and high chairs, leak-proof cloth-nappy systems made out of space-age microfibre and tiny Merino sleeping bags until I felt quite dazed and bewildered. I'd thought I was fairly well qualified to look after a baby. I once reared a litter of puppies from birth, and *they* all survived. Feed them, keep them warm and dry, don't drop them from a height and Bob's your uncle. But judging from all this apparently vital equipment, human babies were a lot trickier.

'This one?' Mark asked me, nodding towards a sturdy-looking wooden cot with removable sides.

'That model has been very popular,' said one of our entourage of assistants.

A woman approached and said diffidently, 'Excuse me, I'm just looking for those little absorbent pads that go in your bra when you're breastfeeding.'

'Supermarket,' said an assistant.

'I'm after the ones you can wash and use again.'

'Over there.' The assistant waved a dismissive hand towards the back of the shop, and the poor customer wandered sadly away. Now, had Mark expressed an interest in breast pads, the whole lot of them would have rushed him to the appropriate aisle and fitted them lovingly to his chest.

'We might just browse on our own for a bit,' I said. 'Thank you so much.'

The entourage withdrew a couple of metres, in a slow and reluctant manner.

'You don't think we should look somewhere else, to compare?'

'A cot's a cot, isn't it?' said Mark. 'And this one looks fine.'

'How would we know? We're rank amateurs.'

'It's not rocket science, surely,' he said, picking up a laminated list of safety features that hung from the side of the cot and passing it to me. 'It's not like if you haven't done your homework you might end up with the amazing patented baby-crushing model.'

I smiled. 'Well, true. Let's take it.'

He picked up a boxed one, and a bevy of assistants rushed forward again to relieve him of it. 'We'll just take this to the counter for you while you keep looking,' said one.

'Thanks,' said Mark. 'What now? Car seat?'

After some debate we chose the only one in the shop that we thought we might be able to figure out how to strap a baby into. Then two sets of flannelette cot sheets, three tiny woollen singlets, a packet of soft muslin face cloths printed with ducklings and – in a moment of heady inspiration – a two-metre square set of canvas drawers on a wooden frame that would serve as baby-clothes storage and front-of-cot screening at one fell swoop.

'I don't think we'll get anything else in the car,' I said, eyeing the box the miracle drawers came in.

'Right,' said Mark. 'Good. We'll call it a day, shall we?'

When the doorbell chimed late that afternoon we were all in bed. Mark was reading *A History of the Arab Peoples*, but Murray and I were merely dozing. We were all three entirely happy, and at the sound of the bell Mark swore and I groaned.

Transferring an armful of limp cat from his lap to the foot of the bed, he rolled to his feet and began to get dressed. He pulled his shirt on inside out and back to front, and went downstairs. I was slower, due to turning my clothes the right way out before climbing into them, and reached the kitchen to see him talking to Alan and Saskia in the front doorway.

'Hi!' Saskia said as I appeared at the top of the stairs. 'How are you?'

'Good. Great. Have you guys got time to come in?'

'This unsociable bastard just told us to piss off,' said Alan. '*Mark!*'

'I did not,' he said. 'I just said that you were asleep.'

'We'll have a coffee, since we've woken you up anyway,' Saskia said, coming in past him and running upstairs. She pecked my cheek and handed me a trendy hessian carrier bag. 'Here. A little house-warming present.'

Being civil to your friend's girlfriend is basic good manners, but going out of your way to welcome someone who's a constant painful reminder of everything you most want and haven't got takes niceness to whole new heights. 'Oh, Saskia, thank you,' I said.

'Now, if it's not you, you can exchange it. There's a card in there somewhere.'

Inside the bag was a tissue-wrapped mohair blanket, clear pale green and soft as a cloud. 'It's beautiful,' I said. 'You shouldn't have, but thank you so much.'

'Look at that: it even goes with your cushions,' said Saskia, smiling at me as she draped the blanket artistically over the back of the couch and rearranged my green shot-silk cushions against it.

'You into cushions too, are you?' Alan asked me, in a voice that suggested a fondness for cushions was somewhere on par with a fondness for the deforestation of the Amazon Basin.

'What's wrong with cushions?' I asked.

'Here we go,' Saskia said wearily.

'You could probably live with one or two on the couch,' said Alan. 'But at our place there's a plague of the little bastards. There are about thirty on the bed, for a start, and they all have to be taken off before you get in. And then they have to be put back when you get up again, all in the right order and at the right angle. Hours of my life that could be spent doing something useful are wasted on bloody cushion arranging.'

'There are three,' Saskia said.

We sat around the breakfast bar drinking coffee and eating chocolate slice, and the conversation moved inevitably on to people I didn't know. By the time you counted up all the men Mark and Alan had played with or against in the last decade, the coaching staff and sports reporters and commentators and Old Boys and Rugby Union executives and wives and girlfriends and goodness only knew who else, the three of them had *thousands* of mutual acquaintances. Outside, the raindrops coalesced on the living-room windows to form tiny rivers, and from time to time the baby stirred as if it was turning over in its sleep.

'Tip, did you talk to that young clown?' Alan asked, taking a banana from the fruit bowl and beginning to peel it.

'Yeah,' said Mark. 'He didn't listen. Very hard to help someone who knows it all already.'

'Which young clown?' Saskia asked.

'Jesse Gallagher. Made the squad out of high school. Seems to think the only reason he's not starting every week is that we're scared he'll show us all up.'

'Ah,' she said. 'One of those.'

'He's the one with the mullet, isn't he?' I asked.

'That's the one,' said Alan. 'Tip used to have a haircut like that, back in the day.'

'Really?'

'Damn straight,' Mark said. 'It was awesome.'

'It was hideous,' said Saskia. 'But I think his all-time low was shaving his whole head except for his fringe, and bleaching it a nasty dirty orange colour. I'll have to find you a picture, Helen.'

'Thank you,' I said. 'What about you, Alan? Did you commit any terrible hair crimes?'

He swallowed the last of the banana, shaking his head. 'Me? I've had the same haircut since I was eight,' he said.

'Except that as he gets older his head hair gets thinner and his eyebrow hair gets thicker,' said Saskia pensively. 'Sometimes I wonder where it will end.'

'When these two got married, one of the women's magazines did a big feature headed *Beauty and the Beast*,' Mark told me.

'Yeah, I've always felt that was unfair,' Alan said. 'She didn't look *that* bad.'

38

THE NEXT FRIDAY NIGHT I STAYED HOME AND WATCHED the Blues–Sharks game from the couch with Murray for company, curled up beneath my new green blanket and chewing my left thumbnail back down to a stub. The game seemed mostly to be a grim arm wrestle between the two forward packs – the commentators talked enthusiastically about old-school physical play and the noble art of scrummaging, but then the commentators had no loved ones at the bottom of those scrums.

It was half past eleven by the time Mark got home, after being stretched and iced and rehydrated. He hobbled off again the next morning to a pool recovery session, returning a couple of hours later to lay himself gingerly down on the couch with his *History of the Arab Peoples* and a bottle of chocolate milk.

I filled a basin with warm water, sloshed in some Handy Andy and got down on my hands and knees to scrub the kitchen floor. This unprecedented behaviour was due not to any mysterious pregnant urge to nest, but to the warnings of my new midwife, whom I'd met the previous afternoon. She was a tiny Asian woman who looked about the same age as Caitlin, with the delicate beauty of a snowdrop and a manner as cold as the North Sea. After kneading my stomach briskly with icy, sharp-nailed hands she had told me that the baby was facing in entirely the wrong direction, and if I didn't want an extremely long and painful labour I would do well to spend the next two months on all fours encouraging it to turn.

'What on earth are you doing?' Mark asked, dropping his book onto his chest.

I looked up, cloth in hand. 'The midwife at National Women's told me I have to spend as much time as I can on my hands and knees to get the baby to turn the right way. At the moment he's looking out, and he should be facing my spine.'

'But he moves around the whole time,' he said.

'Yeah, but he does seem to spend most of his time lying sort of sideways. The midwife said that if the baby engages in the pelvis facing backwards you have a much quicker labour, because then the head presses down square on your cervix, and it's pressure on your cervix that makes it dilate.'

'Well, there you go,' he said, picking up his book again.

I continued to work my way across the floor, tile by tile.

After a few minutes he remarked, 'It's just not right to lie on the couch while your heavily pregnant girlfriend scrubs the floor on her hands and knees.'

'I'm quite happy,' I said. 'But I'll stop if it's spoiling your morning.'

'I suppose I can put up with it.'

'Thank you.'

'You're welcome.'

I finished another tile and crawled forward to wipe the front of a cupboard.

'Hey, McNeil?'

'Mm?'

'Come here.'

Startled by his tone, I looked up again. 'Aren't you supposed to be resting and recuperating?' I asked.

Mark grinned and tossed his book down beside the couch. 'It's amazing how often people forget about the psychological aspect of recovery,' he said. 'It's very important to have strategies in place for relaxing and distancing yourself from the game, or you run the risk of burnout.'

'I see.' I got to my feet and crossed the living room towards him. 'I must say it's a bit disturbing that you're turned on by watching me scrub.'

'It's not the scrubbing. I could see down your top.'

Just then the portable phone at the end of the kitchen bench began to ring, and I turned to answer it.

'Leave it,' said Mark, and I turned back towards him.

The machine clicked on. '*We're not home – leave us a message and we'll get back to you,*' said Mark's voice.

We. He'd changed it.

'Tip, if you're lying on the couch, text me Helen's number, will you?' Saskia said.

I changed direction again and lunged for the phone. 'Saskia? Sorry, I was upstairs.'

'Hi,' she said. 'You wouldn't be up for a shopping trip, would you?'

'Um, sure,' I said, surprised and pleased. I thought Saskia was wonderful, and for months it had saddened me that the nicest thing I could do for her would be to go and be pregnant somewhere else. 'When?'

'Pick you up in half an hour?'

'Sounds great,' I said. 'See you then.' Putting down the phone, I started undoing the buttons on my shirt.

'When's then?' Mark asked, wincing as he pushed himself up to sit.

'She's picking me up in half an hour to go shopping. Hey, lie still.'

'I thought we might go to Parnell,' said Saskia thirty-seven minutes later, executing a neat three-point turn in the driveway. 'My favourite shoe shop's having a big one-day-only sale. And there's a really nice cafe by the Domain.'

'Cool,' I said, buckling myself into the passenger seat. 'How's Alan this morning?'

'Oh, he's fine. Doing his little personal match review session.'

'Does he always do that?'

'Every game,' she said. 'He writes down everything that went well, and all the things he thinks he needs to work on. He's done it since he was about fourteen.'

'Impressive,' I said.

She smiled, and then sighed. 'Yeah. He's a bit of a legend, is Al. He knows exactly what he wants, and he works on it until he makes it happen.'

'Is that what he did with you?' I asked.

Stopping at a red light, she tilted the rear-vision mirror so she could see her reflection and raked her fingers through her hair. She was wearing jeans, canvas sneakers and a hooded sports jacket, and she looked, as always, just exactly right for the occasion. Saskia is one of those amazing women whose track pants and sweatshirts are as carefully chosen and as flattering as their fancy going-out clothes. 'I guess he did,' she said.

'That's really nice.'

'He may well be re-evaluating that decision this morning.' She spoke lightly, but I thought she sounded tired and flat.

'You didn't put another cushion on the bed, did you?' I asked.

She laughed. 'Shit, no, it's not *that* bad. I'm just cranky. Nothing that new shoes won't fix.'

'New shoes fix everything,' I said.

'Don't they just?' The lights turned green, and the car moved smoothly forward. 'I'm late,' she said abruptly.

'Late for what?' I asked.

'Period. Damn it, you'd think I'd have learnt by now not to hope.'

'How late?'

'Two days. Totally insignificant.' She drummed her nails against the steering wheel. 'I'll get it any time now, and then I'll settle down again.'

I opened my mouth to say something uplifting, realised there was nothing even faintly helpful to be said and closed it again.

'Sorry,' she said. 'Sorry, Helen. You're just such a nice person to vent to; you don't say bloody stupid things like, "If it's meant to be, it will be."'

'Fingers crossed,' I said softly.

'Yeah. And hey, we'll have another crack at IVF next year. If we win the World Cup, that is; if we don't, Alan will probably be shot at dawn. Or perhaps lynched.'

I smiled in spite of myself. 'Sorry. I don't think it's funny. I think it's unbelievably hard on both of you.'

'Oh, it's not that bad,' she said. 'People have way worse problems.'

'Yeah, but it's amazing how much that doesn't help.'

'It doesn't, does it?' She rested her head back against the seat. 'Thank God for shoes.'

Saskia's favourite shoe shop was indeed a wonderful place. Inside, I discovered an absolutely beautiful pair of boots, made of silky-soft tan leather and discounted by fifty percent. They looked good with jeans, and would undoubtedly be fabulous with a dress and tights, if ever I managed to achieve so fashion-forward a look.

We moved from shoes to antiques, and Saskia was temporarily distracted from her troubles by the discovery of a set of Venetian glass bowls that would go perfectly with a jug she already had. When we'd had enough shopping we lunched at a cafe so small and exclusive I would never have found it alone, with artfully mismatched crockery and old-fashioned prints of obese, anatomically incorrect farm animals on the walls, and it was after two when she dropped me back home.

I waved as she drove away, and let myself into the house to hear an unfamiliar male voice talking upstairs.

'– to watch it, this is only Super Rugby; you want to be peaking in three months' time, remember. No point in taking stupid risks at this stage, you've got nothing to prove to the selectors.'

There was a noncommittal grunt from Mark.

'Just you remember what happened last time.'

Last time, presumably, was the World Cup semi-final four years ago, in which Mark had played eleven and a half minutes before tearing his right quadriceps muscle and watching the All Blacks lose to South Africa from the bench. How, I thought, frowning as I closed the door, would remembering that make him any less likely to hurt himself in the future?

Upstairs a big, dark, good-looking man in his fifties was leaning against the end of the kitchen bench. He was very like Mark to look at – or, to be accurate, I suppose Mark was like him.

The hair at his temples was flecked most attractively with silver and deep lines ran from his nose to the corners of his mouth, but the two of them had the same bone structure, and the same eyes under slightly slanting eyebrows. Movie-star handsome, these Tipenes; square-jawed and broad-shouldered to a man.

A thin-lipped blonde stood riffling through her handbag in the middle of the living room, and Mark, his face carefully expressionless, was making tea.

'Hi,' he said, looking up as I reached the top of the stairs. 'Have fun?'

'Yeah, it was great.' I smiled at the visitors. 'Hi.'

'Helen, this is my father, Brian,' said Mark. 'And this is Jude.'

'Nice to meet you both,' I said.

'Hello,' said Jude. She was very thin, with wrists like twigs and the leathery skin of the long-term sun-bed devotee.

Mark's father glanced at me, nodded stiffly and turned back to his son. 'How's that shoulder?' he asked.

Somewhat taken aback, I dropped my bags on the bottom step leading up to the bedroom. I hadn't expected the man to fold me in his arms and greet me as a daughter, but a hello in passing would have been nice.

'Fine,' said Mark. 'Tea, Helen?'

'Yes, please.' I went up to the bench beside him, and he smiled at me fleetingly as he reached for another mug.

'What does "fine" mean? Back to normal?'

'Yes.'

His father reached across the bench for his tea. 'So Ted Fraser's off to Japan, is he?' he asked.

'Yep,' said Mark, dunking a teabag.

'He'll do fairly well out of that, I imagine. You should have a think about it yourself.'

Mark, whose contract with the New Zealand Rugby Union had been renewed back in December for another three years, passed me my tea without replying.

'Leave it too long and you'll find you're past your use-by date,' his father continued. 'You'd be a fool not to sign with one of those overseas clubs while they still want you.'

'We'll see in a few years,' said Mark. 'Jude, your tea's here.'

Jude approached unwillingly and seated herself on the edge of a bar stool.

'Have you driven up today?' I asked.

'Yes,' she said.

'It's a lovely road up through the Awakino Gorge, isn't it?'

'I suppose so.'

I gave up.

'What brings you up here?' Mark asked.

'Shindig for her brother,' his father said, jerking his head towards his wife. 'Sixtieth birthday, isn't it? We're staying there the night.' He looked at me. 'So you're a vet, are you? I suppose you like horses.'

'Not much,' I said. 'Cows are more my thing.'

'Right out of luck living here, then, aren't you?' And taking a Swiss Army knife out of his pocket, he removed the toothpick and began to attend to his teeth.

Murray got up from his sunny spot in front of the balcony door, stretched and sauntered across the carpet. He rubbed his chin along Jude's foot, and she nudged him away. Thus encouraged, he gathered himself up and jumped lightly onto her lap. You have to admire the way a cat will unerringly choose the least feline-oriented person in the room to drape himself over; I'm sure they do it on purpose.

'Brian, get this thing off me,' she said breathlessly as Murray settled himself down, paws folded beneath his chest.

'Leave it alone. It likes you.'

I went around the end of the bench and lifted Murray off her lap, and she began pointedly to brush away imaginary cat hairs.

'You should have had that lineout ball at the start of the second half,' Brian said thickly around his toothpick.

Mark rested both hands on the bench top and said, in the tone of a man whose patience is fast evaporating, 'Lucky I've got nothing to prove to the selectors.'

His father took the toothpick from between two back molars and gave him a flat, unfriendly stare.

The visitors didn't stay very long, which was, as far as I could see, the only redeeming feature of the whole experience. Mark accompanied them out and came slowly back upstairs, and putting my arms around him I hugged him tightly.

'Ow,' he said mildly, hugging me back. 'Bruised ribs.'

I slackened my grasp. 'Sorry. I love you.'

'Thank you. You too.'

'Is your father always like that?'

'Yeah, pretty much,' said Mark. 'He was a bit pissed off that I didn't want to buy him his next-door neighbour's farm.'

'I can't think why not.'

'I've already bought him one. Half of one, anyway.'

I looked at him questioningly.

'He had to pay Mum out when she left,' he explained.

I mused for a moment on how it must feel to be regarded by your father – and your brother – as a handy source of cash. 'Your family –' I started, and stopped.

'You'll like Mum,' he said.

'What does she think about the baby?'

He looked a bit blank. 'I'm sure she'll think it's very cute when it's born.'

'She hasn't said anything about you having a baby with some girl you just met?'

'We've been going out for a year,' he said.

'We'd only been going out for a few months when I got pregnant,' I pointed out.

'Don't think it bothers her,' he said. 'Look, my family's not like yours. We don't have a whole lot to do with each other. I see Mum every year or two, and she texts me before a Test match to say good luck, and that's about it.' He let me go and opened the fridge, selecting, after some thought, a block of cheese.

'So how did you end up so nice?' I asked.

'Did I?'

'Yes. And it doesn't really seem like you had much encouragement, growing up.'

Mark cut himself a thick slice of cheese. 'I was bloody lucky,' he said soberly. 'Jack Thornton – he was the Blues' forwards coach when I started playing; he's in Scotland now – took me under his wing a bit. He used to have me round for tea and talk to me about what I was going to do with my life. And then I had Alan as a flatmate.' He broke off a corner of his cheese and tossed it to Murray, who was watching him hopefully from the floor. 'I read somewhere that someone interviewed a whole lot of young blokes who'd done time. They asked them what might have stopped them from going off the rails, and every one of them said, "Someone who gave a shit about what I did."' He smiled at me crookedly. 'It's true.'

39

IN JUNE THE BLUES HAD TWO CONSECUTIVE GAMES IN Australia. I went home to Broadview for a few days while Mark was away, returning with five rubbish bags full of small pink clothes. Em had had them piled ready for me in the hall when I arrived, unwilling to take the risk that I might have a boy and thwart her garage-decluttering schemes. My grandmother gave me a pair of hand-knitted bootees, one a good inch longer than the other, told me I was retaining a lot of fluid and said she supposed rugby players were like sailors, with a girl in every port.

I lunched with Alison and called in to work to catch up on the gossip, where I spent a pleasant hour ventilating a cat for Keri while she sewed up its diaphragmatic hernia. This freed up Zoe to lurk around the corner texting her new man, so everyone was happy.

It's a dreadful thing for a rugby player's girlfriend to admit, but I was secretly hoping that the Blues wouldn't make the Super

Rugby play-offs that year. They did, which meant that Mark spent the last weekend in June in Pretoria and the first weekend in July in Christchurch. And having won both games, the Blues had a home final at Eden Park against the Queensland Reds.

At around seven on the morning of the final, which also happened to be my due date, I woke up, wriggled laboriously to the edge of the mattress and rolled off because it was easier than sitting up.

I was completely over pregnancy. My back hurt, my ankles had vanished and I needed to get up at least three times a night to pee. I felt as attractive as a sea cow, and about the same size. Em had been right: there's nothing like the discomfort of late pregnancy for reconciling you to the thought of childbirth.

Getting to my feet I collected my cell phone from the bedside table and lumbered off to the bathroom.

Mark wasn't home – the team always stayed together in a hotel on the night before a game, even when they were playing in Auckland. I was in the shower when he rang, and as I stepped out to answer the phone I caught my toe and staggered forward against the bathroom vanity. I didn't hurt myself, but I did manage to knock my phone off the sink bench and into the toilet.

I had fished it out and was drying it sadly on a towel when the landline rang. *'We're not home, leave us a message and we'll get back to you,'* said Mark's voice as the answer phone picked up. Then, 'McNeil, where are you? You're not in labour, are you?' I was only halfway down the stairs when he hung up.

Better call him back straight away, I thought, before he had time to worry. And then I realised I couldn't, because I didn't know his number. I never dialled it – I always called him from my cell phone.

I looked up the hotel where the Blues were staying and rang reception, and they wouldn't put me through.

'I'm his girlfriend,' I assured the man at the other end of the line. 'I promise I'm not a stalker.'

'Then might I suggest you try his mobile, madam?'

'I haven't got the number – I mean, it's on my phone, and my phone's broken – look, could you just call his room and ask him to ring ho–' At which point I realised the supercilious prat had hung up.

I did a brief ungainly dance of rage, then called Saskia, whose number was written on the back of the phone book, and woke her up. When at length I got hold of Mark he had reached the hotel lobby on his way home to look for me. He was somewhat curt, as worried people often are.

After this inauspicious start the day passed peacefully enough. Mark came home for a few hours at midday and then left again to do serious match-preparation things, and I took myself out for a long walk with one foot on the pavement and the other in the gutter. (Aunty Deb's tip for bringing on labour – she had also advised me to eat a whole pineapple, but I could picture the potential side effects far too clearly to be tempted to try it.)

At five thirty I was standing at the stove, poaching chicken thighs in ginger broth and wishing I'd chosen a dish that could have been put in the oven and left to do its thing, when the doorbell rang.

'Whoa,' said Sam, looking me up and down as I opened the door.

'Be quiet, or I'll sit on you and crush you like a bug,' I said. 'It's great to see you guys.'

'You too,' said Alison, hugging me. 'How are you?'

'Good. Fat and cranky, but otherwise good. Come up and have a drink.'

'Lovely place,' she said as she reached the top of the stairs. 'Is that your bedroom up there?'

'Yep. Go up and have a look round, if you like. We finished setting up all the baby's stuff last week.' The cot was made up ready and the canvas drawers were filled with tiny clothes. My hospital bag was packed, waiting with the baby's car seat on the changing table, and Mark had hung an animal mobile from the ceiling. I was inordinately proud of it all.

'What's happening at home?' I asked Sam, prodding a chicken thigh with a fork.

'Not a lot,' he said. 'Oh, Jeff Burton drove his tractor off a cliff the other day.'

I twisted experimentally to see if it would make my back feel any better, and found that it didn't. 'Is he alright?'

'He wasn't in it – he got out and forgot to put the handbrake on. Are you okay there, Hel?'

'Sore back,' I said. 'No biggie.'

'You're not going to have this baby in the stands, are you?'

'Sadly, I doubt it.'

'Well, please don't.'

'I went to see the midwife yesterday, and apparently the baby's not even engaged properly yet,' I said. 'I think we're pretty safe.'

Alison leant over the half-wall upstairs. 'Helen, this is great,' she said.

'Thank you!' I said. 'You make such a nice contrast to Dad. He says having the baby in with us will turn us into nervous wrecks.' Such an unhelpful comment, when there was nowhere else to put the cot.

'Why?' Alison asked.

'He says it will either snuffle and snort and keep us awake, or go suddenly quiet so we have to leap out of bed and check it's still breathing.'

'Or it'll yell,' said Sam. 'They do that quite a lot, I hear.'

'Thanks, Sammy.'

He smiled. 'Any time.'

We had dinner, and left the house at quarter to seven to walk to Eden Park. 'How about I drop you off in the car?' Sam asked, watching me make my way slowly downstairs.

'It's only the stairs. I'll be fine on the flat.' In fact my back was now aching savagely and the prospect of a couple of hours on a hard plastic chair had all the appeal of a fish milkshake, but there was no point in admitting it.

The closer we got to Eden Park the thicker the crowds grew. Over forty thousand tickets had been sold and the pre-game fireworks display completely obscured the field with smoke. The poor cheerleaders must have been nearly asphyxiated, although their smiles, from what little we could see of them, never wavered.

It was a breathlessly exciting game. The Reds kicked two penalties very early on, and led until the twenty-seventh minute, when the Blues scored a brilliant, length-of-the-field try that began with Mark winning a Red lineout ball. There was a great roar from the crowd.

Pain stabbed at the base of my spine and I shifted in my seat, trying and failing to ease it.

The crowd erupted again as the try was converted, and gripping the edge of my seat with both hands I pushed myself up to stand. Then I doubled over and collapsed back again, as every muscle in my abdomen went into spasm. A great hot gush of fluid poured down my legs.

'*Fuck*,' I said. There are times when no other word will do. 'Ali –'

She turned towards me. 'Mm?'

'I – I think my waters just broke.'

A lesser woman might have wasted time in exclamations of dismay. Alison merely glanced at the puddle around my feet and turned to Sam on her other side. 'Helen's waters have broken.'

Sam whipped around in his seat. 'You're joking,' he said, with such patent horror that at any other moment I would have laughed.

'We'd better find an ambulance,' Alison said. 'St John's will be here somewhere.'

'I'll go,' said Sam, getting hastily to his feet. 'You get her to the gate.' And he turned and dashed along the row with total disregard for the knees of his fellow spectators.

Alison stood up too and held out her hands to me. 'Let's go,' she said.

I took one agonised look along the long row of occupied seats I would have to edge past, soaked from the waist down.

'Just get up, and I'll put my jersey round your waist,' she said.

Touching though this offer was, trying to hide a pair of sopping wet jeans beneath a small beige cardigan seemed a fairly futile exercise. But I certainly couldn't stay where I was, so I staggered to my feet.

Another contraction hit, and I clutched at the back of the seat in front of me. It was an intense, dragging sensation – it didn't hurt as badly as I had expected, but it was as relentless as being compressed in a giant vice.

346

By now the occupants of all the surrounding seats had entirely lost interest in the game. Everyone between us and the aisle was on their feet, making way for me to get past, and a kindly-looking woman caught my hand and gave it a reassuring squeeze.

'Good luck!' someone called.

There was another shout from the crowd, and as I turned to look out at the field the blue side of the scrum crumpled and collapsed. Mark was somewhere in that heap of men, less than a hundred metres away. He might as well have been on the moon.

'Helen, could we focus here?' Alison said.

'Hang on . . .' They were getting up, resetting the scrum – there was a man still down . . . No, he had blond hair.

'I'm sure you can watch a replay.'

I glimpsed Mark crouching to get back into position and turned back towards the steps. 'I was just checking he's okay.'

The next contraction hit as we reached the top of the stairs. This one was a lot stronger than the last. 'How – long – between?' I gasped.

'Not very long. A minute or two.'

The spasm passed, and I straightened up. 'The midwife said I'd have a really slow labour because the baby was facing the wrong way.'

'You can sue her if you have it in the stairwell,' said Alison, putting an arm around me to help me along the concrete passage.

'I am *not* having a baby in a stairwell.'

'To be honest I'd rather you didn't,' she said. 'You don't feel like you need to push or anything, do you?'

'No, it's like being squeezed, or – or wrung out.'

We reached the head of the steps leading down towards the exit. 'Want to stop and wait for the next one to pass?' Alison asked.

I shook my head and started down, clinging to the handrail. 'We've got to get out before half-time. *Shit.*' This one really *did* hurt, a wave of pain that gripped, built mercilessly and slowly receded.

'Helen!' Saskia called, dashing up the stairs towards us.

'How –?' I started.

'Saw you on the big screen, hon.'

I stopped dead and stared at her in appalled disbelief. On the big screen at the Super Rugby final, live in front of the entire rugby-watching public of New Zealand and Australia. Oh, good God.

'Come on,' said Alison, dragging me on down the stairs. Saskia slipped an arm around me on my other side.

'On the big screen!' I wailed.

My escorts giggled, which seemed unfeeling.

'It's not funny!'

'Sorry,' Alison said. 'Sorry, but honestly, Hel, these things could only ever happen to you.'

Leaving a trail of wet footprints, we made our way through the foyer and across the concrete, where we were met by a pair of security guards. They radioed for an ambulance, but I missed the finer points of the conversation due to another contraction. It was just going off again when the ambulance swept around the corner with Sam running behind.

A plump middle-aged paramedic got out of the passenger side and opened the back door. 'Evening, all,' he said jovially. 'Alright, my dear, in you get. Let's get you to hospital.'

'Do you want me to get Mark?' Saskia asked me.

'I don't – no, not now. Just as soon as the game's over.'

'You sure? I can get Bob to pull him off.'

I shook my head. 'He can't do anything, anyway.'

'I'll grab him the second it's over,' said Saskia. 'Ring me if you need him earlier. National Women's, right?'

'That's right,' said the paramedic. 'Up you hop.'

I didn't, because it's just not possible to climb into an ambulance when your uterus is tying itself in knots. He and Alison helped me up when the next contraction passed, and I sank gratefully onto the narrow stretcher.

'Can you come with me?' I asked Alison.

She looked at the paramedic. 'Is that alright?'

'Yes,' he said. 'Okay, let's go.'

I always thought travelling by ambulance would be, if not fun, at least exciting. It wasn't – it was only horrible. I clung desperately to Alison's hand as we crossed the city, the contractions growing more and more vicious.

At the emergency drop-off zone, the paramedics manoeuvred both me and the stretcher out of the back of the ambulance onto a trolley.

'What's your name, love?' asked a woman in dark blue scrubs, appearing at my elbow.

'H-Helen McNeil.'

'Hi, Helen, I'm Suzie. First baby?'

I nodded.

'And when did your waters break?'

Another contraction gripped, and I curled helplessly around my stomach.

'Half an hour ago,' said Alison. 'Just before eight. She's only getting thirty seconds' break between contractions.'

'Well, you're not messing around, are you, Helen? Breathe through it, love. Just keep breathing, and count until it passes . . . Good girl. Relax. Have you got your pregnancy diary?'

'N-no – I left my bag behind –'

'Never mind. Have you had any health problems during your pregnancy?'

'No,' I said. 'I'll be on your system – my midwife is Grace Ko.'

'Okay, we'll take you up to delivery and look up the details.'

After what felt like miles of brightly lit corridor we ended up in a largish room filled with monitors and bits of technical-looking equipment, like the bridge of the *Starship Enterprise*. It entirely lacked the mood lighting and cosy feel endorsed by pregnancy and birth magazines, but by that stage I don't think I'd have noticed if the orderly pushing my bed had wheeled me out onto a stage and brought in the TV crew from Eden Park to keep filming. And if I *had* noticed I wouldn't have cared. There was only this all-encompassing pain that grabbed and twisted and receded, only to grab again. And again. And again.

Suzie and the orderly lifted me between them from one mattress to another, and she took a length of elastic band from a drawer at the head of the bed.

'You're doing really well, Helen,' she said, leaning over me to push the call button on the other side of the bed. 'Now, this is to measure baby's heart rate, so we know how he's going in there.' She beckoned Alison forward. 'Can you please help Helen up so I can get it under her? . . . Lovely. Well done. We'll just get this set up, and then we'll see how far along you are.'

Another nurse appeared and pulled off my wet shoes, jeans and knickers.

'Lovely,' Suzie said again, snapping on a pair of latex gloves and peering at the printout from the foetal monitor. 'Baby's doing just fine.'

I curled forward with something between a groan and a whimper as the next contraction gripped.

'Nothing bad is happening to you,' nurse number two told me.

'Yes – it – is,' I gasped. What a bloody *ridiculous* thing to say. She'd want to try it from this end.

'No, it isn't. Hold on to your friend's hand. Keep breathing.'

'Helen,' said Suzie, 'I need you to pull your heels up to your bottom so I can check your cervix – it will feel a little bit cold . . .'

It didn't feel a little bit cold. As soon as she touched me, every muscle fibre in my uterus went into spasm, and I thought I was going to die. Through the haze of pain I saw a young man in a white coat put his head around the door and say, 'Nice painful contractions, that's what does it. Just what we like to see,' and if I could have moved I would have leapt off that bed and gone for his throat.

'You're eight centimetres dilated,' said Suzie from the foot of the bed. 'That's wonderful, you're nearly there, you lucky girl. Now would you like the gas?'

'*Yes!*'

The doctor, if that's what he was, came up behind her and peered between my legs. 'Half an hour at least,' he said, and wandered over to look at the foetal monitor. 'Call me when it gets interesting.'

Nurse Two wheeled over a gas bottle with a mouthpiece and a hose. 'Bite down on the mouthpiece and breathe in as your next contraction starts,' she said. 'It will help.' And she followed the doctor out of the room.

It may have helped, I suppose, in the same way that paracetamol may help with third-degree burns. I held the mouthpiece in one hand and clutched poor Alison with the other, and sucked frantically as the contractions built and ebbed and built again.

'Hurts.'

'I know,' said Alison, stroking the hair back off my forehead. 'Mark will be here soon.'

'What's the time?' I wheezed.

'Ten to nine.'

Ten more minutes of game time, and then he had to get here.

'Helen,' Suzie said, 'I need you to stand up.'

The woman must have been out of her tiny mind. I shook my head mutely.

'Gravity will help baby to come down into the birth canal. Come on, sit up.'

'Fuck *off*,' I said. I'd never sworn at a stranger before, but there's a first time for everything.

Unmoved, she unbuckled the foetal monitor and slipped an arm underneath my shoulders. 'Pull her hands,' she told Alison.

They heaved me up to sit on the edge of the bed. 'Wonderful,' said Suzie.

'Have you *done* this?' I demanded.

'Three times, dear.'

'Have you *forgotten*, then?' Another contraction started, and the pain of sitting drove me to my feet. '*God!*' I lurched forward, half falling against Alison.

The two of them grasped an arm each. 'Stand up, Helen,' Suzie said. 'Come on, now, don't be silly.'

I wasn't being silly; it's unreasonable to expect anyone to stand up straight when they're being ripped in half. I screamed.

'Don't push,' Suzie ordered, dropping to her knees in front of me. '*Don't push*; you'll tear if you don't give yourself time to stretch.'

I didn't push, but the baby was coming anyway. It hurt more than I had ever thought that anything *could* hurt – more than anyone could possibly bear – and then something slithered down between my thighs into the midwife's waiting hands, and the pain went away.

'Oh,' said Suzie, lifting a slimy purple squirming thing. 'Oh, you precious wee angel. You little darling.'

The baby opened its mouth and wailed.

40

IT WAS A LITTLE GIRL. SUCH A TINY LITTLE GIRL, WITH damp whorls of fine dark hair and a thick rope of umbilical cord still connecting her to me. Her eyes were squeezed shut and her mouth was wide open, and she flailed at the air with her small fists.

I stood and looked at her, knees trembling and blood running down the insides of my legs, as Suzie got to her feet with the baby in her hands. 'Sit down and I'll give her to you,' she said.

'That's a lot of blood,' said Alison hoarsely.

'I know. Press the call button.'

I sank onto the side of the bed and held my arms out.

'Just lie back, dear, and I'll put her on your chest. Pull up your top – skin to skin, that's the way . . .'

I tugged up Mark's rugby shirt and Suzie laid the baby down on her stomach between my breasts. She stopped crying, and I covered her little body wonderingly with my hands. She was perfect, crumpled and purple and covered in white slimy stuff, but perfect nevertheless. Suzie pressed the call button again and held it, and then hastily put on a fresh pair of gloves to carry out some examination, but I wasn't really paying attention.

'Hello, little one,' I said softly.

Alison leant over me and pushed the call button again. 'Why is no-one coming?' she demanded. She ran to the door and shoved it open. 'Someone get in here! She's bleeding out!'

'Am I?' I asked, lifting my head.

'There's some bleeding, yes,' Suzie said in that very calm, deadpan voice that is supposed to give the impression that everything is under complete control. It didn't.

I had, however, no time to dwell on my imminent death from haemorrhage because just then a whole army of medical professionals arrived at a gallop. The baby was whisked away, and within moments I had an IV line in my arm and a pulse oximeter on the end of my finger, my feet were up in stirrups and a senior-looking doctor wielding a large pair of forceps was poking around between my legs. It was all quite dramatic for a while, but very soon they decided that I wasn't going to bleed to death after all and most of them went away. The young doctor who had approved of my nice painful contractions stayed, pulling up a stool between my legs and donning a pair of surgical gloves, and a nurse fiddled with the buttons on the drip machine.

Alison, who had retired to a corner during the flurry of activity, returned to the side of the bed and took my hand.

'Thank you,' I said.

'You're welcome.' We smiled at one another.

I looked over towards the baby. Across the room Suzie was examining her, moving her deftly from one hand to the other in much the same way as a chef shapes a pizza base, but with infinite tenderness and expertise. 'Is she okay?' I asked.

'She's perfect. I'm just going to prick her wee heel, and you can have her back. *Look* at those beautiful little ears.'

'Suture, please,' said the doctor briskly.

'Did I tear very badly?' I asked.

'It could be worse,' he said, not looking up. A nurse opened a pack of suture material onto the tray beside him.

'Was the bleeding from the tear or from inside the uterus?'

'From the tear,' he said, grasping the needle at the end of the suture material in a pair of needle holders and taking a nice deep bite through my quivering flesh.

'*Ow!*' I cried. 'What the hell are you *doing?*'

He lowered the needle holders and glared at me. 'I don't have to sew you up if you'd rather I didn't,' he said. 'It's your perineum, after all.'

'Have you got something against local anaesthetic?'

'It probably hurts more putting in the local than it does to stitch.'

'How would you feel about having *your* bum stitched up without local?'

'Fine,' he said, throwing down his needle holders. 'Whatever you say.'

Alison, that epitome of mild-mannered gentility, looked him up and down and said, 'That's a fabulous bedside manner you've got there.'

'Local, then,' he snapped at the nurse. 'Let's get this over with.'

There was a thin cry from across the room as Suzie jabbed the baby's heel and pressed a card to the bead of blood. 'There,' she soothed. 'There, precious, all done, and here's Mummy.' She wrapped the baby tenderly in a cotton blanket and put her into my arms.

'She's lovely,' said Alison softly.

She was. She was soft pink now instead of purple, and she opened one dark eye and squinted up at me as if she had wanted for a long time to put a face to the voice. I bent and kissed the top of her head. 'I wish Mark was here.'

And right on cue, the door flew open. Mark tumbled into the room still in uniform, sweating and streaked with paint and with his left eye swollen almost shut. I smiled at him in pure uncomplicated delight and lifted the baby to show him. 'She's a girl.'

But he had stopped short and was staring appalled between my legs. 'Jesus, McNeil,' he said.

'It's fine.'

'It's not.' He looked like he was going to faint. Behind him I caught a glimpse of Sam's shocked face as he recoiled and hastily left the room.

I started to laugh helplessly. This was the moment when, as I lay propped against the pillows with my pale face suffused with joy, Mark should be taking his child in his arms and whispering something about us being a family now. For once, just for *once*, it would have been so nice to achieve the cheesy Kodak moment.

'Don't worry,' said the doctor, his attitude taking an abrupt U-turn. 'It looks much worse than it is. We'll have her stitched up as good as new in no time.'

'Come and look at the baby,' I said.

Mark came up and reached out very, very gently to stroke the little head. Then he took my face in his hands and kissed me, and the moment was perfect after all.

Epilogue

MEGAN ALISON TIPENE IS FOURTEEN MONTHS OLD NOW, with big brown eyes and fine, thick black hair that sticks straight up on end. Mark is her parent of choice. She follows him slavishly around the house and shouts, 'Dad! I *up!*' from her cot every morning at six fifteen, but she quite likes me when he's not home.

Murray appears resigned to the addition to his life of a small shrill person with a taste for cat biscuits. However, he remains steadfast in his dislike of my sisters, who stayed last week while Dad and Em went to Rarotonga for their wedding anniversary.

It has since transpired that last June, Saskia quietly went out and bought herself a home pregnancy test. Then she rushed back to the chemist's and bought another in case she'd done it wrong, found it was still positive and scared Alan nearly to death by casting herself sobbing on his chest during his Sunday afternoon post-game nap. Their little girl is seven months old. She is small and dainty and very cute, crawls as fast as most people can run and puts everything she comes across into her mouth. Her parents are very happy but somewhat exhausted.

Sam and Alison are backpacking around South America, due home for Christmas. Aunty Deb is terrified they'll elope while they're over there and do her out of the chance to be mother of the groom, and to be honest I wouldn't be at all surprised if they did.

Lance is doing his Australian board exams in small-animal surgery and seeing an occupational therapist. I believe he is making good progress with both.

Tamara Healy co-hosts a breakfast show on TV, and recently launched her own fashion label. (Tammi H – a little bit street, a little bit funky. Lots of very short shorts and backless silk blouses with big floppy bows at their necks.) She is engaged to a famous-ish children's show presenter, and *New Idea* have bought the exclusive rights to cover the wedding.

Mark's mother came to visit last summer. She stayed for two nights, and apart from addressing Meg as 'poor wee mite', which I felt was unnecessary, she seemed pleasant enough. Mark's father has yet to meet his grandchild, but we're bearing up pretty well without his input.

I work two days a week at a small-animal practice in Mount Wellington, dropping Meg at day care on the way. It's a nice job, although short on cows, and it keeps my hand in. Nick rings me from time to time, usually when presented with a sick chicken, and assures me I can come back whenever I want to.

After the World Cup we moved into a big, rambling, single-storey house in Grey Lynn. It's a nice house, and it will look even nicer once the builder gets home from his Test match in Argentina and finishes the railing around the back deck. The hole is plugged in the meantime with a row of outdoor chairs and my cow-casting rope, which slightly lowers the tone of the place but does stop the baby from falling into the veggie garden.

I am so happy it scares me a bit.

Oh, and the All Blacks won the World Cup.

Acknowledgements

I'D LIKE TO THANK AUNTY AGGIE, WHO NOT ONLY LOOKED after my children while I finished the manuscript but baked and weeded my garden while she was at it.